THE GUILT TRIP

ALSO BY SANDIE JONES

The Other Woman
The First Mistake
The Half Sister

THE GUILT TRIP

SANDIE JONES

MINOTAUR BOOKS
NEW YORK

This is a work of fiction. All of the characters, organizations, and events portrayed in this novel are either products of the author's imagination or are used fictitiously.

First published in the United States by Minotaur Books, an imprint of St. Martin's Publishing Group

www.minotaurbooks.com

Library of Congress Cataloging-in-Publication Data

Names: Jones, Sandie, author.
Title: The guilt trip / Sandie Jones.
Description: First U.S. Edition. | New York : Minotaur Books, 2021.
Identifiers: LCCN 2021015677 | ISBN 9781250265586 (hardcover) | ISBN 9781250838117 (international, sold outside the U.S., subject to rights availability) | ISBN 9781250265593 (ebook)
Subjects: GSAFD: Suspense fiction.
Classification: LCC PR6110.O6387 G85 2021 | DDC 823/.92—dc23
LC record available at https://lccn.loc.gov/2021015677

Originally published in Great Britain by Pan Books, an imprint of Pan Macmillan

First U.S. Edition: 2021

10 9 8 7 6 5 4 3 2 1

For Lucy.

My daughter and best friend.

My life is all the richer with you in it.

PROLOGUE

The policeman, with his slicked-back hair, stands at the bottom of my hospital bed, staring at me intently.

"So, can you confirm you knew the deceased?" he says, in heavily accented English.

I nod, but even that hurts.

His eyes narrow as he studies me. "Do you remember what led up to this unfortunate incident? Were there any altercations between the guests? Was anything said?"

I almost laugh. Where would I start?

Should I be honest and say everybody was at each other's throats? That it was only a matter of time before something like this happened? That I wish it wasn't me who caused it?

The officer is staring intently, waiting for an answer, and I want to scream "Yes" to all *his questions. But instead I shake my head in bewilderment and say, "No, everything was absolutely fine."*

1

"I can't find it," says Ali, with a slightly hysterical lilt to her voice as she rummages through her bag for the third time.

Rachel feels a hot flush begin to envelop her as she wavers between wanting to believe that Ali's passport is really in there somewhere, and fast-forwarding to what the game plan is going to be if it isn't.

She snatches a look at Jack as he stands at the airport check-in desk, patiently waiting for the growing sense of panic that Ali's creating to be over. They all know that these are the scrapes that Ali normally gets herself into—drama appears to be her friend's middle name—but right now, Rachel's sure they could all do without the anxiety that it's causing.

"When I asked you in the car if you had everything, you said yes," says Rachel, careful to keep her tone light. "You checked off everything, including your passport."

"I know, I know," says Ali, upending her bag onto the polished tiles and dropping to the floor on her knees. She frantically fans through the pages of her current book, empties her makeup bag, and takes her iPad out of its case, leaving no stone unturned in her search for the maroon game-changer.

"I'm sure it was here," she says, as tears of frustration pool in her eyes. "I'm sure I saw it—I just don't understand."

Rachel looks at Jack imploringly, but her husband just shrugs his shoulders as if to say, "*This is* her *problem.*"

"Might it still be at home?" Rachel asks gently. "What about if we retrace our steps back to the parking lot, just to check that you've not dropped it anywhere." She looks at her watch and is grateful that Jack insisted on leaving home earlier than she had wanted to.

"If the traffic's bad, I don't want to be stressing that we've not left enough time," he'd said last night. "*And* don't forget we've got to pick Ali up on the way."

Rachel had felt a sense of irritation creeping in as he'd fussed around her while she deliberated whether to pack the blue or the yellow dress this morning. She'd bristled at his never-ending need to be somewhere before he'd even left, but now she's grateful for his eagerness, because if they need to go back to Ali's place to look for her passport, they may have *just* enough time to do it.

"If I don't get on that plane, Will's going to lose his shit . . ." says Ali, her eyes desperately searching Rachel's and Jack's for an answer they can't give.

"Let's retrace our steps," says Rachel, as she helps Ali scoop up her belongings from the floor.

"Think, just think," says Ali to herself, closing her eyes, forcing herself to focus.

"What time does check-in close?" Rachel asks the bemused British Airways clerk.

"Forty minutes before the departure time."

"And I don't suppose . . ." starts Rachel, not entirely sure where she's going with it.

The woman smiles apologetically with her brightly painted lips. "I can't check in the luggage without everyone's passports."

"Okay," says Rachel, looking around at the five cases that are standing between the three of them. Only one of them is hers and Jack's;

they'd managed to negotiate their way into sharing a single case, on the strict understanding that it was 75/25 in her favor.

"You can't expect me to get everything I need for a four-day trip into one half of a case," she'd moaned as Jack had objected to paying the airline an additional thirty-five pounds just for the privilege of actually taking their belongings on vacation with them.

"Everything you own is tiny. How much room can you possibly need?"

"But I need to take more things than you do," she'd replied, without much conviction because she knew she was going to get her own way. "You only need to take one suit and that's going in a separate carrier, so that means there's more space for me."

He'd smiled and rolled his eyes as he rationed the T-shirts and shorts that were in the pile on their bed. "Why you need to take enough for a month when you're only going for a few days is beyond me."

Looking at Ali's four cases now, Rachel wonders if it's a *year* she's going for. "Okay, so here's what we're going to do," she says authoritatively. "Jack, why don't you and Ali head back to the car . . . ?"

"But . . ." he protests.

"I'll stay here with the cases and wait for Noah and Paige."

"Why don't *I* do that?" asks Jack.

"Because if you don't find the passport, you've got just enough time to shoot back to Ali's. You'll be quicker than I will and besides, you've already got six points on your license, so what's the harm in three more?" She winks at him, trying to inject some much-needed humor into the situation, but his jawline is set and his eyes are fixed on the departures board.

"I'll hold the fort and explain the situation to the others when they get here."

"And what happens if we don't get back in time?" asks Ali breathlessly.

"Then we'll have to get the next available flight," says Rachel, smiling, although the thought of sitting at Gatwick airport for any longer than is absolutely necessary fills her with a sense of dread. "It's only Will we've got to worry about—none of your other guests are arriving until late tomorrow, so we've got plenty of time."

"But he'll be there on his own if we don't make it out by tonight," says Ali tearfully.

"I'm sure he's spent worse nights on his expeditions around Asia," says Rachel. "I don't think a villa in Portugal is going to faze him."

"Jack, would you mind?" says Ali, turning to face him with her best little-girl-lost look. "I wouldn't know how to get back to the parking lot if you *paid* me."

He looks at Rachel as if to say, *"Are you* really *going to make me do this?"*

Rachel doesn't know why Ali seems to rub him up the wrong way so much. They used to get on really well—at least until they stopped working together. It was Jack who introduced her to his brother Will in the first place, so he only has himself to blame for bringing her into the family. But ever since Will and Ali announced their engagement, it's as if everything she says and does irritates him.

Even last night, when Ali texted Rachel that she couldn't sleep because she was sure she heard a noise downstairs, he was unsympathetic.

"Tell her to handle it herself," he snapped.

"That's not fair," said Rachel. "She's in the house on her own, unused to being without Will, and she's spooked."

"Tell her to ring *him* then—she's *his* problem now."

The way he said it struck alarm bells for Rachel, because Jack was usually the first to volunteer to fit a CCTV camera for his parents or a security bolt for Mrs. Wickes next door. She was sure he'd even popped in to check on Ali in the early days when Will was still gallivanting and she was feeling vulnerable. So what had changed?

"She thinks she's heard some glass breaking," said Rachel.

Jack had stopped doing his push-ups on the bedroom floor and turned to look at her with an exasperated expression.

"She lives twenty minutes away," he said. "Do you honestly want me to go all the way over there because she's said she heard a noise?"

"I just know what it feels like when you're on your own late at night," Rachel said, without answering the question.

"Yes, but thankfully, *you* don't make a mountain out of every molehill, like she does."

"She doesn't mean any harm by it," said Rachel.

"Well, let's just hope that this is the *only* mountain she's going to be creating over the next few days."

As Jack and Ali walk back in the direction they came from, with her half-skipping to keep up, Rachel can tell, just by Jack's gait, that he's seriously pissed off. The ice-cold pint of lager that he'd no doubt imagined having with Noah on the other side of security looks highly unlikely. At this rate, the best he can hope for is a lukewarm can on the plane, *if* they make it back in time.

"Hey," says Paige as she dashes across the departures concourse toward Rachel, with her husband Noah following. "Where *is* everyone?"

Rachel throws an arm around Paige's back as she pulls her friend in for a brief hug. "You wouldn't believe it if I told you."

Paige furrows her brow. "Is everything all right? Where's Jack? And weren't you picking Ali up?"

"No; likely to be halfway around the M25; and yes, we did."

Noah looks perplexed as he kisses Rachel's cheek. "So, what's going on?"

"Ali seems to have mislaid her passport," says Rachel. "They've gone back to find it."

Paige rolls her eyes. "Oh God, has it started already?"

Rachel smiles and nods. "It's a bit early in the proceedings, even for Ali."

"What did I tell you?" says Paige, turning to Noah. "I said to him on the way down here that something would happen . . . that there was bound to be one crisis or another."

Rachel looks to Noah, who rolls his eyes theatrically.

"But you know what men are like," Paige goes on, as Noah's mimicking her behind her back. "They're completely oblivious to it all."

Rachel nods in agreement, knowing that when her friend is on one of her rants, it's best to let her get on with it.

"As long as she bats those long eyelashes of hers at them, they let her get away with murder," Paige goes on.

Noah exaggerates a fake yawn and Rachel struggles to keep a straight face.

"I'm going to get a coffee," he says, walking off toward Costa. "Anyone else?"

Paige tuts and smiles. "Honestly, what *do* we do with them?"

Rachel puts her arm through Paige's. "Actually, I'm pleased I've got you on your own," she says, following Noah as he free-wheels Ali's cases across the tiled floor.

Paige stops walking and turns toward Rachel with a concerned expression. "What's up?"

"It's nothing really, but do you remember me telling you a couple of months ago that Jack was being really short with Ali?"

Paige nods. "Yes, you were hoping he was going to snap out of it by the wedding."

"Well, it seems to have gotten even worse and it feels like I'm forever treading on eggshells. I'm worried he's going to say or do something that's going to put a spanner in the works this weekend."

"That's normally my job," says Paige, smiling.

Rachel laughs. "I've come to expect it from *you*, but it's so unlike Jack to have a bee in his bonnet, especially with a woman who's not done anything wrong."

Paige raises her eyebrows questioningly. "You sure about that?"

"Not on purpose, at least," says Rachel. "You know what Ali's like; she can be infuriating, but she doesn't mean any harm by it. She's just one of those people who needs drama to survive."

"Well, as long as it's *her* drama and she doesn't go sucking any of us into it, then she can live it up all she likes."

"Exactly," says Rachel. "But that's not a reason for Jack to get so riled all of a sudden. She's always been like this—even when they were working together. He seemed to like her then, so what's changed?"

Paige shrugs her shoulders. "Maybe he's pissed off because she left his company to go and work for David Friedman."

Rachel wonders if that could be what's getting to Jack. Friedman's entertainment company is a direct competitor to the record company Jack is A&R director at, but with a much higher profile. Maybe seeing his brother's fiancée, a member of his own family, changing sides has dented his pride.

She thinks back to the dinner she and Jack had with Will and Ali at the Groucho Club a few weeks ago. Jack hadn't wanted to go and was unusually quiet all evening until Ali started talking about a new client the company had just signed.

"He's *so* talented," she crowed. "Every one of his songs makes the hairs stand up on my arms. He's going to be huge."

"Uh-oh," said Will, turning to Jack. "Looks like you missed out there, bro."

"I know who she's talking about," said Jack tersely. "It's no great loss to us."

"Are you sure about that?" said Ali, tilting her head to the side. "I heard you were going after him with all guns blazing."

Jack had laughed wryly. "We gave it some consideration, but we decided our roster is strong enough as it is."

"I can't argue with that," said Ali. "Friedman's may be bigger, but you've got a solid reputation for doing the best by your artists."

Rachel winced, knowing that Jack was likely to take Ali's well-meaning words as an attempt to patronize him.

"You can't have it all," Jack said, while signaling to the waitress for the bill, bringing the evening to a premature close.

"Indeed you can't," Ali had agreed. "And anyone who thinks they can, is a fool."

"You might be right," muses Rachel to Paige now as they join Noah in the line. "Though, I'd expect Jack to rise above it."

"I think we're all going to have to display a modicum of patience this weekend, don't you?"

Rachel smiles. "She's getting married," she says, without needing Paige to elaborate.

"She thinks *every* day is her wedding day," says Paige, laughing. "I knew it was going to be bad, but I didn't realize we'd be treated to The Ali Show before we'd even got on the plane."

"Anyway," says Rachel, eager to change the subject. "How's Chloe? Was she okay about being left on her own?"

"Oh, she thinks this is the best thing that's ever happened to her," says Paige. "Don't you remember being sixteen and having the house to yourself? She gets whipped up into a frenzy when we go out for the *evening*, so to be left at home on her own for four days has got her spinning like a whirling dervish."

Rachel can't help but laugh at the thought of demure Chloe being left in charge. If she knew her goddaughter at all, she'd be sick with excitement at the thought of an empty house, yet end up doing nothing with it. Rachel's son, Josh, on the other hand, did exactly the opposite. When she and Jack left him home alone for the first time, he'd seemed so nonplussed that they were worried he was just going to stay locked in his bedroom playing video games for the entire weekend. At least they had been until they saw an open invitation on Facebook when they were thousands of miles away in Santorini, and realized he'd arranged the party of all parties.

"If that girl has a do, I swear to God . . ." says Noah, smiling.

"You can't call it a *do*," admonishes Paige, as she orders their coffees.

Rachel smiles. "I think the correct term these days, if you don't want your kids to laugh at you, is *gathering*."

Paige laughs. "You make it sound so posh with your pronounced 'th.' I think you'll find they don't even call it that now, it's been shortened to 'gav.'"

"How's Josh getting on?" asks Noah. "Does he seem to be enjoying uni life?"

Rachel nods. "I think so, but I'm not sure the work's really started yet. It seems that freshmen's week has extended into a month, because all he's done so far is go out to events and parties." She stops and holds her hands up. "Sorry, gavs."

Noah smiles. "But he's settled into his digs? He gets on with his flatmates?"

"Well, I'm not sure he's been sober enough to work out if he likes them or not," says Rachel, laughing. "Every time I speak to him, he's either on his way out or in bed with a hangover."

"Those were the days," Noah says, ruefully. "It feels like only yesterday."

"That freshmen's week was brutal though," says Rachel. "I don't know if my liver could take that again."

Noah laughs heartily. "What are you talking about? You were the biggest Larry Lightweight out of all of us."

"Er, excuse me," says Rachel, pretending to be affronted. "I think you'll find I kept up with the best of you."

Noah looks at her with raised eyebrows over his double espresso. "What proves that theory wrong is that you remember that we first met at the freshmen's ball."

"Yes, we walked back to our halls together," says Rachel.

"Yet I don't remember meeting you until at least a month later," says Noah. "So, I think that clearly demonstrates how sober *you* were, and how pissed *I* was."

"I can remember many a night where you got me out of a fix because I was too drunk to look after myself." Rachel says it as if it's a badge of honor to prove how cool she really was, but she can tell by the mischievous look on Noah's face that he's about to kibosh her claim.

"That's because that's what you get like after two beers," he teases. "Don't fool yourself into thinking that I wasn't off my head when I was holding your hair back while you vomited. I'd had ten pints by then and was *still* able to hold it together."

"Children, children," says Paige in her best schoolmarm voice. "That's quite enough bickering."

Noah pokes his tongue out and Rachel throws a packet of sugar at him.

"So, what's the plan if they don't make it back in time for the flight?" asks Noah.

"Can we all go home?" asks Paige hopefully. "I've got a ton of work I could be getting on with."

"Don't be so bloody ungrateful," scolds Noah, laughing.

Rachel tracks Jack on her phone. They've been gone over half an hour, but don't appear to have left the airport.

"I'll give him a call," she says. "See where they're at."

"Got it!" shrieks a vision in pink from across the concourse.

"Blimey," says Paige as Ali, dressed head to toe in a magenta jumpsuit, toddles toward them in towering heels, holding her passport aloft. "Woo-hoo! We're back up and running."

Several people in the busy coffee shop turn their heads in her direction. Such is the Ali effect. But Jack, Rachel can't help but notice, is trailing several steps behind, with a face like thunder, pretending not to know her.

"Where was it?" asks Rachel.

"It had somehow dropped into the footwell in the car," says Ali breathlessly. "It must have fallen when I was checking I had everything. Ironic really." She turns to Paige and Noah. "Sorry, I'm such a klutz. Hiiiiii."

She makes a show of greeting them like long-lost friends, with exaggerated cuddles and air kisses, before loudly proclaiming how exciting this all is as she jumps up and down and claps her hands together.

Rachel has to stifle a giggle at Paige's bewildered expression: everything about it screams, "*Get me out of here.*"

She can't help but feel guilty; if it weren't for her encouragement, Paige wouldn't be here, and knowing the part she's played to cajole her best friend into doing something she'd rather not do, momentarily sits heavy on her chest.

When Will had come over to see them a few months ago to ask Jack to be his best man, they'd both been surprised to hear that Noah and Paige had made the proposed guest list. Not that they weren't good friends of his—Will and Noah often got together for a game of golf, much to Jack's chagrin, as no matter how hard he tried, hitting a little white ball with a long stick just wasn't his forte.

"I thought you said you wanted to keep it intimate," Jack had said.

"Yes, there's only forty guests," said Will.

"But Paige and Noah are more our friends," said Jack. "I don't think they'd be offended if you didn't invite them. Plus, you're asking them to take four days out and travel to another country. I know Noah's taken on more work at the university and didn't you say Paige had a big case coming up?" He'd looked to Rachel for back-up.

She'd been about to nod in agreement, but then she'd been struck by how a weekend of imposed purgatory could be turned around if Paige was there too. Instead of spending four days making small talk with strangers, they could eat, drink, dance and pretend they weren't responsible mothers for once. Suddenly, and selfishly, Rachel could see its potential.

"Oh, I don't know," she'd said. "Noah and Paige really like Will and Ali, so I'm sure they'd be flattered to be asked."

Jack had looked at her with raised eyebrows, silently questioning whether they were talking about the same Paige, who was always so quick to denounce Ali's shortcomings.

"Why did you have to push for Noah and Paige to come?" Jack had said later, after Will had left.

"Because it might be an opportunity to spend some time with them," said Rachel. "We haven't been away together for a while, and faced with the prospect of spending four days with your family, they might be just the distraction we need." She laughed to soften the sideswipe. "We could all get a villa together and make a holiday out of it."

Jack groaned. "Why can't he get married here, where we'd all only have to endure each other for the afternoon before going home?"

"Don't be such a miserable old sod," she'd said, going up to him and wrapping her arms around his neck. "Noah and Paige are our friends."

"I'm not talking about *them*," he said. "I'm talking about my bloody *family*. Boxing Day takes enough grit and mettle to survive—why would Will want to impose *this* on us?"

"Because. He's. Not. Been. Here. For. Most. Christmases," said Rachel, punctuating each word with a kiss on Jack's lips. "So, maybe this is his way of making up for it; a chance to get the family to spend some quality time together."

"But four days in Portugal," he moaned, sounding like a spoiled child.

"Oh, for God's sake!" Rachel laughed. "Listen to yourself. Your family will be there. I'll be there—if Noah and Paige come, we'll have a good laugh."

He'd looked at her petulantly.

"You never know," Rachel had said. "You might actually enjoy yourself."

Now, as she looks at his obvious frustration and the strained greeting he gives Paige and Noah, she feels she's manipulated them *all* into doing something they don't want to do.

"Okay, we'd better get checked in," Jack says briskly, grabbing hold of two suitcases and wheeling them away.

Rachel abandons her half-drunk coffee as she follows him—and a sense of foreboding—across the concourse.

2

Despite Rachel trying her best to deter Ali from drinking on the plane, by the time they arrive in Lisbon two and a half hours later, she's four gin and tonics down and has trouble negotiating the steps onto the tarmac.

"I'd have to drink three times as much to behave like she does," Paige says to Rachel as they follow a swerving Ali onto the waiting bus.

"That's because you're hard core," says Rachel, smiling.

"No, it's because *she's* putting it on."

Rachel looks at Ali as she swings herself around a pole. If this is what she's like when she's *pretending* to be drunk, what on earth will she be like when she really *is* inebriated? She remembers Ali telling her that she'd once spent a lost weekend in Amsterdam, going out on the Friday night and not remembering anything until she woke up on Monday morning. She'd boasted that she had to rely on her friend to tell her that she'd danced in a podium cage in a nightclub, tried to put herself in a shop window in the red-light district and had almost been arrested as the first person in the country's history to consume too much space cake.

"It was the most fun I've ever had," Ali had said, although it sounded the exact opposite to Rachel. She couldn't think of anything worse and suspected that Ali would probably agree if she were being honest, but she liked to shock. There was never a simple story where she was concerned. Even an innocuous visit to the dentist recently had resulted in her talking a man out of jumping off a bridge—apparently.

Rachel pulls herself up, ashamed of herself for thinking, even for a second, that Ali may have lied about something like that. But then she remembers what Jack had said after listening to what he was convinced was yet another tall tale. "I think we can safely say she embellishes the truth," he'd said.

Half of Rachel wondered where the harm was in that. Perhaps she *did* see a man who looked like he was about to take his own life, otherwise where would such a story come from? But maybe instead of talking him out of it, she'd merely seen emergency services in attendance and wished she'd been an instrumental part of the action.

"She's had four G&Ts," she whispers to Paige, giving Ali the benefit of the doubt. "*I* might start pole-dancing after that."

Rachel knows that would be the last thing she would do. She'd have been leaning her head back on a toilet-cubicle door until that swaying feeling passed, or splashing herself with cold water well before now. She hates to admit it, because it makes her sound boring, but Noah's right: even when they were at university together, she was never a great drinker.

"She's had *two*," says Paige, without worrying who can hear her. "The third she took to the toilet with her and came back mysteriously empty-handed, and she spilled most of the fourth onto Noah's trousers."

Rachel can't help but laugh. "I didn't know you were keeping such a close eye on her. What are you, the fun police?"

Paige pulls a sarcastic grimace. "You've got to have eyes in the back of your head with that one."

"Aw, come on, we were young once," says Rachel.

"You make it sound as if we're ancient," says Paige brusquely, her advancing years always a bone of contention.

"We *are* compared to Ali."

"She's not exactly a spring chicken," says Paige.

"She's twenty-nine!" exclaims Rachel. "If that's not a spring chicken, I don't know what is."

"Well, *we* wouldn't have behaved like she does at that age," huffs Paige.

"God, I can't even remember what we were doing then," says Rachel thoughtfully. "That was thirteen years ago. It feels like a lifetime away."

"*We*," says Paige, "were being responsible mothers. What would Josh and Chloe have been then? Five and three?"

Rachel nods. "But, looking back on it now, isn't there a part of you that wishes you'd waited a bit longer? I was just twenty-four when Josh was born. I was still a kid myself."

"Are you saying you'd have done things differently if you had your time again?" asks Paige.

The loaded question is impossible to answer. Rachel would never have chosen to have a baby at that age, but sometimes life throws you a curveball and you just have to run with it.

"I wish I hadn't got pregnant so young," she says thoughtfully. "But I would never have done anything about it once it had happened, if that's what you mean."

"But imagine how differently things might have panned out if you hadn't have gotten pregnant," says Paige. "Imagine how different my life would have been if you hadn't."

Rachel looks at Paige quizzically. "How has me getting pregnant back then had an impact on your life? We didn't even know each other."

"Exactly! But if you hadn't gotten pregnant, you and Noah would have gone off on your gap year after university, as you'd planned. God knows how long you would have traveled the world for. God knows who you might have met along the way. Jesus, the pair of you might have even ended up together."

Rachel pulls a face, but her heart is beating double-time. "Well, that would have been weird," she says. "He was my best friend."

"I know," says Paige. "But you don't know where that journey might have taken you. Either way, he would have been unlikely to have found his way to *my* door."

Rachel hasn't ever thought of it like that, but she supposes Paige might be right.

"So, I'm very happy that you had Josh when you did," says Paige, smiling, as they join the line for border control.

"I can't find it," slurs Ali.

Rachel hopes she's misheard her, but Paige's eye-roll tells her otherwise.

"You can't find *what*?" whispers Rachel, always on edge whenever she's in any kind of authoritarian environment; she's the type to go red when she's walking, empty-handed, through customs.

"My passport!" says Ali, far too loudly, as she pats herself down. "I think I've left it on the plane."

Rachel looks at Jack, wide-eyed.

"If you think . . ." he starts.

"What *else* do you suggest?" says Rachel. "We won't get through without it."

"They're not going to let me back on the plane," snaps Jack, but Rachel knows it's not aimed at her.

"Alison Foley!" shouts a voice over the din of three hundred passengers huddled into something resembling an aircraft hangar.

"Yes!" responds Rachel, automatically raising her hand.

A flight attendant, who Rachel recognizes as the woman who discreetly refused to serve Ali another drink, cuts through the line. She doesn't seem surprised when she reaches them.

"This was found in your seat pocket," she says to Ali, holding up the passport.

"I'm so sorry," says Rachel, sounding like Ali's mother. "I should have checked."

"Do you have any other proof of ID on you?" says the pursed-lipped air hostess.

Ali looks at her, momentarily confused, before the penny drops. "Oh, yes!" she blurts out, rooting in her oversized handbag. She pulls out her purse but has trouble with the zip.

"For God's sake," huffs Jack impatiently.

"*All right*, Mr. Antsy-pants," says Ali. "Keep your hair on."

Rachel feels her insides coil up like a spring, pulling back, ready to launch into action, though she's not yet sure whose defense she's going to have to jump to.

She takes Ali's purse from her and finds her driver's license in the side pocket, then presents it to the woman who's inadvertently deciding whether Will and Ali get married in two days' time. An overwhelming sense of relief rushes through Rachel's body as the flight attendant hands Ali's passport back.

"Be careful where you leave it in future," she says, as Rachel lets out the breath she's been holding.

"Thank *you*," says Ali begrudgingly, as if she's been told off by a teacher. Rachel wills her not to say anything more.

"I honestly can't be held accountable for my actions if this is how the whole weekend is going to be," says Jack ominously as he sidles up to Rachel at the baggage carousel.

"Cut her some slack," says Rachel, reaching up to give him a kiss. "She's over-excited."

"You make her sound like a puppy," says Jack, managing to smile.

"In some respects, that's exactly what she is," Rachel says, laughing. "She'll calm down once she sees Will."

"I don't know how he does it," says Jack, shaking his head. "She's a freaking liability."

"I don't want to state the obvious, but this is all *your* fault," says Rachel, with a withering expression. "*You* employed her. *You* introduced her to Will . . ."

"Unwittingly!" he exclaims.

"Ssh!" Rachel laughs, looking around to check if Ali's in earshot, not that she's got the wherewithal to hear.

"She never used to be like . . . *this*," he says, waving his arm about. "It seems to me that she's got a drinking problem. She doesn't know her limits and then becomes this caricature of herself, who spouts garbage."

"Is that all that's bothering you?" presses Rachel, keen to get to the bottom of his disdain for a woman he used to quite like.

He shrugs his shoulders, as nonchalantly as he can. "I just don't think she's right for my little brother and it pains me that he might be about to make the biggest mistake of his life."

Rachel takes hold of his hand. "But I've never seen Will this happy," she says. "And it's your duty as both his brother and his best man to play your part and make this weekend the best it can be."

Jack kisses her on the nose. "You're far too accepting," he says.

"It's easier than being cynical all the time," she says. "That must be *exhausting*."

He playfully smacks her on the behind.

Despite standing up for Ali, Rachel can't help but feel relieved when she spots Will at the end of a long line of holiday reps holding clipboards in the arrivals hall. Thankful that she no longer has to be the responsible adult, she points him out to Ali and watches her zig-zag over to him, feeling like she's handing a naughty child over to their long-suffering parent.

"There's my baby," shrieks Ali as she runs into Will's arms.

They all stand there awkwardly as Will and Ali exchange saliva for far longer than feels necessary.

"Give it a rest," says Jack, jokingly, but Rachel can hear the tension in his voice. If Will knows his brother well enough, he'll hear it too.

"Sorry, it's been a couple of days," says Will, breaking away.

"It's been three!" declares Ali, as if it makes all the difference.

"Hey, bro," says Will, hugging Jack and looking at the group. "How are we all? Good?"

Jack smiles half-heartedly.

"Well, I will be when I get out of these trousers," says Noah, laughing.

"Had an accident, have we?" asks Will, clearly amused by the wet patch spread across Noah's groin.

"Don't even ask."

"So, are we all set?" asks Jack. "What's the villa like?"

"You wait until you see the place," says Will, his eyes dancing. "Man, it's insane."

The tension in Rachel's shoulders dissipates. When Will had told them one of his surfing mates had offered him a villa, so the six of them could stay together, her initial reaction was *Hell, no*. She'd rather be in the hotel with all the other guests than with an already hyperactive Ali in the build-up to the wedding. But Ali had insisted that Rachel be there, "as the sister she never had," to help her get ready and keep her calm. Without a valid excuse that didn't come across as petty, Rachel had resigned herself to it. But her next worry—not wanting to sound like a snob—was that the villa on offer wasn't going to be of the standard she and Jack were used to. He had a rule that they never went on vacation to anywhere that wasn't as nice as their home.

"What's the point?" he'd say. "Where's the sense in me working my arse off and earning good money, to spend the precious time I get off in a place worse than where we live?"

She'd imagined Will's surfer friend having a shack that hung precariously off a cliff, giving a whole new meaning to sea views.

"So, it's okay?" Jack asks again, no doubt aware of the vast difference between his "insane" and his brother's.

"Trust me, it's off the charts." Will smiles.

And Rachel has to hand it to him, as just over an hour later, they pull up at a villa perched on the edge of a clifftop, overlooking the Portuguese fishing village of Nazaré. The imposing glass-and-white walls preside over the terracotta roofs of tightly built houses that line the beach below. The villa's modern, angular features, softened by a swathe of warm light, create an awe-inspiring silhouette against the darkening skies.

"Oh, baby, it's beautiful!" squeals Ali as the minivan moves slowly up the inclined driveway—the lit chrome bollards making it look like a little runway from which they're about to take flight. Rachel nervously grabs Jack's hand as her eyes follow the *calçada* paving until it seems to disappear into the abyss.

Thankfully, the van stops short, though not in time to stop Rachel's hand from growing clammy. Jack gives her a reassuring smile, as if he knows that her mind momentarily saw them all going over the edge.

Noah whistles appreciatively through his teeth as the oversized front door swings open onto a breathtaking double-height room. An open fireplace sits in the middle, its stone-clad chimney reaching up into the vaults of the ceiling.

Rachel feels Jack relax beside her as he looks around the vast space, his fears at what his nomadic brother could have had them staying in immediately allayed.

She'd often wondered how two boys who were brought up together could have such different outlooks. While Jack needed to check his schedule several times a day, and was known to call restaurants to confirm an already confirmed reservation, Will didn't know where he was going to be from one day to the next. If he woke up and felt the need to go to a kibbutz in Israel, he could well be at one by that evening. He'd just throw his meager belongings into a backpack and head to wherever he felt the calling. He was at his happiest spending the night under the stars, with nothing but a stretched piece of tarpaulin separating him from the elements. Hence why Jack—and she, too, she has to admit—are so relieved to be standing here, in front of glass doors that wrap around three of the walls, looking out onto an azure-blue swimming pool lit by underwater spotlights.

Will excitedly pulls back one of the patio doors and invites them to step out onto the polished concrete terrace. There's a saltiness in the air that tells Rachel she's close to the ocean, but it's the crashing of the waves that proves just how close. It's so difficult to get your bearings when you go somewhere new, especially in the fading light, but she knows that, once morning comes, she'll be able to explore and get a feel for where she is. Right now, the roar of the Atlantic resounds in her ears, making her shiver involuntarily.

Jack puts his arm around her shoulders. "It's stunning, mate, it really is."

Will smiles, seemingly relieved by his big brother's appreciation.

"Which one's our room?" asks Ali, hanging onto Will's arm like a limpet. "I hope we've got the honeymoon suite."

Will's eyes light up. "You're not going to believe it," he says, taking Ali by the hand. "Let me show you."

"Well, this is all right, isn't it?" says Jack, taking a deep breath of sea air and stretching his arms up.

"This is better than *all right*, mate," says Noah jovially.

"It's like something out of the *Real Housewives of Beverly Hills*!" Paige laughs, unable to disguise her glee.

"See, I told you it wasn't going to be all bad," muses Rachel as she bumps her shoulder into Paige.

"Let's see if the groom's managed to get any sundries in," says Jack as he walks back into the house.

"Does red wine fall under that category?" asks Noah, following him.

"I bloody hope so!" Jack laughs. It's the first time that he's seemed genuinely relaxed.

"This really is something," says Paige, as she and Rachel stay where they are, looking out into the darkness. The moon is shrouded in thin clouds, casting a sliver of light across the inky-black sea below, and Rachel can't help but shudder again at the proximity of the ocean, and all that lies beneath its surface.

"Here, do you want this?" asks Paige, pulling her pashmina from her shoulders and offering it to Rachel.

"Thanks," she says, gratefully taking it.

Paige pulls the shawl up onto Rachel's shoulders. "You're very forgiving of her, you know," she says.

"Who?" asks Rachel, unnecessarily.

"You *know* who."

Rachel shrugs. "What else am I supposed to do? She's going to be family soon and you know what they say . . . ?"

Paige looks at her with raised eyebrows.

"You can't choose your family . . ." Rachel goes on.

"She should certainly come with an instruction to only take in small doses," says Paige, half laughing.

Rachel chuckles. "I'll give you that, but once the wedding's out of the way, we'll probably not see that much of her. It's poor Will we should feel sorry for."

"Why have we got to feel sorry for *him*?" asks Jack, returning to the terrace with two glasses of red wine. He hands one to Rachel, and Noah gives another to Paige.

"Ssh," says Rachel, pulling Jack toward a sunken seating area. It's only as she collapses into the cushions that she realizes that a firepit is simmering in front of her.

"Don't you find it tiresome?" asks Paige, sitting down.

"What?" asks Jack.

"*Her!*" says Paige, nodding her head in the direction they'd last seen Ali.

Jack takes a large slug of wine.

"She's just so full-on," says Paige. "Even *before* she's had a drink."

"You're full-on, even before you've had a drink," says Jack, laughing.

"I get why she rubs some people up the wrong way," says Rachel, eager to dispel the growing sense that a ruckus is brewing. It often does when Jack and Paige get together, because they're both so hot-headed and keen to prove themselves right that they could argue over the price of a pint of milk. "But I think she's a laugh. The world would certainly be a duller place if she wasn't in it, that's for sure."

"You were moaning about her earlier," says Paige.

"I *wasn't*," says Rachel. "I was just talking about how she seems to wind some people up."

"Namely, Jack," states Paige.

Rachel widens her eyes, wishing she hadn't said anything.

"Whoa," says Jack, holding his hands up in the air. "Don't bring me into this."

"But you *have* got a problem with her?" presses Paige.

"I didn't say that."

"You didn't have to," says Paige. "It's written all over your face."

"And since when were you able to read my expressions?"

Here we go, thinks Rachel, as she brings her feet up under her and swirls her red wine around in its glass. Once they get started, Jack and Paige are like a sparring brother and sister who seem to enjoy getting a rise out of each other. It's good-humored for the most part, the pair of them playing a ping-pong game of banter—each of them desperate to win the volley—but it's been known to get a little out of hand. Rachel suspects it's because they both work in high-pressure jobs and are used to—perhaps even *thrive* on—being constantly challenged by someone else's opinion.

Defending herself, or someone else, is what Paige does for a living—"the Rottweiler with a handbag" is how she's known within the legal profession. If you were ever in trouble, *she's* who you'd want onside to get you out of it. But while her ability to argue her way out of a paper bag may well be of use to someone accused of murder, when the same tactics were used to wage a war on your husband, it could be a little overkill.

Rachel rolls her eyes at Noah and he smiles knowingly back, no doubt wondering, like her, how the four of them could ever be best friends. If a stranger looked at them, they would probably assume that it was her and Noah who were a couple; the pair of them sharing an easy, laid-back attitude that Jack and Paige couldn't even imagine possessing. They were happy just bobbing along, seeing the good in everyone and everything, while Jack and Paige cast a cynical eye over the minutiae of life.

Yet somehow, collectively, it worked. Perhaps because they all got something from each other's spouses that they didn't get from their own.

"So, what's your problem with her?" Paige asks, like a dog with a bone.

Jack looks into his glass, as if he's deliberating whether to say what he's about to say.

"I . . ." he starts, before looking around. "I . . . just don't trust her."

"Why not?" asks Paige.

"P . . ." says Noah, warning her not to push it.

"I've got my reasons" is all that Jack says.

Rachel leans forward, her brow furrowed. "Is there something you're not telling us?"

Jack sighs heavily.

"There's clearly something playing on your mind," says Paige, doubling the pressure.

He looks resignedly between Paige and Rachel. "I think she's cheated on him." His words are almost inaudible.

"*What?*" exclaims Rachel, followed by a deafening silence from Paige. She daren't look to see the *"I told you so"* expression on her face.

"How do you . . . how do you know?" asks Rachel, as her heart breaks into a thousand pieces for poor Will, who's like a brother to her.

"Rick at work," said Jack. "He told me he'd been sleeping with her for a couple of months."

"But does he know . . . ?" starts Rachel. "That she's with Will and he's your brother?"

Jack shakes his head. "When they started going out, I told Ali I didn't want anyone at work to know there was a connection. I wanted to keep everything professional."

"So, this Rick guy didn't know he was revealing anything untoward?" asks Paige.

"No," says Jack. "It was just one of those situations in the pub after work and he said to a few of us that he had been 'banging the hot girl who used to work in A&R,' for want of a better expression."

"Well, when did this happen?" asks Rachel. "Was it recently or before her and Will got together?"

Jack shrugs his shoulders as if he's physically trying to unburden himself of the knowledge he's been carrying for all this time. "He told me in the summer," he says. "I don't know if it's still going on, as he left shortly after."

Rachel can hardly think straight as her mind desperately tries to unravel the news and put it back together in a form that she's happy with.

"Does Will *know*?" she says, when it doesn't work.

"I don't think so," says Jack. "And I don't want him to either."

"You can't let him marry her," says Paige, her voice high-pitched.

"Listen," says Jack, sounding suddenly authoritative. "I've had this going around on a loop in my head for months, wondering what I should do."

Now, it's all beginning to fall into place, thinks Rachel. *He's been so wound up lately.* "But don't you think he deserves to be told?" she offers meekly.

He turns to face her. "You said yourself, that you'd never seen him so happy."

She nods miserably.

"He's a grown man who can hopefully see Ali for what she is," says Jack. "And if he's happy with that, then who am I to stand between them? It doesn't mean I have to like her, but I can put the face on to get through this weekend and I'd ask that you all do the same."

He looks at Paige with raised eyebrows, knowing that she's the most likely to struggle with such a request.

"I've *never* liked her," she hisses.

"I shouldn't have told you," says Jack, raking a hand through his hair.

"I wish you hadn't," says Rachel, wondering how on earth she's going to stand by and let her trusting brother-in-law marry a woman who has been unfaithful to him.

"But you have to promise to keep it to yourselves and not let it ruin the weekend."

"It just goes to show that you never know what goes on behind closed doors," says Noah.

The four of them fall ominously silent when Ali and Will appear at the top of a flight of stairs leading onto a darkened corner of the patio. Rachel immediately feels herself going hot at the thought of them having heard what they've been saying. She searches their expressions for any telltale signs. There are none.

"Oh my God, you guys," shrieks Ali, as irrepressible as ever. "You need to see our room." She claps her hands together like an excited child on Christmas morning.

"Another drink, anyone?" asks Paige, not even trying to disguise her indifference.

"I'll help you," says Jack, getting up. "What are we having?"

"Just a glass of water for me, please," says Ali. "I'm still recovering from the flight." She pulls an apologetic face.

"Will?" asks Jack.

"A glass of red, please, mate."

Rachel watches as Jack and Paige retreat to the kitchen, half-wishing that she'd been quicker off the mark.

"Honestly, guys, our room is *in*sane," squeals Ali. "It's got windows into the pool, so you can see underwater."

"Wow," says Rachel lamely, willing herself out of the stupor that she's become entrenched in. She can't let Will see the change in her, no matter how dramatic the reason.

"So, whose villa is this, exactly?" asks Noah, proving he's better at pretending everything is fine than she is.

Will sits down on the plump cushions opposite Rachel, and Ali immediately plops down next to him, snuggling herself under his arm.

"Funnily enough, it's owned by the family of my business partner back in the UK," says Will, looking up at the villa. It's now awash with cool blue lighting, giving Rachel the vibe of a club that she and Noah went to in Ibiza, the summer after they graduated from uni.

"He and I met through the surfing school I set up down here," Will goes on.

"God, I'd forgotten about that," says Noah.

Rachel hates to admit it, but so had she. Will had had so many failed business ventures and half-cocked, hare-brained ideas, it was probably easier to remember the things he *hadn't* done.

"So, he's who you work with on the water-sports company back home?"

Will nods. "He had the finance to set us up with all the equipment, but it's gone so well that we're fifty-fifty partners now."

"Do you think it's something you'll look to expand even more?" asks Noah.

"I hope so," says Will. "It's all very well having a water-sports company on a lake, but I miss the sea. We're looking at premises down in Newquay, with the hope of setting up a surfing school again."

"I'd love to give surfing a go at some point," says Noah.

Will smiles. "Well, you never know . . ."

Ali bounces up and down in her seat. "Can I tell him?" she says. "Please, please let me tell him."

Will looks at her with such warmth in his eyes that it almost makes Rachel cry. She doesn't care if it's still going on or not: she'll never understand how Ali could *ever* cheat on him. She forces the thought to the back of her mind, because she has four days to get through and she can't feel like this every time she looks at him.

"Go on then," says Will encouragingly.

Ali sits up and looks between Rachel and Noah, her eyes alight with mischief.

"So . . ." she says, drawing it out. "We've got something to tell you."

Jack and Paige return with a bottle of wine and a glass of water, which Paige almost looks pained to offer to Ali. This trip is going to be harder than any of them could imagine.

Ali waits until she has everyone's undivided attention. "We've arranged a little surprise for tomorrow."

Rachel's sure that she hears Paige groan. If she did, Ali chooses to ignore it.

"The boys are going surfing, while us girls are having a yoga session on the beach." Ali smiles and puts her arms in the air. "Woo-hoo, surf's up, dudes."

There's a tangible delay in reaction, and if it weren't for Noah, Rachel's unsure anyone would have said anything.

"That's awesome," he exclaims, eager to fill the void.

Ali flashes a megawatt smile. "Will's going to take you and Jack out and give you a lesson."

"Great," says Jack, desperately trying to show willing. "I haven't been out on the waves for years."

"We'll take it slow to get you familiarized," says Will. "And Noah, I've no doubt that once I show you the basics, you'll be well on your way."

"And while they're doing *their* thing, ladies," says Ali, "I've booked us a one-hour yoga session."

Will blows his cheeks out. "Though, I warn you not to follow Ali's lead unless you want to do yourself some serious damage, because she can get herself into some insane positions."

"I *bet* she can," says Paige, looking as if she has a bad taste in her mouth.

Rachel doesn't need to look to know that Jack's eyes will be boring into her best friend, sending a silent warning to watch what she says.

Ali giggles, none the wiser. "I remember one time we were in Paris and we went to see the Moulin Rouge. I'm ashamed to say that I was so drunk, that I thought I could join the cast, so got up on the stage just before the final curtain and did the splits."

"That must have been some show," says Paige to Will, sarcastically.

"Oh, she wasn't with me," he says.

"It was an ex-boyfriend," says Ali, grimacing. "I don't think he was particularly impressed."

"I can't imagine *anyone* would be, if their girlfriend made a fool of herself like that," says Paige.

Noah laughs awkwardly. "So how long did you have your surf school down here?" he asks Will, in a clumsy attempt to change the subject.

"About eighteen months," says Will. "It's just about the longest I've stayed *anywhere*. But hey, I must have managed to put down enough roots to make this feel like the place I wanted to get married. I know a lot more people here than anywhere else in the world."

"Well, let's give thanks for that!" says Noah, looking up at the house and raising his glass.

"Oh, don't be acting as if butter wouldn't melt," Ali says to Paige, as if Noah and Will hadn't spoken.

Rachel's ears burn with a searing heat as she prays that Paige hasn't heard her, and wills Ali not to say another word.

"You must have done things you're not particularly proud of," Ali goes on, leaving Rachel's prayers unanswered.

She feels Paige bristle as an expectant hush descends, as if they're all waiting with bated breath for an answer.

"I don't tend to make mistakes," says Paige eventually.

"Oh, come on," pushes Ali. "You can't possibly have been this perfect *all* your life."

Noah chokes theatrically on his wine. "Well, there was this time . . ."

"Ah-ha!" shouts Ali triumphantly, as Paige throws Noah a warning look. "I knew it! So, come on, Noah. Tell us what your perfect wife *used* to get up to."

Paige laughs, but it sounds hollow. "I can assure you, I'm by no means perfect." She takes hold of Noah's hand beside her and squeezes it, but Rachel can't tell whether it's for support or to reprimand him for dropping her in it.

Ali tucks her legs up underneath her as if she's settling into a good film, and Rachel winces as she waits to see how Paige is going to play this. Is she going to give Ali what she wants? A glimpse of her old self, in another life? Or is she going to stick to the carefully crafted character she's created for herself in order to get ahead in an industry that has piranhas snapping at your heels at the first sign of weakness?

It was that version that Rachel got to see more often than not these days, as the pressure in the city forced Paige to be someone she never used to be. They still had fun whenever they were together, but it had become more and more inhibited—as if Paige had an impenetrable barrier around her that wouldn't let her fully kick back and relax. As if by doing so, she would reveal a vulnerability she couldn't afford to expose.

Paige drains her glass of wine and puts it back onto the table with a vigor that has both Noah and Jack reaching for the bottle to give her a refill.

"So, what have you done?" asks Ali, unable to let it go.

Paige looks around the group, as if sizing them all up; gauging whether she should say what she's about to say.

"I took drugs once," she says eventually.

A hush momentarily descends over the group before Ali spits out some water. "Are you serious?" Her eyes widen.

"Yep," mutters Paige.

"That *doesn't* count," exclaims Ali. "We've *all* done that! Come on, Noah, what's Paige done that she'd be ashamed to tell us about?"

Noah laughs nervously. "Should I tell them about the time you refused to come down from the podium in Halkidiki, or when you got yourself arrested?"

Paige's jaw involuntarily spasms as she tries to smile, but it doesn't quite reach her eyes.

"Oh my God," squeals Ali. "You got *arrested*? What for?"

Paige clears her throat. "I was at a rally and an over-zealous police officer decided to make an example of me."

"That's brilliant!" says Ali, clapping her hands together. "What were you protesting against?"

"Erm, it was a women's rights march in London," says Paige. "A judge had let off a rapist because he said the victim was too drunk to know whether she consented or not."

"No way," says Ali, without a modicum of conviction. "That sucks."

"Indeed it does," says Paige tightly.

"So, do you consider yourself a feminist?" asks Ali.

"I don't think wanting to see a rapist convicted of his crime makes me a feminist," says Paige. "But believing in equal opportunities and not wanting to be treated any differently because I'm a woman probably makes me one."

"So, you're not a fan of being called darling or being whistled at in the street?" asks Ali.

"Who *is*?" replies Paige. "Anyone who condones that kind of behavior is doing a real disservice to the rest of the female population."

"You work at the Old Bailey, right?" asks Ali.

Paige nods. "Sometimes."

"So, do you feel you have to work extra hard to prove yourself? To prove that you're just as good at your job as your male counterparts?"

"I've worked hard to get to where I am," says Paige. "But I've no doubt I'd be even further on if I was a man."

"Doesn't that piss you off?" asks Ali, as if trying to get a rise out of Paige.

"Yes, but it's the way of the world and, although it's slowly changing, we'll never truly be equals. But it would really help the cause if we could all unite and present a stronger force, so that men know they can't take any of us for fools."

"I think the tide is turning," says Ali.

"*Do* you?" says Paige, seemingly taken aback. "How *can* it be, when there are still some women who continually play up to it? Who feel that the only way to get a man's attention is to play the damsel in distress?"

Rachel sinks further into the sofa cushions as Paige's sharp tone reverberates around the group. She knows her well enough to know that if any one topic is going to get her stoked, feminism is it, and with the new information on Ali, it feels like a firecracker is about to go off.

"God, I hate women like that," says Ali, without any trace of irony. "I've met a few of them in my time."

"Anyway, how's the new job going?" asks Rachel, desperate to change the subject.

Ali laughs. "I've been there over a year now, so it doesn't feel like a new job anymore."

"Gosh," says Rachel, looking at Jack with raised eyebrows. "Has it really been that long?"

"Mmm," he mutters. "Time flies."

Rachel remembers being introduced to Ali as if it were yesterday. She'd gone to meet Jack in the pub after work and Ali was there waxing lyrical about how nice he was and how he'd taken her under his wing.

"Seriously, he's gone way over and above to help me settle in," she'd said.

"That's Jack for you," Rachel had said as the pair of them stood there watching him order a round of drinks at the end of the bar.

"But he doesn't have to," said Ali. "He could easily offload me onto someone less senior, but he seems really invested in my success. I've learned so much from him already."

Rachel had raised her eyebrows in surprise because, if the truth be known, that didn't actually sound like Jack at all. For the past month, all he'd done was complain that he couldn't leave the office much before nine at night. He'd said the company was in the middle of a merger and he'd been working flat-out on supplying all the data and information that was required before the deadline. Which, much to his annoyance, had superseded his day job of finding new musical talent to produce and promote. So, if his workload was *that* full-on,

Rachel had wondered, where was he finding the time to mentor a new recruit?

Despite herself, Rachel hadn't been able to help but reevaluate the woman standing in front of her as she silently weighed up the risk factor. Not that her marriage was prime for sabotage—she and Jack were as tight as any couple she knew—but she defied *any* woman in her position not to at least make an unspoken checklist.

To start with, Ali was blonde, and Rachel had never known Jack to veer away from brunette. She had almost laughed out loud, unable to believe her mind was even taking her down this road, but still she couldn't stop herself from taking in Ali's curves, impossibly tiny waist, and full rosebud lips, that she imagined were the stuff of men's dreams.

Rachel had felt like an ungainly giant standing next to her, but she'd refused to quite literally bow to the pressure of making herself seem smaller, more petite. Yet she couldn't help but wish that she'd worn her long brown hair down, instead of it being in a messy bun on top of her head, and that she'd applied a smidge of lipstick to make herself feel as if she was at least a contender in the race.

The race for what? she'd asked herself as she looked at Jack. *I've already won.*

"Where were you working before?" she'd asked Ali, by way of making small talk, even though she wasn't really interested in the answer.

"I was at Maverick Promotions," said Ali. "And my boss there was a total dickhead."

Rachel had looked at her through narrowed eyes, surprised by her indiscretion.

"How so?" she said.

"He crossed the line," said Ali. "He thought because I'm the way I am, that he could take advantage of me."

"The way you *are*?" asked Rachel, keen to establish exactly what she meant and the threat it might present.

"That I'm outgoing and friendly," said Ali.

Rachel waited for her to add "and because I look like every man's fantasy," but she didn't.

"So, what happened?" Rachel asked, when no more information was forthcoming.

Ali looked up, her piercing blue eyes staring straight through her. "He took me for a fool," she said. "He thought I was just some blonde bimbo who he could silence, due to his position of power, but he was wrong." The tone of Ali's voice as she said those last four words troubled Rachel, though she couldn't quite put her finger on whether it was because he'd treated her badly or because she'd made sure he hadn't got away with it.

"Well, I'm glad that you made a stand," she said, part of her wanting to ask more questions, but equally not wanting to get into it. "Men like him need to know that we won't accept that kind of behavior. We need to push back against these predators."

"Yes, girl!" Ali had declared, before pulling Rachel into a sudden embrace. As Rachel extricated herself, making excuses that she needed to go and help Jack, Ali started making her way toward a circle of men who were becoming rowdier by the minute.

"She's quite a force," Rachel had commented to Jack as he handed her a glass of white wine.

"Mmm, I wonder if she's too much so."

Rachel had cocked her head to one side. "Meaning?"

"Well, look at her," said Jack, taking a sip of his pint of lager and licking the white-foam residue from his lip.

As Rachel had watched Ali coil her arm around the neck of the most handsome of the bunch, pleading with him to dance to Whitney Houston's "How Will I Know," she wondered if Jack might have a point.

"Hey!" said Will, coming up behind her at the bar and squeezing her waist.

"Hi!" Rachel squealed, excitedly pulling him into her for a hug.

"You're back! Ooh it's so lovely to see you—it's been far too long." He flashed her a smile through his thick beard.

"Hey, bro," he said as he leaned in to Jack and they did that macho shoulder nudge thing that men who like to be cool do nowadays.

"Come here," said Jack, thinking better of it and pulling his younger brother in for a proper embrace. "How you doing?"

"Knackered," said Will.

Jack laughed. "How can you be knackered when you've spent the last two months in Vietnam, doing sweet FA?"

Will smiled and rolled his eyes at Rachel, as if to say, *here we go*. "I meant from the flight. Being stuck in economy for twelve hours with legs this long is punishing."

"My heart bleeds for you." Jack sighed theatrically. "What can I get you?"

"I'll have a pint, please," said Will, as he put his arm around Rachel.

"So, what have you been up to?" she asked. "How was your time at the monastery?"

"Intense," said Will. "Let's just say that two months was plenty long enough to know that it wasn't what I wanted."

Rachel had looked at him: so worldly-wise, yet still so vulnerable. At thirty-three, he was seemingly no nearer knowing what it was he *did* want.

He meandered from one low-paid job to the next, flitting between countries and continents as casually as if it were a routine commute. Sometimes, Rachel envied his bohemian lifestyle, his ability to put down roots wherever he landed, no matter how shallow they were. But mostly she worried, like an over-protective big sister, whether he was ever going to be able to settle down in one place long enough to meet someone and start a family of his own.

She could never have guessed that, that very night, her prayers were going to be answered.

"You must miss having such a live wire in the office?" offers Paige now with a hint of sarcasm that only those who know her well would hear.

Jack looks at her with raised eyebrows. "Her absence is noticeable" is all he says.

"Aw, that's so sweet," gushes Ali, leaning over to rub Jack's arm. "I'm pleased that I'm missed."

Rachel squirms on his behalf.

"So, you're working for David Friedman's company now?" asks Noah, no doubt feeling the chill in the atmosphere.

Ali nods animatedly.

"Have you met him yet?"

"Yes," says Ali, smiling broadly.

Paige throws a scathing glance in Rachel's direction that says, "*She's probably sleeping with him.*"

"That must be pretty exciting," Noah goes on. "Is he just like we see him on TV?"

"Nicer," says Ali. "He used to have a reputation as being a bit mean when he first started on the judging panel of *Star Maker* . . ."

"Yes, I remember," says Rachel. "But he's a bit more chilled out now."

"Well, he's even more so behind the scenes," says Ali. "I really like him."

"You'd think that someone like him would be able to spot them a mile off, wouldn't you?" says Paige, almost to herself.

"*Them?*" questions Ali.

"The kind of women we're talking about," says Paige, proving her reputation that once she's got the bit between her teeth, she doesn't let go.

"The women you're referring to don't all wear short skirts and have a sign over their heads," says Ali.

"True enough," says Paige.

"If you're implying . . . ?" Ali starts, before stopping herself.

"I'm not implying *anything*," says Paige.

"Wearing the clothes I want makes me feel empowered," says Ali, sounding a little more authoritative than Rachel has heard her before. "If a man happens to find that attractive or misconstrues it to mean that I'm coming on to them, then so be it, but make no mistake: *I'm* the one in control. Not them."

"You sound as if you're speaking from experience," says Paige.

"Anyone want another drink?" blurts out Rachel, in an attempt to change the subject. She looks to Noah, wide-eyed, but he offers a reassuring wink and a nod to the almost-full bottle sitting on the table.

Ali sighs. "There *was* a time when I foolishly believed that sleeping with someone would further my career. But obviously it only served to cut it short."

"So, you learned your lesson?" asks Paige, almost triumphantly.

"*That* wasn't the lesson," says Ali bluntly. "Finding out he had a wife was."

3

The men laugh nervously, as Rachel and Paige look at each other in shock. Not because Ali had done it, Rachel supposes, but that she'd happily admit to it.

"You're a real ad for the sisterhood, aren't you?" says Paige sarcastically.

"P . . . ," cautions Noah.

"*What?*" she replies haughtily. "I'm just stating the facts."

Noah looks wearily at Rachel, as if asking for an ally in the uphill struggle he finds himself in, and she finds herself torn between the two of them, not knowing who to back.

She takes a deep breath. "If Ali wasn't *aware* she was breaking the code until it was too late, she can't really be held accountable," she offers, hoping it's enough to appease both sides.

"Assuming she stopped it the minute she found out, you mean?" questions Paige, as if Ali isn't there.

"Exactly," says Rachel. "And that's what happened, right?" She crosses everything in the hope that Ali says yes.

"Of course," she enthuses. "What woman would sleep with a man they knew belonged to someone else?"

Noah laughs. "Depends if he's Bradley Cooper or not."

Rachel can't help but love him for trying to break the vicious circle they seem trapped in.

Ali smiles. "Would *you* sleep with Bradley Cooper?" she asks Rachel.

"If *he* was married, or *I* was?"

They all laugh—even Paige, whose edges are being slowly softened by the alcohol. Another couple of glasses should see off all those sharp corners, and Rachel can't get there fast enough.

She looks to Jack, as if weighing up her answer. "Mmm," she muses. "If *he* was married, then definitely not. But if *I* was . . ."

"You are *so* cheap," says Jack, laughing and throwing a cushion at her. "Don't y'all be thinking that it would stop there either. Bradley is one of many on her long list of lucky men she'd get with if she had a hall pass."

"A hall pass?" questions Ali with a vexed brow. "What's that?"

"You don't have a hall pass?" says Rachel in mock shock.

Ali looks at Will, confused and shaking her head. "No, I don't think so."

"I'm not sure there'd be enough passes to go around," snipes Paige, but nobody seems to acknowledge it apart from Rachel, who throws her an admonishing glare.

"So, a hall pass is a one-night-only ticket that's given to you by your partner to spend with a celebrity."

Ali looks at her open-mouthed. "For real?" she gawps.

"No, of course not," says Rachel, unable to believe this girl's ditziness at times. "It's just a fantasy game."

"Ooh," Ali exclaims theatrically. "I didn't have you down for the role-playing type."

Rachel is taken aback, offended by the slight and wondering what it is about her that makes her look like she doesn't enjoy a satisfying love life.

There's only thirteen years between her and Ali, but it may as well be thirty for the way she makes her feel. While Ali's so full of zest and energy, seemingly ready to take on whatever life happens to throw at her head-on, Rachel feels dull and worn-out in comparison.

She self-consciously runs her hands through her hair, questioning whether she looks even older than she feels. She'd always kept her hair long, believing it made her look young and attractive, but perhaps that was only from behind nowadays. The thought of someone seeing her turn around and saying, "God, I thought she was going to be younger than that," makes her squirm with embarrassment. Of course, she chooses not to acknowledge that she still has the figure for someone to make such a mistake.

When Ali looks at her, laughing at something she can't hear because the roar of self-doubt circumnavigating her brain is so much louder, Rachel wonders what she sees. Has all trace of the ambitious career woman, who loved to live spontaneously, all but vanished? Has it been replaced by a wholesome motherly figure who looks like she spends her days knitting and listening to classical music?

But I'm still *in here*, her twenty-one-year-old self silently shouts, as she fingers the buttons on her white shirt, wondering whether, in her efforts not to look like mutton dressed as lamb, she's now dressing like an old lady instead. Her eyes settle on her legs, encased in dark skinny denim, though she doesn't see how slim they are or how long they go on for. Why would she, when she's solely focused on pulling herself apart?

On good days, she can appreciate herself for what she is; a forty-two-year-old mother of one who goes to the gym whenever she can force herself to and eats healthily and whose only vice is a chocolate digestive with her cup of tea every morning. But on bad days, like the one she's only just realized she's having today, she wonders whether it's all worth it, when everyone else will only ever see her as a woman who's past her best.

She'd lamented her fears when she'd met up with Paige a couple of weeks ago, after her own attempt at holding back the years.

"I just think I should try it on my forehead," Rachel had said, as she looked in awe at Paige's wrinkle-free brow. "Just to see what difference it makes."

"You don't need Botox," Paige had said, through a mouthful of garlic bread.

Rachel would probably agree, but she was feeling under increasing pressure to join the thousands of women who were erasing ten years of life and laughter from their faces.

"Nor do *you*, but you still have it done every three months," she said.

"This is my mask," Paige had said. "My poker face for when I'm at work."

"So, it's got nothing to do with wanting to recapture your youth?" Rachel had teased.

"If you're doing it for that reason, then I think that's where it starts to go wrong, because you just keep wanting more and more. Anyway, I don't know why you'd want to turn the clock back—Jack loves you just the way you are."

She was right about that. Jack loved her, warts and all. In fact, he was dead against her doing anything to "enhance" herself, but it still didn't make her feel any more secure when she was around women like Ali.

As she looks at her now, with her boosted bosom and inflated pillow lips, Rachel wonders whether even women like *her* are happy in their own skin. While an onlooker might see a beautiful, overly confident woman, might Ali still see the person who's hiding inside, when she looks in the mirror? If she does, Rachel feels a rare moment of empathy with her. It's exhausting trying to be the person you think you want to be, when all you really want is to be happy being the person you are.

"Be careful what you presume," says Rachel, looking at Ali. "You never know what goes on behind closed doors."

"Steady on," says Jack, laughing nervously. "I don't think anybody needs the rundown."

"Oh, I think we do," says Ali, leaning forward, all ears.

"So, Jack . . ." starts Rachel, to a chorus of "whoas." It's hard to tell who they're coming from among the calls of "*TMI,*" "*go on*" and "*urgh, he's my brother.*"

"Spill," urges Ali, talking to Rachel, but looking at Jack.

"I'll spare his blushes," says Rachel. "But we're having a very nice time at the moment, aren't we?"

Jack looks around awkwardly.

"Come on," says Ali. "You're among friends. If we can't tell our friends about the fun we have, who *can* we tell?"

"You might want to think about keeping it to yourself," says Paige, sagely.

Normally, Rachel would agree with her, but after Ali's assumption that she and Jack are doing the missionary position, and only on Wednesdays, she feels compelled to put her straight.

She wants to say that since Josh had left home for university, all she and Jack ever seemed to do was have sex. They'd shared candlelit baths, being serenaded by Marvin Gaye; she'd unzipped him one Sunday afternoon while he was sitting in the lounge reading the paper, and he'd even interrupted the unloading of the dishwasher last week, apparently unable to wait until they were in bed.

"Well, since Josh has been gone, we've not known quite what to do with ourselves, have we?" She chastises herself for making it sound as if their sex life had been dead up until then. "Of course, once Josh was old enough to go out to parties, we'd have a bottle of champagne with dinner, and a naughty session of foreplay in the living room, just because we could."

Ali shakes her head, as if she's shocked. "I gotta give it to you Rach, you're a dark horse." She laughs to herself. "It's always the quiet ones."

Relishing in her newfound role of surprising people, Rachel goes on. "Though, that came to a rather abrupt end the night Josh and his mates couldn't get into the pub, so decided to come back to ours instead."

She smiles at Jack, but his eyes stay focused awkwardly on the flickering flames of the fire.

His discomfort is enough to stop her from saying that they couldn't get up the stairs quick enough, the pair of them breathless from the sudden interruption and the full-on exertion needed to get out of the lounge before the boys piled in. And that it was only when they had collapsed giggling behind the closed door of their bedroom that Rachel remembered she'd left her knickers on the sofa.

"You forget how it used to be, before kids, is all I'm saying," she says.

"So, normal service resumes once they leave home, does it?" says Paige.

"It's better than normal." Rachel smiles.

"Your Chloe will be off to college before too long, won't she?" asks Ali, her eyes wide, both literally and metaphorically.

"That's the plan," says Noah, crossing his fingers.

"Is that you wishing for your daughter's success, or the promise of more blow jobs?" says Ali, laughing hysterically.

Noah smiles and looks at Will. "I'm afraid to say that once you're pronounced man and wife, you won't know what a blow job *is*. Oral sex and marriage don't make for good bedfellows."

"We're never going to let that side of our relationship go," says Ali, rubbing her hand up and down Will's thigh. "Not even when we have children."

Paige snorts. "You won't have a choice. As soon as you have kids, you're in for eighteen years of worrying whether they're going to walk in."

Ali shakes her head vehemently.

"You mark my words," says Paige, laughing at her naivety. "Your sex life will be confined to unspontaneous fumblings under a duvet when you would both far rather go to sleep."

"We'll always make time for each other," says Ali, kissing Will on the lips.

"Then I suggest you don't have kids," says Paige.

"We want them as soon as possible," says Will, looking at Ali. "Don't we?"

She nods frantically. "We're going to start trying as soon as we're married."

"On our wedding night?" asks Will, laughing.

"Deal," says Ali, putting her hand out for Will to shake.

"I can't wait to be a dad," says Will. "I've never been jealous of Jack for anything, apart from when he became a father. That's the only part of my life that I regret; that I didn't have children earlier."

"Oh, babe," says Ali, leaning into him. "There's still time."

"What if I've left it too late? No one knows how easy or difficult it's going to be until they start trying. What if it takes years?"

"Well, good thing we've got years on our side," says Ali.

He looks at her, panicked. "But we *are* going to start trying straight away, aren't we?"

"Yes, of course, honey," says Ali, as if he were a small child.

Will pulls himself up and takes a deep breath. "Honestly, if I was never able to experience what you guys have with Josh and Chloe, I don't know what I'd do."

"Do they get along?" asks Ali, seemingly wanting to change the subject. "Your two, I mean. There can't be that big a gap between them."

Noah nods. "It's just under two years," he says, looking to Rachel for confirmation. "They used to be really tight, but have gradually grown apart as the teenage years wreaked havoc on them."

"They used to be like brother and sister," remembers Paige.

Rachel coughs, as her wine goes down the wrong way. "They still get along, but there's just a bit of awkwardness there now."

"That'll change again, no doubt," says Will. "In the next few years, once they come out the other side of university."

Ali's eyes widen. "Oh my God!" she squeals excitedly. "What if they end up together?"

"Er, I don't think so," muses Rachel, almost to herself.

"Excuse me," says Paige. "Are you saying *my* daughter's not good enough for *your* son?"

"No," says Rachel, forcing a laugh. "I'm just saying that I don't think that will happen."

"Why would it be *such* a bad idea?" asks Paige.

"It would just be weird. They've grown up with one another. It'd be like getting together with your best friend."

"Yeah, I suppose," says Paige, thoughtfully. "It'd be the modern-day equivalent of you and Noah getting together."

"*Exactly*," says Rachel, throwing her hands up in the air and shuddering for effect.

She's grateful when the *Dirty Dancing* theme song starts playing through the patio speakers, and takes the opportunity to divert the increasingly uncomfortable conversation.

"Ah, this is our song," she squeals, standing up and beckoning Jack, just like she did the first time they met on a crowded dance floor at an eighties night twenty years ago.

"I'm going to marry that man," she'd said to her friend Cass, as she watched him dance the "Love Man" as well as she'd ever seen anyone do. With the exception of Patrick Swayze, of course.

"Yeah, you and every other girl in this place," Cass had replied, laughing.

He'd made his way across the floor toward her as soon as she'd gestured to him. Incredibly, it never occurred to her at the time that he wouldn't; such is the confidence of youth.

"You seem to know what you're doing," she'd said as he'd pulled her in close and they'd gyrated against each other.

He'd smiled, revealing two dimples. "What can I say? I know every song and every dance move."

Rachel had had to restrain herself from taking him by the hand and dragging him to the DJ booth to request "(I've Had) The Time of My Life."

"My husband and I are going to perform the finale as the first dance at our wedding," she'd said.

Jack had looked at her, clearly bemused. "Does he know?"

"No," she'd said. "Because I haven't met him yet."

A year and a baby later, she'd run to him at their wedding reception and he'd lifted her up to the strains of Bill Medley and Jennifer Warnes.

Rachel smiles at the memory now. "Come on, *Johnny*," she says in an American accent.

Jack laughs as he gets up. "Whatever you want, Baby," he says, taking her in his arms and whisking her around the terrace.

She doesn't want to spoil the moment, but they've never been ones to keep secrets from each other—at least she didn't think they were—and she doesn't want to start now.

"Why didn't you tell me about Ali's cheating?" she asks.

He looks at her, before going to speak and seemingly thinking better of it.

"You know you can tell me anything," she goes on, hoping to coax a reason from him as to why he's kept her out in the cold on this.

"I didn't want you to worry about it," he says, kissing her on the forehead. "Because I know how much you love Will."

"But don't you think we should tell him?" she asks, breathing him in as he holds her tight. "So that he has the choice of whether he marries her or not?"

"He may already know," he says, spinning her out and pulling her back in again. She can't help but giggle that he still knows the routine. "Either way, he's happy, and I'm not about to be the one to destroy that, because he might never forgive me."

Rachel can see where he's coming from. "So, we're assuming whatever was going on with this Rick guy is over, as otherwise why would she marry Will if she wants to be with someone else?"

"Exactly," said Jack. "And I'd rather Will be in blissful ignorance, because what he doesn't know can't hurt him."

"May I steal your man from you?" interrupts Ali as she sidles up beside the pair of them.

Rachel looks at Jack wide-eyed as Ali tries to wedge herself between them. Putting one arm around his waist and taking his hand in hers, Ali manhandles him across to the other side of the pool. Reluctance is written all over his face and it looks as if she is dragging a sack of potatoes around the patio.

"Do you know what?" he says, stopping stock-still, as if his feet are encased in concrete. "It's been a long day and I'm whacked."

"Oh, don't be so boring," whines Ali. "Dance with me, at least until the end of the song."

Rachel wonders if *everyone* can see the restraint he's having to exercise, the tension in his stance, the involuntary tic in his jaw. Or do they have to know him as well as she does to know that the pressure cooker is about to explode?

4

"Wow!" says Rachel, as she steps out onto the terrace the next morning, to where Paige, Noah, Will and Ali are already nursing their hangovers.

The ocean stretches out as far as the eye can see and waves bigger than she's ever seen before crash into the cliffs below the villa, with a thunderous roar.

"It's awesome, isn't it?" says Will. "Nature at its very best."

"I can't believe I slept through this," says Rachel, over the rumbling of another swell; the white crest of which is just about to fold in on itself.

She takes herself to the edge of the patio and turns to look back in from the peninsula onto the beach inland. "Is that where we're going?" she says, pointing to the pristine golden sands where surfers are running in and out of the breakers.

"Yep," says Will, walking toward her with a freshly brewed coffee. "We'll jump on the funicular."

Rachel smiles, remembering the cable car she and Noah got stuck in for an hour as it swung precariously over snow-peaked mountains in Chamonix. He'd spent most of it with his eyes closed, begging her to stop rocking it.

"I can't wait to get out there," says Will, looking at the ocean in awe.

"But these waves are huge," says Rachel.

"That's what this area is famous for. Surfers from all over the world come to Nazaré at this time of year, hoping to be lucky enough to ride the big one."

"So, how big is the big one?" Rachel asks, shuddering involuntarily.

"It could be anything up to thirty meters," says Will, his eyes alight.

"I don't think Jack and Noah are able to tackle anything like *that*," she says, her eyes wide with panic.

Will smiles. "I've checked the forecast and it's due to die right down later this morning, so the conditions should be perfect."

"They'll be okay, won't they?" says Rachel, as a sense of unease wraps itself around her.

"They'll have to be." Will laughs. "Otherwise I'm going to be a guest and a best man short."

"Right, who's up for going to the supermarket?" calls out Paige from behind them.

"Yep, give me a minute to get myself sorted and I'll show you where it is," says Will, walking back across the terrace. "Rach, you want to come?"

"Yeah, I wouldn't mind getting some shampoo," she says, taking a sip of her coffee. "The soft water out here is playing havoc with my hair." She lifts up her brown tresses, which are already beginning to dry and frizz from the shower she's just had.

"Okay. Noah and I will go and wait by the van," says Paige. "What about Jack?"

"Well, he was fast asleep when I came down," says Rachel. "So, probably best to leave him."

"Sleeping off a hangover, is he?" asks Ali, laughing wryly.

"Something like that," says Rachel through a forced smile.

"Ali?" Will calls. "Can you grab my wallet from downstairs?"

"Actually, I'm going to stay here if that's okay," she calls back. "I just need to make a couple of phone calls—make sure the yoga's booked and my manicure is sorted for this afternoon."

"Okay, cool," says Will. "Is there anything you need?"

"I can't think of anything," says Ali. "Oh, apart from that sardine paste that they do out here. If you see any of that, grab some and we can have it on toast—it's insane."

"No worries," says Will, laughing. "Give us a call if you think of anything else."

"Will do," says Ali as she disappears down the steps from the patio into her and Will's room below.

"Where's Ali?" Paige asks, as the four of them climb up into the minibus Will has rented.

"She's got some jobs to do," says Rachel. "Says we need to get some sardine paste if we see any."

"I remember her loving that stuff the last time we were here."

"I didn't realize we had the option of staying here and putting an order in," says Paige quietly.

Rachel smiles at Will in the rearview mirror. "So, what time are your mum and dad coming in?"

"Around three," he says. "They're all on the same flight—about thirty of them."

"Have your parents met Ali's parents before?" asks Noah from the front seat.

"Yeah, once or twice. But I'm sure a few bevvies on the plane will get them better acquainted."

"By the time dinner comes around, they'll be ten sheets to the wind," says Noah, laughing. "It'll be a fitting end to your last night as a single man."

"I wouldn't want it any other way," says Will, veering off the dual carriageway.

"So, how are you feeling about tomorrow?" Rachel asks as they pull up outside a surprisingly large supermarket. "Nervous?"

"I'm actually all right," says Will. "I'm a hundred percent sure I'm doing the right thing, so I guess that helps."

"There's not a tiny part of you that's questioning it?" asks Paige.

Rachel and Noah both look at her, as if silently asking why she would need to say that.

"*What?*" she retorts. "It's only natural to feel a smidgen of doubt. I certainly did when I married *you*." She looks to Noah who seems momentarily perplexed by his wife's admission.

"And there's me thinking we were one another's true loves," he says, as he slams the door of the van a little harder than necessary.

"I only had doubts because I wasn't sure it was what *you* wanted," says Paige as they all walk across the parking lot toward the shop's entrance.

Rachel can't help but feel that this is an odd place for a married couple to be having a conversation like this.

"Why would you have thought that?" asks Noah, as Rachel attempts to quicken her pace to join Will, who is just a few steps ahead.

"Because I wasn't entirely sure that it was *me* you wanted to be with."

Rachel's heart feels like it's stopped and if she couldn't see her feet still moving, she'd be sure she was rooted to the tarmac of the parking lot.

Noah laughs nervously. "I don't know why you'd think that."

"Because I really wasn't sure what had gone on between *you* two," she says.

Rachel can feel Paige's eyes burning into her and she's glad her back's to them.

"It seems preposterous now," Paige goes on. "And I'm almost embarrassed to admit it, but you two had such a history together that I couldn't quite believe that it was purely platonic."

Rachel can feel her mouth drying up as she walks faster, overtaking Will at the automatically opening door.

"I mean, it's entirely possible," Paige goes on, laughing. "I can see that now, but eighteen years ago, I didn't know you very well, Rachel, and I was immature and perhaps a little insecure."

Rachel turns to face her as the men busy themselves with the very serious business of selecting the right tomatoes.

"Noah and I have only ever been friends," she says.

"Yes, I know that now, silly," says Paige, bumping Rachel with her shoulder to lighten the mood. "But, back then, you can't blame me for thinking something more had gone on. You were like two peas in a pod, finishing each other's sentences and sharing the same interests. It was pretty intimidating to come into as an outsider."

"But I told you from the beginning that we were like brother and sister," says Noah, his eyes focused on tying the bag of tomatoes.

"Yes, but even still, you were a man and a woman who were so closely in tune with each other that it was impossible—at least in my mind—that something more wasn't going on—or hadn't in the past. It just goes against nature that two people of the opposite sex can be that close without ever taking it one step further."

Rachel forces a smile, but try as she might, she can't stop the memory of Noah's face coming toward her; his lips parting hers as they kiss. She can feel his touch setting her skin ablaze as his fingers trail lightly down her spine.

"*Rachel?*" says Paige, calling her back.

"Sorry," says Rachel, shaking herself down.

"You looked miles away," says Paige, laughing. "I was just asking if we should get some avocados?"

She can feel Noah's eyes burning into her, but she refuses to look at him for fear that it will give something away.

"Erm, yes . . ." she says, when she eventually manages to shrug off the uncomfortable sensation that her best friend's husband is able to evoke in her.

Paige laughs to herself as she feels the firmness of an avocado. "I remember thinking I had to pass the Rachel test."

"Which was?" asks Rachel, unable to believe that, after all these years, they're having this conversation in a supermarket.

"To make sure *you* liked me even more than Noah did," says Paige.

Rachel smiles, but she's not sure how successful that test was, given that on meeting, the first thing she'd said to Noah when Paige went to the bathroom was "She looks like she's got a broom stuck up her arse."

"Now, now," Noah had said, half-smiling. "I've always been nice to Jack, so I expect you to show the same courtesy to her."

"Do you really think it's serious, then?" Rachel had asked.

"Well, I wouldn't have asked you here if I didn't," he'd said.

It wasn't as if she'd been invited to join them, exactly. It had been made to look like Rachel had just happened to be in the same place they were, so she could check Paige out.

"So, why did you ask me if you don't want my honest opinion?"

"I *do* want your opinion—it matters to me what you think—but don't be mean just for the sake of it." He'd looked at her like a stern schoolteacher.

"I don't want her to change anything between us," she'd said sulkily.

"Don't you think *you* having a baby, and getting married, has done that already?"

"I can already tell that she doesn't like me. What have you told her?"

Noah had shifted his stance at the bar.

"Have you told her the truth?" she pressed.

"Have you told *Jack* the truth?" he snapped back.

"Christ, the bathroom's a long way away," said Paige, bursting the invisible balloon that Noah and Rachel had momentarily put themselves in.

"Well, it's been lovely to meet you," Rachel had said, suddenly feeling the need to get out of there. "But I really need to get home to my baby."

"Oh, you have a *child*?" Paige asked.

Rachel could literally see the relief in her eyes. As if being a mother meant that she wasn't a threat to her and Noah's burgeoning relationship.

"Yes," said Rachel, acknowledging that she was probably right. Having a child *had* changed everything, and she'd never do anything to jeopardize Josh's welfare or well-being. She'd learned the hard way how it felt to be the product of a broken marriage and she would never allow him to feel that despair, that guilt, that maybe he'd done something to make his mummy and daddy stop loving each other. That weight of responsibility sat like a lump in her throat.

"He's ten months old," she'd managed.

"Ah, sweet," Paige had said, leaning into Noah protectively.

Rachel had avoided Noah's calls for a while after that, having made the decision that they should both get on with their new lives. He'd met someone, who, on first impression, wasn't ever going to be Rachel's cup of tea. And she was happy with Jack, who, understandably, was none too keen on her continuing to see Noah, despite her protestations that nothing had ever happened between them. Plus, they had little Josh to look after, and he took up more time than she'd ever dreamed possible, so it was only right that she devoted every minute of her day to him. But as one week without Noah turned into three months, she'd decided that she'd rather have him in it *with* Paige, than not at all.

So, she'd set out on a mission to get on with Paige, because without her backing, she had little to no chance of her friendship with Noah continuing. And in the end, it hadn't been too much of a stretch. Yes, Paige was opinionated and hard-nosed, but once you cracked her shell, she could be funny and a great advocate for good. The leap from best friend's girlfriend to best friends, period, was relatively seamless.

But she'd had no idea that Paige had felt she was being put through the wringer.

"I'm sorry that I made you feel that way," she says now.

"It's no biggie," says Paige, smiling. "It was a long time ago and look what came of it. We'd never be here if you and Noah hadn't made as much effort to stay friends."

Rachel looks fleetingly at Noah, but he turns and sets off down the fruit aisle.

By the time they get back to the villa, the midday sun has burned away all the wispy clouds that hung over the hillside that morning.

"It's nice enough to go for a swim in the pool," says Paige as they take a couple of shopping bags each from the back of the minivan.

"There's a door over there that leads straight up to the kitchen," says Will, nodding toward the corner of the carport under the house.

"I'll go round the side," says Rachel. "I want to check the temperature of the pool before I get my one-piece on."

"You wimp!" Noah laughs. "I remember a time when you'd dive straight in, regardless."

She looks at him ruefully. She *had* been that person once, thinking nothing of jostling her way to the front of the line for the three-hundred-foot bungee jump in Cyprus, fearlessly waving to Noah, who lost his stomach on the teacup ride at Disney.

But it wasn't just in the literal sense that she'd once been so daring. She'd stood tall and proud as the president of her university's debating society, always passionate about bringing the topics that mattered to the fore, despite how unpopular it may have made her.

But somewhere along the way, she'd lost that chutzpah, that need to be the best version of herself. She guessed it was around the same time that she gave birth to Josh, and needed to be the best version of a *mother*.

When she thinks how quickly having a baby followed graduation, she realizes she barely had any time to fit anything in between. All thoughts of a teaching career had had to be shelved as she cared for Josh and then, once he was older, she found she didn't quite have the enthusiasm for it anymore. Probably because ten years of looking after her own child had robbed her of the patience she needed to look after anyone else's. Though, now, as time's passed, she wonders if it wasn't more to do with lack of confidence than anything else.

The education system had changed so much that her skills no longer felt relevant, and the thought of going back to relearn everything she needed, to be able to give her pupils a fighting chance, seemed too arduous. But, if the truth be told, there was nothing an English literature degree and wanting to give children the best start in life couldn't have overcome. She'd just needed to *want* to overcome it.

But instead, she'd retreated further into her close-knit group of friends, each of them seemingly content to immerse themselves in their children's lives, to the detriment of all else. Rachel doesn't doubt that, like her, they were all someone else in another lifetime, yet despite yearning for the person they'd lost, they were happily using their offspring as an excuse not to find themselves again.

She wonders if that isn't why she enjoys spending time with Paige; the voyeur in her intrigued by a life whereby you can have it all, if only you're brave enough. She'd had Chloe at twenty-five and was back practicing law by her twenty-sixth birthday. She'd had a baby that had fitted around her life, whereas Rachel had a life that fitted around Josh.

"Don't you want more?" Paige had once asked her, as Josh had moved from infant to primary school. "You've got all this time on your hands. You could do anything you want to do."

"I've got the house to look after," Rachel had said, defensively. "And Jack."

Paige had looked at her admonishingly. "I'm sure Jack's old enough to look after himself," she'd said.

She'd been right, of course, and Rachel had been sure that Jack wouldn't have had a problem with her doing whatever it was she wanted to do, but it was easier to think that he might. "Why would I want anything more, when I can live my life vicariously through you?" she'd said, laughing. "You fight for a murderer's freedom, wearing Louboutin shoes, with a child on your hip, while getting a takeout from the Ivy. I could never lead a life as exciting."

"*Alleged* murderer," Paige said dourly.

Rachel had held her hands up. "Apologies, Your Honor, I stand corrected."

Paige smiled. "Seriously though, there must be something you want to do."

Rachel thought of telling her about her desire to teach at an underprivileged, under-funded school in inner London, believing that she could make all the difference. But she was afraid that she'd be laughed at for setting her aspirations too low.

"Noah says you were quite a force of nature when you were younger," Paige went on. "Before meeting Jack and having Josh."

Had *he?* Had he and Paige sat and discussed what she used to be like? Had he divulged the dreams she'd once had and how instrumental his part in them had been? The thought that Noah had shared the fantasy life they naively believed they would lead had made Rachel's cheeks burn with embarrassment and betrayal.

"We all think we can rule the world when we're young," Rachel had said ruefully.

Yet, fast-forward twenty years, and she's now worrying whether a heated pool will be too cold to lower herself into in her one-piece swimsuit. Even the shift from bikini to swimsuit has passed her by unnoticed. What *has* happened to her?

Suddenly determined to go in, regardless of the temperature, she walks up to the villa's patio doors and slides them across with a renewed vigor. In that moment, a flash of orange silently crosses the mezzanine landing that connects her and Jack's bedroom with Paige and Noah's. It looked like a person, but she only caught it out of the corner of her eye and it came and went so quickly that it could have been a trick of light; the sun's rays are bouncing off all the reflective surfaces, dazzling her and making her feel as if she's inside a turning kaleidoscope.

"Has anyone seen Jack?" she asks, as she goes into the kitchen to find Will, Noah and Paige working together to unpack the shopping and load the fridge.

"Not yet," says Paige, examining the label of a rosé wine. "No sign of Ali either."

"You know the workers from the shirkers," says Noah, laughing.

"So, are you ready to hit the waves?" Will asks Noah.

"I can't wait," says Noah. "Though, I have to admit, as we were coming along the coast road just now, I was looking out there and my stomach somersaulted."

Will smiles. "Yeah, the waves are still looking pretty racy, but we'll stay out of the impact zone."

"You *will* look after him, won't you?" says Paige. "I don't want any broken bones."

"He'll be okay," says Will. "It's Jack I'm worried about. He thinks he's a dude but he's actually a bit of a kook."

Noah looks at him quizzically, and Will laughs.

"Meaning he thinks he's a decent surfer, but he's actually crap, which makes him more of a liability."

"That sounds like Jack," says Paige.

They're all chattering away, but all Rachel can hear is an incessant babble. She's still standing there, in the middle of the kitchen, with a shopping bag in either hand, trying to sharpen her focus on the moving shapes in front of her.

Without saying another word, Rachel puts the shopping bags on the kitchen worktop and walks along the corridor toward the stairs, taking them two at a time. Jack won't be in their room, she tells herself—he'll be outside by the pool. She must have missed him on her way in and he must have had his eyes closed and not seen her. Her chest feels heavy as she crosses the mezzanine and pushes open their door. *Please don't be in here*, she says to herself.

The bed is unmade, the sheets tangled, and their pillows still show the indentations of their heads. She lets out a relieved sigh. What the hell was she thinking? How had she allowed a fleeting image, one that she can't even be sure she saw, to infiltrate her mind and bring about insecurities she never even knew she had? And, even if what she thought she saw *had* been real, it didn't have to mean anything, because Jack wasn't even there.

She laughs at herself as she falls onto the bed, unable to believe that she'd put two and two together and come up with five.

"Hi honey," says Jack, as he comes out of the en suite wearing nothing but a white towel wrapped around his waist. Rachel forces herself not to let her mind wander back down that road.

"You okay?" he asks, though he doesn't even wait for an answer before saying, "How did the shopping go?"

Rachel pulls herself up. "Fine," she says tightly, though she doesn't know why. "Absolutely fine. How have things been here?"

He rubs his brown hair with a towel. "I haven't left this room," he says, without answering the question.

"So, you haven't seen Ali?" she asks, rephrasing the question so that there's absolutely no room for error. "She hasn't been irritating you?"

"No," he says, going back into the bathroom.

"I was thinking . . ." she starts, without knowing where she's going.

"That sounds dangerous," says Jack, laughing.

"Why don't we try and track Rick down?"

"*Rick?*" he calls out, as if it's the first time he's ever heard the name.

Rachel gives him a moment to see if he catches on. He doesn't.

"Who's Rick?" he asks, poking his head around the doorframe.

How can he not know? "The guy who you think Ali had an affair with," says Rachel, trying hard to hide her exasperation and growing sense of unease.

"Oh *him*," he exclaims theatrically. "I wouldn't even know where to begin."

"Well, maybe you should challenge her on it then."

He makes a funny noise. "And what difference is that going to make? It is what it is. She can't undo it and pretend it never happened."

"No, but perhaps she'll deny it."

"Oh, she'll definitely do that!" He laughs bitterly.

"But she might be telling the truth," says Rachel. "It might have just been wishful thinking on Rick's part. A bit of office banter between the lads."

"I don't think so," says Jack. "I know Rick well and he's a pretty sound guy. He'd have no reason to lie about something like that."

"You know him well, yet you *don't* know how to contact him?" asks Rachel, unable to help herself.

Jack comes toward her and picks up her hands, which have been hanging limply by her side. "I shouldn't have told you," he says, looking at her intently. "It wasn't fair to land this on you so close to the wedding. But you pushed me."

"No, I didn't," says Rachel. "Paige did."

"Well, whoever it was, I shouldn't have aired my grievances. But hey, it's out there and now you understand why I don't want to be within three feet of the woman."

Except you just were, Rachel wants to shout. Right here in this room.

She goes to the door and stares out across the mezzanine that overlooks the living room below. Opposite, toward the stairs, is Paige and Noah's room, but as much as she looks, desperate for there to be another door, to give Ali a reason to be up here, there's nothing.

Maybe it *had* been a trick of the light. Perhaps the sun had bounced off the polished concrete walls in such a way that it had created the *illusion* of someone rushing from one side of the mezzanine to the other. Perhaps Ali is still in her room . . . or out on a walk . . . not even wearing orange.

"I'd better go and help the others," she calls out, sticking her head around their bedroom door.

It's then that she sees it; the tiniest dot sparkling in the sun, on the floor, right outside the bathroom. She goes to it and picks it up, examining the perfectly cut diamond. It's only on closer inspection that she sees a tiny hole in the top, as if, until recently, it was a sewn-on embellishment.

She doesn't own anything quite so blingy, so pops it in her pocket and heads back to the kitchen, the whole time telling herself, *convincing* herself, that she couldn't have seen what she thought she'd seen. It was a moment in time—it could have been anything.

Rachel has almost talked herself into believing it by the time she reaches the kitchen.

"Jeez, that dress is *gorgeous*!" Will whistles through his teeth as he picks Ali up and kisses her. "Is it new?"

Rachel doesn't want to look, but her brain already knows what's there and is battling to backtrack against itself; as if trying to convince her that what she knows is there, isn't, and what she knows she saw, she didn't.

"It's a caftan," says Ali, her eyes like saucers as she looks at Will. "And yes, I bought it in Selfridges last week."

"Not many people can get away with that color," says Paige, leaving the words hanging there, so nobody's quite sure whether it's an insult or a backhanded compliment.

"Thanks," gushes Ali, opting to go with the latter.

"Most women end up looking like an escaped convict," Paige goes on, hammering the point home even further.

"It's always been my favorite color," Ali enthuses. "I would have worn an orange wedding dress if I could."

And just like that, Rachel knows that she can no longer pretend to see what she wants to see. She'd wanted to allow her eyes to trick her into believing that Ali's dress, or caftan, is a shade of pink, or even red. She would let her eyes convince her it was green if it meant that it didn't match the flash of orange that she saw leaving her and Jack's room just now. But more than that, she wishes that the diamantés hanging off it weren't the very same as the one that's in her pocket.

5

"Ah, here he is!" says Will, as Jack walks out onto the terrace where they're all sitting around a table laden with Mediterranean fare. Sliced salami, serrano ham, French cheese and olives are laid on platters. The only Portuguese produce is the sardine paste that Will has lined up in the tiny foil pots it comes in, alongside great hunks of freshly baked bread.

"Good morning," coos Ali. "Or should I say, good afternoon."

Jack ruffles his still-wet hair. "Just in time for a hair-of-the-dog," he says, looking past her to Will.

"No alcohol until *after* we've been in the water," says Will, smiling and holding up a can of Diet Coke.

Jack groans like a child who's been told he can't have an ice cream until after dinner.

"How you feeling?" asks Noah, pouring a puddle of olive oil onto his plate. "You were putting in some serious dance moves last night."

Rachel smiles as she pictures Jack twirling her around, the pair of them lost in the moment. But then she remembers what she's just seen and is hit by a sudden image of his head between Ali's legs.

The very thought of it makes her take a sudden intake of breath and she gasps, and everyone's heads turn toward her.

"You okay?" asks Ali.

Rachel can't look at her for fear of seeing her lying on their bed, with her eyes closed and her hands on the back of Jack's head.

"Fine," she says tightly, picking up her glass of water.

"Well, this looks amazing," says Jack, blithely unaware of the all-too-vivid images flashing in front of Rachel's eyes.

"Don't eat *too* much," says Will.

"Blimey, you sound like Mum when we were kids. '*Wait for your food to go down before you get back in that water*,'" Jack mimics in a high-pitched voice.

"You just don't want to be going in after you've eaten a big meal," says Will.

"Isn't that a myth?" asks Noah to no one in particular. "Am I honestly going to drown if I eat all that bread?"

"You'll have to be quick," says Paige, nodding her head in the direction of Ali's full plate.

"Hey, don't knock a girl for her appetite," says Ali, with an edge.

"All power to you," says Paige, retrieving an olive stone from her mouth. "I just don't know where you put it."

Ali smiles sweetly. "I guess I'm one of the lucky ones," she says.

"So, you can eat whatever you like and don't ever put on an ounce?" asks Paige incredulously.

Ali nods. "Pretty much."

"But you must exercise, *surely*?"

"When I feel like it," says Ali, laughing. "Which isn't very often."

"Oh, to be born with a body like this," says Will, giving Ali's pert behind a squeeze.

Ali smiles awkwardly, pretending to be embarrassed.

"Well, I can assure you that I will need to hit the tarmac at *some* point," says Paige. "Especially after all this."

"Did you even bring your trainers?" asks Noah, sounding surprised.

"Of course I did," says Paige, as if affronted by his lack of faith in her commitment to exercise. "Did you?" She's looking at Rachel. "We could go for a run together if you like."

In her mind's eye Rachel can see her trusted Nikes sitting forlornly on their bedroom floor at home, having been booted out of the suitcase, in favor of her hair dryer.

"Are you honestly going to need them?" Jack had asked, as she'd decided on which to sacrifice.

"*I'm* going for a run at some point," he says now.

"You brought your running shoes?" asks Rachel, unable to hide her surprise. "I thought we didn't have enough room."

"I substituted my boat shoes," he says. "I didn't see that I'd need them, and I think I made the right call, because, after all the eating and drinking we're going to be doing, I'm going to have to do *something*."

"I might join you then," says Paige. "Though, I'm not sure I'll be able to match your pace. You'd be best to go out and do three circuits before I join you on the last." She laughs. "Hopefully you'll be knackered enough by then for me to keep up with you."

Jack smiles. "Don't worry, I'll take it slow."

"I'll come with you," blurts out Ali.

It's such a sudden outburst that the whole table turns to look at her. "I need to make sure I can still fit into my dress."

"I don't know when I'll go," says Jack tersely. "It might be tomorrow morning."

"Fine," says Ali. "I'll come with you then."

"I'm sure our yoga session will dispense with any unwanted calories," says Rachel, not knowing whether she's trying to protect Jack or warn Ali off.

"True enough," says Ali. "But there's nothing like a run to get your blood pumping to all the right places, is there?"

Rachel wishes she'd imagined it, but for a split second Jack and Ali lock eyes, as if in that moment, they're the only two people there.

"I wouldn't exactly call my husband a natural, would *you*?" Paige laughs as they watch Will taking Jack and Noah through the basics on static surfboards down on the shoreline. "He looks like he's doing a difficult poo."

Rachel looks on with affection as Noah crouches on bent knees, his expression vexed with concentration. "Let's not write him off just yet," she says. "If I remember rightly, he was a pretty good waterskier back in the day."

"*Really?*" says Paige, as if she doubts it very much.

Rachel wishes she'd kept her memories to herself, as they only serve to remind Paige that Rachel and Noah shared a life before her, and that perhaps she doesn't know her husband quite as well as she thinks she does.

Despite herself, Rachel pictures Noah laying her down gently on a bed, his eyes staring intently into hers, and wonders if Paige isn't wrong.

"Are you sure we should be doing this?" Noah had asked, in between kissing Rachel's neck.

Yes. No. Yes. No had resounded on a loop in Rachel's head as she battled with her trepidation and conscience. Why, in the four years they'd known each other, had they chosen *that* night to cross the line from friendship to something more?

He was going on a year-long trip to Asia the following morning and all they were supposed to do was go out, get drunk and send him off in style. So, how come they were back at her flat about to have sex?

"Come *with* me," he'd said.

"Don't do this," she'd pleaded. "The decision's made."

"But we've been planning this for months—this was our dream."

"I know," said Rachel. "And I'm sorry for letting you down, but it just doesn't feel right for me to go anymore. Not now that Jack . . ."

Noah had stroked her hair from her face. "But you've only just met him. Are you honestly going to put all your plans on hold for a guy you've only known for a couple of months?"

"I don't know what's going to happen," she'd said. "Who *does*? But I just know that right now, I don't want to go halfway around the world and risk never seeing him again."

"And what about *us*?" he'd said, lifting himself off to study her.

She'd pulled herself up onto her elbows. "What *about* us?" she'd said. "You've had four years to work on that, but you chose to sleep with pretty much every freshman who's come onto campus instead."

"Are you saying you've wanted *more*, before now?" he asked incredulously.

How had he not noticed? She'd obviously become too adept at hiding her true feelings, and now he was finally reciprocating them, she didn't feel fully able to. It's what they called Sod's Law.

She'd shaken her head in answer. It seemed easier to lie.

"Why don't you just come with me to Thailand?" he pleaded. "Just to give us a chance of seeing where this might go."

She'd laughed. "And if it doesn't work?"

His hand had trailed between her breasts with a feather-light touch and down her flat stomach.

"I would have lost you *and* Jack."

"But this is a once-in-a-lifetime opportunity, Rach. This is never going to come around again. Before you know it, we'll be chained to a desk and married with kids."

"We're twenty-two," she said, arching her back as she felt his fingers. "We've got all the time in the world."

Perhaps if she'd known then what she knows now, she'd think again, because all of a sudden, time isn't so infinite. It *does* run out, for all of us. Days run into weeks, and months run into years, and we find that the twenty-year-old we thought we'd always be, was lost decades ago.

"Here they go," says Ali, as she lowers herself slowly into a side split on her yoga mat. She demonstrates her suppleness even further by pushing her head forward so that the peak of her baseball cap touches her knee.

Rachel doesn't know whether she should watch *her*, or the men, as they run into the sea with their surfboards under their arms. Will deftly jumps up and straddles the board as soon as he's past the breaking waves, while Jack and Noah struggle to untangle themselves from the leash that's attached to their ankles.

"Oh my God, it's Dumb and Dumber!" Paige laughs, as Noah manages to get himself up onto it, only to fall straight off the other side, while Jack's lying down on his, paddling furiously but going nowhere.

"They call that the dick dragger," says Ali, laughing. "He's going to feel that later on."

There's a tightening in Rachel's chest as she watches the three of them move further toward the monstrous waves.

"He's not going to take them *all* the way out, is he?" she asks no one in particular.

"Don't worry," says Ali. "The waves look bigger than they actually are."

Rachel would imagine that the reverse is true when you're out there and there's one looming large over you.

"Will knows what he's doing," says Ali, as a dark-haired man, with a mustache and a body to die for, approaches them.

"You iz Ali?" he says in broken English.

"Yes," she says without getting up from the splits. "You must be Ramiro."

She throws a glance at Rachel and raises her eyebrows, as if to say, "*Surprise!*"

Rachel groans inwardly. Having to do a downward dog on a busy beach is surprise enough, without being told to contract your pelvic floor by an Antonio Banderas lookalike.

They laugh, though, as he manhandles them all into the bridge position and then instructs them to "*Frust, frust, frust,*" as fast as they can.

By the time he asks them to adopt the lotus pose, Rachel suspects he's actually a comedy act rather than a yoga teacher, and keeps one eye open, on the lookout for what he's going to come up with next.

Her heart lurches as a wave starts building out at sea, rolling and rolling toward a line of surfers straddling their boards.

Her instinct is to shout, "*It's behind you,*" but they know it's coming—in fact, that's exactly what they're waiting for. She wonders for the umpteenth time what would possess anybody to want to do that.

She squints to see if she can pick any of the boys out of the line-up, but in their dark wetsuits they all look the same; like sharks rising up out of the depths. Then she catches a flash of fluorescent green, the topside of Will's surfboard, and sees him frantically waving his arms above his head. She stops breathing as her eyes follow his call to see Jack and Noah floating aimlessly into the path of the rising swell.

She gets to her feet, for all it will do, as the crest of the wave starts curling over onto itself. It's like watching in slow motion as the white water comes crashing down, taking everything in its path with it. A few brave or stupid surfers ride it in, but it gobbles Noah and Jack up and all that Rachel can see are the bright tips of their boards going over and over as if they're in a washing machine.

"No!" she shrieks, running to the water's edge.

It's as if the cycle will never stop spinning, for as quickly as her eyes catch sight of one of them, the other disappears. She imagines them trying to come up for air, but having it snatched away from them as the current whips them back under.

Will is frantically paddling toward them, yelling something that Rachel can't hear over the deafening roar of the next wave crashing onto itself.

A head finally pops up through the foam, but it's impossible to tell who it is. And in that moment, Rachel realizes that it really doesn't matter, as she feels the same intensity of fear for *whoever's* yet to surface.

"Is that Noah?" screeches Paige, holding a hand to her forehead.

"I . . . I . . ." stutters Rachel, rendered speechless.

"Fuck!" says Ali, as Will pulls a deadweight body onto his board.

Rachel's legs wobble beneath her as she attempts to run along the shoreline to where they're coming back in. Other surfers are selflessly making their way toward Will, all of them no doubt aware of the next swell that's building behind them.

"Jesus Christ," says Paige. "They need to get out of there."

The lifeguard, who Rachel hadn't even noticed before, jumps down from his white-painted tower and tears off his yellow sweatshirt as he races into the sea.

Rachel can't help a sob escaping from her throat as she watches helplessly as a group huddles around Will and push him clear of the wave.

"Is it Jack?" cries Paige.

Adrenaline floods Rachel's body as a sense of urgency descends onto the beach.

"*Alguem precisa tirá-lo de lá*," someone shouts. "*Chama uma ambulância!*" yells another.

The more Rachel tries to focus on who the lifeless body draped across Will's surfboard is, the more she realizes that she can't breathe. She imagines a life without Jack and the air rushes from her body. If it's Noah who's in desperate trouble, she'll collapse. The loaded gun spins around and around in her head, waiting for someone to pull the trigger to see if there's a bullet in the chamber.

The water laps up around her knees as Will comes toward her, his soft features twisted into gnarled terror. There are faces everywhere and she searches them, desperately looking for someone she recognizes.

"What the fuck?" is the first thing she says as Will comes into earshot. But he's not listening; he and the lifeguard are laying the limp body onto the dry sand. Her eyes still won't allow her to distinguish the pallid features of the man lying on the ground.

"Oh, Jesus!" comes a voice just a split second before a body slams into her, crushing her with an embrace.

"Jack?" she says questioningly, having to pull away to make sure it's him.

"Oh, God," he chokes.

"What the . . . ?" She starts looking from him, to who she now knows is Noah, lying motionless on the ground. "What the hell happened?"

"We . . . we just got caught out," he gasps. "It came from nowhere and it just . . . it just . . ."

He watches, dumbstruck, as the lifeguard blows air slowly into Noah's mouth.

"Noah!" cries Paige. "Noah!"

Hearing his name called so desperately paralyzes Rachel. She can't move, talk or feel anything apart from a hole opening up inside her chest. A hole so vast that it feels as if it will engulf her.

She wants to go to him, to tell him that everything will be all right, but that's not her place. Paige is with him, as she should be, so why can't Rachel help feeling that it should be her?

Twenty years have passed, and Noah has no doubt developed a whole heap of idiosyncrasies that she knows nothing about, and enjoyed experiences with Paige that she'll never have a window onto, yet, for some reason, she still feels she knows him better than anyone else.

They'd shared so many dreams and been on so many adventures, supporting each other as they negotiated the choppy waters of living away from home for the first time. They'd smoked their first joint together, been chased out of an illegal rave by the police, and been one another's relationship gurus.

Noah has shaped her, made her the person she is today, and without him . . .

There's a splutter, and a collective sigh of relief, as Noah is turned on his side.

"Thank Christ," says Jack, as a sob escapes from Rachel's throat. She throws a shaking hand to her mouth as Jack turns to look at her.

"What the *hell* happened out there?" shouts Will, getting up to face Jack. "I *told* you not to drift. I *told* you to stay close to me."

"We didn't realize . . ." starts Jack.

"There's no *we* in this," argues Will. "*You* know what to do. *He's* the rookie."

"Noah!" calls Paige. "Noah, darling, can you hear me?"

"Did he get taken out by his surfboard?" asks Ali.

"It looks like it," says Will.

Noah opens his eyes and tries to sit up. "Oh, thank God," cries Paige.

"I . . ." Noah coughs, looking around him in confusion. "I'm okay."

Rachel's heart feels as if it's about to burst out of her chest and she can't stop a tear-stained grin from spreading across her face.

"He's going to be okay," says Paige.

Every muscle in Will's body visibly relaxes as the tension seeps out of him. "What did I tell you about eating too much bread?" he says, attempting to laugh.

"Should we cancel the rehearsal dinner tonight?" asks Ali.

Paige looks at Rachel and blows out her cheeks, but she doesn't know if it's a reaction to Ali's insensitivity or Noah's *very* near miss.

6

"Is he okay?" Rachel asks Paige when she comes out to the pool after settling Noah down for a rest.

Jack and Will have gone to see their parents who have arrived at the hotel down the road, and, not one to let Noah's near-death experience throw her off track, Ali's getting her nails done.

"Yes, he's just exhausted," says Paige. "I'll let him sleep for as long as he wants to and if he's not up to going out tonight, we won't go."

Rachel wishes *she* could volunteer to stay here with Noah, but knows that it would look odd.

"Well, that certainly brings home the fragility of life, doesn't it?" she says.

Paige nods. "It certainly does. I honestly thought it was touch and go for a minute."

Rachel feels the pull of tears at the back of her throat as she pictures Noah's lifeless body being hauled out of the water. She goes to speak, but she doesn't trust her voice.

"It's funny what goes through your mind at times like that, isn't it?" continues Paige.

Rachel offers a tight smile.

"It's as if your brain goes into overdrive, questioning your whole existence. I found myself doing a deal with God that if he would just save him, I'd throw everything I have into our marriage."

Rachel can't help but narrow her eyes. "I thought you already were." She looks at her questioningly.

Paige sighs. "I think if Noah and I were both honest with each other, we'd admit that neither of us have been putting enough effort in lately."

"I had no idea," says Rachel, taken aback. "I thought you were happy."

"We are," says Paige. "But it feels as if we're just bobbing along, waiting for something bigger to happen. We could go on like that until our dying days, but is that really enough? Do we not both deserve *more*?"

"So, are you saying you'd consider leaving him?" asks Rachel incredulously.

"I've thought about it," admits Paige. "But seeing him like that today made me reevaluate. Maybe bobbing along is good enough. Maybe I'm looking for something that doesn't exist." She laughs. "I even found myself bargaining with our maker that I'd happily let Noah do whatever he wants to do, just so long as he keeps him alive."

"What? Like an affair or something," asks Rachel, dumbfounded.

Paige nods. "I can't imagine that feeling will last long, mind, but right now, I'd give my permission for anything."

This is so out of character for Paige that Rachel wonders if it isn't her who's had a knock to the head.

"I used to think I'd put his balls in a vise and squeeze very hard if I found out he was seeing someone else," she goes on. "But it doesn't seem quite as big a deal anymore."

Rachel shakes her head and smiles. "I can assure you, this all-new, all-accepting Paige is not going to last the day."

Paige shrugs. "Maybe not, but perhaps this is the wake-up call we all needed."

"*All?*" questions Rachel, panicking that Paige can somehow see within her soul, to where the thought of losing Noah had left its impression. Can she see the emptiness he would have left behind? The void that could never be filled? Can she see that her heart has a crack in it, only superficially filled once she knew he was going to be okay?

Her strength of feeling had even surprised Rachel herself, so much so that she spent those few minutes, that seemed like hours, constantly suppressing every natural instinct to go to him, scream at the ocean, and shout that she was sorry that she didn't go to Thailand with him.

"Maybe we should *all* live a little," says Paige, snapping Rachel out of the one-way tunnel she finds herself in.

Rachel chokes on her water. "What, all have affairs?"

"I'm not saying that," says Paige. "But life *is* short. If Noah wanted to sleep with someone else . . ."

Rachel can't stop herself from imagining Noah's cheek on hers, whispering how much he wants her. His fingers entwined in her hair as his other hand unbuttons her shirt.

"So, what would *you* do?" asks Paige, making Rachel's cheeks flush with color.

"*Do?*" she replies, flustered.

"If you found out Jack was having an affair," says Paige.

Rachel's almost relieved that the conversation has turned to Jack, until she pictures Ali coming out of their room this morning and her indignation returns.

Rachel wavers between needing to tell Paige what she saw—in the hope that she'll say she's being ridiculous—and not doing so, because just the mention of Ali will probably have Paige champing at the bit to prove that she's the woman they suspect her to be.

She shifts on the sunbed and pulls the sweatshirt she's borrowed from Jack over her hands. It smells of him, clean and citrusy, but then she asks herself if she's confusing it with Ali's perfume. She shakes her head, as if trying to dislodge the fragment of distrust she's suddenly developed for her husband of twenty years. Perhaps it's her own guilty conscience that's helping to propel the thought from nothing to something. She's certainly aware that there are double standards at play here, so maybe she's choosing to *pretend* that something might be going on, so she can justify the torrent of forbidden thoughts that are battering her own imagination.

"I wouldn't be able to forgive him," she says to Paige, as the image of Jack's head between Ali's legs flashes into her mind's eye again. "And I honestly don't believe you would either, if it were Noah."

"I think a lot of it would all depend on who he's doing it with."

Rachel looks at her with a vexed brow. "What difference does *that* make?"

Paige pulls her cardigan tighter around her and looks out across the ocean. "I think there are varying degrees of infidelity and the level of forgiveness would depend on which it was."

Rachel scoffs. "You sound like you're in court."

"I'm just saying, I think the mitigating circumstances would need to be taken into account," says Paige, smiling.

"So, what would be the circumstances you'd be willing to forgive?"

"As I say, it would make a huge difference depending on who the woman is. If she was a pretty young thing in the office and he was making a fool of himself *and* me, then I'd struggle to see my way past that. But if . . . I don't know . . ." She waves her hand in the air. "If it were someone like you, who he had history and a deep, meaningful connection with, then I'd like to think that we could all talk it through and find a way to get past it."

Rachel feels as if all her innermost thoughts are being exposed. "That doesn't make any sense," she offers as she desperately tries to shake off the uncomfortable sensation. "If I found out you and Jack were having an affair, it would be the end of everything . . . like immediately . . . that would be it."

"What, you'd be happy to throw our friendship away . . . ?"

"*Absolutely!*" exclaims Rachel, unable to believe she'd be expected to do anything else. "Without question."

"Yet you'd entertain forgiving the floozy in the office?"

"No, but it would certainly be easier to understand, knowing that he'd probably only done it to massage his ego."

"Can I ask you something?" says Paige, before adding, "Without you getting cross?"

Rachel nods.

"Do you think Ali's ever come on to Jack in the past?"

Rachel feels a tightening across her chest, as if Paige knows something she doesn't.

"I think that would be a new low," says Rachel. "Even for Ali."

"But we now know what she's like," says Paige. "And I wouldn't put *anything* past her."

"Even her fiancé's brother?" asks Rachel, desperately looking for a line that even Ali wouldn't cross.

"I'm not saying he'd ever reciprocate . . ." says Paige. "But I just wonder if something has happened, because he's definitely not the same when she's around."

Rachel pictures Ali scurrying across the landing from their room and feels like she's being hollowed out with a spoon, her chest an empty chamber of rib bones. She wants to tell Paige what she saw, but she knows that instead of allaying her fears, she'll ignite them; turning what could well be an innocent interaction into one that has Jack and Ali making love in the shower.

"In what way?" asks Rachel hesitantly.

"He just doesn't seem able to look her in the eye," says Paige.

"And we *know* why that is," says Rachel indignantly. "Because she's cheated on Will."

Paige nods her head. "Yes, but I just wonder if it's something more than that. *She's* different with Jack too."

"Well, maybe she knows he knows," says Rachel, feeling as if she's clutching at straws. "Maybe this Rick fella has told her that Jack knows."

Paige looks away thoughtfully. "Yep, you might be right."

"I *am* right," says Rachel, resolutely.

Paige puts a hand on Rachel's knee. "I'm sorry, I shouldn't have said anything," she says. "It's just that sometimes that girl brings out the worst in me."

"I get that, but she's not really our problem," says Rachel, trying to convince herself more than Paige. "Once this weekend's over and done with, I would imagine Jack will try to put as much space between him and her as he can.

Paige offers a tight smile. "Let's just hope we can all get through this weekend then."

7

"You look absolutely gorgeous," says Jack, as he comes up behind Rachel as she stands in front of the mirror. He smells like he's already had a drink or two with the wedding party up at the hotel.

His hands fall on either side of her waist, fingering the soft silk of her dress as he kisses the nape of her neck. Even after all this time, he still manages to ignite something deep within her with just a touch of his lips.

As if sensing her ardor, a grin spreads across his lips and he looks at her reflection with mischievous eyes.

Rachel swallows the unexpected threat of tears. "Are you happy?" she asks, through tremoring lips.

He laughs, though Rachel can't help but wonder if it's false.

"With *you*?"

She nods as she watches him carefully.

"Of course I am," he says. "I can't believe you even need to ask."

She turns to face him. "If you were unhappy, or wanted something or someone else, would you tell me?"

He shifts, his eyes momentarily flickering to the side before snapping back. "I have never wanted anything more than I want you," he says, kissing her cheek.

"Or . . . any*one*?" Rachel asks hesitatingly.

"*What?*" he exclaims, as if the mere thought is so abhorrent and unnatural that he can't believe she'd even say it out loud. His hands drop from her waist and he walks across the room, facing the floor-to-ceiling glass doors toward the ocean that is shimmering with gold as the sun sets behind it.

His pale-pink shirt is pulled taut across his back, his shoulder blades tense as he cricks his neck from one side to the other. Rachel can feel the tension emanating from him and steels herself for what he might be about to say.

What would she do if he suddenly decided to admit to something happening with Ali, either now or in the past? Would she tell Will what his bride and brother had done? Ruin his wedding . . . his relationship with his brother . . . his life? What if he called it all off? What would he say to the guests? The family would never be the same again.

Her mind whirs with the fallout of the hypothetical scenario.

"Well?" she pushes, desperate to stop the agony from wrapping its tentacles around her and squeezing her until she can't breathe. She'd rather an answer she doesn't want to hear, than be stuck in this state of limbo. "Is there someone else?"

Jack sighs so deeply that it sounds as if it's been sitting there for months, waiting for the right time to be released. As he slowly turns around, Rachel can't help but shut her eyes, in a futile attempt to protect herself from what he's about to say.

"How ironic that you feel the need to ask *me* that," he says, his tone tight and high-pitched.

Rachel pulls back at his inference. "Sorry?" she says, looking at him, confused.

Jack laughs to himself, but makes Rachel feel as if it's aimed at her. "Do you not think I can see straight through you?" he says.

She shakes her head as if to awaken the part of her brain that will make sense of what he's saying. "I'm not with you," she says.

"Do you think I didn't see what happened today?"

"What are you talking about?" she says. "Where? When?"

"On the beach," he says tersely. "With Noah."

She can't help but feel wrong-footed. This isn't the way she'd anticipated this conversation going. "I don't understand what you mean," she says, trying to keep her voice steady.

"I could see the utter fear in your eyes," he says. "I could feel you trembling in my arms."

"That's because it was absolutely terrifying," she says.

"Any more terrifying than if it happened to *me*?" He stares at her unwaveringly, as if expecting an answer.

She tuts. "Why are you being so stupid? You were there—you saw what happened. I would hope you felt just as scared as I did. If you didn't, then there's something wrong with you."

"Don't turn this on me," he says. Hadn't he just done exactly that himself? "My gut reaction was one of guilt; that I was somehow responsible for what happened."

She narrows her eyes. "And *were* you?"

"No!" he exclaims. "I told Noah not to go any further into the impact zone, but he ignored me, so I had to go out there myself to bring him back. His selfish actions put us both at risk." He looks at Rachel. "But you didn't seem too fazed by that. All you were concerned with was making sure *he* was all right."

"Oh, for God's sake, will you just listen to yourself?" she says, exasperated. "In case it escaped your notice, Noah had been knocked unconscious and if it hadn't have been for the quick actions of those around him, he might not have made it out alive."

"I'd taken a battering myself," he says. "But all you seemed to care about was *him*."

Rachel is taken back to the intensity of that moment and instantly feels tears spring to her eyes. Like Paige, she would have given anything to know that Noah was going to be okay—but to the detriment of her own marriage? Yes, probably.

"You're behaving like a child," she says, uncomfortable with the realization that she'd put Noah before Jack. If not physically, then certainly mentally. She would rather have God strike her, Jack, or any of them down, than take away her first love. The shock of what she was prepared to sacrifice lodges in her throat.

"What *really* went on between you two?" he asks, not for the first time. "Because you can tell me that you were just friends until you're blue in the face, but seeing you today suggests it was so much more."

Should she tell him that they'd crossed the line just once, but that it had been the singular most defining moment of her life? That barely a day had gone past when she hadn't transported herself back there, if only for a split second?

"Absolutely nothing," she says, sticking to the agreement she and Noah had made shortly after he'd met Paige. They both knew that if they were to remain friends, in the way they wanted—in the only way they knew how, because after four years of living in each other's pockets, they didn't know how to be any different—they'd have to renounce any notion of something more ever having happened. Because neither Jack nor Paige would allow their friendship to continue if they thought there had ever been an iota of sexual chemistry between them.

"But do you not see the way he looks at you?"

Rachel shakes her head. "You're being ridiculous."

"Oh, come on, Rach, you can't possibly be that naive," he says loudly. "It's so obvious, it's staring you right in the face, and if you can't see it, then you're blind, unless you're choosing to pretend it's not going on."

"I don't even have the words," she says, going to get her gold wedges from the top of the open suitcase that's still sitting on the floor.

"I should be used to it," Jack goes on, "but it's hard, seeing him look at you the way he does. You don't have to be Einstein to work out what he's thinking about."

"After everything that's gone on today, you're honestly going to throw accusations around about how I reacted or how he looks at me?" She tuts as if in disbelief. "Shouldn't your overriding concern be that Noah's okay?"

"Shouldn't *yours* have been to make sure *I* was okay?" he snaps.

"You're insufferable," says Rachel, opening the door. "I'll see you downstairs."

"Hey," says Noah, turning to look at her from where he's standing on the landing, overlooking the living space below.

Rachel shrinks into herself, cringing at the thought of him having heard the conversation she and Jack have just had. By the way he's looking at her, with expectant raised eyebrows, she'd bet that he has.

Every bone in her body wants to go to him, hug him and thank the Lord that he's alive, but Jack has made that impossible by turning it into something it's not.

"How are you feeling?" she asks, careful to keep a few feet between them.

"I feel fine," he says, smiling. "It's certainly swept a few cobwebs away."

"Do you think you're okay to come to the rehearsal dinner?" She doesn't know whether she wants him to say yes or no. It would certainly be easier if he stayed at the villa, if Jack's little outburst was anything to go by, but easy is not what she wants.

"Yeah, I think I'll be okay," says Noah. "I've taken some tablets just to ward off this headache and it's probably wise to stay off the alcohol."

"Good idea," says Rachel. "Perhaps just stick to water to keep you hydrated."

He laughs. "I don't think there's any chance of me being dehydrated," he says, with an unmistakable twinkle in his eye. "I've got half the Atlantic Ocean keeping me afloat."

Rachel can't help but smile. "Well, just take it easy, okay? I think we've had quite enough drama for one day."

"Oh, I don't know," says Jack, coming out of their room and walking past them. "There's always room for a little bit more."

8

“Oh. My. God,” says Paige under her breath.

Rachel follows her eyes to see Ali precariously climbing the steps beside the pool. She’s wearing a skin-tight red dress that leaves absolutely nothing to the imagination.

Rachel instinctively looks to Jack, whose eyes are staying firmly in his head; though she wonders how hard it must be for him to maintain that steely expression. *Any* red-blooded male would find it nigh on impossible not to react in *some* way to how Ali looks, though Jack is so unresponsive that Rachel would hazard a guess that even his pupils would be unchanged if she were to get up close enough to check. So, does that mean that he’s simply not bothered by what Ali says, does or wears, because he doesn’t care? Or has he conditioned himself not to react when his mistress, his brother’s fiancée, looks like she’s serving herself to him on a silver platter?

Mistress? She almost laughs out loud at the choice of words her brain has selected for what was surely a miscommunication on Jack’s part. Yes, there’s no doubt Ali was in their room this morning, but perhaps Rachel hadn’t been clear enough in her questioning. Had he actually said he hadn’t seen her or had Rachel taken it upon herself to assume that’s what he’d implied? She wonders whether there’s a difference.

Ali smiles and totters toward them on towering high heels, and

Rachel can't help but wonder what might be going through Jack's mind. Is he imagining her on all fours with just her shoes on? She knows it would be his thing, as he'd just recently bought *her* a pair of Christian Louboutin red-soled spikes and they'd become something of a staple in the bedroom. They were often the last item she took off, if she took them off at all, as he loved the way they made her back arch. *She* liked wearing them because they made her feel more confident and it was easier to pretend to be somebody else. Though, if she'd known she was only helping him pretend that she was Ali, she may have thought differently.

She looks at him now, unable to believe that he would ever do anything to jeopardize what they have. Why would he? She gives him everything he could possibly want, as he does her in return. They are partners, in every sense of the word; promising to love and to cherish until death do us part, though it only occurs to Rachel now, as she watches her husband's indifference to the blonde vision standing in front of him, that they'd skipped the part of their vows that promised to forsake all others.

No, she screams silently, hating herself for even thinking it. This is Jack we're talking about. A man of principle. A man who has very little regard for *anyone* who resorts to cheating on their other half. He'd once called a guy out at work when his wife had turned up at the office to surprise him on his birthday, only to find that he'd already gone to a swanky restaurant to celebrate with his secretary instead. Jack had covered for him, but he'd gone storming round to the restaurant and taken his colleague to task in front of his shocked assistant.

"I wiped that smug grin off his face," he'd said, as he'd furiously chopped onions that night. "It makes me so bloody mad. Why bother getting married in the first place, if you can't keep it in your trousers?"

Rachel had laughed. "You sound like Paige. Are you sure you're not a woman in disguise?"

She had *never* doubted his integrity for a second and she wasn't about to start now. There were a hundred reasons why Ali could have been in their room this morning; she could have been taking him a coffee . . . asking him what he wanted for breakfast . . . seeing if Rachel was back from the supermarket. They were all perfectly justifiable. So why, then, did Jack deny seeing her?

Desperate to give him an excuse, Rachel wonders if Ali's infatuated with him. If she thinks about it, every time they've seen each other recently, Ali's been desperate to get Jack on his own. The last time they went for dinner, she disappeared to the bathroom as soon as he excused himself, and even that morning, she'd been quick to say she'd go running with him. Perhaps, he's embarrassed by it; ashamed that he's somehow led her to believe that something could happen between them, when all he's done is be friendly. It's not his fault that she doesn't have the filter that most other women have when it comes to how you behave in that situation. She doesn't have a filter in *any* situation.

"Is it too much?" Ali asks now in that little girl's voice of hers.

Rachel hadn't even known she was staring at her. She pulls herself up and forces a smile.

"It's perfect," she says. "You look stunning."

Though Rachel can't help but wonder that if this is Ali's wedding *eve* outfit, what on earth is the day itself going to bring?

"You look gorgeous, honey," says Will, grinning behind her.

"Thank you, baby," says Ali.

"Doesn't she, bro?" says Will, nudging Jack.

"Er, yeah," says Jack awkwardly. As awkwardly as any man would, if he'd been asked by his brother what he thinks of his fiancée's eye-popping outfit. "Yeah, you look great."

Rachel can almost hear the squirm in his voice, not least because he's been put on the spot, but also, she suspects, because he knows this very same woman, who purports to love his brother so much, was in *his* room that morning.

"Okay!" exclaims Ali. "That settles it. Let's get this show on the road." She excitedly grabs hold of Will's hand and pulls her ever-riding dress down with the other as they head back through the house.

"I've never seen Jack look so uncomfortable," says Paige as she follows Rachel into the minibus.

Rachel offers a tight smile. Her own erratic thoughts are enough to contend with, without Paige adding *her* unhelpful opinion to the shitstorm that is raging in her head.

As Noah climbs in, Rachel wills him not to sit next to her. Even though it would normally be the most natural thing in the world, Jack's now made it feel the exact opposite. As if reading her mind, Noah takes the seat in front of hers.

"Who are we waiting for?" asks Will into the dark van.

"Jack just went to grab his jacket," says Rachel.

"And Ali," adds Paige, making Rachel's jaw spasm involuntarily.

It's ridiculous, but when Jack gets in less than a minute later, Rachel wishes the light was on so she could check for any signs that he's been doing something he shouldn't. Though, how she expects that to manifest itself, she doesn't know. Perhaps an untucked shirt, a wipe of his lips, a hair out of place . . .

"*Stop!*" she silently screams as the internal monologue threatens to drive her insane.

"Ooh, you smell nice, Jack," says Paige. "What have you got on?"

"Erm, it's Creed," he says, patting down his hair. "Aventus."

"That's the same one Ali bought me for my birthday," says Will. "How funny is that?"

Rachel can sense Paige's head turn toward her, but she doesn't need to look at her to know what her expression will be saying.

"Right, let's get this party started," shrills Ali as she climbs on board with a bottle of champagne in her hand. She pops the cork and invites everyone to take a swig.

If she were eighteen, Rachel supposes she'd be the first to knock one back, but as a forty-two-year-old mother, she can't help but feel it's all a little tawdry and, if she is honest, a bit beneath her.

"Rach, you're first up," Ali calls out as she passes the foaming bottle back to her.

"No, no," says Rachel. "I'm good, thanks."

"Aw, come on, loosen up," whines Ali. "It's the night before my wedding."

Rachel is still shaking her head as Noah holds out the bottle, the effervescent bubbles forming a froth on his hand. Perhaps she is too "up herself." Maybe if she didn't take life so seriously and had a more devil-may-care approach like Ali, her husband wouldn't feel the need to . . .

She pulls herself back from going down that road. God, this is going to be a long night if she's going to question her husband's fidelity every time he looks at his brother's wife-to-be.

"Down in one, down in one, down in one," Ali sings, encouraging Rachel to be reckless for once in her life and dare to enjoy herself.

Rachel looks around the expectant faces, all of them no doubt wanting her to have a drink for different reasons. An inebriated version of herself means Paige will have a dancing partner, Jack will have a willing participant in whatever roleplay he wants to engage in later, while Will and Ali will be happy under the misapprehension that she is having a better time if she's drunk. She briefly wonders why any of them bother with her at all if she's *that* dull when she's sober. Or is it that *they're* the boring ones and see her as good entertainment value when she's had a drink? It's only Noah, she notices, who turns to look at her with no selfish intentions at all. He smiles with kind eyes, asking nothing of her and expecting even less.

The bubbles go up her nose as she shows willing, but as the warm fizziness trails down her throat she's reminded that she's doing this for everyone but herself.

"Woo-hoo!" shrieks Ali, taking the bottle back as Rachel coughs and splutters. "That's my girl. Oh, Jack, I saw this in town earlier and thought of you." Ali rummages around in her clutch bag.

She produces a three-inch wooden figurine and hands it to Jack, who takes it before examining it.

"What is it?" says Paige, leaning in to take a closer look.

Jack turns it over in his hands before shrugging his shoulders.

"It's the Rooster of Barcelos," says Ali. "Haven't you seen him? He's the Portuguese national symbol; he's everywhere—you can't miss him."

"What did you buy him *that* for?" asks a bemused Will.

"Just as a little souvenir of the wedding and to thank him for being our best man," says Ali, with a smile on her face.

"I think you'll find he would have preferred an IWC watch as a Portuguese memento," says Will, laughing.

Ali slaps him playfully. "This is slightly more meaningful." She tuts. "It's a symbol from medieval times."

"What does it represent?" asks Rachel, because nobody else does.

"It's a fascinating story," says Ali. "When a landowner's silver was found to be missing, the authorities arrested and charged a Spanish pilgrim who happened to be passing through the town of Barcelos. He protested his innocence, but with no other suspects, he was sentenced to be hanged."

Rachel rubs at her head, unable to see the relevance of the preening bird Jack's holding in his hand.

"But, just before his death," Ali goes on, "he went to see the judge one last time to plead his innocence. He pointed to the roasted rooster on the dinner table in front of him and said it would come back to life to sing his innocence. The judge banished him to the gallows, but, just as the noose was being put around his neck, the rooster sprang to life."

"Did it save the pilgrim?" asks Rachel.

"Yes, he was set free," says Ali. "So, the moral of the story is that if you've done nothing wrong, you have nothing to fear."

Rachel looks at Jack, who smiles tightly before putting the figure, which she can now see has red love hearts painted all over its plumage, into his inside pocket.

"We're here!" exclaims Ali, a few minutes later, jumping up and down in her seat excitedly, the low cut of her dress edging dangerously close to revealing a nipple.

"What the hell was *that* all about?" asks Paige as they clamber out of the minibus.

"It's just a rooster," says Rachel wearily, not wanting to hear any more of Paige's theories, especially where Jack is concerned. "There's no hidden meaning."

Paige snorts derisorily. "It's a *cock*," she says. "There's all *kinds* of hidden meanings."

9

It's funny how just a couple of nights ago, the only thing Rachel had to worry about was how they were going to be spending their weekend. To the point that even when a text had popped up on Jack's phone, she'd thought little of it, preferring instead to fixate on whether she was going to be subjected to a rowdy nightclub to celebrate Will and Ali's nuptials or not. But now, all sorts of incidents are flashing up in her brain as she remembers them, suddenly conscious of what they might mean.

"Who's that?" she'd asked, when "*Can't wait to see you*" had flashed up on the screen from where it lay upturned on the vanity unit as she and Jack brushed their teeth the night before they left.

"Er, Will," he said, picking it up and taking it into the bedroom with his toothbrush still in his mouth.

"Why doesn't it say Will, then?" she'd asked, not because she was suspicious, but because she'd thought there might be something wrong with Jack's phone.

"He's got a new number," Jack had said from the other room. "And I haven't got round to saving it under his name yet."

"So, what do you think the venue will be like?" she'd asked, thinking nothing more of it. "I'm hopeful that he'll want to get married somewhere your parents will be proud of."

"Do you honestly think Will's had a say in it?" Jack had asked incredulously.

"Well, I'm banking on his good taste prevailing," she'd replied, in between spitting out toothpaste.

Jack had laughed. "Well, I'm afraid you're going to be bitterly disappointed, because if you think he's had any control over what's happening, dare I say, you're being a little naive."

She'd taken his comment with a pinch of salt, but a lot can change in forty-eight hours and now she's wondering if that's exactly what she's being. Who else would automatically believe that a text message sent to their husband saying "*Can't wait to see you*" would be from his brother?

Paige wouldn't have, for sure. She would have strung Noah up by his testicles until he told her the truth.

As she follows the sign welcoming Will and Ali's guests, she can't help but wonder if she's being taken for a fool.

"Wow," says Paige as she heads through a quaint arch that's decorated with blossoming bougainvillea, its vivid fuchsia petals trailing all the way to the ground.

They walk through to the garden where shimmering fairy lights illuminate the trunks of two tall palm trees, making them look like miniature helter-skelters. Candlelit lanterns hang from branches of cork trees and a gentle glockenspiel tune rings out from the chimes swaying in the breeze.

"Isn't it beautiful?" says Ali happily.

"*Olá bonita,*" calls out a bearded man as he emerges from a low-rise white stucco building. He opens his arms wide as he rushes to embrace Ali, kissing her on both cheeks. "*Como está a noiva?*" he says excitedly.

"Erm . . ." Ali giggles, turning to look wide-eyed at Will.

Will laughs as he shakes the man's hand. "He's asking how the bride is."

"Oh," says Ali. "Good, I'm really good."

"Paulo," says Will warmly, pulling the man in for a bear hug. "How have you been?"

"Very good. Very busy," says Paulo, the unfamiliar words sounding short and clipped on his Portuguese tongue.

"It's stunning," says Will, looking around the walled garden. "Thank you."

Rachel follows his eyes to the open lilies that are lying serenely in a troughed water feature, the stillness reflecting the twinkling lights from the trees.

"Your guest, she is here already," says Paulo as he ushers them toward the doorway of the restaurant.

"That'll be my mother," says Ali, laughing. "I'll put money on it. She wouldn't have been able to wait."

"Yes, I think so," says Paulo, smiling. "We have had a drink already."

"That's definitely my mum," says Ali.

It's not until she's in the restaurant that Rachel shivers, as her body registers the change in temperature from outside. Jack notices, putting an arm around her and rubbing her bare arm. It takes all her willpower not to recoil from his touch that suddenly feels sullied.

As if sensing there's more than just the chill in the air, Jack takes her hand and gives it a squeeze. "You okay?" he asks.

Rachel can't manage anything more than a nod as her brain goes into freefall, wondering what he must think of her. Does he see her as the faithful, docile wife who just sits at home waiting for him to come in from work? Is he bored by the banal conversation in which she has nothing more to offer than telling him who she bumped into in Blackheath Village when she picked up the lamb chops from the butcher's?

She's become complacent, believing that putting a good dinner in front of Jack every night would be enough to keep him by her side. But she can see now that he needs more; he wants a woman with a bit more get up and go. An ambitious streak. A desire to carve a niche out for herself, rather than relying on him for her emotional, practical and financial needs.

She swallows hard. "I was thinking, when I get home, I'd like to start my teacher training." She looks at him, expecting to see a renewed sense of respect in his eyes, but they're devoid of anything. How long have they been like that?

"What would you want to do that for?" he asks, looking around, preoccupied by trying to find the quickest way of getting a drink.

"I just think now would be a good time to pick it up again, seeing as Josh is off doing his own thing."

"But that's why I work as hard as I do," says Jack. "So that you don't have to."

"I know, and I'm grateful, but I just think it's time to do something of my own. I *want* to do something of my own."

He takes two glasses of champagne from a passing waiter's tray and hands one to her. "Is this because of today?" he asks.

She clenches her insides, unable to believe he's going to go there again.

"Life's too short and all that . . ." he says, laughing, as if what happened to Noah was some kind of joke.

"Darling!" calls out a woman, emerging from behind a pillar in a wheelchair.

"Mum!" shrieks Ali, rushing toward her, almost falling onto her lap to hug her.

"Oh, darling, you look absolutely gorgeous."

Ali straightens herself back up and pulls at the various pieces of Lycra that are just about stopping her from being arrested for indecent exposure. "Do you really think so?" Ali asks, forever looking for a compliment, even from her own mother, it seems.

Rachel hears an exaggerated sigh behind her and knows that it's Paige without even needing to look around.

"You *always* look beautiful," says Ali's mother, looking intently at her daughter, as if really trying to drill the words home. Rachel can't help but notice her reaching for Ali's hand and giving it a comforting squeeze. The genuine warmth between the pair of them is unmistakable.

"Mum," says Ali, "this is Will's brother."

"Ah, Jack," she says, not needing a formal introduction, it seems.

Ali smiles tightly as she looks at Jack. "This is my mum, Maria."

Jack takes Maria's hand. "Pleased to meet you," he says, in that false voice he puts on whenever he meets someone new.

It had amused Rachel the first time she'd noticed that slight change in intonation when she introduced him to some friends a few months after they'd started dating.

"Where on earth did the posh voice come from?" she'd asked afterward.

"What do you *mean*?" he'd said, seemingly unaware that he'd come across as anything other than how he normally did.

"There was a complete key change," she'd commented, through fits of laughter. "And since when have you dotted your i's and crossed your t's?"

"I always speak nicely," he'd said, having already discarded the plumminess that had cushioned his vowels and consonants just a few moments before.

"Not like that!" Rachel scoffed. "You sounded like you'd come straight from Eton."

"I can't help it if I was privately educated," he said, smiling. "But class and etiquette are instilled from birth—you can't buy it."

Rachel had shaken her head. "Yet you seem to have spent a fortune on condescension."

He'd stuck his tongue out at her, but he still continued to put "the voice" on whenever he met a stranger; at least until he knew them a bit better.

"It's good to finally have a face to put to the name," says Maria. "I've heard a lot about you."

Rachel wishes that she could replay it, as she's sure the word "lot" was emphasized.

"All good, I presume," says Jack, laughing nervously.

Maria doesn't answer; she just eyes him up and down with a look of . . . Rachel doesn't know what. Is it disdain or a silent appreciation and understanding? She can't quite put her finger on it.

"And this is Rachel," says Ali.

"Ah, I've been so looking forward to meeting you," says Maria, grabbing hold of both Rachel's hands and wrapping them in hers. "After everything that Ali's said about you, I half-expected you to have a shining halo above your head." She cocks her head to the side and squints her eyes. "In fact, I think I can see it," she says, smiling warmly.

Rachel is so overwhelmed by the genuine compassion she feels from this stranger, that there's an unexpected choke at the back of her throat.

Ali had told her about her mother's car accident five years ago, but Rachel wishes she'd asked more questions, and is now riddled with guilt for not showing more of an interest at the time, instead of writing the conversation off as another of Ali's over-exaggerated stories. The admission shames her.

"It's really lovely to meet you too," says Rachel. "How was the trip over here?"

"Well, while you enjoyed the relative luxury of British Airways, we had to endure the indignity of Ryanair." Maria laughs. "Who seem to have taken the idea of a budget airline to a whole new level. I think I might have been more comfortable in the baggage hold."

"We did all right," says a man, chortling as he comes up behind her with a glass of rosé. He extends a hand to Jack. "I'm Ken, by the way. Maria's long-suffering husband."

"Hi, Ken—I'm Jack and this is my wife Rachel." There's that fake voice again. "And these are our good friends Paige and Noah."

They all mutter their hellos and good wishes until there's a natural lull. "So," says Rachel, always keen to fill an uncomfortable silence. "Doesn't it look lovely in here?" She looks around for Ali, who, for all her faults, could never be accused of humdrum conversation.

She's over by the door, hugging Bob and Val, Will and Jack's parents. Even that simple gesture grates on Rachel more than it ever would have done before.

Maybe it's me, she thinks as Val fondly squeezes Ali's cheek like she's a five-year-old. *Maybe I'm the one with a problem.*

As she watches Ali link arms with Val and lead her over toward them, she can't help but feel replaced in Val's affections. They'd always had a good relationship, but it had meant even more since Rachel had lost her own mum a few years ago. She looked forward to their monthly shopping trips and the occasional afternoon tea they treated themselves to every once in a while. But now, Val has a new daughter-in-law to do those nice things with.

Once Ali's deposited Val safely beside Maria like a dutiful daughter-in-law, she heads back to the door and shrieks with excitement as she welcomes more guests.

"Sam! You're here!" she says, throwing herself at an impossibly good-looking young man, while his girlfriend stands beside them, looking—to Rachel—to be grinning with gritted teeth.

Could it be that that's just the way Ali is with *everyone*? Albeit there's no mistaking that she's definitely more like it with men. But there's nothing wrong with that; it just makes her a man's woman. It doesn't mean she's jumping into bed with every guy she sees—*including your husband*, Rachel says to herself, as if she's talking to a third party. It just means that she's more comfortable in their company than that of a woman. When Rachel says it like that in her head, it sounds perfectly plausible. That's not a crime—there are plenty of women like that, though Paige will gladly cook you over the spit roast if you dare to say so.

As if on cue, using the commotion at the door as a distraction, Paige sidles up to Rachel. "Do you think all of her friends are going to be versions of *her*?"

Rachel watches a blonde girl edge herself unsurely through the door, almost as if she's apologizing for being there, even before she's arrived. Her eyes flit around the room and a palpable resignation seems to course its way through her as she forces herself to accept that what she's seeing isn't what she'd hoped for.

"Apparently not," Paige goes on as she watches the same woman hover at the entrance. "Talk about apples and oranges."

Rachel's sure Paige doesn't mean it unkindly, but for all the "every woman is equal" crap she spouts, she's the first to point out the differences in their appearance.

The woman, dressed in a floor-skimming red dress, sees Maria and waves hesitantly, but continues to wait patiently in line to greet Ali, pushing her glasses up her nose as she does so.

"I don't think our lady of the moment is going to be too impressed by her friend's dress choice, do *you*?" says Paige, with a detectable frisson of anticipation.

"Chrissy!" exclaims Ali, throwing her arms around her friend. "Hey girl, we're winning at twinning." Ali pulls herself away and stands beside her. "Sam!" she calls out to the man from the group who came in before. "Look, we're twins! Take a photo!"

"Oh, that's *wicked*," says Paige, looking on.

"What is?" asks Rachel, as Jack hands her another glass of champagne, even though she's not yet finished the first.

"Saying they look like twins and making her have her photo taken," Paige goes on.

"Her friend doesn't look unhappy," says Rachel, watching the pair of them grinning into the camera lens.

"Maybe not, but you can tell Ali's put out about her wearing the same color," says Paige. "Though, it's not as if they bear any resemblance."

Rachel can't decide whether it's meant to be a put-down or backhanded compliment.

"Cheers!" says Noah, as he raises his glass in the air. "Here's to the happy couple."

"I thought you weren't drinking?" admonishes Rachel.

"How does it feel to have your mother out with you?" Jack says, laughing, to Noah.

Noah's jaw spasms involuntarily.

"I'm just going to have the one," says Noah, ignoring him.

"I'll make sure of it," says Paige. "After what happened today, I'll be keeping an extra close eye on him." She kisses Noah softly on the cheek and looks at him in a way that Rachel's not seen her do in years.

"Bloody hell, perhaps I should go drown myself," says Jack. "If it gets you this kind of attention from the ladies."

"It looked like you were giving it a good try," says Paige. "But you didn't quite carry it off with the *aplomb* of my husband."

"Oh, he went for it, for sure," says Jack, laughing. "I've never seen anyone bail under a wave as easily as he did. It wasn't even that big. It was an ankle buster. I even said that to you, didn't I?" Jack knocks back the champagne in his glass and takes another from a passing waiter.

"Was that when we were paddling toward it?" asks Noah, through narrow eyes. "Or when it was smashing me into the seabed on a spin cycle?"

Jack stares at him as he empties another glass.

"But I don't understand why you left Will and ignored Jack when he told you to come back," says Rachel.

Noah shakes his head and laughs sarcastically.

"I thought you said Jack told you to follow him?" says Paige with a furrowed brow.

Rachel's throat constricts and her mouth goes dry. She looks from Noah to Jack and back again.

"Wow!" says Jack. "Are you really going to try and pin this on me?"

"I didn't ignore anyone's instructions," Noah says to Rachel. "I followed them."

10

Despite feeling as though the restaurant is shrouded in a Jack-shaped black cloud, Rachel does her best to ignore it over dinner, throwing herself into conversation with the couple seated to her left.

"So, do you think you *will* start training, now that your son has left home?" asks John, who Rachel has learned is married to Ali's cousin Kimberley. She has no idea why she's told them about her simmering desire to teach, though she guesses she was looking for the encouragement she didn't receive from Jack earlier. That, and the copious amount of wine she's drunk since.

"It's certainly something I'd love to do," says Rachel. "I don't feel like I'll ever forgive myself if I don't at least give it a try." It's definitely the drink talking now because, as much as she knows it to be true, she also doubts she's fearless enough to follow it through.

"I'm so impressed with you ladies," says Kimberley, leaning in. "I wish I had a bit more ambition."

"You can do anything you put your mind to," says John, putting his hand over hers.

"Yes, but that requires confidence," says Kimberley. "I mean, just look at everything Ali's achieved. I'm in awe of her, and a little bit jealous, but I could never do what she does in a million years."

"Of course you could," encourages John.

"She has meetings with David Friedman," Kimberley exclaims. "I could *never* do that."

"Well, I know she works for his company," butts in Rachel, keen for Kimberley not to get too carried away putting Ali on a pedestal she doesn't belong on. "But I'm not sure she has any close contact with him."

"They're like *that*," says Kimberley, crossing her fingers. "He was supposed to be here, but something came up at the last minute."

Rachel doesn't know whether to laugh or cry. "She said David Friedman was going to come to her wedding?"

"Yes," says Kimberley proudly, without a hint of skepticism.

"Uh-oh, talk of the devil," says John. "Here comes trouble."

"Oi you," says Ali, leaning in to give him a hug. She's lost enough inhibitions not to worry about holding onto the top of her dress anymore, but Rachel still has a few left and finds herself constantly wanting to reach out to protect her modesty.

"I'm sorry I've not had a chance to talk to you properly yet," says Ali, as she kisses Kimberley. "How are you?"

"Good," says Kimberley, smiling. "This is wonderful. You look so happy."

"I am," says Ali. "I can't wait until tomorrow when we'll finally be husband and wife."

"It's so exciting that you're about to embark on this new chapter."

"I know," says Ali, with a smug expression. "I can't believe I got so lucky."

"You deserve it," says Kimberley, putting her hand on top of Ali's. "After everything you've been through."

Rachel waits, ears pricked up, hoping for someone to elaborate. It might help explain why Ali's like she is.

"It's been a long time coming," says Ali, sighing. "But it finally feels as if my life is back on track."

Kimberley nods. "It's all about looking forward now," she says. "The future's exciting. A new husband and, God willing, children."

"*Kim*," starts John, as if warning her not to pry.

"Oh, I don't know about that," says Ali, smiling. "I'm not quite ready for kids just yet."

"Wait, *what*?" The words are out of Rachel's mouth before she can stop them.

Ali stares at Rachel with wide eyes and surreptitiously shakes her head. "We've got plenty of time," she says. "There's no rush."

Rachel glares back, knowing that wasn't the plan—at least it wasn't last night, when Ali had professed to wanting children with Will immediately.

Rachel wonders if Ali hasn't got a bigger problem than what they're all making allowances for. Perhaps her tendency to over-exaggerate and need to be at the center of every story is just the tip of a far deeper psychological issue. This isn't the first time Rachel has suspected her of lying, though it's the first time she's caught her red-handed, blatantly changing her tune, depending on who she's talking to. Though she's spoken with such conviction both times, that Rachel can't tell which is the lie and which is the truth.

"If you'll just excuse me," says Rachel, unable to listen to whichever version this is for any longer. She gets up, not knowing where she's going to head, but then she sees Jack leaning in to Noah at the bar, jabbing a finger into his chest. Her heart quickens at the same rate as her feet.

"Is everything okay?" she asks falteringly as she reaches them.

Now she's closer, she can see Jack's features, twisted with anger.

"What's going on?" she asks, as the tension in Jack's shoulders dissipates and he takes a step back. But he doesn't take his eyes off Noah.

"You'd better watch yourself," says Jack, straightening his shirt, as if he's been in a fight.

Noah laughs and Rachel wishes he hadn't. She almost looks out of one eye, expecting Jack to be launching himself at him.

"I'm warning you," hisses Jack.

"Jack!" says Rachel, knowing she's got her work cut out. He's far too drunk and far too angry. "Jack, why don't you go and talk to Paige?"

He looks around unsteadily.

"She's over there," says Rachel, as if she's cajoling one child to go and play with another.

He lurches off and Rachel lets out the breath she was holding in.

"What the hell was *that* about?" she says, turning to Noah.

He shakes his head. "Your husband can be such a prize tosser when he wants to be."

"Is this over what happened earlier?" she asks, not knowing which event she's referring to. Selfishly, she hopes it's the one in the sea rather than the conversation he'd probably overheard her and Jack having in their bedroom.

"He's still maintaining that he told me not to go toward the waves."

"O-kay," says Rachel carefully, not wanting to stoke this unpredictable situation any further.

"And I know I've had a bump to the head, but I clearly heard him telling me to follow him."

"But it must have been incredibly noisy out there," says Rachel, trying to stay on neutral ground.

"I *know* what I heard," says Noah. "He said, 'Come on, this way.'"

"But you must have known it looked dangerous," says Rachel. "If Jack told you to put your head in an oven, you wouldn't do it, would you?" Rachel attempts to laugh.

"No, but I'd lost sight of Will, and in the absence of him telling me what I should be doing, Jack seemed the next safe bet."

"But maybe it was just a miscommunication," says Rachel. "Maybe *he* didn't make himself clear and *you* didn't hear him correctly. I'm sure he wouldn't have taken you out there intentionally."

Noah goes to counter the argument, but seems to think better of it. Instead, he looks at her with soft eyes and smiles. "I hope you're right," he says.

In that moment, it's as if a time machine has picked them both up and dropped them into 2001.

Rachel can see him at the airport, standing under the departures board, begging her to go on the year-long trip they'd planned so meticulously.

"What if this is our only chance?" he'd said.

"But what if I came with you and forever regretted not staying with Jack?" she'd said.

He'd kissed her in answer and for those few minutes she'd wondered how she could even question it.

"I'll wait for you," he said, when they eventually came up for air.

"If we're meant to be, we'll find a way."

"I hope you're right," he'd said.

By the time she saw him again, she was married with a baby, and she's spent the past twenty years convinced she'd done the right thing. Except now, with him looking at her as if he's trying to read her mind, she wonders if she made the wrong decision after all.

She shakes herself down as the unfamiliar, and wholly unwelcome, thoughts wrap themselves around her psyche. She tells herself that this is merely a knee-jerk reaction to seeing Noah unconscious on the beach today. That it's natural to feel panicked and scared when faced with the prospect of losing the best friend she's ever had. All those feelings are perfectly understandable. But what she *hadn't* bargained for was the acute sense of grief she'd felt on realizing that they might never get their chance.

"Could I get a gin and bitter lemon, please?" says an old woman coming up beside Rachel and breaking the spell she's been momentarily under.

Rachel smiles warmly and the woman smiles back, her eyes shining. "What a lovely do," she says.

"Isn't it?" says Rachel. "If this is just the warm-up, I can't wait to see what tomorrow brings."

The woman nods in agreement. "I'm Ali's grandmother," she says. "Are you friends of hers?"

"Well, yes, we are," says Rachel, nodding. "But we're more from Will's side."

"He seems a lovely boy," says the woman.

"Oh, he is," says Rachel. "She's got a good one there."

"He reminds me of *my* boy, looks-wise—when he was younger, of course." She laughs ruefully. "I call him my boy, but he's almost sixty. How on earth I could possibly have a sixty-year-old son, I don't know."

Rachel looks around the room of forty or so people, most of whom are now milling about, or have swapped seats, leaving glaring gaps in the carefully thought-out table plan.

"Is he here?" asks Rachel, looking for who she assumes is Maria's brother.

"Oh no," says the woman. "I'm Alison's *father's* mother, but since their divorce, it's only me she stays in touch with. I'm afraid my son wasn't the best role model. He drank too much, went out too much . . . he really put poor Maria through the wringer until, one day, she decided enough was enough."

"Oh right," says Rachel, making note of another part of Ali's backstory that she'd omitted to reveal. "It's interesting that Will reminds you of your son, then. They say that women often gravitate toward men like their father, even if it's not a conscious decision."

The old woman smiles wryly. "Well, let's just hope that he's only similar in looks, and not personality. As ashamed as I am to admit it, I wouldn't want Alison to end up with someone like my son."

Rachel smiles and puts a reassuring hand over the woman's on the bar. "The only problem Ali will have is trying to keep up with Will's wanderlust." *And his desire for children*, she thinks.

"His *wanderlust*?" queries the woman in a high-pitched tone. "That doesn't sound very conducive to a happily married life."

Noah laughs. "It's not that kind of wander *or* lust. She just means he's always got half an eye on taking off to explore the world. It's how he's always been, but now he's got Ali, he's got someone to do it with, if they both feel so inclined." He takes another large slug of his gin.

"Oh, I see," says the woman, clearly relieved. "It's all such a worry, isn't it? You think they're hard work when they're little, but that's just the start of it. You worry even more when they grow up."

"That's very true," says Rachel knowingly.

"Do you have children, then?"

Rachel nods. "Just the one, though he's hardly a child. Like you say, I can't quite believe I've got a nineteen-year-old."

"So, he'll be going off to university, will he?"

"He's already gone, just over a month ago, and although we all felt he was ready, we miss him terribly."

"Ah, an empty nest," says the woman, looking at them both. "That must be hard."

Rachel offers a smile. "It takes some getting used to."

"Do you have a photo?" asks the woman.

"Oh, yes," says Rachel, taking her phone out of her clutch bag and flicking through to find a picture that shows Josh in all his handsomeness.

The woman takes the phone in her hand, peering closely at the photo before looking between Rachel and Noah.

"Well, there's no mistaking who *he* takes after," says the woman, handing the phone back to Rachel and looking at Noah. "He's the spitting image of you."

"Oh . . . oh . . . no," blurts out Rachel, feeling a heat creep around her neck. "We're not together." She does a frantic backward and forward motion with her hand. "*My* husband's over there." She points to where Jack is sitting next to Paige. "*That's* Josh's dad. We . . ." She starts the flapping motion with her hand again. "*We're* just good friends."

"Oh my goodness," chuckles the woman. "Well, so much for *my* powers of observation."

Noah's mouth pulls back into a tight-lipped grin, but his eyes are alight with shock, burning a hole deep into Rachel. She shifts, uncomfortable under his intense stare, desperately looking for a distraction to ease the strained atmosphere.

She goes to speak, though to say what, she doesn't know, but her throat constricts and her mouth dries up instantaneously when she parts her lips. She wonders if her discomfort is obvious—how can it not be to Noah, who knows her better than most? But when she fleetingly glances at him, he looks at her as if she were a stranger.

"If you'll excuse me," he says, through gritted teeth.

Rachel watches him, her heart pounding, as he weaves his way through the restaurant and out the door.

"It's been lovely meeting you," says Rachel to the old woman, who's happily sipping her gin and bitter lemon.

"You too, dear," she says. "See you for the big day tomorrow."

"Looking forward to it," says Rachel.

Keeping one eye on Noah through the window, she scans the room for Jack and is relieved to see him sitting, deep in conversation, with Paige. Although that will no doubt do little to subdue his truculent mood, it gives Rachel time to pacify Noah, whose mindset worries her even more right now.

She's just about to reach for the door handle when a hand grabs her arm.

"I'm glad I caught you," says Maria.

Rachel smiles at Ali's mother. "I'm sorry, I just need to . . ." She tilts her head to where she can see Noah retreating into the darkness, his arms swinging by his sides.

"Of course," says Maria, letting go.

Rachel shifts from one foot to the other as she loses sight of Noah's white shirt. "It's okay," she says, forcing a smile. "It can wait."

Maria pats the stool next to her and as Rachel dutifully sits down, Maria picks up her hand and holds it tight.

"Just in case I don't get an opportunity to speak to you tomorrow, I wanted to thank you."

"*Thank* me?" says Rachel in surprise. "What on earth for?"

"For looking after Alison; for taking her under your wing and welcoming her into the family. She was beginning to think she'd never meet the right person and then when she did, she was nervous about ingratiating herself."

"*Ali, nervous?* I doubt that." Rachel's head is so full of Noah, and fuzzy with alcohol, that she doesn't know whether she's said the words out loud or not.

Maria smiles, suggesting that she might have. "You see, Alison may come over as confident, but it's just her way of coping."

"Coping?" queries Rachel, not sure that she's interested enough to care. She has a bigger problem to deal with.

"It's just that she's been through a lot," Maria goes on. "And it's all a bit of a front she hides behind."

That's no excuse to be a pathological liar, Rachel wants to say. *To tell your husband-to-be that you're desperate to have children and then behind his back admit you're not ready. To pretend that David Friedman was coming to your wedding, but had to cancel at the last minute.*

"She was bullied terribly when she was younger and she sometimes over-compensates," says Maria, as if in answer. "So, please don't think that how she is on the outside is how she's feeling on the inside. There's a shy and timid girl in there, whose only wish is to be accepted for who she is."

There's an unsettling feeling in the pit of Rachel's stomach: is Maria as naive to Ali, and all that she's capable of, as everyone else?

She almost feels compelled to tell Maria how Ali behaves around Jack, in the hope that she'll allay her concerns. But in light of how she'd greeted him, Rachel fears she'll only stoke the fire instead of putting it out.

"Why was she bullied?" Rachel asks instead.

"Oh, I'd rather not say," says Maria, suddenly flustered.

Of all the scenarios that play out in Rachel's head at that moment, she shocks herself when she settles on an inappropriate relationship with a teacher being the most likely. She can all too easily picture Ali flirting outrageously, encouraging a response and sharing all the sordid details—true or otherwise—with her peers. Rachel imagines it might have made her popular, for a brief moment in time, but as soon as the shit hit the fan, any friends she thought she had would have run for the mountains.

"We had to move schools three times, but the bullying just seemed to follow her wherever she went."

"That must have been very difficult," says Rachel, putting a hand on top of Maria's.

"It was." She sniffs. "But to see her now, as happy as she is, more than makes up for it."

"Will is a wonderful man," says Rachel. "She's a lucky girl."

"And *he's* a lucky man," says Maria, smiling wistfully. "I know she'll make the most loyal and loving wife."

Rachel forces herself not to balk. Clearly Maria doesn't know her daughter quite as well as she thinks she does.

11

"Noah!" Rachel calls out as she tentatively edges toward the orange grove that she saw him disappear into. The citrus scent travels on the breeze, which, despite it having a nip to it, Rachel can barely feel as alcohol and adrenaline rush through her system. "Noah!" she says again, her voice struggling to be heard over the chorus of cicadas singing in the trees overhead.

The light is diminishing into nothing the further she goes, and she can feel the ground underneath her wedge heels change; they struggle to negotiate a bumpier surface—soil hardened by the sun. If she wants to avoid a broken ankle, she knows it would be unwise to go any further. "Noah!" she calls out one more time.

"He was just here," says a slurred voice, the owner of which is only visible by the burning ember of a cigarette end.

"Ali?" Rachel questions falteringly, playing for time to think of what logical reason she's got to be out here looking for Noah rather than enjoying the party. "I was just . . ." she starts, not really knowing where she's going with it.

Ali silently pulls on the cigarette, the orange glow lighting her face. "I've just seen him," she says as she exhales a straight line of smoke up toward the night sky. "He seems pretty shaken up."

Rachel feels a tug in her chest. "Oh, right. Did you see where he went?"

"Over there," says Ali, pointing to a white-walled two-story building, set twenty meters or so away from the restaurant. "That's Paulo's place. I saw Noah heading around the far side."

"Oh, great," says Rachel awkwardly, turning to walk off. "It's been a lovely dinner."

Ali doesn't say another word, but Rachel can feel her eyes burning into her back as she hastily walks toward the soft lighting of a downstairs window. She briefly wonders who's in there, watching television in a language she doesn't understand, living a life so far removed from her own. Have they ever been to London? England, even? She finds it so hard to contemplate that so many other people are going about their everyday lives without ever knowing that each other exists. A dog barks, bringing her back.

"Noah!" she says, a little more quietly this time. "Are you there?"

She turns the corner to find him sitting on a plastic garden chair, with his head in his hands. Shadows are dancing all around him as the branches of the surrounding trees briefly let the moonlight filter in, before gently swaying and blocking it out again.

"I . . . erm." Now that she's found him, she doesn't know what to say.

"What do *you* want?" he says, in a voice so unlike his own that Rachel instantly regrets coming after him.

"I just . . ." she starts, before looking around to make sure no one else is there, least of all Ali, who she hopes is too drunk to even remember seeing her out here at all, let alone who she was looking for. "I just wanted to check that you're okay."

He makes a derisory snort through his nose. "If you knew me at all, you'd know that I'm not."

She goes toward him. He needs to see her, to remember who he's talking to. "Come on," she says, leaning down and taking his hands in hers. "Let's not get all heavy. This is supposed to be a celebration."

"Oh, yes," he says sarcastically. "Let's all watch *another* couple live a lie."

"And what is *that* supposed to mean?" As soon as she says it, she wishes she hadn't.

He looks at her and shrugs his shoulders. "So . . . ?"

"So, what?" she says, even though she's got a horrible feeling she knows what's coming.

His gaze is unflinching. "Are you going to tell me the truth or not?"

Rachel drops his hands and looks at the ground. She'd hoped that this day would never come. She'd almost convinced herself that if it ever did, she'd have a cast-iron alibi. But twenty years on, she has no more assurances to offer than back then.

She'd reasoned in her head that the baby *must* be Jack's; they'd had sex *hundreds* of times, while she'd only been with Noah once. Though, inklings of doubt had crept in when she and Jack had tried to add to their brood. Month after month, year after year, nothing had happened.

"So?" Noah asks again.

"I don't know what you want me to say," she says truthfully.

"Is Josh . . . ?" starts Noah, before taking a deep breath. "Might he be . . . ? *Could* he be . . . ?"

She looks at him, her heart feeling like a ten-ton weight in her chest. "No," she says decisively, surprising herself.

"But that woman just said he's the spitting image of me."

"Is *that* what this is all based on?" says Rachel, incredulously. "A passing comment by a total stranger."

"But she's right though, isn't she? You only have to look at him." He walks away, running his hand through his hair. "Her saying that has made me realize what's been staring at me in the face for all these years."

"Listen to me," says Rachel impatiently, though she knows it's her own frustration that's making her snap. "He's *not* your son."

"How do you know?" he asks, coming toward her, his eyes glassy.

"Because the dates don't add up," she says, though now she can't remember whether she *knows* that to be true, or if she's convinced herself of it ever since.

"It's got to be pretty close, though—it can only be a matter of weeks."

"Well, a matter of weeks makes quite the difference," says Rachel, attempting to laugh, but it comes out more like someone's got a hand around her throat. Perhaps they do. "Look, this is insane. You're allowing a throwaway remark to mess with your mind. Don't you think I would have told you if there was even the slightest chance that you were Josh's father?"

"But what if I am?" says Noah, taking hold of her arms. "What if you've got it wrong? What if he's mine and we should have been together, as a family, for all this time?"

Tears spring unexpectedly to Rachel's eyes as she desperately tries to bat away the thought of it. How many times had she replayed the decision she made two decades ago? Imagined how differently it could have all turned out if she'd gone traveling with Noah, pregnant or not? Everyone has a sliding-doors moment in their life; people assume there are many, but they're wrong. There's only one defining juncture that, depending on which path you take, will determine the rest of your life. And that was hers.

"Don't make this about you and me," she says, her voice catching in the back of her throat. "We had our chance and we made our decisions."

"*You* made the decision for both of us," says Noah tightly.

"That's not fair," she says, trying to pull away from him, but he won't let go. "I spent years waiting for you, and just when I got used to it never happening, you decided . . ."

He lets go of her like he's been given an electric shock. "*Years*?" he repeats.

She takes a deep breath. "You must have known how I felt about you," she says. "I thought I made it pretty obvious."

"While we lived together on campus?" he asks, without waiting for an answer. "When we moved into digs together?"

She nods.

Noah shakes his head, seemingly unable to get his head around this new, twenty-year-old, information. "You mean to tell me that on all the holidays we went on, where I went with every girl who looked my way, you were . . . you were . . ." He can't bring himself to say it.

"Lying there listening on the other side of the wall . . . ?" Rachel says, half-laughing. "Well, yes, but I'm not a masochist. I did put a pillow over my ears."

"But you seemed to positively encourage it," he says. "In fact, you used to say that living vicariously through me meant that you didn't have to put the effort into the opposite sex yourself."

Rachel smiles wryly. "That's called self-preservation."

"So, all the time you were playing it cool, you and I could have been together?"

"I was just hoping that at some point the stars would align."

"Yet when they did, *you* chickened out."

"Noah, it was too late by then," she says, growing exasperated. "You were happy doing your thing and I'd met Jack."

"But I asked you to come to Thailand with me," he says. "*Begged* you."

Rachel sighs. "The downside of us having a platonic relationship for as long as we did was that I knew how you operated with the opposite sex. I've watched you claim victory on countless conquests, heard you say the same words to a hundred other girls that you said to me that night."

Noah goes to interrupt but she puts her hand up. "There was every chance that you'd be saying them to someone else before we'd even reached Bangkok and I wasn't prepared to take that risk; I'd rather be broken-hearted at home with Jack, than a thousand miles away with you and another girl."

"But why didn't you say anything?" asks Noah. "How could I have known how you felt without you telling me?"

She takes his hand in hers again. "What difference would it have made?" she says, softly.

"The world," he says, pushing her fringe out of her eyes. "Because, if you'd told *me*, I would have told *you* I felt exactly the same."

Rachel's chest feels like it's in a vise-like grip, as she looks up at the sky, the blackness alight with twinkling stars.

"It was a long time ago," she says, wishing that her head was clearer. "We've all moved on. You met Paige—if you hadn't, you wouldn't have Chloe. It's the tapestry of life."

"But I want *you*," says Noah, pulling her closer.

The change in tense throws Rachel for a loop. She can deal with nostalgia tangling itself into looking like a missed opportunity. But what she's not prepared for is the here and now: they're both married, they're best friends—and wanting each other *isn't* an option.

He tucks a loose strand of hair behind her ears, his fingers gently tracing the line of her jaw. It feels like she's gone back in time, and is about to make a decision that will change the course of her life. Maybe it *is* possible to have more than one sliding-doors moment.

"I have never stopped loving you," he says, leaning in to kiss her cheek, his lips igniting a heat in her skin that runs deep into her veins. His face is still there, so close to hers, and his hand is nestled at the back of her neck, the pulse in his thumb matching her own.

Rachel closes her eyes as she breathes him in, his smell and touch making her feel as if there are a thousand butterflies about to take flight in the pit of her stomach. She could stay like this forever, trapped in a parallel universe where they could be together. But reality is seeping in, through the hairline chink of light that stands between his lips and hers. She *has* to open her eyes, to separate herself from that life and this, but when she does, she gets a jolt. Standing there watching them, just a few meters away, is Ali.

12

"Noah!" a woman's voice calls out. "Noah, are you out here?"

Rachel freezes, locking eyes with Ali as Paige's voice hangs on the night breeze.

"Hello? Is someone there?" she says, getting nearer.

"It's me," Ali says, stepping into the light.

"Oh, right," says Paige. "I'm looking for Noah. Have you seen him?"

Rachel holds her breath and sways, feeling as if she might pass out.

"Erm," says Ali, drawing it out for what feels like minutes. "No, I don't think I have."

"I can't seem to find him," says Paige. "Or Rachel."

Ali looks behind her to where Rachel's concealed behind an outbuilding. "Ah, that's because she's here," she says.

Rachel's legs feel as if they might give way.

"Oh," says Paige, as Rachel walks unsteadily into her line of sight. "What are you doing out here? Is everything all right?" She looks from Rachel to Ali and back again, trying to gauge the situation.

"We're just having a sneaky puff," says Ali, putting a finger to her lips. "But don't tell Jack."

"You're *smoking*?" asks Paige incredulously. Rachel had never smoked in her life and had often berated Jack and Paige if they went halves on a packet of cigarettes when they'd had a drink.

Ali hands her a lit cigarette as if it were something they did all the time.

"Yep," Rachel says, taking it and putting it up to her mouth. She knows if she inhales, she'll be in all sorts of trouble, so she tightly closes her lips and hopes that the darkness will work in her favor.

"You haven't seen Noah, have you?" asks Paige. "I haven't seen him for a while and after what happened today, I'm a bit worried that I'm going to find him in a heap somewhere."

Rachel hates herself. For allowing the events of the day to get the better of her. For distrusting her husband. For deceiving Paige. But most of all, she hates herself for giving Ali this power to lord over her.

"I saw him about ten minutes ago and he seemed fine," says Ali, taking back the cigarette that Rachel is proffering her.

"Oh, great," says Paige. "Well, once I find him, we're going to make our way home. I don't want him exerting himself too much ahead of tomorrow."

Rachel shudders involuntarily at the well-meaning comment. "I'll come with you," she says, eager to get away from Ali and all that she now knows.

"We're probably *all* ready to go," says Ali, dashing Rachel's plan. "The minivan's out front, so I'll say my goodbyes."

"You okay?" asks Paige as soon as they're out of earshot of Ali. "How come you're best friends all of a sudden?"

Rachel forces a smile. "Just trying to keep the peace," she says, cringing at the irony.

"Who's up for a nightcap?" asks Ali as soon as they get back to the villa.

"Not for me," says Noah as he heads up the stairs. "I'm turning in for the night."

Rachel can't look at him, mostly for fear of what she'll see behind his eyes, but also because she's afraid of what Ali will make of it if she does.

She'd spent the twenty-minute journey back from the restaurant trying to predict what Ali would do with the information she may or may not have. To preserve her own sanity, Rachel has to assume that Ali saw and heard nothing. But the likelihood is that she saw and heard *everything*, and that thought resounds around and around her head on a loop.

Though, to look at Ali now, it's as if nothing has changed. There are no knowing sideward glances or the judgmental raising of an eyebrow. There are no sly digs or inappropriate comments, which only serves to unsettle Rachel even more. She'd rather just know what Ali knows, and what she's intending to do with the knowledge, than be blindsided when Jack no doubt confronts her.

If Ali's going to tell him that there's even a question mark hanging over Josh's head, Rachel would rather have the excruciating conversation with Jack herself, as at least then she'd be able to say what needs to be said with some semblance of accuracy and truth. Though, the thought of telling the man who'd believed he was his son's father for nineteen years, that he might not be, makes her break out into a cold sweat. How duped will he feel when he finds out that the newborn he'd cherished beyond anything else might be another man's baby? How deceived will he feel when he knows that the four-year-old boy he'd taught to ride a bike without stabilizers should have been wobbling his way toward someone else? How will he feel to be told that those three nights he spent on a boys-only camping trip with Josh when he was ten might not have been the father–son bonding experience he'd thought it was?

Josh is Jack's world and the thought of Ali having the power to turn it upside down makes Rachel's insides feel like they're being pulled out of her.

"Who wants what?" Ali asks, shrugging off Will's jacket that he'd wrapped around her when she complained of being cold.

"I'll go," says Rachel.

"Great, I'll have a white wine then, please," says Ali.

"I'll have a beer," says Will, falling down into one of the deep sofas.

"Jack?" asks Rachel, conscious that they hadn't spoken two words since leaving the restaurant. She catches Ali looking at him and has a momentary panic that she might already have divulged her biggest secret.

"I'll have a beer as well," he says sulkily, as he follows Noah up the stairs.

"Where are you going?" she asks, alarmed.

When he doesn't answer, she can't help but go up after him, as her brain fast-forwards to the pair of them having a punch-up on the landing and one or both of them coming crashing down onto the glass coffee table in the living room below.

She breathes out as Noah disappears into his room and Jack keeps walking toward theirs. She silently follows him in and closes the door behind her.

"Is everything okay?" she asks, as he disappears into the bathroom.

"Yes, why shouldn't it be?"

"Just that you haven't said two words to me all night."

"I had a lot of people to talk to," he says abruptly.

Rachel knows that and she wouldn't normally be so needy, but on this occasion it would help to know that he's not avoiding her.

"Is everything . . . ?" she starts, before having second thoughts about opening up a can of worms she'd rather keep shut.

He comes out the bathroom, looking at her expectantly.

"Is everything . . . all right with you and Noah?" she says, wanting to cross her fingers and squeeze her eyes shut.

Her head is such a jumble that she can't remember who knows what, who accused whom, whether she saw Jack and Noah arguing at the bar *before* Noah tried to kiss her or after, and whether Ali had really heard their conversation. . . .

She wishes she hadn't drunk so much because she's unable to time the events of the last few hours, or the order they happened in. That's probably why she's here *now*, looking for reassurance from Jack that all is well in his world.

"He's an asshole," says Jack, which, given the alternatives that Rachel had expected, could have been worse.

"He had an almighty scare today," says Rachel. "We *all* did."

Jack looks at her with raised eyebrows as if to say, *"But you more than most, it seems."* But she refuses to pick up on his insinuation.

"*He's* shocked. *You're* shocked," she says. "I'm sure everything will be fine tomorrow. You just need a good rest."

"The last thing I need is rest," says Jack, coming toward her, his face suddenly alight with mischief.

He bends to kiss her neck as his hands roughly pull up her skirt.

No part of her wants this right now, she's just not in the right headspace, yet she can't help but feel appeased that *he* does. It means that they're okay; that he doesn't know anything she doesn't want him to know, and that even though Ali seems to be doing her best to turn his head, he still wants *her*.

"Jack," she says, pulling away from him.

He grabs her behind, pressing himself up against her. "Come on," he coaxes.

"Everyone's downstairs," she says. "They'll be wondering where we've got to."

"So?"

"So, let's go and have one more drink, say our goodnights and *then* come up," she says, not knowing whether that's her real intention or she's just saying it to cool his ardor.

"Fine," he says stroppily, as he tucks his shirt back into his trousers. "I'll be down in a minute."

As she walks down the stairs, Rachel forces herself to clear her head of any feelings for Noah and any suspicious thoughts of Ali. Though, the fact that the two of them are now intrinsically linked makes it all the harder.

"Oh hi," she says in surprise, when she finds Paige leaning against the kitchen worktop, deep in thought. "You okay?"

Paige smiles. "I was miles away."

"Noah's just gone up to bed," says Rachel, unable to think of anything else to say.

"I'll go and check on him in a minute," says Paige. "But first, I need to tell you something."

Rachel stops pouring white wine into Ali's glass as she tries to guess what Paige is about to say. She can't possibly know about what had just happened with Noah. Ali certainly hasn't had the opportunity to say anything yet and Rachel imagines her first port of call, when she *does*, is going to be Jack.

As she looks at Paige with her heart in her mouth, she can't believe that she'd rather it be about Jack and Ali because the alternative doesn't bear thinking about.

Paige looks to the door before turning back to face her. "There's something going on," she says.

An ice-cold terror floods Rachel's insides. "What do you mean?" she asks. "In what way?"

Paige looks down at her feet, as if contemplating whether to go on. "I was having a cigarette around the back of the restaurant tonight," she says.

Rachel's brain feels like it's being hot-wired, the sparks flying off in all different directions as she backtracks to what Paige might have seen or heard. If she'd witnessed any part of what had gone on between her and Noah, Rachel's sure that Paige, being Paige, would not be calmly standing here, drinking a glass of Merlot. Still, she's too scared to test the theory by asking her to elaborate.

"And so I happened to be outside the open window of the ladies' room," Paige goes on, looking at Rachel with almost a grimace.

Rachel freezes.

"Ali was in there," says Paige.

Rachel's insides contract into a coil, suppressing her airways. "And . . . ?"

"She was talking to someone . . ." says Paige, her eyes unable to meet Rachel's. "About *you*."

Rachel puts the wine bottle down on the worktop and stares unwaveringly at Paige. "What . . . what did she say?" she asks, her mouth drying up.

"She was talking about a situation that I didn't quite catch, and then the other woman said, '*Does his wife know?*'"

Rachel leans against the fridge, desperate for support. Her heart is hammering through her chest as she takes in short, sharp breaths. She forces herself to look at Paige to gauge what else she might know, but there is nothing more than pity etched across her features.

"She could have been talking about anyone," says Rachel, without conviction.

Paige edges closer. "I'd have been inclined to think so, too, if it weren't for what happened earlier in the evening."

Rachel looks at her with wide eyes, urging her to go on.

"Jack and I were dancing," starts Paige. "Just fooling around. I don't know where you were—I couldn't find you."

Rachel pictures herself with Noah and battles to stop the flush of color that is creeping up her cheeks. Yet the harder she tries, the hotter she becomes.

"Anyway, Ali came up to us and whispered something in Jack's ear that made him stop dancing."

Paige looks at Rachel, whose fingertips are tingling with anticipation. She's holding her breath, wanting Paige to get to the point, but closing her ears off to it at the same time.

"Then she leans in to me and says that my time would be better spent looking after my own husband than messing about with someone else's." Paige's nostrils flare. "I mean, what the actual fuck? Who does she think she is?"

Rachel wants to ask what time this happened, so she can ascertain whether it was *before* Ali had seen her with Noah or afterward. As what Paige may assume is a warning to stay away from Jack, might actually be a helpful heads-up to keep an eye on Noah. *With good cause,* thinks Rachel.

"If there *is* something going on between Ali and Jack, I can't imagine she'd make it so obvious," says Rachel, hedging her bets.

Paige raises her eyebrows questioningly.

"What did you say?" asks Rachel.

"Nothing," says Paige. "I was so dumbstruck by her audacity—unusual for me, I admit—that I just stood there, speechless."

"That *is* unusual for you," says Rachel, attempting to smile, but even *she* can tell it doesn't reach her eyes.

"But I'll bide my time, don't you worry," says Paige. "If she thinks she's going to get away with it . . ."

"Look, it doesn't necessarily mean there's anything going on," says Rachel.

"But that doesn't mean she doesn't want it to," says Paige. "Or him, for that matter."

"Okay, but there's a big difference between an affair and infatuation," says Rachel. "And until I'm sure which one it is, I don't think we should be jumping to conclusions."

"So, you're happy to wait it out and see what happens?" asks Paige.

Rachel doesn't know what she wants anymore; as frustrated as she is with Ali's blatant—and somewhat embarrassing—infatuation with Jack, she is yet to be convinced that *he's* doing anything wrong. He's avoiding her, *yes*, but wouldn't anyone, whose every move was being followed and every word was being hung on?

Maybe she'll try to talk to him about it again when they get back to their room. Though, if he's going to throw Noah back in her face again, she'd rather avoid the subject altogether, because, until she knows what Ali saw or heard tonight, she doesn't feel she should be volunteering to put herself in the firing line. Because, if it all goes against her, she won't have a leg to stand on. He'll be able to justify whatever he's done because *she's* done worse. The admission that Jack could have an affair, and she have no recourse, shames her.

But it suddenly occurs to her that although she might not have much to bargain with as far as Jack's concerned, if Ali's not yet told him about Noah, she might have some chips to use against *her.* What price would *she* pay for Rachel not to tell Will about Rick? Or that she has no intention of having children anytime soon? Rachel guiltily exhales as she sees the shimmering light at the end of the tunnel: her quid pro quo.

13

Once Rachel retires to her room, she feels an inexplicable need to speak to Josh; as if somehow the exchange between her and Noah had not only called into question who his father is, but doubted her as his mother too. It's ridiculous, she knows, but after trying so hard all those years ago to dampen down the 1 percent of uncertainty that had snaked around her conscience, it now feels that it's 99 percent certain in favor of Noah, throwing *everything* into question.

She checks the time on her phone, and weighs what Josh might be doing at two in the morning. It being a Friday, he'll most definitely be up, but will he really want to speak to his guilt-ridden mother, who, if she is honest with herself, is only looking for some kind of reassurance?

"*Love you*," she texts instead as she wipes off her eye makeup. She leans in to the bathroom mirror to look at herself as the last traces of eyeshadow vanish. Her mascara, which was advertised as being able to withstand even the longest night, is living up to its promise, the stubborn black paint drawing dark shadows under her eyes.

She looks old, older than she feels, which on a good day is somewhere around twenty-five. *How can you be forty-two?* she silently asks her reflection, before sighing. She can remember her own mother being forty and thinking she was *so* old. Way past being able to go out, get drunk and be attractive to the opposite sex. Yet, incredibly, she seems to have managed all of that in just one night.

As she flips the top of the bin open with her foot, a flash of color catches her eye. Peering closer, she can see that it's the painted rooster, with the vibrant red love hearts on its tail, that Ali gave Jack.

"What *is* wrong with her?" Rachel says aloud as she takes it out. Regardless of whether it's a Portuguese symbol or not, it's not something you would give to your fiancé's brother, and that's without the double entendre that Paige so helpfully observed.

If there's one thing Rachel's sure of, it's that Ali can't know Jack very well, because there's nothing about this he would like. It's ostentatious, indiscreet and, dare she say, a little tacky. It takes Rachel a few seconds to realize that it has Ali written all over it. If she were ever to be immortalized in a sculpture form, this preening figure—so out there and cocksure of itself—would surely be it.

Thankfully, Jack is more refined, more discerning; he'd never dream of giving a gift like this. It's only then, that it occurs to her that if he *were* to give a gift to someone he cared about, he'd take time to get it right, be sure that he chose it carefully.

She doesn't know she's going to do it until she's in the closet, checking the pockets of his two jackets that are hanging there. His wallet must be there somewhere, as she's pretty sure he didn't take it out with him tonight, opting instead to take a bundle of euro notes and a credit card. Though, he hadn't needed either as his parents had generously paid for everything. She finds it in his shorts pocket; the ones he was wearing earlier in the day, but now that she has it, she's not sure what she's looking for. She thumbs through the receipts that make the leather bulge, wondering if she's got enough time to quickly go through them. She'll know it when she sees it; an anomaly among the petrol-station counterfoils and black cab chits. The glaringly obvious proof that he's been somewhere he shouldn't, bought something he shouldn't or done something he shouldn't.

She listens to the noise still emanating from the room below, trying to make out Jack's voice above the cacophony, which, unsurprisingly, is mainly Ali's high-pitched squawking.

"I always *knew* you fancied her," Ali squeals. "You wait until I tell her."

Rachel opens the door a little, straining to listen. "I didn't say I fancied her." Will laughs. "You asked me which of your friends I thought was the most attractive."

"Yeah, and if you *had* to spend a night with one of them, who would it be?"

"So, if you're forcing me, I'd probably opt for Pippa."

"I'll have to keep an eye on you two tomorrow," Ali says, giggling. "So, Jack, what about you?"

Rachel's breath catches in her throat as a loaded silence creeps into the air. She wishes she could see the expression on Jack's face, or maybe Ali's would give more away as she looks at him, forcing him into a corner.

"What about me?" says Jack tightly.

"If you *had* to sleep with a woman you and Rachel know, who would it be?"

The question hangs there, heavily, as the seconds stretch out. Rachel imagines Jack shifting uncomfortably in his chair as he contemplates the safest answer. Ali's clearly only started this to put him on the spot; to see if he's going to admit that it's her he'd have sex with over Paige or any of their other friends. What is she trying to achieve? Apart from making herself look foolish.

Unless, Rachel wonders, it's all part and parcel of their relationship. Perhaps this is what they do to turn each other on when they're unable to physically be together: play sick mind games that risk their affair being exposed; the pair of them aroused by the danger of it being put out there under everyone's noses, all the time thinking they're in control, or that everyone else is too stupid to notice.

"I think I'll refrain from answering that," says Jack wearily.

"Awwww," Ali whines, like a child who's had her favorite candy taken away. "You're no fun."

"Maybe I'm just not in the mood to play tonight," says Jack tersely, his voice coming closer.

Rachel realizes she's still holding his wallet in her hand and rushes to put it back where she found it. There's a part of her that wishes she had time to get herself into bed and pretend that she's asleep, so that they don't have the fight that otherwise feels inevitable. Though, it occurs to her that they'd be having two very different arguments; she'd be demanding to know what the hell is going on between him and Ali, and he'd no doubt harp back to her and Noah. She shudders as she realizes he doesn't yet know the half of it.

Thankfully, he's still not up by the time she turns the lights out, and as she lies down on the bed, looking at her phone, she smiles as she sees that Josh has replied.

"*Love you too*," he says, alongside a goofy photo of himself, with his head cocked to one side, his tongue poking out and each eye going in opposite directions. Despite smiling as she caresses his face on the screen, Rachel can't help the tears from pooling in her eyes as she contemplates the enormity of the lie she may have lived.

She'd told herself twenty years ago that it wasn't so; convinced herself it *couldn't* be so. At the time, the dates had been crystal clear in her head; she'd not seen Jack for two weeks after she'd said goodbye to Noah. But over time, the days had become fuzzy and now she couldn't be sure that her last period had been exactly when she thought it was, which, coupled with Josh's surprise appearance ten days early, all added to the melting pot she'd tried so desperately to stop boiling over.

But now she has to face the fact that that million-to-one chance is a very real possibility. Josh *does* have the same jawline and single dimple that Noah has, and although his eyes are the same color as Jack's, there's just something about the profile of his face that reminds her so much of Noah.

As she lies there, the more she thinks about the similarities, the more she finds. The way they push their hair back from their face. How they stand with their hands on their hips when they're frustrated. Their laid-back demeanor . . .

She runs her hands through her hair and silently screams. What *has* she done?

There's not a morsel of regret attached to spending that one night with Noah. Jack was probably out doing exactly the same, yet, while he might not be able to recall the girl's name if you asked him now, Rachel would be able to describe with a burning intensity how it felt to have Noah make love to her.

Sleeping with him wasn't where she'd gone wrong. Getting pregnant wasn't where she'd gone wrong; just looking at Josh's kooky face on the screen tells her that. No, the only mistake she'd made was passing him off as Jack's child, without question. *That's* where she was at fault.

Stop! she says to herself, banging her hands on the mattress in frustration. *This is crazy*. She'd put these doubts from her mind for years and now she's allowing a passing comment from a stranger to stir it all up again? The invisible barrier that she's relied on to buffer her emotions for all this time has just had a chip knocked out of it.

"That's all this is," she says aloud.

But now that Noah has shown his hand, possibly in the presence of Ali, she feels a gut-wrenching fear that, one way or another, her secret is about to be revealed.

She can't even begin to imagine the damage that would be caused if either of them voiced their suspicions, even if they were proven to be misplaced. She can't remember when exactly they'd decided to not tell Jack and Paige that anything had ever happened between them; she couldn't recall an actual conversation, they'd both just silently decided that it was best kept between themselves if they had any chance of remaining friends. They hadn't exactly lied; they'd just not told the truth.

And for the sake of their friendship, it had been the right thing to do. That part of their relationship was over, almost as quickly as it had begun. And there had been no prospect of it ever being rekindled. Until tonight.

Rachel imagines the shoe being on the other foot and it being Jack and Paige who were best friends before *she* came along. She knows she would have grilled him incessantly, unable to believe that a man and a woman could ever be truly platonic. Suddenly, seeing it from Jack's perspective makes her not only feel guilty, but grateful that he too hasn't asked the question that she realizes has been buried deep in her psyche all this time: "Is Josh mine?"

The devastation that would be wreaked if Jack discovered that the trust he'd shown her had been abused doesn't bear thinking about. The possibility, however remote, that Josh is the lasting legacy of her deceit makes Rachel want to be sick.

She's suddenly reminded of everything she stands to lose. She wishes Jack were here, so that she could selfishly check that her rising panic is unnecessary: be reassured that he doesn't know anything more than he has for all these years about her and Noah; that Ali hasn't felt the need to impart whatever she may have caught the tail end of. Because that's all Rachel is convinced she could have witnessed: seeing Noah, drunk and maudlin, fall into her for an unrequited kiss. That's it. That's the worst-case scenario she will allow herself to believe because anything more makes her brain explode.

She huffs as she turns onto her side in an exaggerated motion, hoping that it will reset her frenzied brain and let her drift off to sleep. But just as her head falls into the pillow, she's sure she hears a splash. She lifts herself up again, listening with both ears, like hunted prey waiting for something to pounce.

There it is again. Leaving the light of her phone on the bed, she tiptoes toward the terrace doors and silently slides one open before stepping out onto the cold tiled floor. She can hear hushed talking and a quiet giggle before she gets near enough to the glass balustrade to look out onto the pool below.

The azure mosaic tiles sparkle as the underwater lighting casts a luminous glow across the soft ripples that the bodies in there are creating. Rachel can make out the silhouette of two people fused together as one, their heads close together, their shoulders half-submerged. She listens to the drawn-out silence they're immersed in, waiting for one of them to say something that she can identify with; that she can identify *them* with. But for the moment it could be anyone: Will and Ali, Noah and Paige, it might even have been her and Jack if he had had his way earlier. She tries to shake any other combination from her mind, yet all she can see, as the shaft of light between the couple closes in even further, is the darkened outline of Jack and Ali.

She doesn't want to watch, but she can't tear herself away, mesmerized by the motion of the water as it swells and falls over the infinity edge, each undulation bigger than the last as the thrusting action in the pool increases.

"Don't stop," she hears a female voice cry.

Rachel's gut twists around itself as the sound of Ali's voice suddenly makes her face clearer. In her mind she can see her, contorting in ecstasy, as Jack brings her to a climax.

As Ali cries out, Rachel is unable to stop herself from grabbing her dress from the back of the chair, wrapping it around her waist and tying it in a hasty bow. Rage and fear propel her across the landing and down the stairs. As she crosses the living room, she imagines what she's going to say when she's face to face with her husband, who she's caught red-handed in the act with his brother's fiancée.

"You fucking bastard!" she'll scream, as she attempts to drag him out of the water. "How *could* you? And with *her*, of all people."

He'll initially deny any wrongdoing as his brain overreacts to the predicament he finds himself in, working a second or two behind the surefire reality of what his wife has just witnessed.

"How could you do this to Josh?" she'll yell, with arms flailing.

"To *Josh*?" he'll reiterate, his tone cold and unforgiving. "Don't you think *you're* the one who has to answer for what you've done to *our* son? For lying to him for all these years; pretending I was his father when you knew damn well that I wasn't."

The confrontation crashes back and forth in her head in the seconds it takes for her to reach the patio doors and throw them open. She knows what's coming. She knows what to expect. So when she finds Ali and Will standing there, naked and shivering, she's stumped.

"Rachel!" he says, instinctively covering himself with his hands.

She immediately senses that she's standing between them and their modesty, and reaches for their towels on the sunbed while her misplaced rage dissipates.

"I'm . . . I'm so sorry," she stutters, embarrassment flushing her cheeks.

Will reaches out one hand to take the towel and she half-throws it at him to avoid him coming any closer. Just a few minutes earlier, she'd wished for more light to shine on the identities of whoever was in the pool, but now she's eternally grateful that it's as dark as it is.

"It's okay." Ali laughs, with a hand on one hip, clearly in no rush to shield herself from Rachel's prying eyes. "We were just having a last get-together before Will goes off to the hotel."

Rachel knows she should turn away, but she can't help but look, desperate to know that Ali is just the same as her. *But*, Rachel muses as her eyes sweep over Ali's perfectly formed hourglass figure, *you're nothing like me.*

In the outfits she wears, Ali's body looks like it belongs to a glamor model, squeezed into dresses that are two sizes too small. But without unforgiving structures holding her in and up, her purest form is breathtaking. Her breasts sit perfectly, accentuated by her tiny waist that nips in before curving into hips that Kim Kardashian would be proud of. She's tanned all over, except for one triangle, making her limbs look long and lean, with not an ounce of excess weight anywhere.

"That's probably because she's been starving herself for the wedding," she can hear Paige saying, as clearly as if she were standing there.

Aware that she's staring, Rachel hurriedly tucks her hair behind her ears, for something to do with her hands, and turns away.

"Yes, of course, big day," she says, without looking back. "I'll see you tomorrow."

14

"Morning!" says Paige as she comes out onto the terrace, dressed in skin-tight leggings and a vest top. With her hair in a high ponytail, she reminds Rachel of a thoroughbred horse, all taut and toned. Their frames aren't that much different, and Rachel knows she could probably look just like her—if only she could be bothered.

"Please tell me you haven't been for your run yet," says Rachel, laughing at how composed Paige looks. That's another reason why Rachel rarely bothers: because she looks like she's been dragged through a hedge backward after exerting herself for just a few minutes. It's too much effort, for too little return, in her book.

"No, I'm just on my way," says Paige, bending down to tighten the laces on her trainers.

"So, you won't be wanting one of these, then?" asks Rachel, picking up a buttery croissant and shoving half of it in her mouth.

Paige laughs. "Has Jack already gone out?"

"Mmm," mumbles Rachel, her mouth still full. "He went about twenty minutes ago."

"He'll be long gone then," says Paige. "Though, it's probably best, as I would never have been able to keep up with him."

"That's the problem with you," says Rachel, smiling. "You give it the big one, pretending you're some fearsome athlete, but actually, you've got all the gear, and no idea."

Paige picks up a croissant from the pile on the table and goes to throw it at Rachel, who ducks.

"Save one for me," she says. "I'll have it when I get back."

"Do you know where you're going?" asks Rachel.

"I think I'll just head toward the beach," says Paige, stretching her arm over her head and bending to the side.

"What a lightweight," says Rachel. "It's downhill all the way there."

Paige pokes her tongue out and sticks two fingers up.

"Don't be too long," Rachel calls after her. "You don't want to miss the wedding of the year."

"Now *there's* an idea," says Paige as she disappears around the side of the villa. "Don't be sending the search party out for me, will you?"

"Enjoy yourself," says Rachel gleefully, grateful that it's not her going, while knowing she'd feel better if she did. "I can't, even if I wanted to," she says aloud, in answer to her guilty conscience. "I wasn't allowed to bring my trainers."

She pours herself a strong coffee from the cafetière and tilts her head up to the sun. The heat works its way through her body, warming her bones, and for a moment, she forgets the events of yesterday and the warped versions that had presented themselves to her throughout the night. It seemed that every time she closed her eyes, distorted faces would appear to goad her.

She remembers going to Will and Ali's wedding in her dreams, but when she got there, instead of it being Will at the altar, it was Jack. The pair of them had turned to face her, with inane smiles on their faces, and when Rachel had looked down at Ali's side, there was Josh, as a child, holding onto her hand.

She'd rushed forward to get him, but an invisible screen had blocked her way.

"Mummy, what is that lady doing?" Josh had asked Ali.

"She's got to do the right thing, before she's allowed in," Ali had said in a cartoon voice.

Rachel had looked all around, screaming to no avail, until Paige appeared. "Have you got something to tell me?" she'd asked.

Even though she knew she was dreaming, the sentiment wasn't lost on her and she'd woken up still full of the conundrum it had presented.

As she swallows the bitter coffee, it occurs to her that if Jack *is* sleeping with Ali, he might be doing it for revenge. Might he know about her night with Noah? Might he have worked out that the date was dangerously close to Josh's conception? What if he's known all along, and has spent the intervening twenty years wreaking his revenge, all the while pretending to be happy?

No, she says to herself as she shakes her head. *That's ridiculous.*

"Hey," says Noah, making her jump.

She looks at him over her sunglasses, but can't bring herself to say anything, her vivid imagination rendering her speechless.

"You okay?" he asks, pulling out the chair opposite hers.

"Fine," she says tersely.

"Look," he says, leaning his elbows on the table to get closer. "I think we need to talk."

"There's nothing to say."

Noah sighs heavily. "I'm really very sorry about last night," he says.

Rachel looks around the terrace self-consciously.

"I'm sorry for what I did," he says. "It really wasn't helpful under the circumstances."

"Have you said anything?" she asks.

His eyes narrow. "To who?"

"Jack," says Rachel, unable to believe she needs to spell it out. "Or Paige."

She's relieved to see him look at her as if she's crazy. "Of course not," he says. "I can't believe you even need to ask."

"Not even at the time?" she adds. "You didn't ever insinuate or allude to what had gone on?"

"No," he says. "More's the pity."

"And what's that supposed to mean?"

"If I had," he says, "it might have saved us all the trouble."

She goes to speak, but the weight of his words sits heavily on her shoulders.

"And nothing was mentioned last night," she asks, her paranoia getting the better of her, "when Paige came up to bed?"

Noah shakes his head. "I was asleep by then."

"Jack didn't come up until some ungodly hour this morning, either. What if she's told them?"

"Who?" asks Noah.

"Ali!" she exclaims.

"Well, if she's told them she saw me trying to kiss you, then I'll hold my hands up and blame it on water on the brain." He laughs, but Rachel remains stony-faced at his attempt at a joke. *Nothing about this is funny,* she thinks.

"And what if she *heard* us?" she asks. "Heard us talking about . . ." She can't bring herself to say it. "What are we going to do then?"

"She wouldn't have heard anything," says Noah. "She was too far away."

His attempt to assuage Rachel's darkest fear is silently appreciated, though she doesn't like to admit that he was too drunk to be able to judge distances, *or* his behavior.

"And if Paige had any inkling of what went on, I can assure you, we'd both know about it by now."

Rachel feels momentarily satisfied. He's right—Paige had seemed completely normal just now.

"She might have told Jack, then," she says, her mind in overdrive. "After Paige had gone to bed." Though, even as she's saying it, she knows that talking is the last thing they'd be doing if they'd unexpectedly found themselves on their own. The thought makes her feel sick.

"Well, have you seen him this morning?" asks Noah.

"He went out about twenty minutes ago," she says, though she doesn't admit that she'd pretended to be asleep when he left.

"Well, there you go then," says Noah, smiling. "I think it's safe to say we're in the clear."

"This isn't a *game*," she says, unable to believe his cavalier attitude.

"I'm not treating it as such," says Noah, turning to look out across the ocean. "I'm sorry for trying to kiss you, but I don't regret it."

"You don't *regret* it?" says Rachel in a shrill voice. "We're both married, and in case it's escaped your attention, our partners are here with us. *They* could have seen. *They* could have heard."

Noah looks at her. "But they didn't."

Rachel tsks. "I would ask that you stay away from me today," she says. "I don't want Ali to see us together."

Noah nods. "So, when are we going to talk about—?"

"Speaking of the devil," says Rachel, cutting him off. "I'd better go and check on her, as we don't want the bride oversleeping, do we?"

"We need to talk," says Noah after her, but she pretends not to hear.

She can feel his eyes watching her as she disappears down the stairs that lead to Will and Ali's room. He's no doubt dismayed at how she can switch off her emotions so easily. She doesn't want him to see that she can't.

"Ali," she calls as she knocks on the bedroom door. "Are you up?"

An image of Ali lying facedown on her bed, unconscious, suddenly floats into her mind. If she was no longer around, then Rachel wouldn't have to suspect Jack of having an affair. But even more than that now, she wouldn't have to fear that her innermost secret is about to be exposed.

She knocks again. "Ali?"

When there's no sound or movement, Rachel quietly opens the door. "Wow!" she says out loud as she's met with a wall of glass holding back the water of the pool. The sunlight is penetrating the surface, sending shafts of light underwater. It's spectacular, though Rachel can't help but feel grateful that she didn't have this vantage point when Will and Ali were in the pool last night.

"Are you in here?" she asks, tiptoeing toward the bathroom.

She steps over a pair of trainers and, as she stops stock-still, staring at them, her heart crashes into a brick wall. She gasps, remembering Ali's insistence that she'd join Jack for a run. She'd pitied her desperate attempt to be with him, so sure that it was nothing but an unrequited infatuation. But everything that has happened since points to it being so much more. Now she pities *herself* for being so naive. They were never going for a run, were they? Though, she'd have expected Ali to at least *pretend* they were.

Rachel falls onto the bed, trying desperately hard not to imagine what the pair of them might be doing. How could they do it to her? How could they do it to *Will*, who she feels even more sorry for? He thinks Ali's the love of his life, yet she's sneaking around with his own brother on their wedding day. Rachel doesn't want to admit it, but whatever it is she's doing to keep both brothers so enthralled, she must be doing it well.

Unable to help herself, she goes to the chest in the corner and slides the top drawer open. Inside is a kaleidoscope of lace knickers and matching bras in every color imaginable. They make Rachel itch just looking at them, but she doesn't suppose they're on long enough for Ali to feel the slightest irritation. Just comparing this to her own underwear drawer, where everything is off-white and 100 percent cotton, almost offers enough reason for Jack to be unfaithful.

No, she says, pulling herself up. *Nothing* justifies what he's doing.

She's about to close the drawer, when a glint of silver in the corner catches her eye. It's partially covered by a barely there thong, which she flicks to one side with an outstretched finger.

There's no doubt about what it is, but Rachel just stands there, hoping that if she stares at it hard enough, it will change into something else. She waits, but no part of the royal-blue bezel, or the second hand that's ticking silently away, morphs into anything other than the watch she bought Jack for their ten-year anniversary.

She picks it up, feeling the weight of it in her hand. It *could* be an identical one, she supposes—perhaps Ali's planning on giving it to Will as a wedding present. But as she slowly turns it over, the engraving on the back is undeniable.

Darling Jack, I'll love you forever, Rachel

Stumbling out of the room, Rachel desperately tries to chase away the video that's playing in her mind's eye. She pictures Ali and Jack lying in each other's arms, spent from a marathon sex session, congratulating themselves on how clever they're being and how easy it is to pull the wool over everyone's eyes.

But they're making silly mistakes and their complacency is about to be their undoing.

She wonders if they even care. Maybe they're banking on being found out because neither of them are brave enough to stand up and be held accountable. Perhaps that's the only way they can see this ridiculous charade of a wedding being called off. Is Jack begging Ali not to go through with it? Promising that they can be together if she doesn't? Or have they decided that her getting married to Will is the perfect cover story for them to be able to continue their illicit affair?

Rachel's breath catches in her throat as she imagines Ali telling Jack about what she saw and heard last night. If they'd ever felt guilt-ridden about what they were doing, unable to sleep for fear their consciences may strangle them in the night, she'd handed them the perfect antidote on a plate.

"I think she saw and heard everything," says Rachel as she rushes back to Noah on the terrace. "And she's just waiting for the right time to say something."

He doesn't respond. He's too busy peering through a pair of binoculars trained onto the beach.

"Mmm, you might be right," he says, slowly and deliberately, as if it's taking all his concentration to look and talk at the same time.

"What are you doing?" she asks, finding it hard to hide her irritation at how blasé he's being about this.

"I just found these on the desk in there," he says, tilting his head in the direction of the living room. Rachel had noticed them yesterday and had been meaning to watch the surfers, assuming that was what they were there for.

"Here," he says, without moving from the spot he's standing on.

"What is it?" she asks, going to him.

He moves himself around her so that she's standing in front of him, the pair of them facing back toward the beach. He carefully takes the binoculars away from his face and without losing the line of vision passes them over Rachel's head into her waiting hands.

She's almost too frightened to look.

"There," he says, pointing. "Just to the right of the surf shack."

Rachel squints through the lenses, holding her breath as if she's watching a horror film, not knowing what's going to jump out from where. "What am I looking for?"

Noah gently moves her head a fraction and *then* she sees it. A turquoise-blue top, just like the one Paige was wearing when she left for her run. Except she's not running. She's standing stock-still, with her hands on her hips, talking to . . .

"Is that *Ali*?" Rachel asks hoarsely, feeling as if the air is being squeezed out of her.

"It looks like it," says Noah solemnly.

Rachel can't think straight. "But . . . I don't understand . . . what are they doing?"

Noah sighs heavily. "Exactly what we don't want them to do," he says.

Rachel's legs turn to jelly, rendering them useless under her weight. She falls onto a nearby chair, but she can't stop them from shaking.

The fear of Ali telling Paige about last night hits her like a ten-ton truck.

"This is all *your* fault," she shouts at Noah.

"*My* fault?" exclaims Noah, jabbing himself in the chest with his own finger. "I haven't been the one keeping this a secret for twenty years."

"And it would have stayed that way, if you hadn't have said and done what you did last night."

Noah sits down heavily in the chair opposite Rachel and puts his head in his hands. "We don't know that's what they're talking about," he says. "We're jumping to conclusions."

Rachel forces herself to ask what else they might be doing, both of them purporting to have gone for a run, even though Ali left her trainers behind. And what is Jack's part in all of this? Where is *he*, if he's not with Ali? The irony that he's probably the only one doing what he said he was going to bears down on Rachel's shoulders.

She brings the binoculars up to her eyes again, as if questioning whether it really is Paige and Ali. For a moment, she thinks they must have both been seeing things, as she can't see any sign of them, but then she trains the lenses to the right of the surf shack, and there they are, deep in conversation. Rachel tries to interpret their body language; Paige is by far the most assertive, with her hands on her hips and her head cocked to the side. While Ali seems to be doing most of the talking, gesticulating wildly with her hands.

For a moment, Rachel allows herself to believe that they've either, quite literally, just run into each other, or, worst-case scenario, Paige is taking Ali to task over how she's been behaving around Jack. Could Ali be offering her an explanation? Might Paige be telling her that she'll be keeping a close eye on her from now on?

It's the best Rachel can hope for as her brain scrambles to comprehend what is happening.

"So, let's assume Ali saw and heard everything last night," she says, breathlessly. "And she's telling Paige right now. . . ."

"Then we're fucked." Noah grimaces as he finishes her sentence.

Rachel's chest hurts at the thought of her best friend finding out she's been deceived all this time.

"We should have told them," she says. "Right at the beginning."

Noah looks at her. "About that night, or about Josh?"

"For God's sake, this has got nothing to do with Josh. *You've* got nothing to do with Josh."

She'll not allow the look on his face to put her off saying what needs to be said. "If we'd just been honest, right from the word go, we wouldn't be in this position. You hadn't even met Paige when we—"

"The only person you needed to be honest with was *me*," says Noah pointedly, crushing the very bones of her.

"*Why* did you have to do what you did last night?" she wails. "Everything would have been fine if you'd just—"

"Ignored the possibility that Josh might be mine," says Noah caustically.

"He's not . . ." she cries. "How many more times?"

"Listen," says Noah, grabbing hold of her arms in an attempt to jolt her out of the downward spiral she's descending into. "Let's think about this logically. Why would Ali want to tell Paige?"

He looks at her with raised eyebrows, waiting for her to see sense.

"They don't even like each other," he says. "Why would Ali want to jeopardize your relationship with Paige? Or Jack, for that matter. She's nothing to gain from it."

Rachel teeters on the brink of telling him how wrong he's got it. That's *exactly* what Ali will be looking to do if she and Jack are having an affair: if there's any part of him that is questioning his loyalty to his wife, that's making him feel guilty for cheating on her, then Ali telling him that Rachel and Noah have slept together will go a long way to assuaging any remorse he may have.

She trains the binoculars on them again, searching in the background for Jack, whom Ali's sure to have told before Paige. Is he waiting in the wings, ready to comfort Paige for the grave injustice that's been sustained by them both? Will they hatch a plan—the three of them together—to wreak their revenge?

Paige might even give their affair her blessing once she finds out her best friend isn't quite the friend she thought she was.

"Paige is going to kill me," says Rachel. "Just after Jack kills you."

The pair of them look at each other and it feels as if time is standing still. Rachel so wishes that it would. Like in those movies, when everything is freeze-framed while the main character goes about putting everyone in the position they want them to be in. But then she wonders if the rewind button wouldn't be more useful here, so that she could backtrack to when her husband wasn't having an affair, and to before his mistress discovered her darkest secret.

15

Rachel's hiding in her room when Jack comes back from the run she was sure he'd pretended to go on. If he was with Ali, he's going to know everything by now, as is Paige. Her heart stops as she contemplates getting through the day with their newfound knowledge emanating from every pore of their beings.

She wouldn't be able to bear it. She'd have to take the coward's way out and go home, with her life in ruins. She'd lose her husband, her best friend, the family she's come to adore and the son she couldn't love any more if she tried. It takes everything she has to stop herself from crying out at the power Ali has over her.

"That was tough," says Jack, sounding unbelievably normal.

She dares herself to look at him. He is suitably puffed out, with sweat staining the collar of his T-shirt and marking the length of his spine on the back.

"The hill coming back up from the beach is a killer," he goes on, as she watches him numbly. "I'm going to jump in the shower."

He groans as he steps under the warm water and, in normal circumstances, she wouldn't mind joining him, but not now. She can't help but wonder if she ever will again.

"Hello," comes a voice from the other side of the bedroom door. "Are you in there?"

The hackles go up on Rachel's neck at the sound of Ali's saccharine-sweet voice, so adept at disguising her ominous intentions. She stays silent, intrigued to see what Ali will do if she thinks Jack's alone. *Jump straight in the shower with him*, she doesn't doubt.

The door handle slowly turns downward and Rachel wishes she had the superpower she so desperately wanted to possess when she was younger, to prove that her little sister was borrowing her clothes and returning them dirty and torn. If she could just be invisible right now, she would be privy to Ali's intentions.

"Oh," says Ali, holding her hand to her chest. "I didn't think you were here."

Rachel offers nothing more than a fixed grin.

"I knocked . . ." says Ali, looking around.

"I guess I didn't hear you," says Rachel tightly.

"No worries," says Ali breathlessly, as if she's been caught out. "I'm glad you're here, because I really need your help."

Rachel looks at her as if she's kidding.

"No, really," says Ali, sensing her disbelief. "My hair won't go right. I've washed it twice and it just won't do anything I want it to do."

"I thought your mum would be here," says Rachel dismissively. "Can *she* not help you?"

Ali shakes her head forlornly. "There's too many steps for her chair, and besides, I want her to see me for the first time when I walk down the aisle."

She looks at Rachel with a quivering bottom lip. "Will you help me?" she begs.

Every fiber in Rachel's being sends out a warning sign. If she knew Ali hadn't overheard her and Noah last night, she'd feel more inclined. If she thought she and Paige were merely discussing the weather on the beach just now, she'd be tempted. If she didn't think there was a very good chance that Ali was screwing her husband then she'd rush to help. But somewhere, deep down, Rachel allows the remote possibility that she might not have done *any* of the things she's being silently accused of. Maybe there's no ulterior motive. Maybe she's just standing in front of Rachel, genuinely in need of her help.

"Okay, I'll be five minutes," says Rachel, giving her the benefit of the doubt one last time, because it suits her to believe that her life isn't about to be driven off a cliff.

"Come in," says Ali tearfully as Rachel knocks on her bedroom door. She's pulling a comb through her wet hair. "Thank you, I just don't know what to do with it."

"What do you *want* to do with it?" asks Rachel.

Ali throws the comb on the dressing table in frustration.

"I just wanted a bit of volume, but my stupid hair is just so thin and fine . . . it won't do anything."

Rachel doesn't think she's *ever* seen Ali's hair do nothing. "So, why don't we try drying it and pin curling it?" she says, picking up the hair dryer. "That way, we can take the clips out once you're dressed."

Ali nods gratefully.

"Are you okay?" Rachel asks hesitantly, knowing that it might be the key to opening the can of worms she so fears.

"Mmm," says Ali. "A bit emotional, but okay other than that."

Rachel deftly separates a section of hair and secures it with a bulldog clip. "But no last-minute jitters?"

"Oh no," says Ali, attempting to smile. "There's no doubt in my mind that Will's the one for me. You know when you know, don't you?"

Do you? wonders Rachel. Are you ever 100 percent sure that you're doing the right thing? She remembers her own wedding day not being quite the occasion she'd spent the best part of twenty years imagining. In her dreams, in fact in the drawings she's sure she still has somewhere, she pictured herself emerging resplendent from a white horse-drawn carriage, in a dress that resembled a meringue, about to marry her Prince Charming. But instead, it had been a rushed affair in a registry office, with her squeezing herself and her burgeoning bump into an unflattering tent-like monstrosity and waddling to the local pub afterward. Though, as much as she regretted the unexpected haste of the day, she never called into question her love for Jack or whether he was the one for her. Besides, she was five months pregnant and the man she'd always thought she was going to marry was on the other side of the world.

"You've got yourself a good man," says Rachel now. "He won't let you down."

Ali raises her eyebrows. "I don't know that you can ever be entirely confident about *that.* Even with the ones you thought you could put money on." She laughs wryly. "In fact, they're the fellas most likely to disappoint you."

Rachel looks at her in the mirror. "Have you been disappointed in the past, then?"

"I've been hurt before," says Ali. "Pretty badly, but it was my own fault."

"How come?"

"I loved someone who wasn't mine to love."

Rachel momentarily stops what she's doing, wondering if this is when Ali's going to confess to an affair with her husband.

"Is this the married man you were talking about the other night?" she forces herself to ask.

Ali nods. "Except I didn't know he was married until I'd fallen in love with him."

Rachel can't help but backtrack to when she'd first met Ali, the same night that Will had been introduced to her. She remembers her waxing lyrical about Jack; cooing about him having taken her under his wing; telling her how he was going above and beyond the call of duty. Had that included inviting her into his bed? Had they already been sleeping together by then? Perhaps her gushing praise had been a clumsy attempt at overcompensating for the fact that she'd just found out he was married, and was about to meet his wife.

As much as she tries, Rachel can't for the life of her remember how she'd ended up at the pub that night. She so rarely mixed with Jack's work colleagues or attended any functions, so there must have been a reason. Perhaps she'd surprised him, thinking it would be a treat, but it had resulted in him having to explain to his uninformed mistress that he had a wife in the wings.

"Do you know, it's three years to the day?" says Ali, interrupting her thoughts.

Rachel raises her eyebrows questioningly.

"That Will and I met," offers Ali in answer.

"Today?" asks Rachel.

Ali smiles and nods.

Of course, thinks Rachel. Three years ago next week would have been Jack's fortieth birthday. The night she went to the pub, she'd been in London shopping for his present, and had called to ask if he wanted to meet for dinner before going home. He'd said Will had just got back from Vietnam and he was going to have a quick drink with him.

"Great," she can remember saying. "Can I tag along?" So, she *had* invited herself.

"So, what happened to the married man?" asks Rachel, unable to stop herself from needing to know more. She hadn't realized she was such a glutton for punishment.

"Oh, I broke it off as soon as I found out," says Ali, seemingly surprised that Rachel would even need to ask. "But even after you've ended things, it doesn't mean that your feelings automatically stop, does it?"

If it's Jack she's talking about, Rachel wonders if he feels the same. Whether he's still holding a torch for her, even though its burning embers ought to have been extinguished by the arrival of Will.

Is that what's happening here? Are they both still reeling from an unfinished love affair, and choosing different ways to deal with it? Is Ali's incessant flirting and Jack's non-compliance their way of navigating their way through the debris of a relationship that has left them both broken?

"I don't know how you can cheat on someone you promised to love and cherish," says Ali. "And I don't know why a wife would put up with it."

Rachel feels like she's being sucked into a vortex, spinning out of control, not knowing which way is up. Her hands tremble as she picks up another section of Ali's hair, unable to believe that she has the audacity to point the finger at *her* for Jack's indiscretions. She should just yank her head back and scream that it takes a strong woman to stand by an unfaithful husband, or one who didn't have a clue anything was going on until twenty-four hours ago.

"Did the wife ever find out?" asks Rachel, her voice shaking as much as her hands. Were they *really* going to conduct this conversation here, like *this*, referring to her in the third person?

Ali's eyes never leave Rachel's reflection. "I'm not sure," she says. "But you always have an inkling if something's going on, don't you?"

Is it Rachel's imagination or was the "you" emphasized? She looks at Ali smiling sweetly in the mirror and tightens her grip on the hair coiled around her hand. She imagines slamming Ali's head into the dressing table, demanding to know what she's doing with Jack. When she admits to cheating on Will, Rachel will promise to keep her secret, just so long as Ali doesn't divulge what she saw and heard last night. They both have a hold over each other, and if Rachel has to make a deal with the devil to release herself from Ali's grasp, so be it.

"Ow," cries Ali, pulling away from her.

"Sorry," says Rachel, coming to her senses and loosening her grip.

"So, you don't think you'd know if something was going on?" says Ali, rephrasing the question.

"It's not always that clear cut," she says, trying desperately hard to keep her voice measured. "I'm sure that there are lots of factors, that on their own don't add up to much, but when they form a much bigger picture . . ."

"So, whether you're the naturally suspicious type, you mean?" asks Ali.

Rachel had never considered herself to be mistrusting, of anyone or anything, least of all Jack.

"I guess that's part of it," she says, playing along to see where this takes her. "Though, I would also imagine that sometimes, it's about whether you *want* to know." That, perhaps, is the category she could be accused of falling into. But is that really a crime? Wanting to hold onto the husband you love by living in staunch denial of what's really going on?

"Wouldn't *you* want to know?" asks Ali, definitely emphasizing the "you" this time.

Rachel fixes her with a steely glare. "*If* there was something worth knowing," she says. "But if it was just a one-sided infatuation that a woman had allowed to get out of all perspective, then no."

"Do you know many women like that, then?" asks Ali, smiling, as if goading her.

"I've come across one or two in my time," says Rachel, refusing to rise to the bait. She will *not* allow Ali to get the better of her; she's not smart enough.

"Is that how you *choose* to see them?" asks Ali. "Because it's easier than blaming your husband?"

Rachel is winded by her unabashed nerve, but refuses to show it on her face. How dare she imply it's all Jack's doing? From her standpoint, all she can see is Ali throwing herself at him, though she's not naive enough to believe that Jack wouldn't have been persuaded to sample the wares. The way Ali displays them, she doubts few men could resist.

"I don't think I need to vouch for Jack," she says resolutely. "I trust him implicitly."

"And what if the shoe was on the other foot?" asks Ali, still coming back for more. "What if *you* were the other woman?"

Rachel's fumbling hands drop the hairbrush onto the tiled floor, her hands instantaneously prickling with sweat from every pore. Hot tears rush to her eyes, teetering on the edge, as her stomach turns somersaults and a gaping hole threatens to open up in her chest. She forces herself to breathe, but there doesn't seem to be enough air to fill her lungs. Every part of her wants to run away, but her feet feel like they're stuck in concrete, and so she's forced to stand there, poleaxed by the realization that this conversation isn't about Jack.

Ali's talking about *Noah*.

16

“You okay?” asks Paige, as they pass on the stairs.

Rachel’s heart thumps in her chest as she looks at her, waiting for her to launch into a well-deserved tirade, but nothing about her suggests that she knows anything more than she did at breakfast this morning; before her run; before meeting Ali on the beach; before Ali might have told her everything she knows. Though, her unsuspecting expression only allows Rachel’s selfish guilt to poison her system even more.

Whenever she’d allowed herself to think about the potential fallout from her and Noah’s secret, she’d only ever thought about how *her* world would be affected: what Jack would do, how Josh would react, what she’d need to do to keep them all together. Seeing Paige’s genuine concern makes her realize what her friend stands to lose.

“I’m not feeling too good,” says Rachel. It’s not a lie.

Paige reaches a hand out to take hold of Rachel’s arm. “You don’t look great—what’s up?”

“I’ve just been helping Ali get ready and I started feeling a bit weird.”

“She has that effect,” says Paige, half-laughing. “Come back downstairs and I’ll fix you something to eat. Maybe you need a bit of sugar.”

Rachel doesn’t want Paige to be nice, because when she finds out she didn't deserve it, she doesn't want her to feel she's been taken for a fool.

"I'll be okay," she says. "I should probably start getting ready anyway."

Paige looks at her watch. "We've got plenty of time yet." She takes Rachel by the hand. "You know what you need?"

Rachel shakes her head numbly.

"Hair of the dog."

"Oh, no, I don't think so," Rachel says, unable to think of anything worse, yet knowing at the same time that alcohol is probably going to be the only thing that will get her through the day.

"Come on," says Paige, pulling her down the stairs. "There's that nice bottle of champagne that we bought at the airport in the fridge. What do you say we crack that open and get this party started?"

Rachel attempts to smile.

"Because you and I both know that we're going to need all the help we can get."

Like the best friends they've always been, they look at each other conspiratorially, knowing it makes sense.

"So how *is* madam today?" asks Paige as she pours half a flute and waits for the fizz to dissipate before topping it up.

It's the simplest of questions, and one that Paige should already know the answer to. Yet she's not giving anything away.

"I thought you'd seen her," chances Rachel, watching her expression carefully.

Nothing changes, apart from Rachel's heartbeat, as Paige shakes her head.

As much as it pains her, she'd rather Paige and Jack just come out with whatever they know, than feign ignorance. Right now, it feels like she's an animal that needs to be put out of its misery and she can't, for the life of her, understand why they would deny her that.

"She's doing okay," she says warily.

"No last minute nerves?" asks Paige, handing Rachel the glass.

"No, she seems pretty set. I don't think she's the type of girl to have second thoughts," says Rachel.

"Well, if nothing else, you've got to give it to her for being so calm. I was a wreck on my wedding day."

Rachel looks at her. "Well, you'd never have known. You seemed an assured, confident vision as you came down the aisle."

"Isn't it funny how different people perceive the same situation?" muses Paige. "As I said yesterday, all I could think about was whether it was what he really wanted."

Rachel feels the first flutterings of discomfort in her chest; like slowly falling sand in an hourglass, each granule gently shifting against one another to push through.

"Why wouldn't it be?" As soon as she's said it, she wants to take it back to rephrase it. Asking a question, especially one to which you don't want to know the answer, is not a strong position to put yourself in.

Paige looks at her with raised eyebrows and it feels as if that hourglass has been turned upside down.

"I've never known Noah to be as sure of anything in his life," Rachel offers.

"He looked like a deer in the headlights," says Paige, half-laughing. "And all the while I was walking down the aisle toward him, I was just waiting for him to put his hand up and say, 'Stop!'"

Rachel smiles. "That's ridiculous."

Paige knocks back half her glass, closing her eyes as the effervescence tickles her senses. "What's even more ridiculous is that when we got to the 'If any person here knows of any just cause why these two should not be joined together,' I was honestly waiting for you to stand up and shout, '*It should be me!*'"

Rachel chokes on her champagne, in the hope that it will distract from the color that is flushing her cheeks.

"What? With my husband and toddler by my side?" Rachel laughs, but she can't help but think it sounds false.

"That was before we became good friends and I got to know you properly," says Paige, making Rachel feel even worse, if that was at all possible.

Unable to stop the tears springing to her eyes, she turns to look out the kitchen window, toward the ocean that is shimmering in the midday sun.

"Hey, hey," says Paige, going to her, sensing something's wrong. "What's up?"

Where would she start? How can she tell Paige that the problem that had seemed insurmountable twenty-four hours ago is now the least of her worries? That, if Ali so chooses, she, Paige, Jack and Noah could be about to have their worlds blown apart? She can't help but acknowledge that however big a mountain looks, when you put it against a bigger one, you realize how easy the first one is to climb in comparison.

"Is this about Ali?" presses Paige.

Rachel nods. "I think you might be right," she says, sniffing.

"About?" asks Paige, looking at her blankly.

"I think there might be something going on between Ali and Jack."

Paige's hands drop to Rachel's sides and her jaw spasms involuntarily.

"I . . . I can't say for certain," Rachel goes on, falteringly. "I'm not a hundred percent, but there's so much that points in that direction, that I have to face the possibility."

"Is it because of what I overheard last night?" asks Paige. "Because I've thought about that and they could have been talking about anybody. I bet half the men in that restaurant are having affairs and keeping it from their wives." She attempts to laugh.

"There's been other stuff too," says Rachel. "Stuff I haven't told you about."

Paige narrows her eyes. "Namely?"

"I saw her coming out of our room yesterday," says Rachel. "When we got back from shopping."

"What?" exclaims Paige, holding Rachel at arm's length.

Rachel nods. "It could have been nothing, but when I walked in a few minutes later, Jack was wearing nothing more than a towel."

Paige's mouth drops open, rendering her momentarily speechless.

"And then I found Jack's watch—the one I gave him for our anniversary—hidden in a drawer in her room."

"I'll fucking kill the pair of them," seethes Paige.

"That's not going to solve anything," says Rachel, attempting to smile.

"I am not going to stand by and let this carry on," says Paige. "She's supposed to be getting married today, for God's sake."

"I know, I know," says Rachel, already wishing she'd kept it all to herself. It will only serve to complicate matters now that Paige is on the case, as she won't let *anyone* get away with *anything*.

"Have you confronted Jack? Asked him how he can possibly justify what he's doing to his brother?"

Rachel doesn't want to tell her that she's already tested the waters and he just used it as an opportunity to throw Noah back in her face.

She shakes her head. "I think I should talk to Ali first."

"Why?" asks Paige. "It's Jack you should be focusing on. He's your husband. Ask him what the fuck he thinks he's playing at."

Rachel sniffs. "I don't know what to do."

Paige's arms wrap around Rachel and she falls onto her shoulder. "I'll deal with this," she says, her voice icy.

Visions of Paige storming across the wedding reception to confront Jack and Ali are all too easy for Rachel to conjure up. Never one to avoid a confrontation, especially with Jack, she can imagine Paige's distorted features as she jabs a finger into his chest, telling him how her best friend is too good for him, and that if he thought half as much with his head as he did his dick, *he'd* realize that too.

"Look, we don't have proof yet," says Rachel. "*I* don't have proof yet."

"You *saw* her coming out of your room," says Paige, sounding exasperated. "She's all over him every chance she gets; she's forever alluding to some kind of private joke; she bought him a cock, for Christ's sake."

"It was a rooster," offers Rachel, as if it makes a difference.

Any one of those, in isolation, wouldn't have caused Rachel a second thought, especially when it involved someone as outgoing and gregarious as Ali. But collectively . . .

"And have you thought that the whole passport charade at the airport might have been exactly just that—a charade?" Paige goes on.

Rachel doesn't need to have the dots pointed out to her; she's already joined them up herself. "I don't want you getting involved," she says. "This isn't your problem."

Paige chews the inside of her cheek, distractedly. "No disrespect, but you've just made it my problem. Why don't *you* talk to Jack, and leave *me* to have a word with Ali?"

Rachel can't think of a worse plan if she tries. If Paige goes in all guns blazing at Ali, Ali would only retaliate by telling her about Rachel and Noah. But then she remembers that they've already had a confrontation—well, a heated conversation, at least—when they were on the beach. If Ali was going to tell her, why hadn't she told her then?

"Have you already spoken to Ali?" asks Rachel.

Paige shakes her head. "About what?"

"About Jack."

"No," says Paige, without missing a beat.

"So, what were you talking to her about this morning, then?"

"I haven't seen her this morning," says Paige, averting her gaze.

Rachel looks at her best friend and wonders why she's lying. A tightness coils its way around her windpipe as she weighs whether to push it. It feels too important a point not to.

"But I saw you," she says quietly, as if hoping Paige doesn't hear her.

"What's that?" says Paige, leaning in.

Rachel coughs to clear her throat. "I saw you on the beach together, when you went for your run."

Paige blinks far more times than is natural. "W-what?" she says, her voice wavering between a laugh and a gasp of disbelief.

"It looked like you were arguing. It was hard to tell through the binoculars."

"You were watching me through *binoculars*?" asks Paige incredulously.

When she says it like that, it does sound a little creepy.

"Well, yes," says Rachel, feeling as if she's been caught snooping. "Noah was watching the surfers, then happened to see you and Ali on the beach."

"Oh," says Paige, seemingly speechless for once.

"So, what were you talking about?" asks Rachel. "Did you just happen to run into each other?"

"Well, I *was* going to tell you . . ." says Paige. "But I wanted to get today over and done with first."

"Tell me what?" asks Rachel.

"I honestly thought she was telling the truth," says Paige, making no sense.

"Who?" exclaims Rachel. "Telling the truth about what?"

"When I went for my run, I saw her and Jack coming toward me on the beach. . . ."

A gasp catches in Rachel's throat. So, she was right—they *had* been together that morning.

"As soon as they saw me, Jack made his excuses, saying he couldn't stop as he was behind on getting everything ready for the wedding."

Rachel's not sure she wants to hear any more.

"And?" she asks, tentatively.

"And," says Paige, unable to look at her, "I had it out with her."

"What did you say?"

"I just asked her what was going on," says Paige. "And she said she was just having a laugh."

"And you believed her?" asks Rachel.

"I was trying to, until you told me you saw her coming out of Jack's room and found his watch in her drawer."

The mention of the watch reminds Rachel of something that doesn't quite add up. "You said she and Jack were *running* together?" she asks, emphasizing the word.

"Erm, yeah," says Paige.

"But she wasn't wearing her trainers," says Rachel. "How could they have been running if she didn't have her trainers on?"

"How do you know she wasn't wearing trainers?" asks Paige.

"Because they were on the floor in her room."

Paige looks like she has a thousand questions she wants to ask, but Rachel doesn't have the energy to answer. "It doesn't matter," she says.

Paige shrugs her shoulders. "I don't know—maybe she has more than one pair—I honestly can't remember."

"But you out and out asked if there was anything going on between her and Jack."

Paige nods. "In not so many words, yes. When she said no, I told her that she'd be wise to rein it in because she was making a complete fool of herself."

"I'm going to ask her outright," says Rachel, turning toward the door.

Paige grabs her by the wrist. "We need to think very carefully about this," she says. "Because if you play it wrong, this whole thing could blow up in your face."

Rachel doesn't need Paige to tell her what's at stake here. Though, it shames her that the fear of Ali calling her out about Noah is far more prevailing than what she might be getting up to with Jack. She shakes her head at the impossible situation.

"I can't get through today, not knowing what's going on," says Rachel. "Constantly waiting for my world to tumble down around my ears."

"But it's not just *your* world you have to worry about here," says Paige. "We've got Will to think about in all this as well."

"I know," says Rachel in a high-pitched voice. "He thinks he's marrying the love of his life. Shouldn't someone tell him she's not who he thinks she is, before it's too late?"

"No," says Paige brusquely. "You have to think of the bigger picture here. No one will thank you for ruining this wedding. Will and Jack will never speak again. The family will be torn apart. Do you really want to be responsible for that?"

Hot tears spring to Rachel's eyes and she lets out a sob. "Oh God, this is such a mess."

Paige pulls her into a hug and rubs her back. "I'm sorry to be so tough, but I'm only thinking what's best for you. You're going to put on your stiff upper lip and go out there today as if everything is under control."

Rachel nods, but her bottom lip is quivering.

"I'm going to be by your side every step of the way," Paige goes on. "And at the first sign of any trouble, I'm going to step in and deal with it."

Paige's palpable loyalty shakes Rachel to the core as she dares to wonder how duped she's going to feel when she discovers that it wasn't afforded to her in return.

17

"There you are!" exclaims Jack as he fiddles with the navy-silk cravat around his neck.

Rachel's insides clench as she looks at the husband she loves in the mirror, unable to imagine how she'll ever let him make love to her again if she finds out he's sleeping with Ali. Though, she doubts he will ever *want* to, if he finds out she slept with Noah, even if it was twenty years ago.

"Here, can you give me a hand with this?" he says.

She walks toward him, her body battling against itself as it sways between wanting to throw her arms around him to beg for forgiveness and wanting to put her hands around his neck to throttle him for being so stupid.

Instead, she ties his cravat and arranges the fabric to sit nicely over his buttoned-up waistcoat. "You look very handsome," she says, honestly.

"I look like I'm going to spontaneously combust at any moment," he says grumpily. "Why on earth we have to wear all this ridiculous get-up when it's so hot out there, I don't know."

"It'd be the same if it were a nice summer's day in England," says Rachel. "You might even be in a top hat there, so I'd count yourself lucky if I were you."

"But isn't that the whole point of getting married abroad?" asks Jack. "It's supposed to be a more casual affair, with the men in linen suits and the ladies in summer dresses."

"It's *their* wedding," says Rachel, stepping out of her dress. "It can be however they want."

"It's *her* wedding," says Jack. "*That's* why we have to have all this pomposity." He shrugs on his jacket, with as much attitude as he can muster, as if the inanimate object is to blame for everything. "If it were down to Will, we'd be barefoot in shorts, drinking bottles of beer by now." He absently looks at his wrist to check the time, but on seeing his watch isn't there, looks at her blankly, momentarily stumped.

"Shit, where's my watch?" he asks.

Rachel's jaw tenses as she shrugs her shoulders as nonchalantly as she can. "When did you last have it?"

"Well, if I knew that, I'd know where it is," he says tersely.

He makes a feeble attempt at looking around the room. Rachel follows him, lifting things up, even though she knows it's futile.

"Do you remember having it on your run?" she asks.

"Mmm, no," he says, rubbing at his chin. "I used my Apple Watch for that."

Rachel watches as he goes into the bathroom.

"I definitely had it last night," he says. "I was wearing it in the restaurant."

Rachel wonders how it came to be in Ali's possession between then and now. Had she and Jack got together after Will had gone back to the hotel? After Ali had already been seemingly satisfied in the pool by her husband-to-be. She wonders what time Paige had gone to bed, knowing she wouldn't have wanted to if it meant leaving Jack and Ali alone together. Perhaps Jack had excused himself first to try to avoid suspicion, and had gone to Ali's room.

Rachel imagines him lying on Will's side of the bed, biding his time until he could be alone with his brother's bride. Would he really be so bold? So desperate to be with her that he'd risk Will's wrath should he unexpectedly come back. He must have been, because why else would his watch have been inadvertently left there? And why else would Ali feel the need to hide it?

"I'll look for it," says Rachel. "You should get up to the hotel, otherwise Will will be thinking he's been stood up by his best man."

"Shame it's not his bride," says Jack.

He huffs frustratedly as he leans in to give her a kiss. "I'll see you at 'the Ali show,'" he says, drawing speech marks in the air with his fingers. "And what a show it's going to be."

He says it with such bitterness that Rachel can't help but wonder if he *knows* something is brewing. As if he knows that it's going to be a party that no one's ever going to forget.

Paranoia seeps through her, like a poison being injected into her veins, as she imagines herself as the star attraction. She pictures Ali standing up to deliver her speech—because there's no chance she won't—but instead of thanking her parents and being grateful for Will, her new husband, she points a finger at Rachel and calls her out for having a child with Noah and passing it off as Jack's. The wedding party will all turn to look at her with sneering derision written all over their faces, but all she'll see is Jack's open-mouthed shock as he sits beside her, utterly bereft.

Rachel tries to shake off the feeling that she's trapped in a waking nightmare, but the malaise is hard to shift as she imagines what she'll do if she's forced into a corner like that. She fantasizes that she'd stand up and storm toward Ali, knocking tables over as she goes, until she's face to face with her.

"Do you want to tell your guests what *you've* been doing?" she'd scream. "With *my* husband!" She'll turn on her heels, without waiting for Ali to answer.

She forces the scene from her head as she watches Jack pick his wallet up from the bedside.

"Why don't you take some euros out of that and leave it here?" says Rachel. "It'll make your pocket bulge."

A split-second look of humor crosses Jack's dark eyes before he pulls out a few notes and throws the wallet into a drawer.

"I know how you feel about her," says Rachel, testing him. "But just remember that she makes your brother happy—*very* happy." She says it in a way that begs to be questioned.

"What's that supposed to mean?" he asks, taking the bait.

"Last night I discovered them making out in the pool," she says, eyeing him carefully. "They were really going at it—and then she stepped out of the water, buck naked, to tell me that they just wanted something to remember each other by before he went to the hotel for the night."

She watches Jack crick his neck as if trying to release the tension that's building up. Knowing that Ali would so unabashedly flaunt what she and Will were doing, right under his nose, will no doubt make him feel like he's in a pressure cooker. Especially if she went running straight to him afterward for a repeat performance.

"So, they couldn't have waited for a few hours?" asks Jack, looking as if he has a bad taste in his mouth.

"Apparently not," Rachel says, smiling. "And why should they? Would *you*, if you were with someone like Ali?"

His jaw spasms involuntarily.

"It must be liberating to be that young and high on life," Rachel goes on. "I wish I was more like her."

"I don't *ever* want you to be more like her," he says sharply.

Is that so you can keep us poles apart? she thinks. *Have the best of both worlds? How does the saying go? A cook in the kitchen and a whore in the bedroom.* Rachel doesn't need to ask which one she is.

He takes one more look in the mirror at himself and shakes his head. "Anyway, I'd better be going."

"I'll see you there," says Rachel. "Try and enjoy yourself."

"Will do," he says curtly, closing the door behind him.

She jumps in the shower, where her racing thoughts don't give her a moment's peace—the how, why and wherefores assaulting her from every angle. But by the time she steps back out, her overriding realization is that, twenty-four hours ago, every single one of the scenarios that are playing in HD and on surround-sound in her head weren't even on her radar.

Sure that Jack is long gone, she pads over to his side of the bed and retrieves his wallet from the drawer. Knowing she can take her time to find any incriminating evidence to prove that he's doing what she thinks he is, she carefully goes through the wad of receipts, placing each insignificant one facedown on the bed to ensure they stay in order. As she discovered last night, most of them are bills for innocuous items such as a meatball marinara from Subway, or a black-cab ride from Euston to Knightsbridge. But nestled in the middle of the stack is one so brash and loud that it literally takes Rachel's breath away.

It's not that, as a piece of paper, it stands out any more than the rest of them. It has no bright colors and doesn't have bells on. But the words at the top send a bolt through Rachel's chest that makes her whole body crumple. She stares at it—hard—waiting for the letters to change into something else, and when they don't, hot tears sting her eyes, mercifully blurring her vision, but she already knows what's there.

Tiffany & Co.

Her brain rushes to conjure up another retailer with the same name, that *won't* mean that Jack's spent two hundred and seventy pounds on a present for his mistress. But the words "silver heart" in the item description and accompanying barcode are hard to ignore.

She throws her hands on her head as she paces the room, unable to fend off the heat that is creeping around her neck, strangling her. She can't do this; she needs some air.

Stepping out onto the balcony, she wonders how she can possibly hold it together. Seeing Noah, resplendent in a pale-linen suit on the terrace below, brings home the utter hopelessness of the situation, because whichever way she turns, there's a reminder of the very deep shit she's in.

As if sensing she's there, he looks up and smiles, holding a glass of champagne to her. "Do you want me to bring one up?" he asks.

She shakes her head vehemently, strands of wet hair slapping her across the face. Pulling the towel tighter around her body, she steps back into the room, forcing herself to think. She can't throw herself into the torturous brouhaha that now seems inevitable, especially when she knows she has little chance of coming out unscathed.

She could lock herself in her room and refuse to come out. She could feign illness, say she must have eaten something off. Christ, the way she's feeling right now, she could even go to the airport and get herself a flight home.

Though, while that might remove her from the here and now, if she has any chance of saving her marriage, she needs to deal with all this head on. Because she can't face a whole lifetime of living in limbo, breathlessly waiting for the tipping point to come.

Fifteen minutes later, she's standing in front of the mirror with blow-dried hair, wearing a belted dress and wedges, though she can't remember doing any of it. As she's putting the final touches to her makeup, a text from Ali pings through on her phone.

Sorry, I need your help again!

What is she supposed to do? Ignore it and play right into Ali's hands by showing her how much their last conversation has unnerved her? *No;* she refuses to give her what she wants.

"It's me," she says, knocking on Ali's door a couple of minutes later.

It opens, but it's not until it closes again that Rachel sees Ali standing behind it in her wedding dress. Her body is encased in a strapless bodice, barely containing her breasts, which seem to be two-thirds out, one-third in. White lace clings to the in-and-out of her waist and follows the curve of her hips. But as it skims her thighs, it loses the lining that has kept her skin from view, revealing her toned and bronzed legs beneath the sheer fabric.

"Well, what do you think?" asks Ali, her voice breaking with emotion. "Honestly."

"Your hair looks lovely," says Rachel.

"But you hate the dress," says Ali, on the verge of tears. "I must have put on a few pounds since the last fitting because these weren't so . . ." She eyes her breasts like an enemy. "And my arse wasn't so . . ."

Rachel has a straight choice. Get this day over and done with by making the least amount of fuss possible, or railroad into it, starting here and now, until not a semblance of the happy event is left. Though, even as she's thinking it, she knows she would have done the latter *before* now, if that was the kind of person she was.

"Your dress is . . ." she says, trying to find the words. "It's stunning . . . you look stunning."

"You're not just saying that?" asks Ali, sticking her bottom lip out the way she does. "You really think Will will like it?"

"Is that who it's for?" asks Rachel, unable to stop herself.

Ali laughs nervously. "Who else do I need to impress?"

Rachel takes a deep breath, unable to decipher how long her pride is going to let her hang out to dry for. "Primarily, you should be doing this for yourself," she says, swallowing the litany of barbs that so readily leaps to her lips. "He'll adore it, but he adores you more, so *you* need to be happy first and foremost."

Ali looks down at herself. "I never imagined I'd *ever* wear a dress like this." She dabs at the tears falling onto her cheeks with the back of her hand. "God, I swore I wouldn't get upset."

Rachel wouldn't have expected anything less. She has no doubt that histrionics will follow her around for the entire day.

"You're bound to feel emotional," says Rachel. "It's a big moment."

"You don't understand," says Ali, fluttering her hands in front of her eyes in a futile attempt to stop crying. "I just can't believe I'm here. About to get married. In *this* dress."

Rachel smiles tightly.

"Listen, I need to tell you something," says Ali, picking Rachel's hands up and holding them in hers.

It's as if Rachel's heart has stopped pumping. Is she really going to do this now? Here, as she's standing in her wedding dress?

"What is it?" she asks shakily.

"It's really important to me that you know . . ."

"Yes?" If this is going to happen, she wants it over and done with as quickly as possible. She knows the pain won't be any lesser, but it will allow her to start rebuilding the rest of her life, whatever that's going to look like, because, as crazy as it sounds, it feels like she's been stuck in this state of limbo forever.

Ali looks down at the floor, and Rachel wants to slap her, to make her hurry up, if nothing else. "I just need you to know that, whatever happens, I want us to promise that we'll always be friends."

Rachel's lips stick to her gums as she forces a smile. "What could possibly happen that would mean that we wouldn't be?"

"You know how families can be," says Ali. "Brothers fall out, people mess up. But you've been so kind to me since I've been seeing Will, and I want you to know that I'll be forever grateful for that. I'll always be here for you in return, no matter what."

Ali pulls Rachel in for a hug, throwing her arms around her and holding on, as if her life depends on it. "Thank you," she says, pulling away with tears in her eyes. "Oh, bloody hell, I'm going to cry again."

Rachel looks at the woman standing in front of her, like *really* looks at her, as if she's trying to get a glimpse into her soul, to see if what she's saying is heartfelt. But Ali's fixed smile thwarts any attempt to see what's behind it, leaving Rachel to surmise that it's probably all a crock of shit.

"Anyway, we should probably get going," says Ali, turning away. "Can you just do the top buttons on this corset? It's barely letting me breathe, let alone reach around to do it up."

Rachel hooks the silk loops over the three buttons and smooths down any errant fabric. "You're good to go," she says.

Ali steps into a pair of peep-toe stilettos, the lace of which matches her dress, and picks up the posy of fuchsia bougainvillea and white clematis from the chair.

"Oh my God!" she shrieks, just as Rachel puts her hand on the door handle. "I almost forgot."

Rachel turns to see her picking up a delicate silver necklace off the dressing table. "He will absolutely kill me if I don't wear this," says Ali, holding it out. "Could you just put this on for me?"

Rachel takes the chain, the weight of its significance bearing down heavily on every part of her. Her hands shake uncontrollably as she attempts to open the fiddly clasp and pass it around Ali's neck.

The silver heart lies perfectly flat between Ali's clavicles, while Rachel feels like hers has been torn out of her chest, and is flatlining on the floor.

18

"You look lovely," says Noah as they meet in the hallway.

"Our car's ready," she says, desperately trying to keep her voice from wavering. "We should get going if we're going to be there before Ali."

"Rach," he says, taking hold of her wrist as she turns to go out the front door.

"Don't." She doesn't even attempt to look at him.

"You can't just pretend this isn't happening," he says.

"I'm going to do exactly that," hisses Rachel in a hushed voice.

"Hey, you two," calls Paige from outside. "Let's go."

"Coming," says Rachel through a false smile.

"You okay?" asks Paige, casually putting a hand on Rachel's leg once they're in the car.

She nods.

"If at any time it gets too much, just say the word and we'll split, okay?"

Rachel looks at her, unable to believe that she deserves such a good friend. The nicer she is, the more wretched Rachel feels about the secret she's been keeping for so long. It's as if she's living on borrowed time because she knows that once Paige finds out that she and Noah have been lying all this time, there's going to be no pulling her back from the storm of fury she's going to rain down on them.

But for now, Paige smiles warmly, making Rachel's blood turn icy cold. She searches Paige's eyes for a hidden agenda, a sign that she knows more than she's letting on, but all she sees is a naivety that only serves to show Rachel how toxic her own thoughts and actions are. Her chest rises and falls at the enormity of how selfish she's been, wanting her perfect little life to continue without ruing the consequences of something she did twenty years ago. And how dishonest she's been, to profess that Josh is Jack's child, when there may be even the slightest chance that he isn't.

"Thanks," says Rachel, barely audibly.

"What's going on?" asks Noah. "Is everything all right?"

Paige looks at Rachel with raised eyebrows, as if asking permission to bring him up to speed. Rachel finds it hard to believe that she hasn't already, but if she had, then the topic of conversation would have been different on the terrace. If Noah had the slightest notion that Ali and Jack were at it, he would most likely have already taken Jack out by now. He wouldn't stand for Rachel being treated like that and he would most certainly have taken the opportunity to tell her how she deserves better. No, he can't know, and she doesn't want him to because it will only make things even more complicated than they already are.

"I'm just not feeling all that great," she says in answer to Noah's question. "I think I might be coming down with something."

"I can always bring you back if you don't feel up to it," he says.

"*We* can always bring you back," Paige chips in. "I'm not sure that Noah's got it in him to last the whole day."

"I feel okay, actually," he says. "I'm looking forward to a drink."

Paige tenderly cups his face in her hand. "Well, just take it steady," she says. "No more scares. I don't think I could go through that again."

Noah smiles. "Sorry to give you such a fright."

Paige takes his hand. "Just don't make a habit of it," she says.

Rachel feels like she's playing a bit part in somebody else's movie. She's never seen Paige like this and if it wasn't so ill-timed, it'd almost be funny.

The car tips forward as it descends a steep track; the imposing cliffs on either side feel as if they're closing in on them, creating a pinch point that makes it look like the end of the road drops straight into the sea. Rachel briefly wonders what would happen if the brakes failed, and can't stop herself from putting the window down, just in case: she's seen enough films to know that it's often the only escape once a car's submerged under water.

"O-kay," says the driver as he mercifully stops just short of the end of the dust track. If he'd gone just a few meters farther they'd be on the decked terrace in front of them, the only thing that seems to separate land from sea. He makes a point of pulling up the handbrake, hard.

"It's here," he says, gesturing to the left, toward a simple wooden shack of a restaurant with whitewashed paneling and a corrugated-iron roof.

"How the hell did they find this place?" asks Noah to no one in particular as he pays the cab fare. "It's in the middle of nowhere."

"It's as if we could just dive off the side and straight in," says Paige, in awe as she steps out and looks at the sea as it glistens in the afternoon sun. "It's so freeing."

Perhaps it's a reflection of Rachel's inner turmoil that she doesn't share Paige's sense of liberation. Instead, she finds the ominous cliffs suffocating; the black-winged Alpine swifts menacing as they circle overhead.

She's tempted to ask the driver just to take her back to the villa, knowing that the next chance she has of getting out of here, her life may well be very different.

Noah leads the way across the flower-festooned terrace toward an uneven wooden staircase, ravaged by the salt water at high tide. The juxtaposition between the optimism of the cerise bougainvillea and the rickety platform that looks like it might collapse at any moment sends shivers down Rachel's spine.

"Are you sure it's safe?" asks Rachel as she steps from the relative security of the platform onto the precarious staircase. It had looked like the steps could lead to nowhere but the sea, yet as soon as Rachel's at that vantage point, she can see a tiny crescent of golden sand, a sheltered cove protected by rock formations that rise out of the water, forming an arch at one end and a bank of caves at the other.

Just shy of the water's edge is a white gazebo that looks like a dainty bird's cage, set in front of six rows of chairs, each festooned with bright-pink flower garlands. It looks stunning, but Rachel refuses to say that, as if doing so will somehow condone what Ali's doing.

She spots her parents-in-law: Bob, and Val in her big hat, beaming from ear to ear as they chat with Will and Jack, so immensely proud of their two boys. How would they feel if they found out one of them was betraying the other in the worst way possible?

A red carpet meets them at the bottom of the stairs and thankfully accompanies them, high heels and all, down the aisle. Rachel can't wait to see how Ali manages to negotiate the unlevelled sand hidden underneath in those lace stilettos of hers.

"Rachel, you look gorgeous," says Val. "A vision in yellow."

"Thanks, Val, you look lovely too," says Rachel, smiling as she ducks under the broad brim of her mother-in-law's hat to give her a kiss on both cheeks.

"She'll have someone's eye out with that at some point today, I'm sure," jokes Bob.

Rachel laughs. "You're looking very dapper as well, Bob. You okay?"

He kisses her as if he's still unaccustomed to it, even though that's how they greet each other every time. He goes in for two when she's pulling away after one, and there's that awkward moment when neither of them is sure what to do. "You're matching the sunshine today, kid," he says, by way of filling the split-second silence.

"You know me . . ." she says, looking down at herself, hoping that she doesn't look like a great big round yellow blob. "Always trying to bring a little sunshine into the world."

Bob smiles before extending his hand to Noah.

"You've met Noah and Paige before, haven't you?" Rachel asks.

"Yes, a couple of times over the years," says Bob, before shaking Paige's hand.

Val does the same. "You're Rachel's friend from university, aren't you?" she says to Noah.

Just the association being acknowledged makes Rachel's nerves jangle. She imagines him replying, *And lover actually, albeit just once, though there's every chance it resulted in me fathering the grandchild you dote on.*

"How's the groom feeling?" she says, turning to Will. "You okay?"

She knows that Jack is standing beside him, but can't bring herself to look at him, knowing that if she does, she's likely to want to punch him in the face.

Will shakes himself down, as if trying to rid any last-minute doubt. "She *is* coming, isn't she?" he asks apprehensively.

"Of course she is," says Rachel, while keeping everything crossed that by some divine intervention she isn't. It won't make what Ali and Jack are doing any less painful, but it *will* make the fallout a lot easier to deal with if she's not already married into the family. At least for Will, in some small way.

"You okay?" asks Jack, as if sensing something's wrong. She can *think* she's hiding it all she likes; congratulating herself on how she's going to be able to keep this under wraps until the wedding is over. But Jack will be able to tell from the set of her jawline, the lack of eye contact and the way her lips are pressed tightly together that she's not happy.

"Fine," she says tightly. "Will, where do you want us to sit?"

"Erm . . . anywhere," he says, looking up toward the top of the wooden stairs, desperately searching for confirmation that his bride is going to turn up. "Anywhere in this row." He points to the chairs behind his.

Rachel glances across the aisle to where Ali's family is congregated and catches her mum's eye. They nod their heads at each other, but

Maria, Rachel notices, holds her gaze for a little longer. Rachel wonders if she knows what her daughter is up to, if she's even positively encouraging it.

Will suddenly whacks Jack with his arm and hurriedly turns to face the ocean, implying that Rachel's wish has been denied: Ali is here. A lone singer, whom she hadn't even noticed before now, launches into a cover of Norah Jones's "Come Away With Me."

"I cannot *wait* to see what she's wearing," hisses Paige next to her. "Although perhaps I should rephrase that to what she *isn't* wearing, because that is bound to be the order of the day."

Rachel stays focused on the waves as they edge ever closer to the gazebo, and wonders if it might save her the trouble if a tsunami came and washed them all away. She immediately hates herself for allowing the abominable thought to even enter her head.

She watches Jack's shoulders, so rigid in his fitted jacket, as if he's forcing himself to stay facing forward. His hands are clasped in front of him and a vein throbs in the side of his neck. If anyone were looking on, they'd think *he* was the groom. Rachel can't stop herself from wondering what he must be thinking. Has he begged Ali not to go through with it? Promised her that they could be together if she doesn't? Or was this turning him on? Knowing that once today is over, he'll be able to shag his brother's wife.

She thinks back to last night, in their room, when he'd wanted to have sex, and a tiny glimmer of hope ripples through her that she might have gotten this all wrong. If he was so hung up on Ali, why would he want to make love to *her*? She almost laughs out loud at her naivety when it dawns on her that that was *precisely* why he was desperate: he'd been watching his mistress strut around all night, in a dress that left absolutely nothing to the imagination, and no doubt Ali had teased him mercilessly whenever she could get away with it too, showing him what he was missing out on. Who knows? Maybe they even managed a quick fumble when no one was looking. Which would all go to prove why Jack would have been climbing the walls by the time they got home. It wouldn't have mattered who it was; he'd probably have just closed his eyes and pictured Ali anyway.

The thought makes her feel sick and if she had a knife right now, she'd fancy shoving it right between his twitching shoulder blades.

As the singer reaches the end of the second chorus, Ali appears at Rachel's side, just as Will—and Jack—turn around to see her for the first time.

Rachel can't decide who is going to give the most away with that initial glance; she doesn't suppose Ali would be stupid enough to look at Jack before Will, so Rachel concentrates on every flicker of emotion that crosses her husband's face. His eyes drink her in, his gaze so intense that it could set a person alight. Ali must be able to see it, feel it . . . the whole goddamn congregation must be able to feel it.

But if they do, they pretend not to. There are ah's and aw's as Will smiles proudly and takes Ali's hand in his. Her mum bursts into noisy sobs the moment she sets eyes on her daughter, theatrically throwing kisses for Ali to catch. "Look at my baby," Rachel overhears her saying to the row behind her.

Jack pulls at his restrictive collar as the ceremony gets underway, the heat of the occasion seemingly getting to him. He breathes heavily and clenches and unclenches his fists, as he no doubt questions why Ali's putting him through this arduous torture.

When the registrar asks if there is anyone present who knows of any reason why Ali and Will should not be married, Paige digs Rachel in the ribs. She daren't look at her, as she honestly doesn't know whether she's referring to today's proceedings or harping back to her own wedding day when she was clearly expecting Rachel to stand up and object. She can't think about either right now as she's concentrating solely on the twitch that has appeared, involuntarily she presumes, in Jack's jaw. She silently begs him to throw his hand in the air, to put her out of her misery and to negate the responsibility from being firmly on her shoulders.

But it's too late.

"I now pronounce you husband and wife," says the registrar, as Stevie Wonder starts blaring out "Signed, Sealed, Delivered (I'm Yours)."

"Great," says Jack, as he and Rachel follow the happy couple back down the aisle. "Now I need a fucking beer."

"Don't we all," pipes up Paige from behind them.

"What can I get you?" Jack asks as he strides purposefully toward a pop-up bar set up at the back of the beach.

"If they're doing gin and tonics, I'll have one," says Paige. "But otherwise, wine or beer, whatever's on offer—I'm not fussy, as long as it's cold."

"Rach?" asks Jack.

"Rosé, if they've got any," says Rachel tersely.

"I'll come with you," says Noah.

"You know you're not going to be able to keep this up all day," says Paige, as the men drop out of earshot.

"Can't I?" challenges Rachel.

"So, I'm assuming things haven't improved any?"

Rachel snorts derisorily. "They've gotten worse."

Paige looks at her wide-eyed. "Have you spoken to him?" she asks.

"I don't need to," says Rachel. "I found—"

"Wasn't that a lovely service?" comes a voice, next to them.

Perturbed by the interruption, Rachel turns to see Ali's friend—the one who was wearing the red dress the previous night. Her smile is twitching with nerves and her eyes flit around anxiously.

"Oh, hi," says Rachel. "It's Chrissy, isn't it?"

The woman nods and breathes out a palpable sense of relief.

Rachel offers her hand and introduces Paige. "So, you're a friend of Ali's?"

"Yes," says Chrissy. "We were at school together."

Rachel feels Paige come alert, the lawyer in her ready to pounce, as if knowing what Ali was like back then will somehow shed light on why she's a homewrecker now.

"That must have been a blast," says Paige. "I can't imagine what she was like back then."

"How long have *you* known her?" asks Chrissy, deflecting the implied question.

"Long enough," says Paige.

Rachel throws her a warning glance, and Paige looks at her as if to say, "*What?*"

This is going to be harder than Rachel thought and she bitterly regrets telling her *anything*. It's hard enough keeping a lid on it herself without having to worry about Paige, who, it has to be said, is far more unpredictable. It had seemed like a good idea at the time—she'd probably done it in the hope that Paige was going to talk her out of the downward spiral she'd gotten herself in, except she'd somehow fanned the flames. It wasn't her fault—she was only doing what a good friend would naturally do—but Rachel wishes she'd kept her suspicions to herself, at least until she'd worked out exactly what she was going to do about them.

"I'm married to Will's brother Jack," Rachel says to Chrissy, whose confused expression suggests she's waiting for Paige to elaborate.

"Oh," says Chrissy, visibly relaxing. "So you and Ali are now sisters-in-law."

Rachel nods, unable to comprehend how any kind of sister could do what *she's* doing. "Yes, I suppose we are."

"Cool," says Chrissy. "You're going to have so much fun. She's such a great girl."

Rachel and Paige snatch a glance at each other.

"So, you've known each other forever," says Paige.

Chrissy smiles. "Since primary school. We met when we were nine and have been as thick as thieves ever since."

"What was she like when she was younger?" asks Paige. "I assume not the same as she is now."

The line of questioning is making Rachel feel uncomfortable and she wonders how far Paige is going to go.

A perplexed expression crosses Chrissy's face as she mulls it over. "I guess not, but so much has changed between then and now that I suppose it's impossible to stay the same. But for Ali, it's all been for the good—mostly."

"Mostly?" presses Paige.

"Well, compared to what she was like back then, she's definitely come out of her shell." Chrissy smiles, as if remembering fondly. "We were so similar when we were growing up—I think that's what drew us together."

"I can't imagine you ever being similar," says Paige disparagingly.

Chrissy, in her floor-length maxi dress, seems to shrink into the ground. Her knees bend, her shoulders round even more than they do already and her head dips, as if she's trying to make herself invisible.

"We wouldn't say boo to a goose," she says quietly. "She was even shyer than I was."

Paige laughs falsely. "And now look at her."

They all turn to where the most noise is coming from, knowing that that's most likely where Ali will be—right in the middle of it.

"Oh my God," she shrieks, as her family circles around her. "I honestly thought I was going to pass out. When the registrar said, 'Do you, Alison Foley, take Will . . .' I could feel myself swaying and thought, *I'm gonna go!* I don't know how I didn't."

Will walks over to the group and they all cheer and crowd round for hugs and celebratory pats on the back. "Please may I introduce my husband," shrieks Ali, holding a glass of champagne in the air. "Woo-hoo!"

"I've never seen her so happy," says Chrissy, smiling reflectively. "It's so wonderful to see."

"Especially after everything . . ." says Paige, leaving it hanging there.

Rachel looks at her, dumbfounded, wondering where the hell she's going with this. She can suddenly visualize Paige in her wig and gown, commanding a court room in a criminal trial. If she followed this line of questioning at work, she's sure the judge would accuse her of leading the witness. For a moment, it feels like Chrissy isn't going to take the bait, and Rachel breathes a sigh of relief, but a part of her hopes that she might, even if it's just to give her a tiny window into Ali's world, and the slightest explanation as to why she would do what she's doing with another woman's husband. *With her husband's brother.*

"Exactly," says Chrissy. "The accident hit her really hard."

"Her mum's, you mean?" asks Rachel.

Chrissy nods. "She still blames herself, no matter how many times Maria tells her not to."

Rachel desperately tries to claw back any nuggets of conversation that she'd had with Ali on the subject, but there's little to glean. Either Ali hadn't divulged the details, or Rachel hadn't bothered to listen.

"That must be an awful burden to carry," offers Paige.

"It doesn't help that she came out of it unscathed, of course," says Chrissy. "I honestly think she would have coped better if she'd been injured in some way. Because at least then she would have gotten what she thought she deserved."

Rachel audibly gasps and instinctively goes to put her hand to her mouth, but Paige stops it in mid-flow, discreetly taking hold of her wrist and lowering it, as if a show of emotion might detrimentally affect whatever Chrissy says next.

Whatever Ali may have told Rachel about the accident, she'd certainly not confessed to being the driver and causing it. *Who would?*

Had she momentarily lost her concentration? Been going too fast and lost control? Rachel shudders at the thought that she might have been drunk, having convinced her mother that she was fine. But then she would have been arrested and would no doubt be carrying a criminal record. Rachel looks to Paige, wondering if she's thinking the same thing.

"She should be thankful," says Paige, taking a gamble. "It's a miracle that she was able to walk away from the wreck that was left. Not many people would have survived it, let alone come away unhurt."

Chrissy looks at Paige for a moment, as if wondering how much she knows and how far she can trust her.

"Well, it was thought that her weight cushioned her from much of the impact," says Chrissy.

"Her *weight*?" repeats Rachel, unable to see how someone so slight could be protected against the ravaged metal of a stricken car.

Chrissy half-laughs as she looks down at herself. "Yes, apparently there *are* some advantages to being morbidly obese."

Rachel's mouth drops open as her brain struggles to compute what Chrissy's suggesting. *Morbidly obese? Ali?* That just wasn't possible. She'd always been slim, hadn't she? *"I guess I'm one of the lucky ones,"* she'd said just yesterday.

"I don't understand . . ." she starts, before Paige cuts her off by saying, "She's done *so well* to lose it all."

"Yes," agrees Chrissy.

"Have you got a picture of you two?" asks Paige, as casually as she can. "It'd be great to see you as teenagers together."

Chrissy's hand instinctively goes to the bag that's hanging across her, as if creating a barrier. "Erm, I don't think Ali would be too happy about me showing pictures of her past to all and sundry," she says, shifting from one foot to another.

"Ah, no worries," says Paige. "It's just that she's already told us about what she went through back then. In fact, she mentioned her weight just the other day, didn't she, Rach?"

Rachel nods, but she and Paige both know that it wasn't in the way that Chrissy might imagine.

"I'd love to be able to put it into context," Paige goes on. "But I'm sure she'll show me when she's got a minute, once she's back from honeymoon and all that business."

Chrissy looks around furtively, as if she's about to give out class-A drugs in a school playground.

Rachel hopes that she's not going to get her phone out, because there's nothing to be gained from either her or Paige seeing the photos.

"I'll just show you one quickly," says Chrissy as she flicks a finger over the screen. "If Ali has already spoken to you." She looks directly at Rachel.

Rachel wants to shake her head and tell her to put it away. She doesn't want Ali's lifelong friend to get into trouble for revealing something she hasn't chosen to herself. But then she wonders if it's not *Ali* that's let *Chrissy* down, by pretending to remove any semblance of the person she once was.

19

"Can you believe it?" says Paige as soon as they're out of earshot of Chrissy.

The photo had shown her and Ali, as early twenty-somethings, sitting in a back garden on a sunny day. At first, it was impossible to tell who was who, as they were both so far removed from the women they are today. But slowly, Ali's sunburned features had presented themselves from under a mane of frizzy red hair.

"I mean, she was huge," Paige goes on, as they go in search of Jack and Noah and a much-needed drink.

"It doesn't matter how overweight she was," says Rachel impatiently. "It's why she lies about it. That's the bit I don't get."

"She can't stop herself," says Paige. "She lies about everything. That's why we have to take her denial that anything's going on with Jack with a pinch of salt."

Rachel grimaces at the reminder, but a part of her wonders if Ali's propensity to lie might actually work in her favor. It would certainly cast doubt on any revelations she cared to expose about Rachel and Noah.

"Here they are!" exclaims Jack, leaning on the bar with a beer in his hand. Rachel had hoped that he might pace himself today, but if a few pints help to restore the equilibrium with Noah, she's all for it.

"We were waiting for you to bring us a drink, remember?" Paige bites back. If Rachel knows Paige at all, she knows that it's going to take all her resolve not to show her indignation at what Jack's doing with Ali. Even in the best of circumstances, they had a cat-and-mouse relationship, taking turns to dangle the cheese. But with this time bomb ticking noisily underneath them all, it just feels like a matter of minutes before Paige lights the fuse.

"Oh, sorry," says Jack playfully, knowing that's the perfect way to rile Paige. "You don't seem the type to wait on a man for *anything*."

She looks questioningly at the glass of rosé he hands her.

"No gin and tonics, I'm afraid," says Jack in response. "Just wine and beer."

"Here," says Noah, passing an identical glass to Rachel.

She knocks the warm liquid back in two hits, desperate to feel its effects, trusting that it will numb her jangling nerve endings enough to enable her to get through this afternoon and evening.

"Ladies and gentlemen," announces a loud voice. "Mr. and Mrs. Hunter would like to request that you make your way up to the restaurant for the wedding breakfast."

"Let's hope we'll be able to get a decent drink," says Paige tightly. "And let us pray that we'll be sitting together."

Rachel groans inwardly. She'd never been a fan of sit-down meals, where you were forced to make small talk with a total stranger for three hours, knowing you'd never see them again. She understood why it naturally fell that way whenever you got everyone from two people's lives in the same room, but it didn't stop the feeling of dread that consumed her as she counted down the minutes until she'd be back sat on her couch, wearing pajamas and watching an entire series on TV. Today, though, she's thousands of miles from home, so that isn't an option.

As she looks at the table plan at the door, she's got her fingers crossed that Paige and Noah *aren't* on her and Jack's table. Because the atmosphere is toxic enough, at least to her, and she can do without the added tension of wondering whether Paige might divulge Jack's secret before Rachel's ready to share it. And she certainly doesn't need Noah's eyes burning into her, whenever Josh comes up in conversation. If she had *her* way, she'd even rather be sitting on her own without Jack, because it gives her no pleasure to watch him hang himself.

The restaurant is pitched precariously on the cliffside, supported by what look to be ill-fitting stilts. Some long, some short, others clearly retrofitted in an effort to replace those that had been ravaged by the sea salt and heat of the summer sun. Rachel wishes she'd not seen the underside of it, as not only does it make her apprehensive about sitting in it for the next few hours, but it also reminds her of the state of her marriage, which for all intents and purposes *looks* solid, yet is on very shaky ground below the surface.

The terrace, next to it, seems to be a newer addition, with more robust posts holding it up, out of harm's way and the sea's natural course. But the watermarks on the supports are evident, and Rachel shudders to think that at some point in the next few hours, the waves that are gradually claiming back the beach will be well over and above her head, creeping ever closer to where they'll be dancing the night away.

She can't make her way back up the rickety staircase fast enough and, as if sensing her unease, Jack puts his hand on the small of her back, in an attempt to make her feel secure. She couldn't feel any less so if she tried, both literally and metaphorically.

"You okay?" he asks with a wide smile when they reach the terrace that has now been set up with bar tables and outdoor heaters for when the sun goes down. She gives a curt nod as she looks up the dirt track that cuts a swathe through the rocky ridges on either side of it. It's so steep that it was no wonder the taxi had been able to cruise down, seemingly without power. She wonders what it would take to get herself back up it and into the nearest village, *wherever* that may be. She hopes it would be far enough away from here to make her feel less like she is being suffocated from the inside out.

Despite its shoddy undercarriage, the restaurant itself is beautiful. Three of its sides are open to the elements, and the late afternoon sun is streaking across the round tables that are adorned with crisp white tablecloths, a centerpiece of bougainvillea and a tissue-wrapped favor on each place setting.

Paige is already across the driftwood floor in search of her place and Rachel can't help but feel relieved when she sees her disappointed face.

"Please be seated where you find yourself," reprimands Ali's mum, as Paige surreptitiously attempts to move her place name to where she'd rather be. She pulls a face behind Maria's back as she's forced to stay where she is.

"Rachel," says Ali's mum, with a warm smile that lights up her eyes. "You're over at the front, at the table next to the bride and groom."

Rachel can't help but wonder how complex the relationship must be between Ali and her mum since the accident. How could you ever forgive yourself for causing someone you love so much pain? Taking away their ability to ever walk again? And how could Maria not spend the rest of her life blaming her daughter for what she'd done? Yet despite it all, Rachel doesn't think she's ever seen a pair as close as they are, though the memory of Maria's words, "*It's all a bit of a front,*" rings alarm bells loudly in her ears.

As Rachel weaves her way through the tables toward the magnificent sea view, the fragrant aromas of fish and garlic remind her that she's hungry, and with the amount she's intending to drink, she knows it's only sensible to eat as much as she can now if she's going to avoid making a scene she doesn't want to make.

"Hello," says the man next to her awkwardly. "I'm Neil."

Rachel takes the hand he offers, and once again wonders about the absurdity of the intimate situation they've been forced into. She's never met this man before, yet for the next few hours, he is her only outlet, as she is his, unless they want to endure a painful and unnatural silence. At least when you're faced with this situation on an airplane, it's commonly accepted that you either make eye contact or you don't. But at weddings that's not an option you can really choose.

"Rachel," she says, through a controlled sigh. "Nice to meet you."

As it turns out, innocuous conversation is just what Rachel needs. Neil, a mechanic, and his wife Liz, a doctor's receptionist, give her a blow-by-blow account of how they've left their three-year-old at home for the first time, and the banality gives her a temporary respite from the nightmare she's trapped in. Thankfully, the nerves of having to deliver his speech ironically render Jack, on her other side, almost speechless for the duration of the meal.

The sound of cutlery clinking against the side of a glass gradually stills the room and all eyes turn to Will, who's already gazing adoringly at Ali.

"I can't believe I get to call this incredible woman my wife," he starts, to a rapturous round of applause.

Rachel forces herself to put her hands together, but she looks about as enthusiastic as Jack does.

"From the first time I laid eyes on Ali, I knew she was the one for me," says Will.

Which is surprising, thinks Rachel, seeing as she was hanging off another man's neck at the time.

"After years of being in the wilderness . . . ," he goes on.

"Quite literally," one of Will's friends heckles.

"I was thinking more from a companionship point of view." Will laughs. "I didn't think I'd ever meet my soul mate. But here she is . . ." Ali fans her face with her hands in an attempt to stop her tears from falling. Will tenderly wipes them away with his napkin. "And she is the most generous, thoughtful and funny person I've ever met. We have had such a laugh together and there have been times when I've been lost for words at how kind and caring she is."

Rachel catches Paige's wide-eyed look of disbelief.

"Just last week, when we found out that her grandmother wasn't going to be well enough to fly out here, Ali's immediate reaction was to postpone the wedding. It didn't matter at what cost, she just knew she didn't want to get married without her gran here to see it. But, with a little persuasion on my part, and a lot from her family, she agreed to go ahead on the condition that we recreate a mini version for Grandma Nettie when we get back home."

Ali's mum claps and dabs at her own eyes as she looks at her daughter with so much pride that she might burst. Rachel wonders how much more of this sanctimonious bullshit she's going to be able to take.

"But of all Ali's admirable qualities, it's her loyalty that astounds me the most."

There's a snort from behind Rachel, at the exact same time as the wine she's got in her mouth threatens to splutter from her nose. She doesn't need to look to see who it is. Will gives Paige a few seconds to stop coughing and, as the clock ticks down, Rachel's getting hotter and hotter.

"So, yeah, as I was saying," Will continues. "Ali's loyalty knows no bounds. When we met, I had just returned from another voyage of self-discovery in Vietnam."

"You took ten years longer than the rest of us to find ourselves," calls out the same heckler.

"Yes, I am aware of that, thanks," says Will. "And, let's be honest, my prospects weren't great. As Ben has so helpfully pointed out, I've been a nomad ever since leaving university, with nothing of any relevance to show for it on my résumé. Ali had a good job and I'm sure her friends told her not to waste her time on a no-mark like me." He looks around at the few women of Ali's age, who all shake their heads and utter their disagreement. "Well, thank you, ladies, but frankly I wouldn't have blamed you. Yet somehow, some way, Ali decided it was worth backing me, and there hasn't been a single day in the last three years that she's made me feel it's a decision she regrets. She has stuck by me, through thick and thin—waiting patiently for me to get my act together."

Ali grabs hold of his hand and looks up at him, her face full of devotion. Rachel empties her glass of red wine, not knowing who she feels sorrier for. Herself or Will.

"Thank you for the loyalty you've shown and the trust you've put in me," he says to her, amidst much ah-ing and aw-ing. "I will never let you down."

He leans down for a kiss and the guests applaud and raise their glasses.

"To the happy couple," says Jack, taking it as his cue to stand up. He clears his throat, and Rachel almost delights in how difficult this is going to be for him. Though not nearly as difficult as it's going to be for her.

"I'll keep it short," he says. "As I know you'll all be keen to get your dancing shoes on, but I just want to say a few words about having Will as a brother."

Will groans and puts his head in his hands.

"Well, not so much a brother, as an acquaintance, who on the odd occasion he's bothered to call me in the last ten years, shows up on my phone as 'Will . . . you lend me a hundred pounds?'" The line gives him the laugh he'd hoped for when he'd practiced on Rachel the night before they left, when her world was a thousand light years away from the one she finds herself in now. When she'd lain there in bed, watching Jack as he strode up and down at the foot of it, pointing to her whenever he delivered what was supposed to be a humorous line.

She'd kept her face deadpan for all four of the puns, until, exasperated, he'd thrown his piece of paper in the air.

"You're supposed to laugh," he'd sighed.

"Well, maybe I just don't find you funny," she'd jested.

"No?" he challenged. "So, you don't think I can make you smile?"

"Nope," she'd said, as his head disappeared under the end of the duvet. She'd spread her legs as her book that had been lying dormant on her chest dropped to the floor.

"Still not smiling?" he'd mumbled through the quilt.

"Uh-uh," Rachel had managed as she arched her back.

She looks at him standing beside her now and can't help but wonder how many times he's made Ali smile like that.

Bile rises, burning the lining of her throat with a poker-hot ferocity. If she stays here, she's going to purge the remnants of her lobster casserole all over the table. With her face burning, more from embarrassment than the pressure of holding it in, she pushes her chair back and scoots behind a bewildered Jack toward where she hopes the toilets are. There are two doors; one's clearly the kitchen, so she opts for the other, without looking back to see the trail of onlookers she might have left in her wake. Shutting herself into a cubicle, she pours cold water on the insides of her wrists and wills herself to calm down. But she can't shake the image of Jack's head buried between Ali's legs from her mind.

"Rach!" comes Paige's voice through the door. "You okay?"

Rachel lets her in and falls into her arms. "I can't do this," she says.

Paige stiffens. "Do you want me to take you back to the villa?"

"I don't know. I just don't know how I'm supposed to carry on and pretend that everything's normal, when the best man, *my husband*, is fucking the bride." She knows she's had too much to drink as she's lost all volume control as well as the propensity to care who might hear.

"Okay," says Paige, backing Rachel onto the closed toilet seat. "You've got two choices here; you either find a way of getting through the next few hours without driving yourself insane, or we'll say that you're sick and I'll take you back."

"I should have stopped it," cries Rachel, ashamed to acknowledge that if Ali didn't have what she has over her, she would have. But instead of giving Will the chance to get out of a marriage that is destined to fail before it has even begun, she'd taken the coward's way out, too scared of Ali's recrimination; selfishly saving her own skin at the expense of Will's. "He's not done anything to deserve this and he's going to be so devastated when he finds out he's been betrayed by his brother *and* his wife. It's him I'm most worried about in all of this. I couldn't give a shit about Jack or Ali, or even me, but *he's* done nothing wrong."

Paige looks taken aback. "Er, neither have you."

Rachel has never felt more compelled to tell Paige about Noah than now. She *has* done something wrong. So *very* wrong, and now, quite rightly, she has to suffer the consequences. She's under no illusions about the double standards she's currently living by.

"Paige, listen . . ." she starts.

"No, *you* listen to me," says Paige, crouching down to Rachel's height. "Will is *not* your responsibility. Ali's got form—she's done it before and, no doubt, she'll do it again—that's just who she is. What *you* now need to do is to find out if anything's going on between her and Jack, because if it is, I swear to God . . ."

Rachel nods, willing herself to get her act together. To gather the strength and resilience she needs to get through the rest of the day.

"I assume you haven't said anything to Jack yet?" asks Paige.

"I haven't had the chance, but I will, tonight or tomorrow, depending on how drunk he's planning on getting."

"And have you thought about what you're going to do if he admits it?"

A lump instantaneously forms in Rachel's throat. "I need time to think about that," she says.

"Can you live with a man who's been unfaithful? Or are you always going to be thinking that, every time he's late from work, he's with *her*?"

"I don't know," she cries. "What if he wants to be with her?"

"If he wanted to be with her, and her with him, then she wouldn't have just married his brother, would she?"

"I just don't know what to think anymore."

"Whatever's going on, it needs to be stopped," says Paige in a threatening tone. "Because I won't stand for it."

"Anyone would think he's *your* husband," says Rachel, laughing snottily.

"I'm only thinking about you," says Paige, rubbing her hands up and down Rachel's arms. "Do you want your husband back or not?"

Rachel wasn't aware that he'd gone anywhere . . . yet.

"So, are you going to put your big-girl pants on and go out there, or am I calling a taxi?"

Rachel stands up, shakes herself down and peers into the badly lit mirror. She rubs at the streaks of mascara that are smeared under her eyes and pinches her skin to get a rush of color to her cheeks.

"Here," says Paige, handing her a lipstick from her bag.

Rachel takes it, twisting the silver casing in her hand, trying not to cry again. "I don't know what I'd do without you," she says, hugging Paige to her.

"I'm sure you'd manage." Paige laughs.

"No. I don't think I would."

"Well, good thing you don't have to, then."

As the two women walk out of the bathroom Ali momentarily stops what she's saying. Rachel's not remotely surprised that, as uncustomary as it is for the bride to give a speech, Ali has taken it upon herself to give one. Another chance to be in the spotlight, just in case she's not been in it enough already.

Jack looks at Rachel like a six-year-old boy whose mum's come late to the nativity play, but once she's sitting beside him, he softens and rubs her back.

"Are you all right?" he whispers.

Rachel nods, the bitter taste in her mouth rendering her speechless.

"So, all that's left to say," Ali goes on, picking up a champagne glass, "is that William Hunter, I love you and I can't thank you enough for choosing me to be your wife."

As the diners stand to toast the couple, Ali throws a hand in the air. "Oh my goodness, I almost forgot . . . Jack, where are you?"

Rachel stiffens as Jack squirms beside her.

"Ah, there you are," says Ali, as if she'd not known where he'd been sitting for the past three hours. "Jack, ladies and gentlemen, is the person I should *really* be thanking."

Rachel falls back down into her chair, feeling like the air's been sucked out of her.

"Yes, please sit," says Ali, motioning with her free hand.

"It would be remiss of me not to mention Jack, because if it weren't for him, none of us would be here right now. I was working for Jack when he introduced me to his brother Will, and I will be forever in his debt. Though, that's not to say I'd ever work for him again."

The audience titters nervously while Jack stays focused on the bitter cup of coffee in front of him.

"I certainly hope he's a better husband than he is a boss, Rachel," Ali goes on, before dissolving into a schoolgirl giggle.

Rachel's ears go hot as she feels forty pairs of eyes turning to look at her, their laughter easier now that they've worked out who the butt of the joke is supposed to be. She grips at the tablecloth, desperately trying to find the strength to stand up, to put a stop to this and tell everyone that Ali already *knows* he's not a better husband. How can he be, when he's having sex with *her*?

She half expects Jack to stand up and defend her; tell his mistress that his wife is off-limits, but of course, he doesn't. He just sits there, with the tightest of smiles stretched across his face, and white-knuckled fists clenching his napkin.

"So, thank you, Jack," says Ali. "For *everything*. I hope I'm able to pay you back, tenfold."

Every word grates into Rachel's consciousness, the meaning behind each one, hidden from all but her, and most likely Paige, who she can't bear to look at. How could any woman be so audacious as to wrap up promised pleasures to her lover in a veiled speech at her wedding?

"But until then," says Ali, as if affirming Rachel's worst fears, "let's get this party started!"

20

"I'm just going for a smoke," says Jack as the restaurant staff begins to move tables to make way for a dance floor.

"I'll join you," says Paige tersely.

Rachel looks at her wide-eyed, in silent warning.

Paige, her jaw set, as if she's in court and about to deliver the blow to the jugular, surreptitiously shakes her head, as if to say, *"I know, don't worry."*

As Rachel watches the pair of them walk across the emptying restaurant and out onto the terrace, there's a part of her that wishes Paige *would* take him to task. She has a way with words that Rachel could never begin to emulate. She'd be able to deliver the ultimatum clearly and succinctly with no room for error or misunderstanding on Jack's part. He either stops whatever he's doing with Ali and begs for forgiveness, or he chooses to be with *her.* The very thought of him leaving sends shooting pains across her chest and she struggles for breath. Josh would never forgive him, she knows that much, but then he'd never forgive *her* either, if he found out the father he was mourning wasn't his father after all.

"Hey, you okay?" asks Noah, coming over just as the table in front of her is taken away. She hasn't even noticed that she is almost the last person on a chair.

"You still not feeling well?"

"Erm, no," she says, getting up. "I feel a bit sick."

"Could it be something you've eaten?" he asks, his voice full of concern.

"Well, if it's something I've eaten, then we're about to see everyone else drop like flies too." It's an attempt at a joke, to ease the tense atmosphere, but it comes out like a sarcastic barb.

"I want a paternity test," says Noah.

Rachel's blood feels like it's stopped moving, her heart shocked into submission. The whole room and all the people in it seem frozen in time, in suspended animation. Will has his head thrown back, laughing heartily; Chrissy is in the throes of being twirled around by a waiter; and Ali . . . Ali is looking directly at Rachel and Noah with a knowing expression.

"Don't be ridiculous," she says through a forced smile, refusing to give Ali any more power to wield over her.

"I need to know if Josh is my son," says Noah.

Her head snaps round to face him; she's so incensed that she doesn't care who might be watching anymore. "And have you thought about what *he* might need?" she hisses. "What do you suppose would happen to him if it turned out you were his father? That Chloe is actually his half-sister? How do you think that would make him feel? But yet, like everybody else, all you can think about is yourself. How *you* need to know. How it will make *you* feel. Well, guess what? This isn't just about you."

"Are you honestly telling me that it has never occurred to you?" asks Noah.

"Yes," she lies. "Why would it?"

"Because it's a very real possibility," he says, his voice high-pitched.

She shakes her head in disagreement, though she's not convincing herself, let alone anyone else. "Whatever you may remember of that time is wrong," she says.

"I remember that you cut off all communication while I was away," says Noah. "How could you not have had the decency to at least tell me what was going on? Why would you have denied me that?"

"Because it had *nothing* to do with you," she snaps, desperately looking around for a way out of the conversation.

"So, I went from being your best friend to a stranger who wasn't entitled to know that you were pregnant and getting married?"

Rachel shifts from one foot to another while she thinks of a logical reason to counteract his argument, but the only one she can think of is the truth. So instead, she lies.

"You were on the trip of a lifetime," she says. "You didn't need to be bogged down with the minutiae of my life back home."

"You didn't tell me because you knew there was a good chance that Josh was mine."

She looks at him exasperated, but tears are springing to her eyes as the skeleton in her cupboard falls out and lands in a jumbled mess of bones at her feet. The relief at having someone to share the burden with is almost as powerful as the fear of the consequences.

"I would *never* share the results with Josh," Noah says, leaning in closer as the strains of Ed Sheeran's "Thinking Out Loud" start up. "I just need to know."

Rachel looks out at Paige and Jack, deeply engrossed in animated conversation, and wants to scream that, actually, it doesn't matter anymore, because whatever Jack is doing with Ali, it will pale into insignificance if it turns out Noah is right.

"And how do you think that would sit in your marriage?" asks Rachel, acerbically.

"Paige would never know," says Noah.

"But *you* knowing would affect your relationship—it has to. And Paige is my best friend. It would change everything."

"Maybe everything *needs* to change," says Noah, looking at her.

"Ladies and gentlemen," comes an announcement over the speaker. "Would you please welcome Mr. and Mrs. Hunter onto the floor for their first dance."

Paige comes up to them with a fixed smile on her face, though Rachel can tell it's fake from a mile off. "Can you get me a gin and tonic, please?" she says to Noah.

"Yep, sure," he says resignedly. "Rach?"

She looks at her half-full glass of wine, disappointed that her emotions are still crystal clear and her feelings on high alert. "I'll have a gin as well, please," she says, hoping that it might be what's needed to numb her nerve endings.

Noah's not even a meter away when she turns to Paige. "You didn't say anything, did you?"

Paige shakes her head, exasperated, but Rachel can't tell if it's because of Jack or the fact that Ali and Will are recreating the dance from the song's video. The audience stands watching, transfixed by the grace with which Ali moves and the obvious hours they've both put into rehearsing. If Rachel could concentrate for more than a second, even she would admit to being captivated.

"Not exactly," says Paige quietly, when she eventually finds her voice.

"What's *that* supposed to mean?"

"I just told him what it looks like," says Paige. "That the way Ali's behaving is going to raise a few hackles, and that he might need to have a word with her, because it's only going to be a matter of time before you or Will pick up on it."

"And what did he say to that?" asks Rachel, her heart thumping in her chest.

"He said she was just a silly little girl who didn't know what she was doing."

Rachel inhales sharply as relief floods through her, closely followed by the realization that he was never going to say anything else. He'd never be as stupid as to incur Paige's wrath by admitting it; it'd be worse than her own.

"And you believe him?" asks Rachel.

"Well, considering we know her to be a pathological liar, then yes.

Perhaps she's wishing it so hard, she believes it. That's what I think folk like her do."

Rachel nods thoughtfully as Noah hands her a fishbowl glass with a straw and a long cucumber shaving sticking out the top of it. *This should do the trick.*

"You okay for a drink, darling?" asks Jack as he sidles up to Rachel and puts an arm around her waist. She can't help but notice the tumbler he's holding, with an inch's worth of whiskey in it—the drink he refers to as alcoholic's ruin, because it's so strong, you only need one.

"Yes," she says, holding up her glass. "Is everything all right?" she asks as he knocks his Scotch back in a single hit.

"Yeah, good," he says, planting a kiss on her cheek. "Anyway, never mind me." He looks at her as if he means it. "How are *you* feeling? Any better?"

She nods, but if the truth be known, there's still a gnawing in the pit of her stomach.

"Why don't we get out of here?" he says.

"What, *now*?" she exclaims. "The best man can't leave before the first dance is over. What excuse would you give?"

The cheers from the wedding party surrounding Will and Ali on the dance floor drown out Jack's reply.

"Just when you think you've seen it all . . ." she says bitterly, nodding toward Ali as she jumps up into Will's arms and he spins her around.

Ed Sheeran stops singing and the audience claps and whoops as Ali throws her hands up in the air.

"We should go away," says Jack, talking to Rachel, but his eyes are still on Ali.

"We *are* away," she says sourly.

"No, not like *this*," he says. "Just you and me, somewhere warm, somewhere secluded, where we can just be on our own together, without all this nonsense."

Rachel wants to believe that that's what he wants, but as she follows his eyes to where Ali's kissing Will, she can see his frustration, *feel* it. His eyes narrow and his jaw spasms involuntarily, his body unable to hide the envy, of wanting something he can't have.

Ali is giddy as she twirls off the dance floor toward them. "Phew, I need some air," she says loudly, fanning herself.

"You were incredible!" Ali's friend calls after her as she walks out through the door to the terrace. She brushes the comment off with a look that says, "*Oh, stop,*" quickly followed by one that says, "*I know.*"

"We should get something booked up as soon as we get home," says Jack. "Maybe the Maldives, where I can have you all to myself." He flashes her a smile that normally gets him anything he wants, but she doesn't feel like giving it to him today.

"Let's see," she says, noncommittally.

"I'm going to get another drink," he says, going to walk away.

"Why don't you have a soft drink?" says Rachel.

He looks at her as if she's mad. "Why would I do that?" he says, over his shoulder.

"Just because the evening's only just started and you don't want to peak too soon," says Rachel, looking over at Noah and Paige at the bar. "We could all do with pacing ourselves a bit."

She doesn't know whether she includes *them* to make Jack feel she's not singling him out, or whether she really means it. In all honesty, it's probably the latter, as any one of them getting too drunk and loose-lipped could be dangerous.

Her insides coil as she watches him walk toward the bar, but at the last minute he swerves toward the door to the terrace. The door that Ali had walked through just a few seconds before. He's either getting exceedingly desperate or terribly careless in his pursuit of her. She wonders if it's perhaps both. The thought of that almost hurts her more than what he's physically doing.

She takes a giant swig of her G&T and grimaces, her throat unaccustomed to European measures. But the very next second, a warmth is running through her chest and across her shoulders, loosening the knots that have been making her feel as if she's bound by an invisible rope.

She starts to make her way across the dance floor that is still littered with guests eulogizing about how wonderful Ali is. Rachel wonders if they'd still feel the same if they knew she was cheating on the husband who'd just held her tight, looking as if he depended on her to complete him.

She pretends in her head that she's just going to the bathroom, but she knows she's got to go past the very same door that Jack and Ali have just walked through to get there. She looks to the back of the restaurant, where Noah and Paige are deep in conversation, and alternates between whether she wants to alert Paige to what she's doing or not. It would be useful to have the back-up if she stumbles across what she fears she's going to stumble across. But if Paige is with her, Rachel knows she'll lose control over the situation, as Paige won't be able to hold back. *No,* she needs to do this on her own.

The door to the terrace is within touching distance, but she could still easily walk past and go to the bathroom or bar instead. She tries to fight the urge, convincing herself that she'd prefer to be kept in the dark about whatever it is they're doing than be faced with the deceit in real time. She wonders whether she could pretend that none of this ever happened. If she and Jack could go away to an idyllic island and work through their problems. But that would mean that she has to swallow her pride and she's not sure she can do that.

As she pushes the door open, a cool fresh breeze whips around her body. The wind's really picked up since they've been inside and she holds onto her skirt to stop it from billowing up. As if on legs that aren't under her control, she steps onto the terrace that is littered with a slew of smokers, huddled together under the outdoor heaters.

Now that the sun is setting, the sky is a swirl of blue and orange, descending into burned amber the closer it gets to the horizon. Rachel remembers when she and Jack went to Santorini a few years ago—

their first vacation without Josh—and walked to the top of Oia to witness what the locals call "the best sunset in the world."

"Can you hear it?" Jack had said, as they'd sat on a stone wall, along with a hundred or so other awe-struck tourists.

She'd looked at him, full of love and excitement at what this new phase in their life would bring. With Josh fast becoming an independent teenager, they could certainly look forward to more trips like this, and the warm feeling that the thought evoked had wrapped itself around her.

"Hear what?" she'd asked, smiling.

"The sizzle as the sun disappears into the ocean."

Her chest physically hurts at the thought he could be saying that to Ali now. There's no sign of either of them on the terrace, and she casts an eye over the beach below. The cliff face is now highlighted by neon-pink strobes from a laser beam, masking the multitude of darkened crevices within. Any one of them would be perfect for the two of them to hide in. Though, with the tide coming in so quickly, the water would soon flush them out.

Rachel imagines Ali floating facedown in the rising water and can't help but feel satisfied by the thought of her not being around to create havoc anymore.

Removing her wedge shoes, Rachel starts to descend the wooden staircase onto the beach. Feeling the sand between her toes, she sees a notice nailed to a precarious-looking crag, *PERIGO DE DESMORONAMENTO,* and then written below, *BEWARE OF FALLING ROCKS.*

More horrific images of Ali's head, smashed to a pulp by a dislodged boulder, do little to incur any sympathy within Rachel, and she wonders what the hell's wrong with her. Hating a woman for sleeping with your husband is understandable. Wanting her to die an incredibly grisly death isn't.

Going against her better judgment, Rachel stays close to the base of the cliffs, edging her way toward the first cave. She can hear *some-*

thing, but with the sound of the crashing waves creeping ever closer, it's difficult to be sure what it is. Birds soar overhead, squawking as they make their way home to their ledges further up the rock face, and there's a faint pounding from the bass of the music reverberating from the reception.

It all merges into a cacophony that threatens to drown out the very thing she came looking for. Though, she wonders if that's not such a bad thing, as to actively seek out proof that your husband is being unfaithful must surely be masochistic. Yet still she pushes on, as if seeing it for herself is the only way she will believe it. The first nook is barely deep enough to obscure one person, let alone two, so Rachel moves onto the next, just a few meters on. She peeks around a jutting rock to see that it's dark and forbidding, too deep to see the back wall, but there are voices coming from within. Rachel cranes her neck to hear Jack, whose speech is slurred, yet there's no mistaking the wrath of his words.

"If you ever do that again, I swear to God, I'll . . ."

"You'll *what,* Jack . . . ?" comes a female voice. Rachel knows that it's Ali, but she so desperately wants it not to be. She begins to step backward, wishing she could just go back to twenty seconds ago when she still just had suspicions.

"Don't push me," spits Jack.

"No, come on, tell me," presses Ali.

"I mean it. If you threaten to expose what's going on one more time . . ."

"I'd like to see it," says Ali, her voice unwavering. "If you want me to stop, you know what you've got to do."

"Do you have any idea what it will do to Rachel?" says Jack. "This will destroy her. Do you really want to be responsible for that?"

"I think you'll find Rachel is far stronger than you think. Either that, or she refuses to acknowledge what's going on right under her nose, because I've certainly left enough clues."

There are two breaths of silence before Ali screams and Rachel turns to run, unable to comprehend what might be happening. But she's only put one foot in front of the other when she stops stock-still. No matter what Ali's done, she cannot, *will* not, stand by and let a man hurt a woman, for *any* reason.

She heads back to the cave, rushing in, shouting Jack's name. As her eyes take a couple of seconds to adjust to the darkness, she can just make out his arm in the air, about to bear down.

"*Rachel?*" he says, as if in disbelief.

Ali's eyes are wide and scared as she looks from Jack to Rachel and back again, as if unable to weigh whether she's come to help *him* or *her*.

"What the *hell* do you think you're doing?" Rachel screams at Jack, needing to hear his excuse for lashing out at Ali, far more than why he's sleeping with her.

"I . . ." he stutters, letting his arm drop.

"What's going on?" Rachel asks, not knowing who she wants to answer.

"It isn't . . . it isn't what it looks like," says Jack, stumbling back, as if in shock. Though Rachel can't tell if it's because she's made an unexpected appearance or that he realized what he was about to do.

"Tell her, for fuck's sake," screams Ali, her voice echoing around the cave.

Jack's jaw spasms involuntarily as he looks at Ali with such intensity that a sob catches in Rachel's throat. She's *never* seen him look at anyone the way he's looking at her and she can feel her marriage being washed away with the tide that is lapping at her feet.

"Not like this," he says, his voice breaking.

"How many more chances do you want me to give you?" says Ali, her voice, in contrast, strong and steady. "Either you do it, or I will."

"I . . . just . . . ," stutters Jack. "Please . . . I just . . ."

How could Ali, who Rachel had written off as being nothing more than a silly young girl, have so much hold over Jack that she has turned him into a crumbling wreck? How has she worked her way under his skin to such an extent that he's unable to string two words together? This isn't her Jack; this is a different man entirely.

Despite feeling hollowed out inside, Rachel forces herself to stand tall; to be more like Ali. "Is somebody going to tell me what's going on?" she says, sounding far more authoritative than she feels. She looks from Jack to Ali and back again.

"I'm sorry," says Ali, looking at Rachel with tears in her eyes—the first time that she's shown any regret or remorse. "I tried to stop it, honestly I did."

It takes all of Rachel's restraint not to launch herself at her, to tear the hair from out of her stupid head and to rip the tacky dress she's just worn to proclaim her love for someone else, off her back. But that would make her no better than Jack and despite everything, she *has* to be a better person than he is.

"How long's it been going on?" she asks, her mouth feeling as if it's full of cotton wool.

Ali looks to Jack, but he's turning around in circles, agitatedly raking at his hair. "At least eighteen months," she says. "That's why I left the company. I *had* to."

Rachel's mouth drops open. She thinks of all the things they've done in the past eighteen months: the words they'd exchanged, the dreams they'd shared, the love they'd made, and it all suddenly seems sullied. Like she's been living a lie, or worse, been unknowingly immersed in someone else's.

"Please!" shouts Jack, as if he knows he's fast losing the chance to claw Rachel back from the precipice she finds herself clinging to. "I need to do this *my* way." He looks at Ali. "Without you here."

Ali laughs acerbically. "I don't trust you to do it *your* way," she says, lifting her dress up to avoid the lap of water that is easing its way toward her with every break of a wave. The tide is coming into the cave so rapidly that it won't be long before they'll have no choice but to swim out.

"Why don't you think of Rachel in all this?" he snaps, finding his voice again. "What might be best for her?"

"Don't you think that's what I've been doing?" says Ali.

"Oh, yeah," says Rachel sarcastically. "You've gone all out to do right by me."

Holding her dress at her knees, Ali walks to Rachel. "I'm so sorry," she says tearfully. "You have to believe me when I say I tried everything in my power to put a stop to it."

"If you don't get away from me," sneers Rachel. "I swear to God . . ."

She watches Ali wade out of the cave and turns to Jack, whose face is sallow, devoid of color. She imagines slapping his cheek hard and the red blush it would create.

"Do you want to tell me what's going on?" she asks, once Ali's gone.

Jack's manically rubbing at his head, back and forth. He goes to speak, but seems to think better of it.

"I'll ask again," she says firmly.

"She . . ." he starts.

Rachel waits, with her hands on her hips, refusing to make this any easier for him.

"When she first started working for me, she made an advance . . ." He leaves it there, as if waiting to gauge Rachel's reaction.

She can't help but laugh. "And let me guess . . . you were powerless to resist?" It's a question she expects to be answered.

"I . . . I tried, but you know what she's like."

"Poor you," says Rachel, without a modicum of sympathy.

"Anyway, I kept refusing her and one night, when I'd had too much to drink—I think you and I had had a fight . . ."

Rachel scoffs. She knew it was somehow going to be *her* fault.

"And that night, I kissed her," says Jack.

Rachel raises her eyebrows expectantly, wanting him to go on, but not wanting to hear it.

"And ever since then, she's been pushing for more. Blackmailing me by threatening to tell you if I don't give her what she wants."

Rachel shakes her head, trying to make sense of what he's saying. "So, have you given it to her or *not*?"

"No!" he exclaims, his voice so loud that it reverberates around them. "Of course not. You know I'd never do that."

Rachel looks up at the cavernous ceiling, waiting for the patience she so desperately needs to be bestowed upon her.

"So you're saying that all you've done is kiss her?" she asks incredulously. "Once?"

"Exactly!" he says. "And ever since, she's been making out that there's something going on, when I swear to you, there isn't."

Rachel can't believe what she's hearing. "But that doesn't even make sense," she says. "Why would she do that?"

"Because she's stark raving mad," he says, throwing his hands in the air. "You know what she's like. You've seen how she behaves. This is what I've had to deal with."

If he thinks she's about to feel sorry for him, he's got another think coming. "So, you're saying she's deluded? That everything she's just said is garbage?"

"Yes!" says Jack. "Yes, she's got it in her head that something's going on, but you know what she's like, Rach. She's mad."

She wonders if he thinks repeating himself will make her believe him more. It doesn't. It just makes him sound as if he's clutching at straws.

"So this is why you didn't want Will to marry her?" says Rachel.

Jack nods.

"So, what about Rick?" she asks.

He looks at her with a perplexed expression.

"The man you said she'd had an affair with," says Rachel, having to jog his memory yet again. "Does he even exist?"

Jack shakes his head. "No, I just needed to give you a reason for why I hated her so much, but without having to admit that I'd been stupid enough to kiss her."

"You said I'd be destroyed," says Rachel. "I heard you."

"Yes, because that's the kind of thing I have to say, to keep her from losing her mind and going on the rampage. I really don't know what she's capable of, and right now it's a balancing act, at least until we get through this and are back at home. I don't want Will to know that I kissed her, even though it was before they even met."

It's a long shot, but Rachel wonders if there's any way he *could* be telling the truth. Every single seed of doubt that has been sown into her mind has been planted by Ali. From having to retrace her steps to find her passport, to her being in their room, to inviting herself on Jack's run, to finding his watch in her drawer. It's all been one-way, with Jack having played no part in any of it.

And she *does* know what Ali's like; she's a liar and a fantasist who will stop at nothing to get what she wants, even if it means taking down the people she supposedly loves in the process. Look what she did to her own mother. God knows what led to the horrific events of that night, but Rachel can bet her bottom dollar that it was Ali's selfishness that has resulted in Maria being bound to a wheelchair for the rest of her life.

Nothing is as it seems in Ali's world, so why would Rachel think she and Jack could escape the storm that seems to prevail wherever she is?

"You have to believe me," Jack pleads, as if reading her mind. "You know what she's like. You've seen it with your own eyes. She can't stop herself. The woman is a pathological liar."

Rachel laughs at herself for wanting to give him the benefit of the doubt. She knows that if any of her friends were in this position, she'd scream at them to "wake up!" But somehow, when it's your own marriage on the line, it's not so clear cut.

"That's what I've been dealing with," he says. "Haven't you ever asked yourself why she's no longer working for me?"

"She just said that she had to leave because it all got too much," says Rachel, reading between the lines.

"I got her fired," says Jack bitterly.

"You *fired* her?" says Rachel, shocked at the admission. "You said she gave her notice in when she was offered the new job."

Jack shakes his head.

"What grounds did you fire her on?" asks Rachel.

Jack sighs heavily. "She just wouldn't leave me alone, but I could hardly go to the boss and complain that I was being sexually harassed by a woman, could I? He'd laugh me out of his office."

"Why didn't you tell me?" asks Rachel.

Jack looks down as the advancing tide fills his footsteps as quickly as he leaves them. "Because you'd probably do the same," he says.

Rachel likes to think she wouldn't, but without knowing what she now knows, she has to admit that she might have.

"So . . . so what did you do?" she asks.

"I had to do some digging," he says. "To see if I could find something, *anything*, that meant I could fast-track her out of the door, and out of my life."

"So, what did you find that proved conclusive enough to fire her?" asks Rachel.

"She lied," says Jack, bluntly.

Rachel tuts and shakes her head. "Why doesn't that surprise me?"

"She put down a fictitious job on her résumé," Jack goes on. "I was determined to get something on her that would stick, and I did."

"How did you find out it was fake?"

"I just called all the employers she said she'd worked for and they all stacked up, except one, who said they'd never heard of her."

"So, there's a gap in her career that's unaccounted for?" asks Rachel.

"Two years," says Jack.

"What could she have been doing that meant she had to make something up?"

"It doesn't matter," says Jack. "It gave me enough to dismiss her on the grounds of obtaining employment fraudulently."

"But don't you want to know *why*?" muses Rachel, feeling that they might be on to something; something big that could be the death knell for Ali's hours-old marriage. "Aren't you intrigued to find out what she's hiding? Because she's definitely hiding *something*."

"I honestly don't care," says Jack tightly. "I just wanted to be rid of her and that gave me the chance."

"But what if . . . ?" starts Rachel, her mouth working faster than her brain. She pauses, waiting for it to catch up. "What if she was *inside*?" Her eyes widen as the possibility dawns on her.

Jack laughs. "What . . . prison?" he asks, his voice high-pitched.

Rachel nods. "It's not too far beyond the realms of possibility, is it? Knowing what we now know about her—the lengths she'll go to, to get what she wants."

Jack's eyes flit rapidly from side to side as he contemplates what Rachel's saying.

"She might be a professional fraudster—a con woman who got caught out. Or she might have been convicted of stalking," offers Rachel, warming to the theme. "They take that pretty seriously these days."

"I don't think so," says Jack.

"She was driving the car when Maria was injured. If she'd been drinking, they'd have put her in jail and thrown away the key."

"If she'd been in prison, we'd know," says Jack.

"How?" asks Rachel. "You only checked her references when you wanted her out. Most people would do it when they were considering hiring someone *in*."

"Nobody does that anymore," says Jack, by way of defense. "You glean more from someone's social media accounts than from talking to an employer who can barely remember them working there. The job she went to never bothered to ask me for a reference either."

"So, it's the blind leading the blind," says Rachel. "No wonder she's gotten away with it for so long. You've all allowed her to—and now she's got her feet under the table of *our* family." Her voice wavers as she thinks of Josh and what Ali might have seen or heard. "She could be capable of *anything*."

Jack goes to her and takes hold of her shoulders. "I think she's already done her worst, as far as we're concerned."

Rachel wishes she felt as confident.

"Why haven't you told Will any of this?" she asks. "Why wouldn't you warn him who he was marrying before it was too late?"

"I tried!" he exclaims. "But he just wouldn't listen. She's done the same to him as she's tried to do to me. But Will's weaker than I am and he's let her win. He's desperate to have kids, and doesn't want to leave it too late."

"She doesn't want children yet," says Rachel, as if to herself.

"What?" says Jack. "But the other night . . ."

"I know what she said to us the other night, in front of Will, but I heard her telling her cousin that she's not ready."

"The fucking bitch," seethes Jack. "How can she do that to him?"

Rachel thinks about it for a moment.

"See, this is what I'm talking about," says Jack, jumping in on her thoughts. "This is what we're dealing with."

"You had your chance to put a stop to this," says Rachel, feeling the ice-cold water lapping at her feet. "If you'd been honest—with me, with Will—you could have stopped him marrying her."

"It's not too late," says Jack.

"Of course it's too late!" cries Rachel, ashamed of the part she's played in this. How had she let her stupid insecurities come between her and her husband? If she'd confronted Jack when she should have, all this would have come out sooner, and together they would have had a chance to let Will know the mistake he was about to make.

Jack takes her hand. "We should get back before we're missed," he says, attempting to laugh. "And before this place fills with water."

21

"What's going on?" asks Paige when Rachel approaches her and Noah.

"You're not going to believe it," says Rachel, giddy with relief. She finishes the gin she'd left on the table and picks up her handbag from the back of a chair. "Let me just go and sort myself out and I'll bring you up to speed."

She takes herself off to the ladies' room where she finds Chrissy standing outside a closed cubicle door.

"Are you . . . ?" starts Rachel, pointing to the open cubicle beside her.

"Oh, no," says Chrissy. "Go ahead."

Rachel doesn't really need to go, she just wants access to the mirror to make sure she doesn't have mascara running down her cheeks, but with Chrissy in the way, there's not enough room, so she locks herself into the cubicle and checks her phone while she waits.

"Come on, Ali," she hears Chrissy plead. "Whatever it is, you can't let it upset you on your wedding day."

"I'll be fine," sniffs Ali. "I just need a minute."

"Okay," says Chrissy. "I'm right here."

"Actually, could you leave me?" says Ali. "I just need to be on my own."

"Well . . ." starts Chrissy, clearly not sure if it's wise to leave Ali alone.

"Honestly," says Ali, sensing her hesitation. "I'm fine. I'll be out in a second."

"Okay," says Chrissy reluctantly. "I'll just be outside by the bar."

Rachel hears the door open and close and a few more sniffs coming from next door. She doesn't know whether to bolt out of there to avoid Ali—after all, she has nothing left to say to her—or let her go first.

The door unlocks and a tip-tap of shoes crosses the tiled floor. Water runs and the hand dryer blasts hot air into the tiny space. When it turns off, Rachel waits for the door to open and close, but there's only silence. No movement. No tip-tap. Nothing—just an ominous stillness.

It's beginning to feel awkward, like a standoff, with only a flimsy sheet of Formica to witness who will break cover first.

Rachel doesn't want a confrontation, but she's not going to hide in a toilet all night. She smooths down the fabric of her dress and takes a deep breath as she prises the lock and opens the door. If Ali is surprised it's her, she doesn't show it. In fact, she's standing purposefully against the basin, as if waiting for her.

"Excuse me," says Rachel, tightly.

Ali moves aside and exhales. "I just wanted to say I'm sorry," she says.

Rachel rests her hands on the edge of the sink, lets her head fall and laughs.

"What's so funny?" asks Ali.

"Is that honestly all you've got to say? You're not usually one to be lost for words. I expected more from you, quite frankly."

Ali looks at her quizzically. "Has he *told* you?"

Rachel, feeling her temper fraying, turns to face her, their noses just an inch apart. "Yes," she shouts. "Yes, he's told me."

"And you think it's *funny*?"

"If I don't laugh, I'll cry," says Rachel. "Because it is so fucked up, that I can't even begin to understand why you would have done it.

What did you think you were going to achieve? Did you really think you were going to coerce Jack into submission?"

"I don't know *what* I was thinking," says Ali, her bottom lip beginning to wobble. "I just wanted him to be honest with you, because believe it or not, Rachel, I really like you."

Rachel laughs sarcastically again. "Wow, really? Well, then I'd hate to see what you do to your enemies."

"What are you going to do?" asks Ali.

"About *this*?"

Ali nods nervously.

"Well, we're going to ride this out, for Will's sake, while we're here, but once we get home, I don't want you anywhere near me or my family."

"Seriously?" asks Ali, tearfully.

"Seriously," mimics Rachel. "Though, I can't guarantee that Jack will be able to hold back until then. He has every intention of telling Will what's been going on."

Ali screws her face up. "Why does he need to bother Will with this? I've kept it to myself for months, out of respect for you and, for some illogical reason, Jack. Why would either of you want anyone to know about this? He really has no shame, does he?"

Rachel leans in toward Ali, her teeth grinding against each other, in an effort to stop the vicious diatribe that is threatening to project from her mouth. "If you come anywhere near my husband again, I will not be held responsible for my actions."

"I assume you're going to say the same to *her*." Ali spits the last word out as if it's venom.

Rachel stops and looks at her, her patience hanging by a thread. "*Her?*"

Ali dries her tears and looks at her wide-eyed. "He hasn't told you, has he?"

Rachel doesn't want to give her the satisfaction of saying no.

"Oh my God," says Ali, looking at Rachel's slack-jawed expression. "The bastard's not told you the truth."

Rachel straightens herself up. "He's told me what I need to know," she says, suddenly feeling like a fish out of water. "That you've been harassing him for months, years even, refusing to take no for an answer."

"You think *I've* been going after *Jack*?"

"I don't *think*. I *know*. And it all makes sense, the constant innuendos, the smutty gifts—though, how you pulled off the necklace ruse this morning, I don't know, because there's no way you could possibly have known that I would find the receipt."

Ali fingers the heart hanging around her neck. "What are you talking about?"

"*Don't* play dumb with me," spits Rachel. "Did you think that by pretending something was going on, it would make it true?"

"I don't . . ." stutters Ali, shaking her head. "I don't understand."

Rachel laughs cattily. "Taking him off at the airport, asking him inflammatory questions, giving him inappropriate gifts, trying to go for a run with him. It's desperate behavior by someone who isn't used to being told no."

Ali closes her eyes and takes a deep breath.

"But guess what?" Rachel goes on. "He's *not* interested."

"I didn't do *any* of that to try and make you think something was going on between us," says Ali, looking confused. "I wanted to put him on the spot; to make him feel under pressure to do the right thing. The questions and gifts were all designed to let him know that time was running out."

"You gave him a cock covered in love hearts, for Christ's sake."

Ali sighs. "I gave him something that illustrated a strong moral compass; to show that those who have done nothing wrong have nothing to fear. But those who do . . ." She trails off.

Rachel shakes her head. "And trying to get him on his own all the time? How do you justify that?"

"I just needed to talk to him in the hope that he'd see sense," says Ali. She looks at Rachel, her eyes pleading to be believed. "I'm sorry, I didn't even think about how it might have looked, but I can assure you, it was never meant to allude to something going on between us."

Rachel's eyes narrow. "So what *was* it done for?"

"As a warning," says Ali, "to let him know that if *he* didn't tell you, I would." Her voice tails off at the end.

"Tell me *what*?" Rachel shouts, losing her patience.

"That he's having an affair."

"For God's sake, what is wrong with you? He's not having an affair with *you*."

"Not with *me*, no," says Ali.

Rachel laughs incredulously. "Well, who the hell with, then?"

Ali looks upwards, as if asking for help. "Well?" shouts Rachel impatiently.

"Paige," says Ali, in barely more than a whisper. "He's having an affair with Paige."

The floor spins and Rachel feels like she's being sucked into a vortex, as she falls backward. Ali grabs hold of her arms and backs her onto the closed toilet seat. Rachel's hands instinctively strike out, looking for something to grip onto, but all they can find is the frictionless cubicle wall, which they slide down.

"What . . ." she starts when she eventually finds her voice.

"I'm sorry," says Ali. "I wanted him to tell you."

Rachel pushes herself against the cistern, hoping and praying that someone comes in and drags this psychopath off her.

"What kind of fucked-up world do you live in?" hisses Rachel. "You can't help yourself, can you?"

"I'm telling you the truth," says Ali.

"You're *incapable* of it," cries Rachel. "You've done nothing but lie since we've been here."

"I've only ever tried to protect the people I care about," says Ali.

"The only person you care about is *yourself*," says Rachel, pushing herself up and walking toward the door, unsteady on her feet. "You're nothing but a fucking liar, and I'm warning you to stay away from me, my family and my friends."

"She's *not* your friend" is the last thing Rachel hears as the door closes behind her and she finds herself, dazed, on the edge of a dance floor filled with people with their hands aloft, singing to Neil Diamond. Jack, Paige and Noah are staring at her, their faces etched with concern, from the other side.

22

Without even realizing what she's doing, Rachel finds herself standing behind the DJ deck, with him looking at her expectantly.

"Can I borrow the mic?" she says.

"Eh?" he questions, not understanding her.

"Give me the microphone," she says in clear, clipped syllables.

She reaches across his turntable to pick up the bulbous-headed mic and taps it three times with her finger before sliding the needle off "Sweet Caroline." The music comes to an abrupt stop as the scratching grates around the restaurant and guests cover their ears.

They turn to Rachel, waiting for her to say something, but she looks at them blankly, not knowing what she's going to say herself. Ali comes out of the cloakroom, looking around in confusion. She freezes when her eyes settle on Rachel.

"I just want to talk about Ali for a second," says Rachel, her voice projecting further than she'd expected. Her mouth dries up as she moves the mic further from her lips.

Everyone's faces look strange, like they're staring at her from inside a bottle, their features distorted by the curvature of the glass. Maria's is the only one she recognizes, though she can't quite read her expression. Is it panic?

"You see," Rachel goes on. "She's not quite who you all think she is."

Jack moves across the floor toward her, like he's skating on ice, while Ali just stays rooted to the spot, poleaxed, with her mouth open.

"Please tell me it's not just me," Rachel asks the sea of faces, in a room where you could hear a pin drop.

"Rachel," Jack says into the bewildered silence.

"What?" she snaps.

"Don't do this."

"Why not? They need to know. *Everyone* needs to know."

Jack laughs awkwardly, as if he's dealing with a drunk, forgetful elderly relative. "But now's not the time," he says. "Later. We're supposed to do this later."

Reality hits her then, as Jack's attempt to pretend she's gone too early on a planned announcement sinks in.

The forty or so gawping onlookers suddenly come into sharp focus with Will at the forefront, smiling as he waits naively for Rachel to sing Ali's praises. How can she shatter whatever warped illusion he has of the woman he's just married?

She almost drops the mic in shock, unable to believe that she's taken leave of her senses. *What the hell was she thinking?*

"Sorry," she mumbles as she shakily hands the microphone back to the DJ. Jack takes hold of her arm and guides her over to where Noah and Paige are standing.

"Have you *completely* lost your mind?" he hisses, through a fixed grin.

"She can't keep being allowed to get away with it," says Rachel, still defiant, but grateful that somebody has stopped her from saying anything more. "I bet everybody here will be relieved it's not just them she does it to."

"What the hell's going on?" asks Paige, looking from Jack to Rachel and back again.

"God knows how many relationships she's destroyed—friendships she's ruined," blurts out Rachel. "I'm not going to let her do it to mine."

Paige looks at Jack with raised eyebrows. "I thought I told you to sort this out."

"Oh, it's got even better since then," says Rachel, no longer caring who knows what anymore. "Apparently it's not Ali he's having an affair with."

"O-kay," says Paige hesitantly, looking at Jack. "So, that's a good thing, no?"

"Do you want to know who she says he *is* having an affair with?" Rachel's talking as if Jack isn't there. It's easier that way, as it fools her into thinking they're not talking about the man she's loved for the past twenty years.

All three of them look at her expectantly.

"*You!*" she says, laughing and pointing at Paige.

"*What?*" the three of them say, in unison.

"That's what I mean," says Rachel. "She's wrecking relationships. You should have let me say what I was going to say."

Paige looks like she doesn't know whether to laugh or cry. "Well, that's just . . ." she starts. "I don't even have the words . . ."

"Well, where has she got *that* idea from?" asks Noah, looking from Paige to Jack and back again.

"It's a long story," sighs Jack. "But it goes without saying that it's completely untrue."

"Of course it is!" snaps Paige.

"It seems she's got form," says Rachel, the four of them staring at Ali across the restaurant. "This is what she does. She must be so unhappy with herself that she throws hand grenades into as many other people's lives as she can."

Paige's lips pull into a tight line as she looks Ali up and down, her hostility apparent. "She knows I've never liked her," she says snidely. "I guess this is what she does when someone doesn't dance to her tune."

"Oh, come on," says Noah. "This is all a bit melodramatic, isn't it?

I mean, I know she's a live wire and sails a little close to the edge sometimes, but she's never crossed the line."

"That's because, like most men, all you see is her sweet smile and big tits," says Paige, crudely.

"Oh, right." Noah laughs tightly. "She's one of those women, is she? How do you describe them again, Paige?"

She looks at him blankly, but there's tension pulsing in her jawline.

"Ah, that's it," says Noah, as if he's just remembered. "You'd refer to her as a *man's* woman."

"Well, I think this quite clearly demonstrates that she's not a woman's woman," says Paige.

"So, that's all this is, is it?" he asks. "A spiteful vendetta against you because you're a fellow female who's dared to show your obvious disdain toward her?"

"Clearly," snaps Paige. "What else would it be?"

"Okay," says Rachel, stepping in. She hadn't quite thought about the effect her announcement would have on Paige and Noah. "Look, I don't think it's anything against Paige per se. It's a much bigger picture that centers around Jack, it seems."

Noah raises his eyebrows in a silent question.

"It's honestly too complicated to go into now," says Rachel.

"I'm going to talk to her," says Paige, going to shoulder her way past Noah.

"I don't think that's a very good idea," says Jack, grabbing hold of her arm. "There's all sorts of things going on that you don't know about. For Will's sake, I suggest we all just get through the rest of the evening, as best we know how, making as little fuss as possible."

Paige laughs acerbically. "What? And let her get away with telling my best friend that I'm having an affair with her husband?" She's still tugging at Jack to release his grip on her.

"For the moment, yes," says Jack authoritatively.

"But you *are* going to deal with this?" says Paige. It's a rhetorical question.

"And you *are* going to tell Will what's been going on?" adds Rachel, piling the pressure on him.

Noah snorts. "Isn't it a bit late for that?"

"I'll deal with Will," says Jack. "But not now."

"Isn't this just wonderful?" says Ali's mum, as she approaches them, misreading the mood completely.

They all fix false smiles on their faces, with the men already beginning to edge discreetly away so they don't get caught up in whatever else she's about to say.

"I mean it's just breathtaking," she goes on, looking out across the fuchsia cliffs as they descend into a sea of the same color. A full moon has now replaced the sun, but it's the neon pink of lasers that's reflected in the inky black water.

"It is," agrees Rachel, at a loss for anything else to say.

"She so deserves this," says Maria, as if to herself.

"I'm going to get another drink," says Paige, curtly, obviously unable to listen to anyone singing Ali's praises. Rachel's going to find it hard to stomach as well if Maria intends to go down that line.

As Paige moves away, Maria turns to face Rachel and looks at her so intently that it makes Rachel shift her stance in an effort to snap her out of it.

"Please don't hate her," says Maria.

"Ex-cuse me?" says Rachel, unable to believe that Ali's mother is in on this ridiculous charade as well. "Do you have *any* idea what she's been doing?"

Maria nods. "She's told me what's going on and I'm sorry, I truly am, because you seem like such a nice person."

"Mrs. . . ." starts Rachel.

"Please, call me Maria," she says, putting her hand on Rachel's arm. "It might not seem like it right now, but she's only trying to do the right thing by *you*."

Rachel looks at her through narrowed eyes, trying to put herself in her position as a mother. Without knowing what part of Ali's catalog of deception Maria is alluding to, it's hard to judge whether she'd try and make the same excuses for Josh if she had to. Does she know, for example, that her daughter has been essentially blackmailing her former boss? Trying to force him into a predicament that he doesn't want to be in, or else she'll tell his wife that it's happening anyway? Does she know that now that Ali's on the ropes, she's accused another woman of having an affair with him? An allegation so potentially damaging that it could have a devastating effect on *two* families.

"No disrespect, but I don't think you have any idea what your daughter is capable of."

"You know," says Maria, leaning in. "When I had my accident, if Alison hadn't been there for me, I wouldn't be here today."

Rachel looks around, hoping for an escape opportunity to present itself. *This woman is clearly as deluded as her daughter.*

"When they got me into the hospital, I had a twenty percent chance of survival," she goes on. "Unbeknownst to me, Alison had already been told that I had a hundred percent chance of losing my leg."

The admission takes Rachel so by surprise that she can't help but look at the two shins and sandalled feet that appear from below Maria's long floral skirt.

"False," she says, tapping on the prosthetic.

"I'm sorry," says Rachel. "I didn't realize."

"As I say, if Alison hadn't made the sacrifice that she did, I honestly wouldn't be here now, so just know that whatever she does, it's always from a good place."

"*Sacrifice?*" asks Rachel, unable to help herself. "If she hadn't been driving, *you* wouldn't be in a wheelchair."

Maria pulls her head back, her expression vexed with confusion. "Alison *wasn't* driving," she says. "I was."

"But I thought . . ." starts Rachel. "I thought Chrissy said she'd found your accident hard to deal with because she blamed herself."

Tears spring to Maria's eyes. "Only because she called that night to ask me to pick her up from a party. I'd fallen asleep in front of the

TV, so I was a bit disoriented when the phone rang. She could tell and told me she'd get a cab, so that I could go back to sleep. But I wasn't having any of it." She looks at Rachel and smiles. "The thing is, your children grow up so quickly that it's just nice to be needed, even when they're adults. And it wasn't that late, so I didn't think twice. But it was pouring rain outside and as we were coming back, a car came out of nowhere on the other side of the road and smashed straight into us."

"So, it wasn't Ali's fault?" says Rachel, almost to herself.

"Of course not," says Maria. "And it pains me that she still thinks it is. She couldn't have done anything more for me if she'd tried. She stayed by my side, twenty-four-seven, for two years after my accident."

Rachel feels her body swaying; it's as if she's outside, looking in. She has so many questions, but she's afraid the answers are not going to be ones she wants to hear.

She pictures Ali's résumé, with the two-year period she'd so readily allocated to "Serving at Her Majesty's Pleasure," being replaced by "Caring for Her Sick Mum." It doesn't quite have the same ring to it, and it most certainly doesn't fit in with the warped caricature of Ali that Rachel's created in her head.

"So, she gave up *work*?" asks Rachel, her voice wavering.

Maria nods. "She was doing so well—her career was going like a train—but she packed it all in for me. That's why I'm pleased she's doing so well now—least of all, it makes me feel less guilty for holding her up. But she wouldn't have it any other way."

Rachel smiles as a swirling pool of nausea works its way up from her stomach.

"Just look at all these people," says Maria, waving her arm around. "They've known Alison since she was a little girl—they've been with her through thick and thin and I bet you everything I have that they would all tell you that she is one of the most loyal people they know."

Rachel would bet even more that Paige, who looks like she's sucking a lemon while staring intently at Chrissy's phone, isn't one of them.

"She might not always go about it the right way," Maria goes on. "But it's always well-intended and with your best interests at heart."

Rachel almost laughs out loud at Maria's skewed perception of the woman who's doing her utmost to destroy her life. And as she makes her excuses to leave the conversation, she wonders if the protective matriarch in front of her might be just as much of a fantasist as her daughter. *Perhaps that's where Ali gets it from?*

23

"Are we having a good time?" asks the DJ over the speaker, just as Rachel reaches Jack and Noah at the bar.

No! screams a voice in her head as she orders a gin and tonic.

"Yes!" yell the revellers on the dance floor, throwing their hands in the air to prove the point.

"Okay," says the DJ. "Al-eee, where are you?"

He turns the music down, until just the faintest beat can be heard among the low hum of muted conversation.

"Ali?" Will calls out across the dance floor. He stands on tiptoes to see over the heads of the revellers who are still trying to move to the music, even though it can barely be heard. He shrugs his shoulders at the DJ.

Heads turn expectantly as the bathroom door opens, only for a palpable sense of disappointment to descend when Ali's grandmother comes out.

"I think I saw her go outside," offers Chrissy.

"Where's Paige?" asks Rachel quietly, noticing that she's no longer with Chrissy.

Noah shrugs his shoulders and Jack pulls an impassive expression, both seemingly oblivious to the relevance of Ali and Paige both being missing at the same time.

"Where the *hell* is Paige?" Rachel hisses.

As if they cotton on at precisely the same moment, they both turn to look at her with their mouths open.

"Shit!" says Jack, slamming his glass down on the bar. He goes to move toward the door to the terrace, but Rachel takes hold of his arm.

"Don't," she says, under her breath.

He shrugs her free and rushes to follow Will outside.

"Ali?" Will calls out into the darkness.

"Paige!" shouts Jack, his voice so taut with tension that Will turns to look at him, puzzled.

"Are they together?" he asks.

"I don't know," says Jack, rubbing the back of his neck.

Rachel shivers as the waves crash against the bottom of the wooden terrace they're standing on. There's no way either of them would have gone down onto the beach, as the tide has come in so far that it no longer exists.

She looks up to where a wide ledge nestles under an overhang of the cliff, and can just make out two figures standing on the craggy outcrop. In this light, it's impossible to know if they're moving toward her or away, or even if it's Ali and Paige at all, but who else is it likely to be?

She nudges Jack and nods in their direction, careful to keep the rising panic that he must surely feel too under wraps. If Will catches on that the pair of them are at loggerheads, he's going to want to know why, and despite everything, Rachel desperately wants to spare him that heartache—at least for today.

"Paige!" Jack calls out, displaying no such conscience, as he trips over himself to get to them.

"Is that Ali with her?" asks Will, his high-pitched voice showing the first sign of concern and confusion.

The silhouettes seem to move closer toward one another, as the gap of muted light between them is snuffed out. Rachel shudders as she imagines Paige's barely contained fury at being dragged into this sorry state of affairs. She was used to clearing up other people's messes, not being embroiled in her own. But as much as Rachel would like to pretend that this is all about Paige taking Ali to task over her behavior and the wicked lie she'd spouted, she's not naive enough to believe that Ali won't retaliate with the ace that is up her sleeve. Perhaps that's why she didn't tell Paige on the beach earlier today—because she knew she'd need to save it for this precise moment.

A scream echoes across the cliffs and Rachel holds her breath, picturing Paige, so incandescent with rage that she can't stop herself from lashing out. She imagines Ali falling and turning through the air. Over and over she goes before disappearing into the icy sea below.

Rachel covers her ears, knowing that if anything happens to Ali, it's going to be *all* her fault.

"Paige!" shouts Jack, sounding as if he's being strangled.

As he rushes toward them, his legs look like they're wading through syrup while the upper half of his body falls over them in its effort to get there. Just as he's about to reach the shadows standing on the cliff edge, he seems to run out of steam, as if he's suddenly aware of what it might look like if somebody were to put two and two together. For starters, they might question why he's left his wife's side to run to another woman's aid. But the debate that's raging in Rachel's own head is, which one of them is he trying to rescue?

She watches as the three of them stand there and wonders if this is the moment that her life implodes. She imagines Jack and Paige looking at each other, openmouthed in shock, as Ali reveals what she saw and heard last night. Her heart beats double time, waiting for Jack to howl into the darkness like an animal who's just had its newborn snatched by a predator. Even if Josh *is* his, she'll *never* be able to make this right. She's suddenly aware that despite everything that Ali has done, *nothing* compares to the consequences of what one night, twenty years ago, could bring to bear.

Her brain wants to run to them, but her body won't let her; too scared of what she will be met with when she gets there. She looks at the fifty or so meters between them and wonders how so little distance can stand between her and her future. Would it make a difference if she were to offer her heartfelt apologies? Would it save her marriage? Her friendship with Paige if she were able to defend her actions? If she explained why she honestly thought that burying the remote possibility was the best thing to do—for *all* of them.

A hand slides into hers and she turns to see Noah standing beside her, his vexed expression matching her own.

Despite knowing she should pull her hand away, she leaves it there for a moment, because she needs to. It reminds her that there is one person who might still be standing beside her when this is all over. She can't help but wonder if he might ultimately be the most important.

Suddenly, Paige emerges from the darkness, her face like thunder, as she strides toward them purposefully, with Jack trailing behind her. Rachel drops Noah's hand as if she's been given an electric shock and goes toward her.

"*Bitch*," snaps Paige, when their two paths collide.

An icy hand reaches into Rachel's chest and wraps itself around her heart, squeezing until she can no longer feel it pumping. She goes to defend herself, but her mouth has dried up and she doesn't know where she'd even begin.

"You need to get out of my way," Paige says to Noah, who is blocking her in a misguided attempt at placating her.

Rachel looks at him wide-eyed as they both silently acknowledge the deluge they're trying to hold back.

"I mean it . . ." says Paige, locking eyes with him.

"Paige . . ." starts Rachel.

Paige spins around to face her, with flared nostrils. "*What?*" she yells.

"I'm sorry," starts Rachel, terrified by this version of her best friend, one she hasn't seen before. But then she doesn't know what else she should have expected. "I can't begin to understand how you must be feeling . . ."

"You have no fucking idea," says Paige.

Rachel wants to shrink into herself, away from the toxic atmosphere of everyone having held a secret in for so long that it now feels like they're all about to spontaneously combust.

"I just . . ." says Rachel, not knowing where to even start. "I just want you to know . . ."

Paige shakes her head, as if in an effort to clear the poisonous thoughts that are trapped there. "I'm sorry," she says, sighing deeply. "I shouldn't be taking it out on you."

"Wh . . . what?" asks Rachel, numbly, as her knees threaten to buckle with relief. She holds onto the door to the restaurant for support, not wanting to count her chickens before they've hatched. "What happened?"

Paige takes a deep breath in and out. "She really is quite something," she says. "I don't think I've ever met someone so divisive in all my life."

"What did she say?" Rachel asks, before tensing her shoulders up in the hope that they might reach her ears and render her deaf to the answer.

"I won't let her get away with the lies she's peddling," she says, shaking her head. "She's going to pay."

"I can understand you being angry," says Rachel. "But this isn't the way to deal with it."

"You honestly expect me to let that liar get away with it?" asks Paige, exasperated.

"No," says Rachel, daring to believe that Ali's not told her about Noah and Josh. "No, of course not, but there is a time and a place. And here and now isn't it."

Paige suddenly grabs hold of Rachel's arms and turns her to face her. "You know that Jack and I aren't . . ." It's as if she can't bring herself to say it. "You do know that, don't you?"

"Of course," says Rachel, her voice high-pitched.

"Are you okay?" asks Jack, coming up to them. It's only when Rachel turns to look at him that she realizes he's talking to Paige.

Rachel stands there, between her husband and her best friend, yet feels like she's a million miles from anyone. Jack's fraught with an unnerving panic. Paige is as incensed as Rachel's ever seen her. Both of them are seemingly oblivious to the fact that even while she's trying to comfort them, it's *her* world that's falling apart at the seams.

Guests are beginning to bristle, as if they know something's amiss, but are not quite sure what. It would help enormously if the DJ put a record on to distract everyone's attention from what may or may not be going on outside. But in the absence of music, they're craning their necks to get a better view.

There's no escaping the fact that Will is clearly comforting Ali, as he wipes her tears and looks at her earnestly. Eventually, after taking a few deep breaths, she comes back into the restaurant to a round of applause.

"Ah," says the DJ. "Here she is."

Will accompanies her to the middle of the dance floor, keeping her close to him. Rachel knows him well enough to see that he's concerned about what's just gone on, but Ali's attempting to make light of it by forcing a smile.

"So, here we have it," says the DJ, in broken English, blissfully unaware of the edginess that's crept into the proceedings. "A surprise for you, Ali."

The big TV behind him comes to life and David Friedman is on the screen, sitting in a monochrome-designed room, wearing his trademark jeans and white T-shirt.

"Ali," he says into the camera, as everyone gasps and turns to look at her. It seems that Rachel isn't the only one who thought the David Friedman story was just another far-fetched fantasy that Ali had concocted as truth. She can't help but wish that it was.

David flashes a megawatt smile. "I just wanted to send you a message to say that I'm so sorry I couldn't be there. I know you'll have a fantastic time and I wish you and Will many congratulations as you embark on this new and exciting chapter of your lives. Will, you're a lucky devil and you better treat her right, otherwise you'll have me to answer to."

Will smiles and pulls Ali in even closer.

"You think you're coming back to work next week," David goes on. "But as much as I need you here, I'm going to have to muddle through without you, because you're going to Barbados!"

Ali cups her hands to her mouth in shock. "What?" she says, looking at Will with tears in her eyes.

Will nods. "We're staying at his place for a week," he says, as everyone cheers and claps.

"Oh my God," says Ali, disbelievingly.

Rachel's stomach turns over as reality hits home. The knowledge that Ali had told the truth about knowing David, even playing *down* how closely she clearly works with him, goes against every natural instinct in her body. This isn't supposed to happen. This isn't who Ali is. She's a liar and a fantasist—who tells untruths as easily as reciting the alphabet.

Despite the oppressive heat in the restaurant, Rachel's blood feels icy cold, her fingers and toes numb. She wiggles them just to check that they're still functioning, so disconnected does she feel to her body. Her brain wants to fast-track forward, desperate to join up the dots, but she refuses to allow it because she doesn't want to see the picture it will draw.

"Wow, how cool is that?" coos Chrissy beside her.

Rachel smiles tightly as she looks around for Jack. She's not surprised to see him at the bar, in an animated discussion with Paige. As she walks toward them, her legs not feeling like her own, she wonders if their conversation will change between now and when she's standing there beside them. By rights it shouldn't, but Paige abruptly stops talking when she approaches.

"Jack, can I talk to you for a second?" Rachel asks.

"Yes," he says, without moving.

Rachel looks from him to Paige. She doesn't suppose there's anything she can't say in front of her, especially now that she's so deeply immersed in whatever the hell is going on.

"I know where Ali was for those lost two years," she says, desperately trying to keep her voice from wavering. "The period she assigned to a fictitious company on her résumé."

Paige tuts. "She just can't help herself, can she?"

Jack raises his eyebrows, silently asking her to elaborate.

"She was caring for her mother," says Rachel. "After her accident."

Jack looks like it doesn't make any difference to him, but to Rachel, it's a whole world's worth.

"Do you think it matters?" he asks, bluntly.

"Yes and no," says Rachel, failing to understand why Jack's being so belligerent, with *her* of all people.

"She lied in order to get a job, and that, in my book, is enough."

"But you can understand why she felt the need to do it," says Rachel.

"All she had to do was be honest," says Jack.

"But you would never have employed her if she had been," says Rachel. "You've admitted to me that you've avoided taking on women of a certain age, or those you suspect will be looking to have a baby in a couple of years. If you knew, for just a second, that Ali had a responsibility to care for her mum, you wouldn't have given her the time of day."

"Why are you even trying to stick up for her, when she's done what she's done?" asks Paige.

"I'm not sticking up for her," says Rachel. "I'm just trying to understand what's happening here."

"I'll tell you what's happening," says Jack. "That bitch over there has been harassing me for nigh on three years, and when she gets called out on it, she claims that I'm having an affair with my wife's best friend."

"Is that how long it's been going on?" asks Rachel, looking from Jack to Paige.

"What?" says Jack irritably.

"The supposed affair between you." She leaves it hanging there, not knowing what she wants either of them to do with the insinuation.

"We are *not* having an affair," barks Jack, looking at Paige.

"I wasn't talking about you two," says Rachel. "I'm referring to the affair that you say Ali is claiming to have had with you."

Jack coughs and takes a swig of his drink. "That's when she started hassling me, yes."

"So, *before* she'd met Will?" asks Rachel, double-checking the facts.

Jack thinks about it before nodding. "Yes, but I don't see why you're obsessing over the semantics because whichever way you look at it, you're dealing with a pathological liar—pure and simple."

Rachel shakes her head. "Yet the selfless act of looking after her mother only makes her a better person."

Jack and Paige look at her, their expressions etched with confusion.

"And the lie we *thought* she told about David Friedman appears to be true," Rachel goes on.

"What's your point?" asks Jack.

"My *point*," says Rachel, battling to keep her frustrations under control. "Is that it's already been proven that she's not quite the liar we had her down for."

Jack laughs disbelievingly.

"So, I'm left wondering what else she's said that might not be fabricated."

Jack looks from her to Paige, like a rabbit caught in headlights.

"Hi, excuse me," comes a voice from behind Rachel.

She swings around to find Kimberley standing there, Ali's cousin who she sat with at dinner the night before.

"Oh, hi," she says, trying to curb her irritation at the untimely interruption.

"I'm really sorry to bother you," Kimberley goes on, "but I just wondered if everything was all right." She's speaking to Paige more than Rachel.

"This is Ali's cousin, Kimberley," offers Rachel.

"Hello," says Kimberley unnecessarily. "I'm sorry, I don't mean to be poking my nose in, but when I saw Ali out there with you a little while ago, she seemed to be upset."

Paige's jaw tightens.

"Is she okay? Has something happened?"

"She's fine," says Paige haughtily. "A few too many drinks have got her a little over-emotional, that's all."

"Oh," says Kimberley, smiling, visibly relieved. "That's hardly surprising—it's a big occasion."

"It's certainly that," agrees Paige, taking a cigarette and lighter out of her clutch that's on the bar. "Can someone keep an eye on my bag? I'm going outside."

"I'll join you," says Jack hurriedly, as if worried he'll be left alone with Kimberley.

"I didn't mean to interfere," Kimberley says, fretting that she's caused offense.

"You didn't," offers Rachel, as she pulls Paige's bag toward her. "I'm glad I've got the chance to speak to you, actually."

"Oh?"

"Can I be open and honest with you?" asks Rachel.

Kimberley's brow furrows in anticipation of what she might be about to say. "Of course," she says.

"Have you ever . . . ?" Rachel starts, before asking herself if this is really the right thing to do.

Kimberley looks at her wide-eyed, waiting for her to go on.

But Rachel knows she shouldn't, because it will be crossing a line that she would never normally cross. Yet if those perimeters hadn't already been infiltrated, she wouldn't be *in* this position.

"You're family," says Rachel, with a smile to soften what she's about to ask. "So you've known Ali for a long time, and you know her well."

Kimberley nods. "We've grown up together."

"So, have you ever felt that she . . . ?" Rachel racks her brain for the best way to put it. "That she embellishes the truth a little?"

Rachel wants to close her eyes because she's afraid that Kimberley's horrified expression will confirm that it's just *her* world that she's messing with. And right now, it would be a great source of comfort to know that she fucks with everyone's.

But shockingly, and rather unexpectedly, Kimberley throws her head back and laughs. "She's the biggest exaggerator I know," she says. "But that's what makes her so fun and exciting to be around."

This isn't going as well as Rachel hoped. She's going to have to spell it out to her. "Last night, at the restaurant, I heard her tell you that she wasn't ready to have children."

At this, Rachel notices, Kimberley balks, showing the first sign that she may have hit some common ground.

"But just the night before, she was telling Will that she couldn't wait to start a family with him and that she wanted to start trying immediately."

Kimberley pulls herself up, as if doing so will better equip her to deal with the mud that Rachel's slinging.

"It's a pretty big deal," Rachel pushes on. "She's either desperate for them or she isn't, but to lie to Will about something so important on the eve of their wedding is callous and cruel."

Kimberley nods her head as if she's in full agreement. "I understand your concern," she says. "But I really don't think you should be too worried about what she said to Will."

Rachel looks at her, taken aback. "But if she's lied to him—"

"She hasn't lied to him," says Kimberley, cutting her off.

"But how do you know?"

"Because she lied to *me*," says Kimberley. "And I don't blame her."

Rachel can't get her head around what Kimberley's saying, or why she's so accepting of the fact. How is Ali always seemingly forgiven, no matter *what* she does?

"I'm sorry," says Rachel. "I don't understand."

Kimberley wipes a tear away. "Oh goodness, I'm sorry," she says, as if embarrassed.

Rachel can't help but put an arm around the woman's shoulders. "I really didn't mean to upset you."

"It's not you," says Kimberley. "It's just the situation. I just feel so sad that she felt the need to lie. It's my fault. I made her do it."

"What do you mean?" asks Rachel. "How can her lying to you be your fault?"

Kimberley takes a deep breath. "I lost my baby six months ago."

"Oh my God," gasps Rachel.

"I was almost full-term, but for reasons we'll probably never know, it wasn't to be."

"I'm so sorry," says Rachel, feeling gut-wrenchingly horrified that she's making this woman, who she barely knows, recall the most unimaginable pain possible.

"Ali was with me when it happened, and she stayed by my side until my husband was able to get home from where he was stationed abroad."

Rachel can feel a tightening at the back of her throat, but she doesn't know whether it's in response to what Kimberley's been through or the realization that Ali might have had a reason for lying.

"She's been truly incredible ever since, making me laugh with her escapades and crying with me when I needed her to. I've been a limpet on her resources, selfishly draining her boundless optimism, when she should have been looking forward to *this*." She looks around. "Of course she wants children—she's *always* wanted them—I've just made it very hard for her to admit that lately."

A panic is beginning to engulf Rachel, a vise-like grip that is snaking its way around her chest, making it difficult to breathe. "So . . ." she manages. "She lied to *protect* you?"

Kimberley nods. "Yes, but that doesn't make her a bad person."

No, it doesn't, thinks Rachel as she numbly walks away. In fact, it makes her an even better person than most.

She looks out onto the terrace and sees Jack and Paige together, as if through new eyes. Jack's face is intense as he looks at her, dragging hard on a cigarette, before tilting his head up skywards to exhale a perfectly straight line of smoke into the night sky.

Paige is more pensive, surprisingly unconfident in her own skin, taking small furtive puffs and expelling them quickly. They look like a couple with a big problem. Rachel can't help but wonder if it's her.

"What the hell's going on?" asks Noah, coming up beside her. They both silently look out at Jack and Paige for a moment.

Rachel turns to look at him. "I don't think she's told them," she says, unable to believe Ali might have kept her mouth shut.

"She definitely hasn't," says Noah. "Because Paige has just apologized and told me she loves me."

Rachel doesn't know which of those anomalies leaves the bitterest taste. She pulls herself up, surprised by her own feelings.

"Apologized for *what*?" she asks.

"I don't know yet," says Noah. "That's all she said when she came back in." Rachel raises her eyebrows, and Noah smiles. "I know, it unnerved me too!"

"Seriously," she scolds. "You don't think there's anything in this, do you?"

"What, between Jack and Paige?"

Rachel nods.

"Why would you even think that?" he asks, as if it's the most preposterous suggestion he's ever heard.

She looks at him as if to say, *"They'd probably say the same about us."*

"The impression I get is that Ali lies about everything," says Noah. "So, no, I don't think there's anything going on. Though, why she'd feel the need to say there *is*, I don't know."

Rachel bites on her lip, wondering how she could even think to ask the question, but for some reason she can't let it go. "How has Paige been?"

Noah looks at her over his glass of wine, as if he can't quite believe she's asking it either. "In what way?"

"Has she been her normal self?" asks Rachel. "Or has she seemed . . . I don't know, off?"

"Are you asking me if I think my wife is having an affair with your husband?"

"I'm asking you if anything has been amiss recently."

Noah shrugs his shoulders. "She's had a lot of work, but that's nothing new."

Rachel nods. "Late nights?"

"Yes, but like I say, that's nothing new."

Rachel thinks back to all the late-night shifts Jack's been putting in at work recently; the dinners that have had to be put back in the oven; the plans that have had to be canceled; the nights where the Christian Louboutins have gone back in their box because she was tired of waiting.

"Jack had to stay in town the Wednesday before last," she says, as if to herself.

Noah's face suddenly changes, as if the enormity of such a possibility is dawning on him for the first time.

"It's nothing," she says, shaking herself down, unable to believe she's allowed her mind to go there. "It's nothing."

"I think you're barking up the wrong tree," says Noah gently. "Though that's not to say that I would put it past Jack . . ."

"To have an affair?" she asks.

Noah's silence speaks volumes.

"So, you're saying you think he is?" she asks.

"I just wouldn't be surprised" is all he says, but it feels like he's forcing himself to stop there in case he divulges something he shouldn't.

"If you know something . . ."

"Come on, Rach," he groans. "You're putting me in an impossible position."

"You're supposed to be *my* friend," she says.

He tilts his head to the side, as if offended by her questioning his loyalty. "You know better than to ask which side of the fence I'm on."

"Do I?" she asks, knowing she's playing devil's advocate. "Because from where I'm standing, it's not looking too clear cut."

Noah smiles wryly. "Don't make this about you and me. You know my stance on this. You know how I feel about Jack."

Rachel looks at him, taken aback. She has *no* idea how he feels about Jack, because they've never discussed it. "Wouldn't this be a good time to tell me?" she asks.

He looks down at his feet, as if weighing the pros and cons of divulging what he's clearly been keeping hidden. Rachel wonders if it's based on just the last few days, or whether he's got years of disclosures to make.

Noah confirms it's the latter when he says, "I've never thought he was good enough for you."

Rachel laughs tightly at the sweeping statement. "Is that Jack specifically, or would that judgment befall any man I happened to fall in love with?"

"I've only ever wanted you to be happy," he says.

"And until I came here, I was!" she says, her voice high-pitched.

"Exactly," says Noah. "That's why I've always kept my opinion to myself because you would only have held it against me."

"Jack's treated me well," she says.

"Until he didn't," he says, finishing the sentence for her.

Rachel feels the sting of tears in her eyes as she looks at him. Good, dependable Noah, who always gives it to her straight. Except now, just for once, she wants him to sugar-coat it and lie, because that feels like the only way she's going to get through this.

"Do you think he knows what we did?" Rachel says, feeling like she can't breathe.

"*What we did?*" repeats Noah. "You say it with such disdain, as if it was the worst thing you've ever done."

"It was!" she snaps, as a tear falls onto her cheek. "I've never regretted anything as much as I regret that."

The shock on Noah's face makes her feel sick, as if she's been punched in the stomach. The hurt in his eyes is decades old, and since the beginning of time, when *he's* hurt, *she's* hurt. To know she's caused his pain breaks her. She wants to take it back, to tell him the truth: that that night was incredible, that he'd made her feel the most special she'd ever felt, that it was everything she had imagined it would be. But that would only fan the fire that's burning precariously close to their fingertips—the ones that are clinging onto a perilous ledge, desperately trying to hold on.

"Well, just for the record," says Noah quietly. "The only regret *I* have is that I couldn't persuade you to come away with me."

"Just because you didn't get what you wanted doesn't give you the right to question Jack's loyalty. *I* made the decision to stay."

"Because of him," says Noah bitterly.

"I *loved* him," she says, though even before the words are out, she knows it was a close-run race.

And now, as she watches Paige's Tiffany heart bracelet slip down as she stubs out her cigarette, she's wondering if she backed the wrong horse.

24

"Ali," says Rachel quietly, almost hoping she doesn't hear her.

"Hey, sister-in-law," says Will drunkenly, noticing her between them and pulling her under his arm to join in a rendition of "New York, New York."

"Hey," she says, forcing herself to sound upbeat. "Are you having a good time?"

"How can I not be?" he says, looking lovingly at Ali, who is discreetly inching away from Rachel. "Look at my gorgeous bride!"

Rachel smiles. "She looks beautiful, doesn't she?"

"She sure does," Will slurs.

"And that necklace is gorgeous," says Rachel. "Was that a gift from you?"

Will smiles broadly. "Yep, I left it under her pillow for her to find this morning."

Rachel's heart sinks, at the realization that Ali being Jack's mistress was the better option. Because, as bizarre as it seems, that's preferable, given the alternative.

"Could I have a word?" she says to Ali, who is still actively trying to put as much space between them as she can.

Ali looks at her apprehensively.

"Please," begs Rachel.

Ali gives an almost imperceptible nod and leans up to kiss Will. "I'm just popping outside for a minute," she says.

He stops dancing and seems to sober up in an instant. "Is everything all right?"

Ali nods and smiles, but he still looks to Rachel as if needing extra assurance.

"Yes, I just need to borrow her for a couple of minutes," says Rachel.

"Okay," he says, turning around to link arms with his friends who are all kicking their legs in time with the music.

Rachel leads the way out of the restaurant, turning right so as not to end up joining Jack and Paige on the terrace. She finds herself at the back of the kitchen and anxiously fiddles with her wedding ring for the few seconds it takes for Ali to join her.

"I'm not going to stand here and get abused" is the first thing she says as she comes around the corner.

Rachel holds her hands up, as if in surrender. "I know, and I'm not intending to. I just want to ask you a few questions."

Ali looks around warily, as if checking her escape route if she needs one.

"Have you ever slept with Jack?" asks Rachel.

"*No!*" says Ali, as if appalled by the mere suggestion.

"But you think he's sleeping with Paige?"

"I *know* he's sleeping with Paige."

Rachel swallows the taste that's souring her tongue. "How . . . ?" she starts, before clearing her throat. "How can you be so sure?"

"Because I've seen them together, more than once," says Ali, looking at her feet. "The first time was when I was working with him."

Rachel clamps a hand to her mouth. "It's been going on for *that* long?"

Ali nods. "I don't know *how* long exactly, but I first saw them over eighteen months ago."

"Where?"

"I just happened to be behind him as I walked home one evening and he met her outside the Ham Yard Hotel."

Rachel tsks, hoping that Ali's put two and two together and come up with five. "That doesn't necessarily mean . . ."

"He kissed her," says Ali quietly. "In a way that you don't kiss your wife's best friend."

Hot bile bites at the back of Rachel's throat as she pictures it, the image so alien that their faces melt as soon as their lips touch.

"Why haven't you told me before now?" asks Rachel. "I thought we were friends."

"We are," says Ali. "But you and Paige are a lot closer and I had no idea how you would take it from me. I didn't want it to ruin what we had, especially once I knew I was going to be part of the family." She looks to Rachel for some semblance of understanding, but Rachel is too shaken to give it.

"It had to come from *him*," says Ali, spitting the last word out. "But no matter what I did to make him do the right thing, he refused."

Rachel looks at her, too stunned to speak.

"So I gave him an ultimatum that he had until the wedding to end it with her, or I'd tell you, because I couldn't bear the thought of all six of us being together, for what should have been a happy occasion, knowing what was going on between them."

"So that's what all the furtiveness has been about?" asks Rachel, dumbfounded.

Ali nods. "I gave him one final warning at the airport on our way out," she says.

"When you lost your passport?" asks Rachel, the pieces slowly falling into place.

"I hadn't, but I thought it was the only chance I was going to get him on his own."

Rachel remembers Jack striding back into the terminal with a face like thunder.

"I told him that if I felt, for just one second, there was still something going on, I'd tell you when we got back."

"And?" asks Rachel, ashamed that she doesn't know the answer herself.

"I'm so sorry . . ." starts Ali, as Rachel's heart cracks.

"Please, no," Rachel begs, as if doing so means Ali will change the narrative.

Ali grimaces, clearly wishing she weren't the one delivering the devastating blow. "I'm so sorry, but they were together last night."

Rachel crumples, falling into the wall for support. "They couldn't have been," she cries. "You're wrong."

"I wish I was," says Ali. "After Will left for the hotel, it was just the three of us left. I was never going to leave the two of them on their own, but I was so tired and neither of them were going to give in. So I went to my room and waited for a while, hoping that when I went back up, they'd have gone to bed. They weren't in the living room where I'd left them, and for a moment I thought that whatever they had was over. That they'd taken my threat seriously and put an end to it."

The weight on Rachel's chest starts to lift, just a little, as she allows the possibility that none of this is as it seems.

"But I could smell smoke," Ali goes on. "And I followed it up to the roof terrace."

"Roof terrace?" questions Rachel, desperate to find a flaw in her story.

"Yes, there's a jacuzzi on top of the villa," says Ali. "I only found the stairs by accident, not knowing where they led, but they were up there."

Rachel wants to ask what they were doing, but Ali's face says it all.

"I tried to go back to sleep, knowing that I had no choice but to tell you when we got home, but I couldn't bear the thought of you finding them there, doing what they were doing."

Something lodges in Rachel's chest, making her feel as if she can't breathe.

"So I got back up again to confront them, but they'd already gone." Ali looks repulsed. "And all that was left to show for their indiscretion was Jack's watch."

Rachel shakes her head wryly. So *that's* where she'd gotten it from.

"You were in our room yesterday," says Rachel, keen to hear what Ali's excuse for that is. "When we came back from shopping."

Ali nods sheepishly. "I told him he was skating on thin ice."

Rachel looks at her inquisitively.

"The previous evening when we were all sitting around the fire talking, he and Paige were texting each other."

The blatant deceit winds Rachel. "While we were all *together*?" she says. "Right in front of me?"

Ali nods. "You wouldn't have noticed, but knowing what was going on between them, I could see it a mile off."

"They could have been messaging anyone," reasons Rachel.

Ali shakes her head. "When I asked Paige what she'd done that she wasn't particularly proud of, she typed a message on her phone. Jack's screen lit up and he smiled as he read it."

Rachel dreads to think what it might have said. "That could be pure coincidence," she says.

"When I pushed you to share what you and Jack were getting up to in the bedroom, Paige told you to keep it to yourself."

Had she?

"And she refused to look at him or talk to him for the rest of the night," adds Ali. "As if she was surprised that you had such an active sex life."

"Did she know you were on to them?" asks Rachel.

"Well, I assumed that Jack would have told her, but she seemed shocked when I confronted her on the beach this morning."

"*That's* what you were talking about?"

Ali nods with a confused expression. "She *told* you I'd spoken to her?"

"She said that she was warning you off Jack," says Rachel.

Ali shakes her head. "I wanted to give her the same chance that I'd given Jack: to end it or I'd tell you. But she just laughed and turned everything around on me. Telling me that I'd gotten it all wrong. That the only reason I was making something out of nothing was because I wanted Jack for myself. It seems that, like you, she presumed that something might be going on between us."

For a split second, Rachel is comforted by the loyalty Paige had shown in her attempt to save her and Jack's marriage, but then she is hit by the harsh reality of it not being *her* relationship with Jack that Paige had been trying to protect.

"What were you doing there? On the beach."

"I knew she was going to meet him," says Ali. "Do you remember how they mentioned going for a run, so casually, over lunch yesterday?"

Rachel frowns. "And you jumped straight on it and said you'd go too."

"To try and stop them from having time alone," says Ali animatedly. "I knew what they were up to and I just couldn't stand by and let it happen."

Rachel thinks about how Jack had manipulated her into not bringing her trainers, how Paige had nonchalantly asked if he'd already left, and her body language as Ali had spoken to her on the beach.

"I followed Jack down to the beach and knew she'd be close behind, and sure enough, twenty minutes later, they met."

"But maybe they just happened to bump into each other," says Rachel, clutching at straws.

"Have you not heard anything I've been saying?" asks Ali, not unkindly. "They'd *arranged* it like that. They kissed when they met and held hands as they walked."

"But Paige said you and Jack were together on the beach."

Ali laughs wryly. "She would, wouldn't she?"

"So where did Jack go?" asks Rachel.

"Well, as per usual, he scooted off, like the spineless wonder he is," says Ali bitterly.

"And he hadn't told Paige you were on to them?"

Ali shakes her head. "No, I don't think so, otherwise she would have been better prepared. It was only when we were out there"—she tilts her head in the direction of the cliffs—"that she seemed to realize that I would follow through on my threat to tell you."

"Which is probably why she reacted the way she did," says Rachel.

Ali nods and a tear escapes onto her cheek. She raises a shaking hand to wipe it away.

"I thought she was going to throw me off the edge. She had me by the shoulders and went to push me." Her shoulders cave in and her chest convulses as she sobs. "I'm sorry," she cries. "It's really shaken me up."

Rachel refrains from going to her, a part of her still not convinced that she's telling the truth. Yet how can she *not* be?

Tears spring to Rachel's eyes as she realizes that all the time she thought Paige was looking out for her, feigning concern that something was going on between Ali and Jack, she was only ever protecting her own interests. She clenches and unclenches her hands, desperate to feel something in her numb stupor.

"Does Will know . . . ?" she whispers. "Does he know what's going on?"

Ali shakes her head. "I haven't told him because I was hoping that Jack would come to his senses. I thought if Paige was out of the picture, we could go back to how the four of us used to be and I didn't want Will to lose respect for his brother. Though, I'm beginning to regret that now because if I'd been honest from the outset, he wouldn't have insisted she come to the wedding, and we wouldn't find ourselves in this situation."

Rachel looks at her through blurry eyes.

"What are you going to do?" asks Ali.

Rachel sniffs and wipes her nose with the back of her hand. "First, apologize," she says. "I've thought the very worst of you, only to find out that you're probably one of the kindest, most considerate people I know."

Ali looks at her suspiciously, waiting for the killer blow that's sure to follow.

"I'll deal with Jack and Paige in my own way," Rachel goes on. "But I just want to ask you one more thing."

"Sure," says Ali, quietly.

"That thing with Noah," says Rachel, not knowing how best to broach it. "Whatever you may have seen or heard last night wasn't what it looked like."

"Noah's a lovely man," says Ali.

"Yes, he is," says Rachel. "We go back a long way."

Ali nods her head knowingly. "You must have made quite a pair."

Rachel doesn't like her intonation. Among everything else that's going on, she could really do with knowing that whatever Ali *thinks* might be going on between her and Noah is nothing more than it is.

"We're good friends," says Rachel.

"You know he's still in love with you, don't you?"

Rachel looks around, panicked, as if *that's* the line in this whole conversation she doesn't want anyone to overhear.

"I . . ." she starts. "I don't know what you mean."

"It's not a crime to have had other relationships before getting married," says Ali. "But it is a crime not to follow your heart."

"It's not like that," says Rachel.

"I think you'll find it is for Noah," says Ali.

Rachel feels fresh tears spring to her eyes.

"And I don't doubt that you feel the same," Ali goes on.

Rachel pulls herself up, waiting for the autopilot she's trained so well to kick in. She'd come to rely on it over the years, to protect her from the feeling she got whenever she'd see Noah and Paige together. In the beginning, it was like a red-hot poker being driven into her chest; a pain so intense that she didn't think she could be part of his life anymore. But the thought of never seeing him again was too much to bear, and so she had learned to build an invisible barrier around herself, that had, until now, kept her true feelings at bay.

"It's not like that," she says again, though with little conviction.

"You've not done anything wrong," says Ali.

Rachel's eyes fill with tears. "I have," she says, wiping them away as they fall onto her cheeks.

"Do you *know* for sure that Josh isn't Noah's son?" asks Ali, looking at her intently.

The weight of the question bears down on her, pinning her to the wall. So she *had* heard it all.

"No. I don't know—he might be—but I don't think so. I just . . ." She falls to the ground with her head in her hands.

"Ssh," says Ali, coming to kneel beside her. "You did what you thought was right. I'd have done the same, and if anyone tells you any different, they're lying."

"Ali?" calls out a voice that sounds like her mum. "Are you out here?"

"Coming!" Ali shouts back. "Will you be okay?" she adds sincerely.

Rachel nods as she pulls herself up and brushes her dress down. "I'll be fine." She sniffs, wiping under her eyes. "Thank you for everything that you've tried to do for me, even when I couldn't have been easy to help."

"I'm just sorry I couldn't do what I set out to do," says Ali, pulling her in for a hug. "But I'm always here if you want to talk."

"Ali, come on," shouts her mum. "The fireworks are about to start."

"Go on," says Rachel, forcing a smile. "Go and enjoy yourself. It's your wedding day."

"Are you sure?" asks Ali, reluctant to leave her.

"Yes," says Rachel. "Go and start your new life, because this part's over."

They squeeze each other's hands, and Ali's gone.

25

Everyone is out on the terrace by the time Rachel feels strong enough to emerge from her hiding place. She's surprised to see that, while her entire life has crashed down around her ears, everyone else is still going about theirs, without a care in the world.

The wind is whipping up again, and hearing the sound of the Atlantic waves crashing against the underside of the structure they're standing on makes Rachel shiver. She can no longer see the caves further along the cove, lost to the dark and the rising tide that is steadily climbing the cliff face.

She glances around for Jack, but doesn't want to see him, because she doesn't know how to look at him anymore. If she sees Paige, there's no way she can disguise what she now knows and the thought of having to go back to the same house, and then travel home tomorrow on the same plane, fills her with a dread so unsurmountable that she can't even begin to comprehend it. It's almost as if something even bigger than what she's dealing with needs to put itself between the now and then, because without it, she can't see a way through.

"Oh my God," cries Ali. "But how . . . ?"

"It's okay," says her mum, pulling her in tight. "It's going to be okay."

Rachel looks on with a sense of dismay. It must be her grandmother, who was too unwell to travel. Her heart breaks along with Ali's.

"But how could that happen?" asks Ali.

"I don't know," says Maria, as the pair of them look fervently at a phone. "But it's definitely come from her."

Rachel can see the rising panic behind Ali's flickering eyes as she looks around.

"Chrissy!" she calls out, having to shout above the sound of the sea and bass of the music that's still playing inside. "Chrissy!"

"Is everything okay?" asks Rachel, going over to her, feeling compelled to offer help in any way she can. Though, she can't dispel the growing sensation that this might have something to do with her. It seems that *everything* has something to do with her.

Ali looks at her, with wide eyes, as if momentarily weighing whether she can be trusted or not. Rachel nods at her, to silently assure her that she can.

"What is it?" she asks gently, putting an arm around her shoulders. She looks to Maria, who has tears in her eyes.

Ali shows Rachel her mother's phone where the photo of her and Chrissy as teenagers is presented in glorious technicolor.

"I don't understand," says Rachel. "What's the problem?"

"Th-that's . . ." starts Ali, before looking to her mum, who nods slowly. "That's me."

"Yeah, I know," says Rachel ambivalently.

Ali's mouth drops open and she physically takes a step backward, holding a hand to her chest. "*How* do you know?"

"Because Chrissy showed me earlier," says Rachel, without thinking. Though, even if she had, she'd have never been able to foresee the problem.

Ali looks at her mum, unable to stop her bottom lip from sticking out. Giant tears teeter on the rims of her eyes, reminding Rachel of a six-year-old Josh, when a bully had stopped him from using the slide in the park.

"How *could* she?" cries Ali.

"Who?" asks Rachel, still none the wiser what the problem is. "What's happened?"

"Look!" says Ali, her voice high-pitched. She swipes down from the photo of her and Chrissy to show one of her today, in her wedding dress, with the text message, "*The two faces of Ali Foley. Who knew?!?*"

Rachel looks at it, confused. "*Chrissy* sent you this?"

"Erm, Ali . . ." says Kimberley hesitantly, as she approaches them with her phone in her hand.

Rachel knows what's coming.

"I'm not sure why, but I've just received this . . ." She shows them the screen with the same message and images.

"Sh-she's sent it to *you* too?" cries Ali, hoarsely. "So, who else . . . ? Who else has she sent it to?" Her arms flail and she spins around with her hands on her head.

"Darling, please," says her mum. "Please try to stay calm."

"How can I?" says Ali. "I've spent all my life trying to leave that time behind and now it's back to haunt me . . . on my wedding day!"

"It was a long time ago," says Maria. "You don't ever have to go back there again."

"Is that why you were bullied?" asks Rachel, unable to understand why kids are so cruel to each other.

Ali nods.

"She's always struggled with her weight," says Maria. "It was only a few years ago, after the accident, that she decided to do something about it."

"But you told me that you never had to worry about what you ate," Rachel says to Ali gently.

"Because I didn't want you to think any differently of me," says Ali.

"But I would never have," offers Rachel.

Maria takes her daughter's hand. "You have to understand that it was a life that she worked hard to get away from. She never had anything to be ashamed of in her appearance, but she couldn't stand how it reminded her of being bullied. She never learned to love herself the way she looked back then, and so she left the physical person that made her so unhappy behind and forged a new identity. She created a persona she could feel proud of and what you see now is that woman. She wears the clothes she wears because she never dreamed she'd be able to, and she speaks her mind because she's not used to anyone listening. She's always felt invisible and now she feels seen."

Rachel looks at the woman in front of her with new eyes. All this time, she'd had Ali down as being vacuous, so full of her own self-importance that she was unable to relate to anyone else. Yet, behind the facade of over-confidence, and under the pretense of having skin as thick as a rhino's, she's fighting to get away from a past that plagues her every waking moment. She can see it now, as the real Ali emerges from the shadow of the caricature she's invented to protect herself.

"You are a good person," she says to her. "Don't ever feel you have to lie or make excuses for the person you are or the person you once were."

Ali shrugs her shoulders pitifully. "But everyone's going to see that picture," she whispers.

"So what?" says Rachel, taking hold of her arms and turning her to face her. "The only people who really matter are here with you right now and they know what you've been through because they've watched you grow up. Anyone else who's got a problem with it can go swivel on this." Rachel sticks her middle finger up and Ali laughs.

Rachel looks at Maria, who's nodding and sobbing into a tissue. From one mother to another, Rachel can see that she'd rather have gone through it herself than have her daughter hurt *so* much, that all these years later, she still feels the effects.

"Will!" Ali calls across the terrace to where he's standing with his back to them.

Rachel can only imagine the turmoil going on inside Ali's head as she reconciles how best to tell her new husband that she's not always looked the way she does today.

He turns around with a concerned expression, as if knowing just by the way his name was called that his new wife is upset.

"Will, have you got my phone?" asks Ali, unable to keep her voice steady.

He comes toward them, rifling in his inside pocket.

"Yeah," he says, handing it over. "Is everything all right?"

Ali unlocks it and her face instantly crumples. "She's sent it to me too. She must have sent it to everyone."

"I'm going to see what she's got to say for herself," says Maria, heading back in the direction of the restaurant.

"Er, what's going on?" asks Will.

Ali looks at Rachel in exactly the same way as Josh did in the park that day, unable to comprehend why someone would be so horrible.

"It's Chrissy . . ." she starts. "She's sent this picture to everyone's phone."

Rachel waits for him to ask who it's of and what it's got to do with Ali. But as he squints at it, all he says is, "Why would she do that?"

"I don't know," cries Ali. "But now everyone will know."

He takes hold of her face with his hands and smiles. "What does it matter *who* knows that you used to look like that?"

Rachel lets out the breath she was holding. He already knows. Of course he does. That's why they're a couple who are going to survive. Because they have no secrets from each other.

"When are you going to get it into your head that being the person you were back then has made you the person you are now?" he asks, smiling. "The way you handled that made you the strong, incredible woman you are today."

It doesn't sound like the first time Will's had to dispense this speech, and Rachel's heart feels as if it might burst.

"Their weakness made you strong," he says in between kissing her. "Their jealousy made you selfless. Their bitterness made you sweet."

Ali's sobs dissolve into whimpers as his wise words sink in.

"Ali!" calls out Chrissy, breathlessly, as she runs toward them. "I don't know how . . . I'm so sorry . . . it doesn't make any sense."

"I can't even look at you right now," cries Ali, her tears returning. "After everything we've been through together . . . how could you?"

"But I didn't . . ." pants Chrissy. "I swear to God . . ." she says, looking as if she's about to pass out. "This wasn't me. I would never have done this to you."

"It came from *your* phone," says Ali accusingly.

Chrissy shrugs her shoulders and shakes her head, speechless.

"Well, if *you* didn't do it, who did?"

An uncomfortable, but not altogether unsurprising thought begins to whir around Rachel's brain.

Ali's looking at her, as if she's asking herself exactly the same thing.

If she's capable of sleeping with her best friend's husband, then she's capable of anything.

"I saw her," says Rachel, as if to herself. "She was looking at Chrissy's phone."

Chrissy looks from one to the other, desperately wanting to be let in on the conspiracy theory that's gathering pace. "Who?" she asks.

"Paige," says Rachel. "The friend I was with earlier."

Calling her a friend already sounds so alien now.

"She was with you at the bar a little while ago and you were both looking at your phone."

"Yeah," says Chrissy, not seeming to grasp what's being suggested. "She wanted to see the photos I'd taken of the wedding."

"Jesus," says Rachel, exhaling. "She must have sent it without you noticing."

Chrissy thumbs through her sent messages and looks up ashen-faced. "I'm so sorry," she says to Ali. "She's sent it to everyone on my contact list."

"Wait, Paige has done this?" asks Will, his face clouded with confusion. "Why would she do something like that?"

Ali looks to Rachel, as if seeking permission to tell him. Rachel nods.

"She's not quite who you think she is," says Ali.

His perplexed expression is wiped off by an icy spray of sea water that washes over the side of the terrace—an ominous warning of how high the tide's come in.

Yet while he and everyone else yelps in shock, instinctively turning away, Rachel finds herself stepping closer to the edge. She looks into the swirling water just a few meters below as it batters the underside of the terrace. What had it done with the beach they were sitting on this afternoon? The caves they'd stood in? The staircase they'd walked down? Even the sign warning about falling rocks that had seemed so high when she was down on the beach is now about to disappear just below her. It's as if, one by one, they're being magicked away, lost in the depths of the choppy waters, only to reappear when the ocean feels ready to give them back.

She wonders if the waves have ever reached the restaurant, which is just a little higher, and, if they have, whether the lobsters in the tanks were able to set themselves free. She entertains the bizarre idea, as she knows it's the only way she can hold off having to decide what she's going to do about her husband sleeping with her best friend.

Because there's no doubt in her mind that Ali's telling the truth. Yet instead of feeling hurt or angry, Rachel feels stupid. How could she have allowed herself to be deceived by two people she thought cared for her? How had she lived the life she thought she should live, when deep down she knew she wanted the life she gave up? Now that she really asks herself the question, she thinks that if she hadn't become pregnant so quickly, she and Jack most likely wouldn't have lasted. But family is everything, and she'd vowed to do whatever she could to ensure they stayed together. But what was it all for? Why had she suppressed her feelings for the man she truly loved? Spent years beating those emotions out of herself, so that every time she saw Noah, she wasn't taken back to that night, with a yearning that threatened to tear her apart. The thought that Josh *may* be Noah's son, and they could have been together as a family for all this time, makes her want to throw herself into the swell of the waves. She'd done what she thought was the right thing to do by everybody. Why couldn't Jack and Paige have demonstrated the same respect?

A tremendous bang makes her jump, as the night sky is set alight with a flash of pink and white. The million colored sparkles burst out from their cardboard rockets, reigniting again and again, before falling into the inky abyss.

As the sky falls black again, Rachel can see the streams of smoke weaving their way through the darkness, leaving floating gray wisps. But within seconds, another telltale whistle of a burnt-amber light soars up from what she can only imagine is a boat out at sea. It resembles a weeping willow tree as it explodes, reflecting in the water below.

In that split second, the ooooh's that are coming from behind her turn into strangled screams that slice through the air. Rachel instinctively turns around and is blinded by a dazzling light that seems to be heading toward her. Her brain goes into overdrive as it battles to catch up with what others are already beginning to work out. The beam is definitely moving, and fast, but there are people in the way, she can see their outlines in the headlights.

Headlights? So it's a car, and it's showing no sign of stopping. She wants to scream, but it's as if she's trapped in a nightmare and no sound is coming out. She wills it to veer left, so that the restaurant takes the brunt of the impact, but she freezes as she thinks of the staff and DJ who are no doubt still inside.

The engine screeches, stuck in first gear, and Rachel prays that it won't have enough power to reach the terrace. But it's already here. She can hear the thud of bodies hitting the unforgiving metal, see them being spun up into the air. It's all happening in slow motion, but yet she can't seem to reach anyone before they're hit; can't save them from this faceless horror that is picking them off and taking them out, one by one.

The revving is deafening, competing against the roar of the waves, as the machine gets ever closer. What looked like a single beam separates into two round circles of light as it nears, blinding Rachel to anything beyond. She can't see what car it is, what color it is, or, more importantly, if anyone's in it.

It's almost upon her now, but there's nowhere for her to go, other than diving over the side of the terrace and into the sea. But it's rocky and she's likely to be taken by the ocean without trace if she gives it the chance.

She thinks of Josh, pictures his smiling face, and wonders how he'll cope without her. She doesn't want to leave him, miss out on seeing him graduate, get married and have children of his own. In that moment, she is comforted by the fact that he'll still have his dad by his side, but then terror rips through her as she realizes that Jack might already be lying somewhere, mown down just a second before her. Where is he? When did she last see him?

She cries out in fear for Josh, more than herself, as the car reaches her. She moves, but not fast enough, to stop it from slamming into her, sending her spiraling out of control. It feels like she's flying through the air, oddly serene as she floats above everyone else already on the floor. She's sure she catches a glimpse of Noah's pale-linen suit as she spins and she searches frantically for his face, knowing that if her eyes are going to be forever closed from this point, *his* face is the last thing she wants to see.

She tenses everything, squeezing every muscle tight, waiting for the impact to come. When she crash lands, she's sure she must be dead, as there is nothing but a pain-free silence all around her.

But the whirring scream of the car as it goes airborne brings her around, and she watches as it's momentarily suspended in mid-air before plunging into the sea.

There are cries of pain and calls for help all around her, but as much as she feels compelled to go to them, she takes a second for her own self-assessment. She tentatively moves her arms up toward her head, waiting for the agony to manifest itself in whichever limb has been struck. She doesn't quite believe that her head is still on her shoulders until she feels it with her hands. Working her way down her body, she pats herself, checking that everything is still where it should be. Her fingers instinctively recoil from a warm, wet patch at the top of her leg, and as she allows herself to focus, a deep, rhythmical throbbing starts beating from her hip.

She winces as she pulls herself up into a sitting position, looking around at faces wearing expressions identical to her own, none of them yet believing what they've just witnessed and in too much shock to move.

Rachel's buoyed to see that there are more people standing than on the floor, though Ali's mum is the only one she immediately recognizes. "My baby, my baby," comes a blood-curdling scream, as she reaches a figure lying motionless on the floor. Rachel can see the white dress literally turning red in front of her eyes.

"Noah!" Rachel calls out, her tears mixing with the salty sea spray, stinging her face. "Noah!"

Like a celestial being, he emerges from the open-mouthed crowd, running toward her and falling to his knees. "Oh my God," he cries. "Are you okay? Please tell me you're okay."

She nods. "What the hell happened? Have you seen Jack? Where's Paige?"

He shakes his head. "I don't know," he croaks. "It came out of nowhere. I don't know where they were. I don't know where they are."

Rachel's aware of frantic movement all around her, as staff emerge from the restaurant with their hands on their heads and the wedding guests begin to call out in disbelief.

"Kimberley!" comes a desperate voice. "Ali!" cries another.

"Will?" Rachel shouts. "Will, is that you?"

She sees him stumbling around, disoriented. "Go to him," she says to Noah. "See that he's okay and find Jack and Paige."

"The *serviços de emergência* are coming," calls out one of the waiters. "Please, be calm. They are here quickly."

"Stay where you are," says Noah, squeezing Rachel's hand. "Help is on the way."

Rachel nods as he leaves and she looks around, trying to match the bloodied outfits that just a few seconds ago had looked so glamorous to their owners.

A man, just a few meters away from her, groans as he comes round. Seeing the color of his trousers, and having made the observation earlier that it was only Will and Jack in dark suits, Rachel goes to get up, desperate to get to him. But she screams in pain as her leg buckles beneath her and she falls heavily to the ground.

"Jack!" she says, wanting to shout, but forcing herself to stay calm. He looks to be a minute or two behind her and she wants to give him the same moment she gave herself, to feel for what hurts and assimilate what has just happened.

As Jack rolls himself over, Rachel has to stop herself from recoiling in shock. One half of his face is covered in blood; the flesh that normally covers his cheekbone is flapping and his front teeth look to have gone through his bottom lip.

"Don't move," says Rachel, using her arms to drag herself along the floor toward him. "I'm here and help is on its way."

He groans. "Please," says Rachel. "Please don't try to talk. You're going to be okay. I promise."

Those that had been floored by sheer terror and shock begin to stand, as if not quite believing they can. They pat themselves down and sob as they hug one another, the adrenaline that had coursed through them just seconds before now dissipated, leaving them drained and emotional.

"Paige!" calls out Noah, as he moves ever more frantically around the terrace, turning people to face him, as if he wouldn't recognize his wife from behind. "Paige!"

"*Aqui, bebe um pouco de água*," says a man kneeling down next to Rachel. She gratefully takes the bottle of water that he's offering.

Blue flashing lights descend down the hill, the noise of the sirens piercing the eerily quiet atmosphere. As men in red jackets, with *Bombeiros* written across their chest, race onto the devastating scene, Will breathlessly explains in broken Portuguese what happened. It's only as he uses his raised hand to describe the car going off the terrace and into the sea that Rachel acknowledges that if the car is now underwater, so is whoever might be in it.

Rachel looks out to the black thrashing ocean, which offers up no clue whatsoever to what's just happened. A chill rushes through her as she imagines the submerged vehicle sitting on the seabed, the water rising second by second as the driver thrashes to get out. It would be impossible to see, the cold and the dark so disorienting that even if the car had landed the right way up, you'd never know it.

No, Rachel tries to convince herself: it was a runaway, it had slipped off its handbrake and come hurtling toward them in a million-to-one freak accident. It couldn't have had a driver because that means that person is still in there.

"Paige!" calls out Noah again, increasingly desperate.

"*Precisamos de saber quem está presente,*" says the *bombeiro*.

Will rakes a hand through his hair. "Yes, I can give you the guest list, but we need ambulances. My wife . . ." His shoulders collapse as he kneels over Ali, lying motionless on the ground. "My wife is unconscious . . . *inconsciente*."

"Okay, okay," says the *bombeiro*, issuing instructions to his crew and gesticulating toward the sea.

"Jack," says Rachel, pulling herself up beside him. "Can you hear me?"

Jack groans as he slowly brings one hand up to his other arm.

"I'm here, Jack," she says. "But please try not to move, okay?" Relief floods through her as she looks up to see men carrying stretchers running down the hill toward them. "The ambulances are here, but you must stay still."

He makes an inaudible noise that sounds like he's gargling blood.

From the shocked stillness of just a few minutes ago, there is now a palpable sense of panic. For every limp body that is on the floor, there is someone by their side, comforting them. But then Rachel catches sight of a shoeless foot, twisted at an unnatural angle, with no one there to show they care.

"Chrissy!" she breathes, then calls out to the men in hi-vis jackets. "Hey! Over here." She crawls toward Chrissy, dragging herself along on her elbows, like an enemy in combat. "It's okay," she says, grimacing as the pain in her leg shoots through her consciousness. "Chrissy, it's Rachel. Can you hear me?" There isn't even a flicker of movement and Rachel cries out, unable to help herself. "Chrissy, stay with me. Please, somebody! Over here!"

Two men lean down beside the stricken woman, checking for her pulse. Rachel can only presume that they can't find one, as they start talking loudly and quickly. "Chrissy!" she calls out again, as tears stream down her face.

She shuffles out of the way as more paramedics move in like worker bees around honey, each of them working in synergy in an attempt to revive Chrissy.

"I can't find Paige," says Noah desperately, kneeling down beside Rachel.

"Well, she's got to be here somewhere," says Rachel, looking around. "Where was she when it happened?"

Noah shakes his head. "I don't know. I think . . ." He runs a hand through his hair. "I thought she was with Jack."

In that moment, Rachel suddenly remembers all that had gone on before, and her already-splintered heart breaks in two. Before the fireworks: Paige on the terrace with Jack, pretending to anyone looking on that they were casually enjoying a cigarette together—the bracelet on her wrist saying otherwise.

Had they still been there when she'd come around the corner after speaking to Ali? She shakes her head, trying to place them, but the terrace had been full by the time she'd arrived and she hadn't been able to see them *or* Noah.

"I saw them out here when I was inside at the bar," says Noah. "But by the time I came out, there was no sign of them. I don't know where they were."

Rachel pulls herself toward Jack, who is lying on his back on the deck with his eyes open. "Help is coming," she says. "Just a couple more minutes."

Jack manages a shivery nod. "Can he have your jacket?" Rachel asks Noah.

"Don't *you* need it more?" Noah says, taking it off.

Shock's setting in, freezing her to the core, but she shakes her head, taking the jacket and laying it over Jack's chest. He winces, despite her barely touching him, making her wonder what other injuries may lie beneath the surface.

"Where's Paige?" she whispers close to his ear, conscious of how loaded the question is.

His eyes flicker and slide toward her.

"Was she with you?" she asks, not wanting him to exert himself. "When it happened?"

"Sh . . ." he starts, the one syllable clearly causing him pain.

"Blink once for yes," says Rachel. "Twice for no."

He has to exert all his energy into closing his eyelids and opening them with purpose. Rachel and Noah watch intently, both of them desperately hoping that he blinks again to say she wasn't with him. Because if she was, where is she now?

Rachel shudders as she tries to fend off the terrifying thought that Paige might have been knocked into the sea—which, as the waves crash against the terrace, doesn't look like it will give anyone up easily.

26

Noah's is the first face Rachel sees when she comes around from the anesthetic and, for a moment, she thinks she's still under its influence. His features are softened, as if she's looking through a blurred lens, but as the focus sharpens, she sees his brow is creased and he has bags under his eyes.

So many thoughts railroad her brain, though she's unable to separate the flashbacks from a dream she thinks she's had. A car is up in the air—she can see its underside—yet when it crashes into the water, she's inside, thrashing to get out. She gasps, as if desperate for air.

"It's okay," says Noah, as if able to see her innermost thoughts. "You're safe now."

"Where am I?" she asks raspingly.

"You're in a hospital in Portugal," says Noah. "You've had an operation on your leg, but you're going to be just fine."

He looks like he hasn't slept for days; is that how long she's been out for? And if he's by *her* side, waiting for her to come round, does that mean he doesn't have his own wife to watch over? And where's Jack? Shouldn't *he* be here?

She suddenly remembers him lying next to her, shivering, with blood covering his face.

"Jack?" she breathes, going to pull herself up. The needle in the back of her hand tugs and she winces.

"Ssh," says Noah, gently holding her down. "He's okay. He's being patched up, but he's going to be okay."

She allows herself to fall back into the pillow, trying to recall at what point the party turned into a nightmare. She sees flashes of Ali and Jack in a cave, Paige going to push Ali off the cliff, Josh as a baby in Jack's arms, Noah and Josh laughing and drinking in a pub . . . all the images bombard her fragile brain and she's unable to determine which of them really happened and which she's imagined.

"Where's Paige?" she asks, fearful of the answer.

Noah drops eye contact and stares intently at the bedsheets.

"Where *is* she?"

He shakes his head. "We don't know," he says quietly.

She goes to pull herself up again. "What do you mean, you don't know?"

"She's wasn't on the terrace," he says. "The police think she could have been knocked into the sea."

"Is everybody else accounted for?"

Noah nods.

"So, it's just Paige who's missing?" she asks incredulously.

"And the driver," says Noah.

They both look away from each other, neither of them prepared to even begin to acknowledge that it could be one and the same person.

"What the hell happened?" cries Rachel, the enormity of the situation bearing down on her.

"I don't know," says Noah. "They were going to recover the car at first light." He looks out of the window at the pink-tinged sky. "So we should have some answers any time now."

"Mrs. Hunter?" comes a voice.

Rachel looks up to see a man knocking on an invisible door at the foot of her bed. "May I come in?"

Rachel nods, assuming that he's a doctor, in his beige chinos and open-necked pale-blue shirt. Dark hair curls around his collar and he offers the kindest of smiles. The sort that heals people.

"I am Afonso Da Silva from the police department," he says, taking Rachel completely by surprise. He extends his hand before realizing that hers is otherwise occupied by the IV drip. He nods, almost imperceptibly, to Noah, implying that they've already met.

"This is Sophia Casimiro," he says, turning to the woman who's just appeared beside him. "She is assisting me in this incident."

Rachel wonders what an "incident" means in Portugal. He didn't say accident, crime or inquiry, so it gives her no clue as to what they're actually investigating. Might it be a missing person case, while they search for Paige?

"I have spoken with your consultant," the policeman goes on. "And she thinks you might be well enough to answer a few questions."

Rachel looks at Noah, who gives a small nod.

"I still feel a little bit woozy, but I should be able to tell you anything you need to know."

Da Silva's brow furrows. "I'm sorry, woozy? I'm afraid I don't understand."

Rachel manages the tiniest of smiles. "Just a little sleepy from the surgery," she says.

"Ah, my English is not that good, I'm afraid."

"It's better than my Portuguese," offers Rachel.

"Okay, so while Ms. Casimiro speaks with you, perhaps, Mr. Collins, you would come with me?"

"Oh no," says Rachel. "It's fine. I'm happy to talk to you with Noah here. In fact, I'd prefer it."

"I will be needing Mr. Collins to accompany me for just a few moments," he says, holding a hand out to encourage Noah to leave.

"Do you know something?" he asks, getting out of his chair. "Have you found her? Have you found Paige?"

"Please, Mr. Collins," says the policeman patiently. "Come with me."

Noah turns to look at Rachel wide-eyed and terrified, as if they're leading him to the gallows.

"Have you found her?" Rachel asks the policewoman who is getting a notebook out of her crossover bag.

"They will have news soon," says the woman, sitting down on the imitation-leather armchair next to Rachel's bed. "If I could, please, ask one or two questions?"

Rachel knows they know more than they're letting on. "Is she alive?" she asks, in desperation.

"Senhor Da Silva will be giving answers," she replies. "But I would like to know where you were when the car came?"

Rachel tries to brush off the fear that's creeping through her veins, pretend that it's a perfectly reasonable question under the circumstances. Though, if it had been a fluke runaway, she doubts the police would need to know her exact whereabouts.

"I was on the terrace," she says carefully, considering her position both literally and metaphorically. "I had been talking to Ali, the bride, and we were called to watch the fireworks."

Casimiro makes a note. "Where are you and . . ." She looks down. "Alison Hunter when you are talking?"

Rachel's eyes narrow, wondering why it could possibly be relevant. "Around the back of the restaurant," she says, slowly. "By the kitchen."

"So, that is to the left of the terrace, as you come down the hill?"

Rachel rubs at her forehead, trying to remember. "Yes, I think so."

"And why were you there?"

Even though she knows she's done nothing wrong, Rachel can't help but feel that every twitch and nuance is being analyzed by the woman. Unlike her colleague, her face is deadpan, giving nothing away. Her small, dark eyes are empty of everything, except judgment.

"We were talking, away from the loud music," says Rachel, her mouth drying up with every word she utters.

"About what?" asks the woman, tilting her head to the side.

"Rachel!" comes a voice.

"Maria," shrills Rachel breathlessly, as she appears through the curtain. "Where's Ali? Is she okay? Please tell me she's okay."

Maria's eyes fill with tears. "I don't . . . I can't . . ."

"Where is she?" asks Rachel.

"She's in surgery, but . . ." Her shoulders convulse as she sobs. "She's in a bad way. They don't know if . . ."

"It'll be okay," says Rachel authoritatively. "She's going to be okay."

"I'm sorry, but you are Alison Hunter's mother?" asks Casimiro.

"Yes," says Maria quietly. "Yes, I am."

"I would like to ask you some questions, just as soon as I am finished here."

Maria nods. "Of course, I'll be waiting for my daughter to come out of surgery."

"Thank you," says Casimiro. "I will come and talk to you in time."

Maria backs herself out of the cubicle, shaking her head inconspicuously, as if silently trying to communicate with Rachel.

"So, can you remember what you were talking about?" asks Casimiro, urging Rachel to carry on.

Rachel forces herself to trawl through the debris in her brain. She'd thought Ali was having an affair with Jack . . . but then she can see Ali in the ladies' room, telling her that he was sleeping with Paige. She can visualize herself laughing at the ridiculous suggestion.

She shakes her head. "No, it's fuzzy, I can't quite remember."

"And Mrs. Paige Collins wasn't with you?"

"No," says Rachel.

"So, afterward, when you had finished talking, you came out onto the terrace to watch the fireworks, yes?"

Rachel nods her head, wary of where this is going.

"And do you remember seeing Mrs. Collins then? Was she on the terrace?"

Rachel closes her eyes, desperately trying to recall those few moments before it happened. It was dark, but there was enough lighting to be able to see silhouettes, and faces you knew well enough. But as much as she tries, she can't see Paige anywhere.

"No, she wasn't," says Rachel.

"And Mr. . . ." says Casimiro, looking at her notes. "Jack Hunter, your husband?"

"He was there," says Rachel adamantly.

"You saw him before the car arrived?"

Rachel can see Jack in the morning suit he'd complained about, the pair of them not knowing that it was the only way she was going to be able to identify him later. "Yes, he was definitely there," but even as she says it, she wonders why she wasn't standing with him if he was. She remembers seeing the fabric of his suit, going toward him, but then . . . *no.* She shakes her head in an attempt to retrieve the recollection.

"No, actually it wasn't until *after* the car had hit us that I saw Jack."

"You are sure?"

"Yes, but he must have been there, otherwise he wouldn't have gotten injured so badly."

"And Mr. Noah Collins?" asks Casimiro. "He didn't show very many injuries. Was *he* there?"

Was he? Rachel knows she *wants* to be able to place him, even though she's not yet sure what it will mean if she's able to. Will it exonerate him from whatever the police are trying to determine, or implicate him?

She takes herself back to when she joined the other guests on the terrace after talking to Ali behind the restaurant, and can still feel the deep-rooted contempt that flooded her veins. Every fiber of her being had bristled with a stinging hostility as she looked around . . . but for *who*?

Another jolt and she can see herself with Noah, but not on the terrace. They're somewhere else and he's trying to kiss her and is asking for a paternity test. Blood rushes to her head as she's hit by the sudden recollection of what had happened. She falls back onto the pillow as the pieces begin to fall into place.

"Noah was the first person I saw after I'd been hit," she says.

"But you didn't see him *before*?" presses Casimiro.

"No," says Rachel, feeling weary.

She's relieved when Noah returns, though he looks worse than he did ten minutes ago: sheet-white with red-rimmed eyes.

"Are you okay?" she asks.

"I'm going," says Casimiro, hastily standing up and putting her notebook back in her bag. "I will be leaving you to take time."

As soon as she's left, Noah takes hold of Rachel's hand and squeezes it, his tears flowing freely.

"I've seen her," he manages between sobs.

"Oh, thank God," says Rachel. "Is she all right?"

He shakes his head. "She's gone, Rach."

"Wh-what?" she almost screams. "No . . . no, she can't be."

"I've just had to identify her," says Noah. "They recovered her from the water."

Rachel's world spins and she clutches hold of the bedclothes to save herself from falling off. *No. No. No.* This isn't real, it can't be. If she wasn't already lying down, she'd pass out, her body temporarily shutting down to protect it from the shock. Her head lolls back onto the pillow and hot bile stings the back of her throat. She grabs the cardboard bowl from the side and vomits into it.

"The car must have knocked her in," cries Noah.

"Or else she felt she had no choice but to jump out of its way," says Rachel. She can't refer to it as a car, as she's unable to relate to how an everyday object could become a devastating killing machine.

Noah's shaking his head, as tears stream down his face. "I should have protected her, but I can't even remember her being there. The last time I saw her she was with Jack."

Rachel can see the pair of them standing on the terrace, and watches in slow motion as Paige's heart bracelet glistens as she stubs out her cigarette. It's the tiniest thing, but it's the catalyst that unlocks the memories that have been locked away. Suddenly, the conversation she'd had with Ali comes back to her with crystal-clear clarity; the scenes shuttering in front of her eyes like a 1940s homemade movie.

Rachel looks at Noah, already in his own world of hurt and pain, and wonders how she can possibly contemplate making it worse. But the truth can't be hidden forever, and if she doesn't reveal it now, it will have much further-reaching consequences when it *does* come out. "They were having an affair," she says numbly, as the details slowly seep into her consciousness.

"Who were?"

"Jack and Paige," cries Rachel.

Noah's head jolts up and he looks at her wide-eyed. When he goes to speak, nothing comes out. She squeezes his hand, for all the good it will do.

"I'm sorry," she says, feeling somehow responsible.

"Are you serious?" he says, his voice high-pitched.

"Yes," says Rachel meekly.

Noah shakes his head, as his shock and pain metamorphose into anger. "What the fuck . . . ?" he exclaims, standing up, sending his chair scraping against the worn laminate floor.

"Please, don't," she begs.

"Have you told the police?" he asks, as he paces up and down, not knowing what to do with himself.

Rachel shakes her head. "Not yet, because everything was so hazy when I was talking to them. But it's all gradually coming back, and now that Paige is . . ." She can't bring herself to finish the sentence.

"They need to be told," says Noah. "It might make a difference to their investigation."

"Investigation?" repeats Rachel naively.

"Into Paige's . . ." He doesn't seem to be able to say the word either. "A car doesn't randomly start up on its own, point in the direction of the terrace and start rolling toward it at speed."

"But who would do such a thing?"

Noah rubs his hand manically through his hair. "I don't know," he says. "I just don't know."

"So you think we should tell them that Jack and Paige were . . ." asks Rachel, unsure what to do for the best.

Noah falls onto the chair and puts his head in his hands. "Do you know for sure that they were?"

"Ali told me," says Rachel.

"But I thought we were disregarding that as Ali being Ali?"

Rachel shakes her head as the memories become clearer with every passing minute. "She told me everything, just before the accident. I heard it in all its technicolor glory."

"And you believe her?" asks Noah.

"Does it really matter anymore?" cries Rachel.

"Excuse me," says Da Silva, peering around the curtain. "May I?"

Rachel nods as Noah buries his head in his hands.

"Is there any news on my husband?" asks Rachel, her voice unsteady.

"He has a dislocated shoulder, a torn tendon in his arm and some facial injuries," says Da Silva. "They have him in surgery now, but he will be okay, I think."

"So, you've not spoken to him yet?" asks Noah, without even looking up.

"No, we will be speaking to him about the evening's events as soon as we're able to." Da Silva looks between them. "I know this must be a very difficult time, but I just need to ask you both again, so I am completely clear, that neither of you saw Paige Collins before the accident."

"I-I've just told your colleague," Rachel cries. "The last time I saw her was when I left the restaurant to talk to Ali. Paige was outside talking to Jack, my husband."

"Why were they outside?" asks the policeman.

Noah's mouth pulls tight and his eyes darken, as though he's about to say or do something he might regret. Rachel puts a hand on his in an attempt to silently caution him, and his jaw slackens, as whatever incriminating statement he was about to make dissipates.

"That was probably about fifteen minutes or so before it happened," Rachel goes on.

"And you?" Da Silva says, turning to Noah. "When did you last see your wife and where was she?"

Any fire that remains in Noah's eyes fades as he processes the loaded question. He rubs his chin, bristling his five o'clock shadow that seems to have grayed since yesterday.

"She was out on the terrace, talking to Jack," he says. "By the time I went outside to watch the fireworks, I couldn't see either of them."

"And you didn't see them again," asks Da Silva, "before the car came?"

Noah shakes his head.

"I don't understand why it's so important," says Rachel. "What does it matter where Paige was? Isn't it enough to know that when the car hit her, she was thrown into the water?" A sob catches in her throat.

Da Silva grimaces. "I'm afraid it's not that simple."

Rachel and Noah both look at him, waiting for him to elaborate.

"Because Mrs. Collins's body was found in the car."

27

Noah locks eyes with Rachel, his fear, anger, sadness and confusion mirroring her own.

"B-but . . ." she stutters, unable to make any sense of what's going on.

"How . . . ?" starts Noah.

"That's impossible," manages Rachel. "That can't be right."

Da Silva looks at her resignedly.

"Sh-she couldn't have been in the car," Rachel mumbles, hoping that if she says it enough it'll be true.

"I'm afraid she was, and I need to understand what happened and why she was there."

"Well, she . . ." blusters Rachel, desperately looking for answers herself. "She must have been making an ill-fated attempt at getting home. She wouldn't have been used to being on the wrong side of the road. She might have gotten confused with the gearshift being on the right instead of the left. There are myriad reasons why she may have been disoriented. It was dark, she'd been drinking, the fireworks went off. The list goes on . . ." She's scrabbling around for any other reasonable justification as to why Paige would have been in that car, and, if she *was*, how this terrible accident could have occurred. Because whichever way Rachel looks at this, it *has* to have been an accident, as the alternative doesn't bear thinking about.

"Did anything unusual happen at the wedding or the party afterward?" asks Da Silva. "Were there any arguments or problems?"

Rachel's head throbs, the beat of a banging drum reverberating as her pulse quickens.

"*Senhor Da Silva, posso falar com você, por favor?*"

Rachel looks up to see Casimiro's grave face peering around the curtain.

"Excuse me for just one moment," says the policeman.

As soon as he's out of earshot, Rachel turns to Noah, with a look of utter horror on her face.

"Oh my God, it's *my* fault," she croaks.

"*What?*" exclaims Noah. "How can it be?"

Rachel shudders involuntarily as she looks at Noah. "What if she overheard me and Ali talking about what happened between us?"

"Ali *knew*?" asks Noah. "So, she *did* hear everything you and I said?"

Rachel nods, struggling for breath as she imagines Paige hidden from view around the back of the restaurant, but still within easy listening distance. What might have gone through her head if she heard Ali's observation that Noah and Rachel were still in love with each other? That Josh might be Noah's child?

"She heard it all," says Rachel, not knowing whether she's referring to Ali or Paige.

"Well, did you put Ali right, like you did me?" he asks. "Did you tell her there was absolutely no chance Josh could possibly be mine?"

A tear falls onto Rachel's cheek. "I told her the truth," she says.

Noah raises his eyebrows. "Which is?"

"Which is that I honestly don't know."

His eyes, which already hold so much pain and angst, appear to take on a truckload more.

"So, you always knew there was a possibility," he says quietly.

"No!" she exclaims, desperate for him to understand. "I've always assumed Jack was his father because . . ."

Noah looks at her, waiting.

"Because I wanted him to be," she says, when she can't think of a better answer.

"Because it was easier," says Noah.

Rachel wipes a tear away. "Yes," she says honestly. "I guess it was."

"And now?" asks Noah.

"Now, *everything's* being called into question and I don't know *what* to think anymore."

"We don't know that Paige heard anything," says Noah.

"Why else would she have done what she's done?" cries Rachel, unable to keep her voice down.

"You're jumping to conclusions," he says.

She shakes her head vehemently. "*I* made her do this," she says. "She was coming for *me*."

Her chest convulses as she sobs and Noah takes her hand in his.

"Are you saying she did this on *purpose*?" asks Noah hoarsely. "That she *targeted* us?"

Rachel tries to stop her mind from fast-forwarding, but it's like holding back a freight train. There are so many faces, scenarios and possibilities crowding her brain that she has to wait for the fog to clear to think straight.

"*Me, you, us*—I don't know who she would have felt more betrayed by."

"Fucking hell," says Noah as his head falls into his hands.

"What am I going to do?" cries Rachel. "Should I tell them?"

Noah's praying hands touch his lips as he processes the question.

"We've done nothing wrong," he says eventually.

"We've kept a secret for twenty years." Rachel sniffs.

"It won't help anybody if we start dredging up the past now," says Noah.

"But it will offer an explanation for why Paige did what she did," says Rachel. "What if Ali doesn't make it?"

She thinks of Maria and the heart-wrenching pain she'll endure at the loss of her only child. Every mother and child's relationship is special, but their bond was unlike anything Rachel had ever seen. They'd been through so much already and come out of it all the stronger, but Maria would never get over losing the daughter who gave up so much for her, only to have her life snuffed out on what should have been the best day of her life.

"I may as well have killed Ali myself," says Rachel. "She had no part to play in this; she was only doing the right thing by me, and look how I've repaid her."

"You've got to stop doing this to yourself," says Noah.

"If anything happens to her," she says, ignoring him, "I'm going to have blood on my hands."

"This isn't our fault," says Noah angrily, though Rachel knows it isn't aimed at her.

"I apologize," says Da Silva, reappearing around the curtain looking even more thoughtful and serious than when he went out. "So there is nothing you can think of that may have started this catalog of events?"

There is so much at stake here, Rachel feels like she's standing on a bridge, deciding whether to jump or not.

"My wife and Jack Hunter were having an affair," says Noah, making the decision for her.

Rachel looks at him, unable to hide the shock of his confession.

Da Silva raises his eyebrows. "I see . . ." he says, though it feels like there's more to come.

"Both Rachel and I found out at the wedding reception," Noah goes on while the policeman listens thoughtfully.

"And how did that make you feel?"

Rachel and Noah look at each other, both of them seemingly unable to put it into words.

"I understand," says Da Silva. "Perhaps you can tell me how you came to find this out."

"I don't see why it makes a difference," says Rachel. "Because it has nothing to do with what's happened."

"It might," says Da Silva.

Rachel shakes her head. "Paige would never have done this intentionally," she says, willing herself to believe it.

"I'm not suggesting she did, but we have to look at all the possibilities."

"There are no other possibilities," cries Rachel.

"You have escaped very lightly," the policeman says to Noah. "Did you see the car coming?"

Noah nods. "I heard it before I saw it," he says. "I suppose I just instinctively jumped out of the way."

"So, you didn't see who was in the car?" asks Da Silva.

"Well, no," says Noah, looking confused. "But it was obviously my wife." He chokes on the last word.

"And you, Mrs. Hunter? You weren't able to see who was in the car?"

She shakes her head. "I just remember the lights blinding me, so I couldn't see who was driving, but I think it's pretty conclusive, don't you?"

"That it was Paige Collins?" offers Da Silva.

Rachel nods.

"Not necessarily," he says.

Noah and Rachel look at him quizzically as he sighs heavily.

"Because it appears that someone else may have been in the car with her."

28

The last thing Rachel remembers before falling asleep is that she didn't think she'd ever be able to sleep again. Now, as her eyes flicker open, she's met by darkness, but she can make out an unfamiliar dim light filtering in from somewhere beyond her bed. It occurs to her that she might be in a hotel—she's definitely not at home, she can tell by the acrid smell and strange beeping noises. Her throat is parched and she reaches to the right, where she'd normally keep her water, but there's a spiky tug in her hand that immediately makes her recoil.

There's a hum of voices, barely audible at first, but as soon as she concentrates, she can separate two accents. It feels as if she's playing a lead role in someone else's dream and, desperate to get herself out of it, she blinks really hard. It's always worked before, when she's trapped in a nightmare with no other way out. But as much as she squeezes her eyelids together, she still doesn't wake up in her own bed.

Jack's here, though—she can hear him, talking quietly, so as not to disturb her. Then she remembers the villa they were staying in and she realizes he must be downstairs.

She swings her legs off the bed, but a searing pain shoots from her hip, making her fall back against the pillow. What the hell's going on? Jack's voice seeps into her consciousness, his words becoming clearer, as if he's getting nearer. She goes to call out but she stops herself when she hears him say, "She's my soul mate."

"So, you would do anything to protect her?" asks another voice, heavily accented.

"Of course," says Jack. "She's the love of my life. We're going to spend the rest of our lives together."

"So, you're planning to leave your wife?" asks the other male voice.

There's a loaded silence as Rachel's befuddled brain momentarily plays catch-up.

"Yes," says Jack. "But it's complicated because Paige is my wife's best friend."

The name pierces Rachel's heart like a knife, as reality hits her. The wedding, the arguments, the blood, the thrashing waves as the car disappeared into the murky depths. Her lungs struggle to inflate as she gasps for air, making her feel as if *she* was the one in the water. Tears sting her eyes and she bites down on her clenched fist, for fear of crying out.

"Do you remember what happened to you, Mr. Hunter?" asks the man, who Rachel now recognizes as Da Silva.

Jack sighs. "I know that I was hit by a car that just came out of nowhere."

"Do you remember where you were just before the accident?"

"I was on the terrace," says Jack, sounding as if he's in pain.

"And Paige Collins? Do you remember where *she* was the last time you saw her?"

"I . . . I don't know," says Jack. "Look, what's this about?"

"I'm afraid I have some difficult news to tell you," says Da Silva.

"What is it?" asks Jack, his voice high-pitched. "Is it Paige? Is she okay? Please tell me she's okay."

A heavy silence fills the air as Da Silva contemplates how to answer.

"Do you not want to know how your wife is first?"

"Yes, of course," snaps Jack.

"Your wife—she is fine, but I am afraid to say Paige Collins was not quite so lucky."

"What do you mean?" asks Jack, panic-stricken. "Where is she? What's happened to her?"

"Mrs. Collins's body was recovered a little while ago," says Da Silva.

Jack lets out a strangled cry. "No, she can't be. She can't be."

"I'm sorry."

"Was she hit?" asks Jack. "Did the car hit her? Who's the driver? You need to find the driver." He's verging on hysterical.

"Her body was found *in* the car," says Da Silva.

"What the *hell*," cries Jack. "But why? Why would she do that?"

"I'm not entirely sure she did," says Da Silva.

"What?" Jack chokes. "What do you mean?"

"It appears Mrs. Collins might not have been alone in the car."

There's a sharp intake of breath. Rachel doesn't know if it's hers or Jack's as she's suddenly reminded of what she'd already been told.

"Are you suggesting that someone . . . ?" Jack chokes. "Someone did this on purpose . . . to hurt her?"

"We're looking at all lines of inquiry at the moment, but if you have any reason to think someone might have had cause to do such a thing, I'd be grateful to hear it. I understand your wife and Noah Collins found out about your affair at the wedding party?"

"They *did*?" answers Jack, almost in question. "Erm . . . erm, yes . . . yes, they did."

"Did *you* tell them?"

"Er, no, I was intending to, but someone else got there first."

"And who was that?"

"Ali," spits Jack, with such venom that it makes Rachel shudder.

"Alison Hunter?" asks Da Silva, double-checking. "Why would she do that?"

Jack makes a strange snorting sound. "Because she's been threatening to do it for months. She's jealous of Paige. Jealous of what we have."

Rachel can imagine the confusion that must be clouding the policeman's features. "Why would she be jealous?" he asks.

"Ali and I had a thing," says Jack, resignedly. "A little while back."

"An intimate relationship?" asks Da Silva.

"We slept together a few times," says Jack.

Rachel's head falls back onto the pillow. So they'd lied, though she doesn't know who she's most disappointed in: Jack or Ali.

"I called it off when I started seeing Paige about two years ago," he goes on. "But Ali couldn't handle it and she's been blackmailing me ever since."

"So, it's fair to say Alison Hunter disliked Paige Collins?"

"With a vengeance," says Jack.

"Do you think she is capable of causing Paige harm?"

"Without a doubt," says Jack, making Rachel gasp.

"But Alison Hunter was found on the terrace and is critically ill," says Da Silva.

"Well, maybe she . . ." starts Jack. "I mean, God, she could have driven the car and jumped out at the last minute."

There's a moment's silence. "That is a possibility," says Da Silva eventually.

"It's more than a possibility," says Jack. "It would explain why she's so badly injured."

"Mmm," muses the policeman. "I will certainly bear it in mind. But tell me, what was your wife's reaction to this news? How did she take it?"

"As you can imagine," says Jack stiffly. "Rachel's pretty calm normally, but understandably she just saw red. She went completely crazy—I've never seen her so angry."

"What did she do?"

"She was shouting and swearing, telling me I'd never see our son again. Then she started hitting me in the chest with her fists."

The blatant lie makes sweat spring to every pore on Rachel's skin and her mouth instantaneously dries up, making it impossible to speak, even if she wanted to.

"Did she confront Paige about the affair?" asks Da Silva.

"She was definitely intending to," says Jack.

"Do you think your wife . . . ?" starts Da Silva before leaving it hanging there.

Rachel's chest feels like it might explode as she waits to see if the man she loves, who she thought loved her, is about to incriminate her in a murder.

"I don't know," cries Jack. "I just don't know *anything* anymore. Rachel was mad, *really* mad, but she surely wouldn't do something . . . something like this." He takes a deep breath and Rachel imagines him grimacing and tilting his head to the side as he adds, "*Would* she?"

She stifles the sob that she can no longer hold in, with a hand over her mouth. How could he do this to *her*? *And* the others, by picking them off, one by one, loading them up with a motive, when all of them were struck by the car itself. All of them except Noah, who was first on the scene to help those who had been tossed aside like rag dolls.

Her windpipe feels as if it's being squeezed by the people she loves the most, as it occurs to her that Noah *was* the only one of them not to have been injured. She doesn't want to allow the thought to infiltrate her exhausted brain, but as much as she tries to push it away, it only comes back at her even louder.

"Rachel said she was going to tell Noah what was going on as well," Jack adds, almost as an afterthought.

"And did she?"

"I'm tired," says Jack, sidestepping the question.

"I'm sorry, I won't keep you from rest for much longer," says Da Silva. "Just a couple more questions, then I will leave you to sleep."

"I begged her to wait until we got home, so as not to ruin my brother's wedding, but she was insistent that he know."

"So, she told him?"

"Yes," says Jack. "She must have, because the last I saw of him he was walking up the hill, away from the restaurant. I guess he'd gone to let off some steam."

"You were happy that he was leaving?" asks Da Silva.

"I was relieved that he wasn't going to make a scene," says Jack. "I've been on the wrong side of his temper before and believe you me, I'd happily avoid it."

"So, he's known to get angry?" asks Da Silva.

"With me, yes," says Jack.

Rachel listens in disbelief as one lie after another trips off of Jack's tongue.

"Because he's always seen me as the one who took Rachel away from him. They were college sweethearts and he's never gotten over losing her. So, finding out that I'm now having an affair with his wife would have sent him over the edge."

If he realizes his Freudian slip, he doesn't apologize for it.

"Oh my God," wails Jack suddenly, sounding like a wounded animal. "This can't be happening. None of this makes any sense."

"I'm really sorry to push you, Mr. Hunter, but just one more question, if I may. Can I ask if you recognize this?"

Rachel wants to throw herself off the bed and through the curtain to see what Jack's being shown.

"That's . . ." starts Jack before clearing his throat with a cough. "That's *my* watch. Wh-where did you find it?"

"It was on the floor of the front seat of the car, Mr. Hunter."

29

"It was a beautiful service," says Rachel to Ali's mum.

"Thank you for coming," says Maria, tearfully. "I know it couldn't have been easy. It's not easy for any of us."

Maria hugs her tightly, as if she never wants to let her go.

Rachel hugs her back even tighter. "I can't thank you enough," she says.

"What for?" asks Maria.

"For everything." Her eyes meet Maria's. "If it wasn't for you and Ali . . ."

Maria nods as a tear falls onto her cheek. "I knew, as soon as she told me about Jack and Paige, that he didn't deserve you. She knew it too. She couldn't bear to see them hurt you, but she really didn't know what to do for the best. She honestly thought that threatening to expose their affair was the right thing to do, but look how that turned out."

Rachel takes hold of Maria's hand. "But if you hadn't overheard Jack and Paige talking on the terrace just before, we'd never have known what happened."

Maria sniffs and wipes a tear with a tissue. "As soon as she told him it was over, I knew he was going to do something. He was so mad, though I could never have imagined in my worst nightmare that he was capable of such . . . such horror."

"I wonder why she called it off," says Rachel, almost to herself, like she had a thousand times before.

"It sounded as if the incident with Noah the day before made her realize just how much she loved him," says Maria.

Rachel can't help but flinch at the irony that it made her realize the very same thing.

"Though, she couldn't have known that Jack wasn't going to take no for an answer," says Maria.

"But to tell her that if *he* couldn't have her, no one could . . ."

"I know," says Maria. "I hear him saying that in my head all the time and it chills me to the bone."

"I can't stop myself from thinking . . ." says Rachel, choking back tears.

Maria gives her the strength she needs by giving her hand a squeeze.

"About what Paige must have thought when she got in that car with him. Did she think they were just going to talk? That he was going to drive her somewhere to make her see sense? Even as he drove at speed toward the terrace, did she think that it was just scare tactics and he'd stop before it was too late?"

"Yes to all of those, I'd imagine."

"I hope she didn't know that he was going to keep going," says Rachel. "I hope it all happened so quickly that she had no idea of the coward that he was."

"I would imagine, like the rest of us, she knew *exactly* what kind of man he was even *before* he jumped out. It was just too late for her to do anything about it."

The battle to hold back her tears proves futile. "I'm so sorry," says Rachel. "It's all my fault. None of this would have happened if it wasn't for me. If I'd just stopped digging, forcing people to tell the truth . . ."

"Listen to me," says Maria. "You can't allow yourself to think that what happened was your fault. There was no one else to blame but Jack."

"Yes, but if I'd just left it alone, then we'd all be none the wiser, and Ali wouldn't have . . ." She chokes on her words.

"She was always going to do right by you, no matter what," says Maria.

Rachel smiles gratefully. "Here she is," she says as Ali approaches them in a flowing white dress that falls in rivulets to the floor. "You look absolutely gorgeous."

"Though, hopefully a little more conservative this time," says Ali, laughing as she looks down at the sweetheart neckline that just shows the very top of her cleavage. "But it's all for Grandma Nettie, so it's a sacrifice I'm willing to make."

"I'm so pleased she got to see you and Will do it all over again. How are you? How have you been?"

Ali wrinkles her nose. "Not too bad, considering the extent of my injuries. I'm still getting the odd headache, but apparently that's very common after a brain trauma."

Rachel nods solemnly.

"But," says Ali, smiling widely, "my physio says there's no reason why we can't start trying for a baby."

"Oh, that's wonderful news," says Rachel, welling up at the thought of her and Will as parents.

Ali laughs. "Chrissy cried when I told her as well."

"How's she doing?" asks Rachel.

"She's getting stronger all the time. She wanted to come back for today, but I told her it would be too much."

"So, she's still in Portugal?" asks Rachel.

Ali nods. "Yep, still in Portugal. Still in love with Paulo's son!"

Her optimism, as she offers a winning smile, is infectious. "What about *you*?" she asks, with a nod to Noah, who's talking to Will behind her.

Rachel can't help but grin. "It's still early, but I'm as happy as I can ever imagine being. *And* I've just started my teacher training."

"I'm so thrilled for you," says Ali. "And Josh and Chloe?"

"They're doing okay," says Rachel. "The anniversary last week was really hard because, whichever way you look at it, Chloe's lost her mother and, essentially, Josh has lost his dad."

"Has he?" asks Ali, tilting her head to the side.

Rachel knows what she's implying. "Yes," she says. "He has."

Ali offers an awkward half smile, as if she doesn't know if that's good news or not. If Rachel were honest, she's not quite sure herself. But at least it means the past twenty years haven't *all* been a lie.

"I was just saying to your mum, if it weren't for you two . . ."

Ali takes her hand as Rachel chokes on the words. "He would have been found guilty no matter what," she says.

"Perhaps," says Rachel. "But thank you for taking the stand and telling the truth. It couldn't have been easy."

"I wasn't going to let him get away with saying what he said about me," says Ali. "I've had a lifetime of it and I'm not going to put up with it anymore."

Rachel can't help but be buoyed by her chutzpah. "But if you hadn't shown him for the liar he was . . ."

"I don't think me telling the court that I'd never kissed him and had certainly never slept with him got him convicted of manslaughter," says Ali.

"But by all of us working together we were able to show what he was capable of," says Rachel. "*We* got justice for Paige."

"I think the watch got justice for Paige," says Maria. "He was never going to be able to explain how it came to be in the car."

Rachel steels herself, knowing she needs to tell them that *she* could.

"I . . ." she starts.

"That's because there *was* no other explanation," interrupts Ali, taking Rachel's hand and looking at her so intently that it feels as if she can see straight through her.

Perhaps she can.

EPILOGUE

Up until that moment, I thought I'd wanted Rachel to tell me what I already knew. But just as she was about to, I suddenly realized it wasn't important anymore.

It didn't matter that I'd seen her put Jack's watch into Paige's bag when she was standing at the bar. I'd greatly admired her for it at the time, cheered by her courage to call Paige out by showing her what she'd done and what she stood to lose. I'd hoped that Paige would read the inscription on the back and be reminded of the grave error of judgment she'd made. It would never have made things right, but knowing Rachel as I know her, she would have gone to the ends of the world to try and forgive her husband and best friend for their betrayal.

But they didn't deserve to be forgiven and if my silence made her see that, then I'm only too happy to have helped seal their fate.

ACKNOWLEDGMENTS

As always, the first thank-you goes to my agent, Tanera Simons at Darley Anderson, who makes me feel as if I'm the only author she looks after. Nothing is ever too much trouble, and she always has my best interests at heart. I'm not much of a businesswoman; it's the reason I make up stories for a living, using my fictional world as an excuse to escape the real one. But she has one foot firmly in both camps, and I will be forever grateful to her for always having my back.

The same can also be said for the rest of the team at Darley Anderson: Mary Darby, Georgia Fuller, Kristina Egan, Sheila David, and Rosanna Bellingham, who all somehow manage to turn my scrawled ramblings into a paid occupation. I've got the best job in the world—thank you!

This is the fourth book I've worked on with Catherine Richards, my amazing editor at Minotaur Books, and it feels like we're really getting into the swing of things now! As ever, she has waved her magic wand over the initial drafts of *The Guilt Trip*, but I hope that with each book, I've honed my craft, so that I'm closer to delivering what she's expecting the first time around! Thank you for your patience!

Also to Gillian Green, my editor at Pan Macmillan, who seamlessly picked up where Vicki Mellor left off. Thank you for your support and enthusiasm. I feel very lucky to have had the valuable insight of two brilliant editors.

Writing a book is easy compared to what goes on behind the scenes. Many thanks to Nettie Finn, Joseph Brosnan, Sarah Melnyk, Matthew Cole, and Becky Lloyd for everything that you do.

A big thank-you to all the Alis out there! We probably all know someone as spirited and irrepressible as her and, if we're honest, might even have gone out of our way to avoid them. But I have thoroughly enjoyed writing her character and I vow to be "more Ali" in the future!

To my friends and family, for once again allowing me to go into my writing hole and not come up for air until I was done.

After months of scratching our heads for a title, *The Guilt Trip* quite literally tripped off my son's tongue over dinner one night. It says everything that this book is about and is absolutely inspired. Thank you, Oliver!

And lastly, saving the biggest thank-you for you—for buying this book, reading it, and talking about it. You have no idea how much I appreciate your ongoing support and I hope you enjoyed it.

A DELETED SCENE FROM CHAPTER 14, A FLASHBACK SHOWING MORE OF THE HISTORY BETWEEN NOAH AND RACHEL

As she swallows the bitter coffee, it occurs to her that if Jack is *sleeping with Ali, he might be doing it for revenge. Might he know about her night with Noah? Might he have worked out that the date was dangerously close to Josh's conception? What if he's known all along, and has spent the intervening twenty years wreaking his revenge, all the while pretending to be happy?*

No, *she says to herself as she shakes her head.* That's ridiculous.

She was pretty sure Jack didn't even know she'd seen Noah that night. It was so early on in their relationship that she didn't need to offer him chapter and verse on where she was going and who with. Though she remembers thinking, as she'd stood with Noah at the departure gate the next morning, that she would owe Jack a phone call if she decided to get on that plane.

There had still been seats available. She had her passport in her bag, always at the ready with it as ID when stores refused to sell her alcohol because she looked so young. She had enough money in her bank account to buy a holdall and some cheap clothes when she reached Thailand.

"Let's do this," Noah had pleaded, in between kissing her, long and deep.

Rachel had closed her eyes, feeling light-headed with the intensity of the emotion that was ripping through her. It was what she'd wanted for so long, fearing that no one would ever come close to the man she called her best friend, who she'd secretly put on a pedestal as being untouchable. But all of a sudden, he was quite literally within touching distance and last night was the most incredible thing that had ever happened to her.

Yet it was still *Noah,* and the downside of having a platonic relationship with the love of your life is that you know how they operate with the opposite sex. Hadn't she heard him say the same words that he'd said to her last night to a hundred other girls? "I've never felt like this." "I want you so badly." "You mean everything to me."

In the heat of the moment, she'd believed every word, but standing on the airport concourse, in the cold light of day, she could envisage him saying them to someone else before they'd even reached Bao Tao. And then where would she be? *No.* She'd rather be broken-hearted at home, and give it a shot with Jack, than a thousand miles away, alone, with Noah as he chased some other girl.

"Hey," says Noah, making her jump.

A Q&A WITH THE AUTHOR

What gave you the idea of a sinister undercurrent among friends at a destination wedding?

Knowing that *The Guilt Trip* was coming out in the summer months, I really wanted to capture the vacation vibe. I love that my novels are considered great beach reads, and I wanted to write something that everyone could relate to while lying by a pool, soaking up the sun. Although it was originally about a group of friends going on vacation together, I added the wedding element to give the plotline more depth, which in turn leads to the catalyst where each of the characters feels as if they have something to lose. Once that fear is instilled in them, you can crank up the tension and watch them all implode.

Was it fun to write about the coast of Portugal, a place that seems pretty far from menace and chills? Did you have to do a lot of first-hand research?

Portugal is one of my favorite destinations, and it is always my first choice if I'm looking to go away for a few days. I tend to head to the Algarve at the southern-most tip of the country, but *The Guilt Trip* is set in Nazaré, up on the west coast, famous for its record-breaking surfing. I based it there because I have a real love-hate relationship with the ocean. I can while away hours looking out from land, in awe of its beauty. But I'm not so comfortable when I'm in it, and the Atlantic waves that hit Nazaré are so fierce that they give me palpitations just watching them. That, for me, is where the sense of menace and chills comes into play: when the sea unleashes its full power, taking out anything in its path.

Do you think the COVID pandemic has changed the way people (especially readers) think about travel?

Yes, definitely. I think the pandemic has had a profound effect on how we view travel. We've taken it so much for granted in the past that now, not being able to go where we want when we want has left many of us feeling as if we've had our wings clipped. And without the ability to travel, we've had to rely even more on books for the escapism we naturally crave. Reading other people's stories means we can go anywhere in the world we want and boy, have we needed to be taken far, far away this past year.

Would you say that travel brings out something in people, such as a certain kind of tension?

It definitely brings *something* out in people! In the main, I think traveling is quite a stressful experience; from the packing, to leaving home without feeling you've forgotten something, to the lines in the airport, to finding space on the plane for your bags . . . it all gets people worked up. Then, if you throw in having to go on vacation with someone you don't particularly want to go with, which is how most of the group in *The Guilt Trip* feel about Ali, it's inevitable that fireworks are going to go off!

Are there any other luxurious places where you've thought, *This would be perfect for a psychological thriller*?

I'm determined to find a way to use the Maldives as the backdrop for a psychological thriller! It's the most magical place on earth, and I'm sure I could find a sinister story amongst the pristine beaches, crystal-clear waters, tropical fish, first-class staff, and the most amazing seafood I've ever tasted in my life! I might have to do a few more research trips, just to make absolutely sure I get every detail right, but I'd suffer it for my craft!

DISCUSSION QUESTIONS

1) The prologue of *The Guilt Trip* begins with an unknown character being interviewed by a police officer. How does this set up the rest of the book? What do you think about this in retrospect, now that you've finished reading?

2) Within the first two chapters, we've met our main cast of six: Rachel and Jack, Noah and Paige, and Ali and Will. What was your initial sense of their relationships with each other? How have the six of them settled into certain roles within the group?

3) Our protagonist, Rachel, has her own ideas about how their group of family—both chosen and biological—fit together. In chapter 2, she states, "Perhaps . . . they all got something from each other's spouses

that they didn't get from their own." Leaving aside the eventual reveal that makes this statement quite ironic, do you think this does occur in relationships? Is this desire necessarily disloyal or dangerous?

4) Rachel is a self-described optimist, and we see events unfold from her point of view. How does this aspect of her personality influence her reading of certain situations? How did Rachel's point of view influence what you thought might be going on? Would you consider her an unreliable narrator?

5) From early on, Ali is presented as a bit manipulative and prone to white lies. Eventually, she seems to be a full-fledged villain. How do Ali's own actions—and secrets—lead to her being viewed this way? Imagine if the book was told from her perspective: What moments might have stood out to Ali that Rachel glosses over?

6) Once the cast expands to include other weddings guests, like Ali's mother, Maria, and friend Chrissy, Rachel learns information that doesn't fit with her "warped caricature of Ali" (chapter 22). Why did Rachel create—and try desperately to sustain—this caricature in the first place? Can you think of a time you have tried to fill in the blanks of another person's life and eventually been surprised by the truth?

7) The vast majority of *The Guilt Trip* takes place over one wedding weekend. Why do you think the author chose such a celebratory event as the backdrop for a novel of suspense?

8) The novel ends with another secret kept: how Jack's watch ended up in the car. How does this final twist change what you thought was the "truth"? Do you think this new truth, shared now between Rachel and Ali, will ever be revealed?